# HORIZON

TOR BOOKS BY FRAN WILDE

*Updraft*
*Cloudbound*
*Horizon*

# HORIZON

## FRAN WILDE

**TOR**

A TOM DOHERTY ASSOCIATES BOOK
NEW YORK

HORIZON

Edited by Miriam Weinberg

A Tor Book
Published by Tom Doherty Associates
175 Fifth Avenue
New York, NY 10010

www.tor-forge.com

Tor® is a registered trademark of Macmillan Publishing Group, LLC.

The Library of Congress Cataloging-in-Publication Data
is available upon request.

ISBN 978-0-7653-7787-6 (hardcover)
ISBN 978-0-7653-7789-0 (ebook)

Our books may be purchased in bulk for promotional, educational, or business use. Please contact your local bookseller or the Macmillan Corporate and Premium Sales Department at 1-800-221-7945, extension 5442, or by email at MacmillanSpecialMarkets@macmillan.com.

First Edition: September 2017

Printed in the United States of America

0  9  8  7  6  5  4  3  2  1

*To that place near Worton, Maryland,*
*where I first learned how to fly.*

# ACKNOWLEDGMENTS

Completing a trilogy is intense and emotional. I will miss this world, and these characters (I may visit sometimes!). I'll take with me many memories and much gratitude for everyone I've met on this adventure. To get here, many things had to go right, and so many people helped along the way.

To you, the readers and fans of the Bone Universe who've shared your love for these characters and this world, I could not do this without you.

To my editor of four years, Miriam Weinberg: a most glorious and brilliant partner in rhyme and crime; and to everyone at Tor who makes this possible—Irene Gallo, Patrick and Teresa Nielsen Hayden, Tommy Arnold for the gorgeous covers, Jamie Stafford-Hill for the layout, Patty Garcia, Lauren Hougen, Anita Okoye, and everyone in PR, sales, printing, and distribution. To my beloved copyeditor, Ana Deboo: thank you especially.

To Barry Goldblatt, without whom. (No, that's not a typo, that's a statement of fact.)

To my first readers, Aliette de Bodard, Eugene Myers, A. C. Wise, Siobhan Caroll, A. T. Greenblatt, Stephanie Feldman, Sara Mueller, Sarah Pinsker, Chris Gerwel, Lauren Teffeau, Kelly Lagor, Nicole Feldringer, Sandra Wickham, Laura Anne Gilman. To Kevin Hearne and Chuck Wendig (they know what they did).

To Viable Paradise and Taos Toolbox, thank you for showing me the way.

To b.org especially. To Natalie, Bear, Celia, Jodi, Arkady, Elsa, Kat, Annalee, Jeffrey, Bo, Cee, Ilana, Oz, Ann, Nanita, Matt, Beth, T, Amy, and Sylvie, for balance. To Jennifer, Wendy, Sara, Nancy, Dan, Jeff, Claudia, Jack, and Mike, for community. To Charlotte and Terry, Becky, Mark, Shveta, Jack, Chris, Eric, Blair, Alex, Kate, Tiffany, Stacey, Dan, Juliette, and Lydia; and Melissa, Josh, and Noa, for friendship.

To Susan and Chris, Beth, Jeff, Kalliope, Raq, and the rest of my family.

And most especially, to Tom and Iris. You are my reasons.

And to you, thank you for joining me on this adventure.

# PART ONE

## THE FALL

# 1

## MACAL, ABOVE

*⌁ As bridges burned, Mondarath fought above the cloud . . . ⌁*

Each night, our city dreamed of danger, crying out for help I could not give.

Wind rippled between towers, flowing along tense borders. Since Allmoons, fighting had spread: Tower versus tower. Quadrant against quadrant. Blackwings versus blackwings. Blackwings against towers, and against quadrants. Even the trade gusts grew dangerous, between northwest and southeast, near the cracked Spire, and around the city's edges.

This night, I joined Mondarath's guard. I flew the city's disturbed winds, looking for danger.

As tower leader, it was my duty to keep Mondarath safe. But I was more than a leader. In the dark, I clicked my tongue fast against the roof of my mouth, echoing. The hard-won Singer skill, learned when I was a fledge, revealed more fliers riding the gusts than usual.

I whistled my windsigns: "Magister," "councilor." Nearby, Lari, one of Mondarath's best guards, whistled back "all clear."

"On your wings, Macal," she whispered.

"Silence," I whistled in reply. *Stick to windsigns.*

We didn't know where or when the blackwings from the

southwest would try to attack next, but I was positive they were out there flying the darkness too.

Evidence of their visits accumulated along our borders—mysterious fires, cut bridges—as if they wanted us isolated and afraid.

Now, on the shortest night before Allsuns, my guards and I flew the darkness, echoing, trying to keep the bridges safe and the city whole. We kept alert for skymouths too, for bone eaters that had been seen near the Spire, and for our friends who had disappeared into the clouds—my brother Wik, Nat and Kirit, Ciel and Moc, Elna, Beliak, Ceetcee, Doran. Even Dix. So many lost. So much to guard against. So much to protect.

Especially this night. Tomorrow was a market day.

Mondarath and the surrounding towers desperately needed supplies. We needed to connect and trade. We needed a market badly.

Last Allmoons, after the council fell from the sky, battles roiled the south and blackwings chased Wik and his companions below the clouds. They'd fought Dix to save our city, then disappeared far beneath it. There'd been few markets since.

One night, the clouds had pulsed blue in almost-patterns, and goosebumps had risen on my arms. But there'd been no sign of the lost even moons later. And once the blackwings took the south, there had been few markets. Too risky.

Now we had to face the risk.

When I echoed again, I sensed the northwest's towers rising around me—Mondarath's broad tiers just below, then Densira's slim, graceful form to the east. Viit was a sturdy monolith south of us, and Wirra a wisp in the distance.

My echoing, required for night flying, and the sharp hearing that came with training as a Singer Nightwing long ago, brought the city's unrest to my ears all the time. Nights like these were the worst. Nightmares twisted the wind around distant towers rising pale and tall in the darkness. Dreams and hunger teased whimpers from children sleeping close together, even at Mondarath. Fear gave a hitch and a stutter to Sidra, my partner's, breathing.

I tipped my left pinion and turned back towards Mondarath, completing my circuit of the upper tiers. Time to venture lower, then return to my own bed before Sidra discovered I was gone once again.

The moonset began to silver the cloudtop below our tower.

I sensed wings approaching fast and low. A flier was trying to circle Mondarath unseen, heading for the tower's far side.

"There," I whispered. "Got you." Whistling windsigns in rapid order—"defend," "lowtower," "attacker"—I rallied the guards who flew with me. We dove in a knife formation, chasing the blackwing from the shadows.

"I'm friendly!" a young voice said—high-pitched and very frightened. "I'm alone."

"A lie," I said. My guards dropped their net, thick with the smell of muzz, over the flier's dark wings. "Blackwings are never alone. Bind this one tight."

As the stars faded in the sky, the flier ceased struggling. Mondarath no longer left anything to chance. My guards drew the muzz-laden ropes closed around the blackwing.

Wary and searching the horizon for more attackers, I circled near a lowtower balcony, echoing. I found no more wings in the sky.

᠎᠎᠎          ᠎          ᠎

"Whom do you fly for?" I shook the blackwing awake. In the dark, they might not see my marks, or know I was a councilor, but they knew they'd been caught. Lari lit an oil lamp and held the fretworked bone container so that light glared in our captive's eyes. She handed me a skein of Lawsmarkers.

The blackwing squinted and fended me off with a hand. "I fly for no one now! I came for help!" I saw his face. His eyes wide with fear. *Good.*

Our guards continued to search the night for more blackwings, to guard the crowded tiers filled with family and refugees above us. Meanwhile, the setting moon outlined everything in silver: the balcony, Lari's watchful pose, the net draped over the prisoner, the prisoner's worn black wingset.

Lari snorted. "You should have come in daylight."

The young blackwing shook his head. "I told the quadrant leader I'd go, that I'd do what he wanted tonight. He's a powerful blackwing. But I wanted to leave Bissel too. I needed to leave. There is too much infighting." He sounded miserable. I would too, in his position.

A second guard stepped closer. Three of us, surrounding the boy. Six more flying close formation just beyond the tier.

"What should we do with you? So many laws broken." I shook the Lawsmarkers so that they clattered. "Blackwings don't hesitate to drop a Lawsbreaker into the clouds. They don't care which tower's Lawsmarkers you're wearing either."

The blackwings had first appeared in the southwest as Grigrit councilman Doran's guards. Doran was dead now, but the blackwings had grown in power, then splintered into groups once their secretive leader, Dix, had disappeared. They were not forgiving of Lawsbreakers.

"Please," the boy whispered. He knelt on the bone tier beneath the net. "Please. My aunts are in danger too. Blackwings fight amongst themselves. I had nothing to eat. I had to fly."

I leaned closer. "What's your name?" The boy smelled of sweat and muzz, but something rang true in his words. His eyes were hollows; his shoulders shook. "What did the blackwing quadrant leader ask of you?"

"My name's Urie," he whispered. "And the quadrant leader told me it was important to start as many fires as I could to disrupt the markets."

I put the Lawsmarkers in my satchel and pulled out a strip of dried goose meat. Handed this to Urie. "Bring him water, Lari. Keep him bound."

My guards did as I asked. Urie chewed on the dried goose as if it was the first food he'd tasted in a long time.

The blackwings had sent a boy to his death. Tower against tower. They'd asked him to do the unspeakable, alone, and they hadn't even fed him. They probably thought a feeling of importance was food enough.

I'd have deserted them too.

"You might have a better chance here with us, Urie." I kept my voice soothing, as I would with fledges. I wanted him to tell me everything. "You can do a very important thing for the city now. Tell me. Are there more of you?"

Urie nodded, eyes wide. "Six blackwings for Mondarath. Coming from the north. Before dawn."

ᚲ  ᚲ  ᚲ

"Put five more guards in the air," I ordered. "Tell six to come here." We had twenty guards, counting myself.

I lifted the net and took Urie's wings. "Make any disturbance, and you will not be with us long," I warned.

The fear in his brown eyes gave me pause. He was barely older than some of my flight students. I didn't like scaring fledges. But these were difficult times. The young man—an infiltrator? a traitor?—nodded his understanding. He curled up in his robe, bound and miserable.

The overnight breeze shifted to a brisk predawn gust. The best traders had always flown around the city's outer edge in the early morning when the winds were fastest. Today's wind snapped Mondarath's makeshift market banners gleefully, and buffeted the few birds we had remaining.

But the wind carried on its back a taint, familiar and dreaded: smoke. I sniffed again and the scent was gone. Had I imagined it? Misjudged a morning cookfire?

I envied those who could still sleep in the tiers above, even restlessly.

There would be no sleep for me now.

The market would go on. We'd stop this attack before it began. With Urie tethered on the balcony, we had an advantage. We knew they were coming. The other towers would know too.

I pulled a bone marker from my pocket and scratched a message. "Take this to Amrath, then Varu," I told the nearest guard. "Warn them of the danger. Tell them every remaining guard goes up in the air now. Even those still in training."

We would make our stand. Our market wouldn't be like the big Allsuns markets of old, but it would be a market nonetheless. Once it succeeded, we could hold more, better markets. Our bellies would fill with different foods, our ears with news from other towers. Our nightmares might ease. We would become a community again.

No longer isolated. No longer hungry.

But if we failed, there wasn't much farther to fall.

In the air beyond the balcony, a shadow moved, its swift passage catching my eye. Another blackwing?

No. A large gryphon diving through the air, a wild kavik swooping around it, screeching.

Watching the spectacle, I tried not to see the birds as an omen. Singers had catalogued omens once, used them to weigh their actions in order to hold the city together. Though I was Spire-

born, I'd left long ago to become a tower Magister, then a councilor. It had been many Allsuns since I'd followed their ways.
Now with the Spire ruined and the Singers disgraced, the city
had become a barbed collection of doubts and distrust.

The guards I'd summoned joined us on the low tier.

I separated six out, including Lari. "We'll fly north and east
beyond the city's edge." The wind was quickest from that direction. While Urie might be lying, we would soon find out. "We
will find the attackers before they can surprise us. The rest will
guard Mondarath, and our captive blackwing."

At the balcony's edge, facing away from the city's towers, I
tightened my wingstraps. Sidra would be furious when she
woke. She'd tell me I needed to be a leader now, not a hero.

Leaders did what was needed. I leapt, and my guards followed me, echoing, back into the night sky.

When we were well east of Mondarath and the city's outer
edge, I spotted a tight formation of blackwings below us, flying
against the silvered clouds. They'd begun their turn. We would
not have the advantage of surprise for much longer.

"Hawk," I whistled, and my guards shifted into the formation,
fast and sure.

As we approached, the blackwings seemed to fold in on
themselves. One flier looped around to overtake another. I
saw the gleam of a knife in the moonlight. Their formation
burst apart as the second flier spun defensively and the other
four tried to stay out of the way.

"A weakness," Lari whistled, using an old sign for wingbreak.

Indeed there was. "Hold formation until we break them
up. Lari, with me." I tucked my wings and dove hard, an old
wingfighting trick that sent me tearing between the two fliers
just as the attacker turned, preparing to slice his victim's
footsling.

My dive disrupted the gust they rode and sent the attacker

into a tumbling spin. His knife flew from his fingers. The other blackwing dodged and then circled back.

The air erupted with cries as Lari engaged the blackwings who'd tried to stay out of the fight. My guards dove quickly to help her. Six pairs of green and blue wings spun and dove among four pairs of black, then three.

With a scream, a defeated blackwing disappeared into the clouds.

The blackwing who'd nearly had their footsling cut rose on a gust. They dove, shouting, right past me. Came close enough that I could hear the black edge of a wing flap on the wind. I saw the fighter's face: dark skin, darker tattoos around her eyes. She flew straight at her attacker, anger overtaking fear.

Locking my wings, I joined her in pursuit. No matter who lost, it would be one less blackwing to fight later.

I pulled a glass-tooth knife and slashed at the attacker's black silk wings. While he focused on dodging me, the woman on his tail destroyed his footsling.

The silk parted with a ripping sound. The attacker dropped fast.

Now there were only three blackwings gliding the wind beyond the city. Seven still from Mondarath.

The tattooed blackwing whistled to her remaining companions, and they dove for the clouds. Moments later, we saw them skimming the brightening mist, taking a fast circuit of the city back to the southwest.

"Pursue?" Lari whistled.

"Back to Mondarath," I signaled. "To guard the tower . . . and the market."

❧ ❧ ❧

We circled slowly back up, tired from the fight and still on the lookout for more blackwings.

When I landed on the upper tier, crowded with Mondarath families and the refugees we'd taken in from other towers, I noted the guards had already tied Urie to a grip on the far edge. My escort on the night raid began to arrive, sunrise illuminating their blue and green wingsilk from below, outlining the bone battens and wingframes in a soft glow.

"You did well." I bowed to each of them as they landed. As dawn tensed the sky, they clasped my arms. We'd stopped the attack. Now we stared into the clouds for any further sign of friend or foe.

As the tier began to wake, unaware of what had transpired, I loosened my wingstraps again.

Once more, I was a Magister and councilor. A teacher and a leader. The sun was coming up. And today's markets had to be flawless. I had a different duty now.

Walking as silently as possible across my tier, I shucked my wings from my shoulders. I stepped carefully between sleeping forms arrayed in crowded geometries of legs, heads, and arms on my tier. Children and adults lay on mats and with their cheeks pressed against the hard bone floor. Finally I reached the silk and down mat I shared with Sidra. She still slept, though fitfully.

I set my wings beside the mat and wrapped a sleeping quilt around my shoulders as if I'd just woken. Padded on silk-bundled feet to the cooking area where I found myself a bone cup in the nets hung from the tier ceiling. Poured it full of old chicory from a goosebladder. With a sip, sour and sharp, the exhaustion from the fight was chased away.

The night watch was done. As morning broke above the clouds, I would stand with my tower, my citizens, no matter what came.

# 2

## KIRIT, BELOW

*⁓ While far beneath, four struggled to rise again,
proud. ⁓*

The night we fell out of the clouds, and all those that followed,
I fought against my dreams.

In the dark, I dodged sleep by singing of wind and wings with
Ciel, Nat, and Wik. The city groaned and wheezed beside us.
When we ran out of songs, Ciel quieted, then slept, her head
pillowed on my leg, her hair caked with grime.

I sharpened blades. Nat paced. Wik leaned back against
the city's foot, and I leaned against him. The cloud above us
blocked the stars. A spare breeze barely ruffled my robe until
a drizzling rain began. We sheltered beneath what remained
of our wings.

When exhaustion won me too, I dreamed only of the ground.

Here, we could not escape the dust and the dead. Not even
in sleep.

Some nights, my mother, Ezarit, walked with me, silent, her
face obscured by clouds, her wings broken. Some nights, the
blackwing Dix attacked us again and again from above.

Their ghosts were always gone by morning.

Tonight, they fought each other, circling, then clashing overhead. They trailed behind me, singing The Rise.

Dreams trapped me the way thirst, pain, and loss caught us

all. Ezarit and Dix wrapped their arms around me, and I fought them, thrashing.

Wik whispered, "Kirit, shhhh." He lowered his voice to keep from disturbing Ciel.

Too late, his niece kicked and cried out for her brother. "Moc! Fly!"

"Shhhh," Wik whispered to her too. He sat guard against our nightmares until we settled back to uneasy sleep.

Too soon, the sun broke the horizon. Light spilled across mud and grime, illuminating the body of the dying city. Time to wake again.

That morning, like many before, bone eaters watched from high perches as we fed the city rotting animals and garbage. The city's thick gullet took it all in. It spat out the cracked bones.

The giant black birds carried the marrow away.

The thick odors of the city curled around us. As the sun rose higher and the day heated, the smell grew worse. Rot and waste, bird and bone. No matter how hard we scrubbed our skin with the ground's unfamiliar dust, we stank. Our moods followed suit. Wik grumbled and muttered.

Ciel swore at me as we passed each other, her arms empty, mine burdened. "Clouds, Kirit, we can't keep this up forever."

Dreams and waking wound through each other now. But in daytime, the heat and stench of our surroundings felt true, in the way dreams are rarely true. The long days beneath the clouds and nights of hard-fought sleep turned everything slow and nightmarish. Our only comfort was each other.

The worries that lurked below Ciel's words felt like the old songs. Her curses became cadence, then verse. *We break the bones, we miss the stars, clouds, Kirit when can we go home.*

"This is our punishment, since being cloudbound didn't kill us," Wik said in passing. "Our way to appease the city."

My breath caught. Such worry in Wik's eyes.

"Do you really hold with that tradition? We broke no Laws."
I said it loud enough for Ciel to hear too.

"Kirit," Wik said, reaching out, then stopping. "We broke all
of them."

That was truth, and I knew it in my heart. We'd broken
War, Trespass, Treason. We'd thrown ourselves down from the
city to the midcloud. We'd been driven down farther by the
blackwings, and—worst of all—I'd hastened the city's death,
instead of saving it.

My shouts had cracked the Spire, had killed the towers and
sickened the city below.

Now we had to keep it alive for as long as we could. To help
the bone eaters keep the city fed, though food was growing
scarce.

Now we appeased the city on the ground, without cease.

᠍ ᠍ ᠍

Those first sleepless days after we fell, we watched our city
sicken further. We worried as it settled deeper into a pained
crouch. I'd tried to help the bone eaters keep the city fed and
alive. "We'll do as they do," I said, following the giant black birds
to a midden heap.

The bone eaters noticed us following. Saw us lift the carcass
of a gryphon and drag it back to the city's mouth. One dove at
Wik while he dragged the large bird.

After three trips to the midden, the bone eaters began to
swoop lazily, calling at us as we hauled rats, gryphons, and larger
creatures to the city's mouth. Their shadows grew smaller as
they roosted higher on the towers, out of range of our arrows.
Some left for other cities on the horizon. A spare dozen cackled at us from the towers above. But the city still lived.

Nat reappeared from behind the city's shoulder, carrying his
own burden. He ignored our feathered audience. Pressed his

ear against the city's thick, enormous hide near where I scavenged. "Barely breathing."

Weeks ago, we hadn't been able to escape the bellows sound of its breath.

"*Barely* is still alive. It chews, it breathes and digests," Wik said, frowning at Nat.

"And craps. Don't forget," Ciel said, her voice a blend of disgust and sorrow at our fate.

It was true. Sick green rivers of the stuff heating beneath the sun mixed with sharp ozone and rotten-egg scents. My stomach, too empty to do more, flipped in protest.

"We keep the city alive until we can get a message above the clouds." I put force behind each of my next words. "They need to know it's sick."

"Not just sick." Ciel tucked her chin and climbed the city's claw, all the way up to a ridge on its massive shoulder, using a tether we'd tied there for that purpose. "People need to evacuate. But who would want to live down here?" She avoided a sore spot and disappeared around a fold in the city's stinking flesh.

"They won't have a choice," Nat said. He patted the city's foreleg.

The city could not feed itself. Hadn't been able to for a long time. The towers on its back had crushed its massive bulk into the ground. The crouch was the city's survival pose, and its trap. If it hadn't sunk to its haunches long ago, it would have toppled.

Because it had settled this way instead, it could no longer move.

Motion caught my eye: Wik, giving the city's maw a wide berth. I could see his figure through its open jaw, framed by teeth and sunlight. His Singer-gray robes were shredded, his skin dulled and highlighted with dust. Grime crusted the silvered skymouth-ink tattoos on his cheekbones.

Wik didn't meet my gaze. He heaved a gryphon in, muttering, "I'm agreed this can't last."

The city's tongue wrapped the morsel, and its jaws crunched closed.

For as long as I'd known Wik, he'd been the stoic one. Solid, like a tower against the wind. Now he muttered when he thought no one could hear him with the city making such noise.

"We agreed to stay and care for the city, all of us," I said. He nodded and kept working.

Despite his muttering, Wik worked harder than anyone. His face was gaunt with the effort, but his determination rarely wavered.

That was part of his inheritance as a Singer—his ancestors had maintained the city's culture for generations without flinching from the task. They'd taught each tower, and each citizen, what was necessary to keep the city safe. But they hadn't known what was below the clouds any more than the rest of us. They'd maintained traditions established long ago: the dead flown to the city's edge and dropped. Living Lawsbreakers too, during Conclaves. Those who disobeyed were weighted and flown, wingless, through the clear blue sky and into the never-ending clouds. They were called cloudbound, and they appeased the city. We'd learned to praise their passage and their service.

Now we knew what had happened to the cloudbound, knew they'd fallen far beyond the cloud and were brought to the city by bone eaters. But not yet by us.

I writhed. No time to think about that.

While we each walked our own circuit to find food to feed the city, Nat sometimes disappeared for long stretches of day and night. He left us like the bone eaters had, with more work. We'd grumbled at first, then searched for him. Found him trying to carve stairs in the bone ridge.

Now we let him vanish without complaint.

At the rate he was going, even with our help, it would take generations to work his way back up the steep bone ridge and into the cloud.

"You're worse than your bird," Wik chided Nat, not unkindly, when he returned. A point of contention between them.

Nat could still not convince Maalik to fly high enough to take a message to the rest of the city. The bird had fallen from the clouds just as we had, when the wind faded. Since then, Maalik was unable, or unwilling, to fly far from us at all.

Now Nat's frown deepened. "I know we need a messenger. But until Maalik can fly again, or we can, stairs are a start."

I would have launched myself at the clouds at that moment. Would have made myself a messenger for them. I did not care about falling or crashing. But there was the problem of wind and wings. We had neither.

Wik caught me looking up, flexing my fingers in missing wing grips. He put a steadying hand on my shoulder. "We'll sort it out." But he stopped grumbling only when Nat opened his satchel. A baby gryphon carcass was stuffed inside.

"Keep the city fed, Kirit?" Nat deadpanned. "The first Law of the undercloud." Even when he tried to joke, I could hear the pain in his voice.

"Not a Law," I answered before Wik could. "A necessity, for now."

It was such a small deed, and so large. And we ourselves were the size of silk spiders, compared to the city. Smaller.

Our prior lives above the clouds faded to dusty memories, as did the old Laws, the old songs.

My feet, scuffing the ground's uneven expanse, made a beat for the song in my head, childish and repetitive: *It can't die, it won't die.* The bone eater up on high cawed at me, mocking. Maybe sizing me up for a meal. Might be I'd die before the city.

We'd found live birds and scraggly weeds to eat. Even Maa-lik had sampled some of the weeds, but spat them out. And the stagnant water hadn't killed us off yet, though it was difficult to get used to the taste. When it rained, we filled our water sacks to the brim, then emptied them just as quickly. But my stomach had long ago stopped growling. We were starving.

We knew we couldn't last. Still, we focused all our efforts on keeping our city alive.

That was the way of nightmares.

\ \ \

When Wik reappeared once more around the city's flank, his face looked ashen beneath the sweat and dust. "There's been a small Conclave, far to the south."

A Conclave. That meant more cloudbound to appease the city.

Ciel sounded crestfallen. "A Conclave? Why? The city hasn't roared in so long. Who would claim to appease it?"

Nat rushed to us. "Who fell?"

Wik shook his head. "I couldn't see." The cloudbound were unrecognizable on the ground, they fell so far. Still, Wik's face was as expressionless as bone. "We must use that."

"You'd debase them further?" Ciel protested.

Wik rounded on her and Nat. "Do you want to live? Do you want to give the others the chance to live? What do you think has happened to Conclaves before now? The bone eaters will help, but we can speed the process up."

Despite myself, I shivered. We'd both nearly been Conclave sacrifices. Many we'd loved had died that way. Wik caught and held my gaze. "Be strong for the city."

His words were spare, but the burning sensation in my stom-ach was not. Wik had been working near the city's mouth earlier. He'd had a silk-wrapped burden then. I realized he'd already begun to feed the city its awful meal. One the city had been eating for centuries, with the help of the bone eaters.

*Be strong.* I would. I had to.

❧　❧　❧

That evening, as the sun's last rays slipped below the distant ridge, Wik and I found Ciel standing on the city's brow, spinning a turn, as one would for flight practice. Arms out, empty. No silk wings, no battens, no grips.

She stepped into a slow curve of mimicked flight, fingers moving invisible wing controls, hooking and lifting the air.

When she caught me watching, she dropped her arms.

My heart sank. We'd lost so much. All of us.

"I don't want to forget how," she said, her eyes welling.

"We'll find our way back into the clouds," I promised, knowing we might not.

Ciel, no longer a child, wouldn't meet my eyes.

We went to sleep hungry that night. In the morning, after awful dreams, we caught a change on the horizon. Variations in the slow-paced movements of the creatures crossing the long stretch of desert.

I spotted the motion at the same time as Wik, but he was the one who yelled, "Look!" He was the one who caused the giant black bone eaters to lift, startled, and crap everywhere again. I ran out of the way, climbed up the rope to the city's shoulder, and saw clearly what Wik had noticed.

In the distance, large, gray shadows moved slowly across the dust, highlighted by moonlight.

More cities. Smaller than our own. We watched the first city bite the second with a fierce lunge. That motion had caught Wik's attention.

We'd watched these cities since we'd hit the ground moons ago. We'd seen them walk to the distant ripple on the horizon that had to be a body of water.

We'd seen them run at each other and fight, their massive bodies and the short bone ridges on their backs looking impressively graceful for all their bulk.

"They won't make good homes if they fight," Wik worried. But we still watched, looking for one with towers high enough to fly from and short enough to scale.

We'd named them, trying to tell the differences between them. None had spires as tall as our city. Most were relatively small. The one we called Nimru was pale, like its tower namesake. Another, Corat, had spires that twisted a little crooked, like Corit tower. These two cities had been feinting at each other for days, loudly.

Our own city had no name. Ciel refused to name a dying thing, worried that doing so was bad luck. That it would speed the city's passage.

Now with one bite, Corat's wobbles and tremors increased, its spires swaying slowly back and forth. A beginning of new nightmares. Corat collapsed to its knees.

Nimru moved carefully away from the long shadows that the kneeling city's towers cast across the dirt.

The sight stilled my voice in my throat and turned all my hopes to ash. What were we doing here, working towards that kind of end? Our city would one day wobble, then fall like this.

But we couldn't warn anyone above. We'd tried to climb the bone wall, but overhangs and bone spurs blocked our upward passage. We tried to help Maalik fly again, and failed. Without the bird, we had no way to communicate with our friends and family in the clouds.

The best we could do was keep feeding the city, keep it alive until Maalik was better, or we found a place to climb that worked.

We could watch Corat die in the meantime.

Over the dark half-night, when the sun was above the cloud, we heard an enormous crash.

When the sun came down once more over our own city's bulk, it lit the plain. Nat stared, his profile in shadow, shoulders hunched.

Corat lay on one side, flesh already sloughing in the sun, spines collapsed and scattered across the ground. Enormous clouds of dust hovered around the city. As we watched, Nimru peeled Corat's flesh and dragged it away. Then the flocks of bone eaters began to descend.

"That must be how our city grew so big, being the strongest and fastest," Ciel said. "Eating everything it could."

"Our city had help growing this large," Wik said. "Our ancestors must have been feeding it for generations. Even before they started to raise the towers."

No one mentioned that raising the towers was what had crushed the city to the ground.

"Do you think they've always been here?" Ciel asked. No one answered her. We didn't know.

I was too captivated by the sight of spires crushed into ground to add anything to the discussion. The real enemy was not other cities, it was gravity.

When our city died, it would fall just like Corat. Collapsing on its side. I held my thumb and forefinger up at right angles and looked at its towers now. There was a slight list. No real change from when we fell from the clouds, as far as I could tell. Judging from our days watching cities in the distance, there'd come a time when our city listed from side to side. A warning period. We had to get above the clouds before then. To get to Elna. To reach our friends, and their friends.

But how? And if we managed to convince them to come

down, what would we do then? We'd been living in the shadow of the city for moons now, with no real way forward.

In the dust on our city's hide, Nat began to sketch out the landscape. The precipitous height our people had raised the towers to. The city's size. "What will happen to the towers high above the clouds when our city falls?"

I imagined how hard they would hit when they struck the ground. I felt that impact deep in my gut.

"When that happens, everyone who is still on the towers will die," Wik said, sparing no one the news. Not even Ciel.

Days ago, Nat took Maalik up as high on the bone ridge as he could climb, then up the stairs he'd cut. He'd held the bird in the air and gently tossed him.

We'd watched Maalik press himself into the air, up-up-up, then falter. Then the whipperling fell back into Nat's outreached hands.

Nat stroked the bird's head after the attempt. "It's okay. We'll try again. We'll make it."

Without Maalik, we couldn't warn Djonn and the others in the midcloud. Unless we had a way up. Even carving steps in the bone ridge on the city's back, which we'd begun to do at night while it slept, was too slow.

Now Wik wrung out the silk rag I'd tied across his forehead, letting the dampness run onto his lips. I swallowed, realizing my own thirst, noting the cracked lips of my companions. We were growing tougher, but still, our sweat was more salt than water. As I tied the rag again, my ragged fingernails caught on the worn-through fabric. The bones in my wrists stuck out, highlighted by the sun as I twisted the knot.

He touched my hand, gently. I shivered. We'd grown lean trying to save the city. We'd grow leaner still when it fell.

"We have to find a place to live," Wik said. His eyes said much more: *This isn't living.*

"We shouldn't just start looking for other cities," Nat said, coming up behind us with another armload of garbage and offal. "We need more time."

I squinted at him. "Where would you have us go if the city dies?"

Nat's forehead wrinkled. "What happens to the towers if it dies?" He pointed. "I know you have no family up there, Kirit, but I do. Ciel does!" He turned his back to us and stared at the sunset.

Ciel stared at Wik. "What about Macal? What about Moc?"

"I am thinking about them," Wik said. Ciel threw up her hands.

"Nat." I raised my hand to touch my friend's arm. He pushed me away without looking at me.

"You haven't cared about anything in so long that you can't understand something beyond survival. And Wik's willing to follow your lead."

That hurt. Worse than a broken bone. Worse than losing my home. I cared so much I couldn't breathe.

I wanted to heal the city, to put things back the way they'd been before I'd shattered the Spire.

A horrible thought began to dawn on me. "You think that I killed the city."

Nat didn't turn. "No." He didn't elaborate.

"Then what?" My voice echoed in my head. He did think that.

He turned his head slowly. "It's not what I think. It's what I know. I know we're not going to leave them stranded up there, not knowing what's going on."

A bone eater crouched on a high-flung bone spur, staring at us. Feathered bulk and a sharp-hooked beak framed the hungry look in its eyes. It screeched. Ciel shivered, and my own skin crawled at the sound.

Could I kill it with a single shot? Recover the arrow? Could we eat it?

Survival, yes. But I had to think beyond that. To keeping my friends alive.

Other bone eaters, those that hadn't flown away recently, perched darkly on the city's spines, cackling. If I'd had a stronger bow, or more arrows, I might have taken a shot. The raptors were bigger than anything else we might find for the city, and for us. If they wouldn't work, they could still help us. We were that desperate.

The city's stomach rumbled beneath its skin. A belch issued from its nose and mouth, thickening the air with stench. The rumble jarred us to the ground, but it was a good sign. We had a fair span of time before it would need to eat again. And we'd have plenty of warning, as the city would regurgitate the bones it could not digest first.

The day grew warmer; the smell intensified.

I settled back into the city's shadow, hoping for rest, but knowing sleep would bring worse dreams.

# 3

## NAT, BELOW

*When monsters clashed, the groundbound watched
a city die.*

I hated the ground, the absence of sky and wind. But truth was,
I hated falling more.

On the ground, at least, there wasn't far to fall.

Stranded below the heavy clouds, my feet fought the uneven
earth. My lungs tightened in the dusty air. Frustration roiled
my gut.

I hated feeling trapped. Especially when those I loved most
remained high above. When they didn't know the danger, and
I could not reach them to help.

We were failing.

Failing felt worse than falling. Worse still because I wouldn't
fall this time; my family would.

As the distant, wounded city, Corat, collapsed to its knees, I
wanted to fly from the ground. To break open the clouds. To go
home.

Beside me, Ciel gasped as Corat wobbled. "That could happen to us." She meant to *them*. To Moc, to Beliak and Ceetcee,
to Elna and Aliati, trapped in the clouds.

"It won't. We won't let it," I said, fast. But how could we stop it, trapped below the clouds? The ground had caught us. Fear had us too.

In the dark, the earth shook and we tasted dust on the air. I watched as Corat's shadow slipped to one side, then crashed, and the dust boiled higher.

When the sun returned, Nimru drove forward and tore its claim from the fallen city's side. We watched the smaller city die, fall, and be devoured.

We slept and woke and slept again. We would not give up.

At night, Ciel cried out in her sleep. Kirit and Wik whispered to each other. I huddled in my cloak alone.

In the next daylight, two bone eaters screeched and took to the skies around Nimru, followed by more of their flock. They swooped and darted, their cries filling the air.

Nimru lifted its head and turned slowly. Towards us.

"Nat, what's happening now?" Ciel said wearily. The sun had passed far above the cloud, and the light had dimmed. The ground shook as Nimru stepped away from Corat. The bone eaters swooped, seeming to encourage it to hunt again.

The sun sank too slowly below the cloud. By the time the city had finished its turn and began moving inexorably towards us, a dozen diving bone eaters surrounded it. Its towers blocked the sun's light.

"How many arrows do we have left?" Wik asked, watching Nimru focus on us.

*How much time do we have?* Time enough to run, surely, but we would abandon our home, our families, in doing so.

Ciel and I had carved more arrows when we could, but they lacked fletching. "Not nearly enough." She ran to get her supplies. *How much time?*

Nimru's bone eaters dove and swooped again.

The few bone eaters left on our city began to screech on their roosts. How many were there? A dozen? Ten?

Our city was immobile. Our bone eaters vastly outnumbered. This was another way a city died.

Kirit paced the length of the city's neck, looking as if she wanted to launch herself right at Nimru. Wik knelt on the city's brow, right hand held out, measuring distance, time.

How much time did we have? Nimru began to pick up speed. Ciel set a finished, fletched arrow down. Picked up another one. *Too slow.*

I looked over the city's side, at the tracks and divots around its body. This wasn't the first time our city had been attacked. We'd just been too high up to notice before.

What had kept the city defended before?

The swirling black cloud around Nimru was my answer. Its bone eaters were close enough to call out now. Raucous. Maalik shivered against my chest.

Our city had once hosted a similar flock of bone eaters. We'd seen them. We'd helped them. And as we had, our city's host of bone eaters had dwindled significantly. On the hunt for more food, better resources.

I groaned when I realized what we'd done.

"What?" Ciel said, trying to sharpen more arrows as we tracked the monster.

"Before we began helping, our city was ringed with bone eaters. They protected the city, even when it couldn't move."

"So?" Ciel said.

"I see ten bone eaters roosting on the city now. They're not enough." Not by far.

Wik turned to look at me. "We chased them away."

We drove them away, and now we had to become like them. Fierce and daring. We had to defend the city from another of its kind. Without talons or claws. Tiny by comparison. Without wings.

Slowly, unstoppably, Nimru—one we'd watched cross the horizon, one we'd watched kill and eat another city so recently—was coming for us.

# 4

## MACAL, ABOVE

*⌐ Pulled apart, towers weakened, unless a bridge was tied. ⌐*

Overhead, more of Mondarath's guards circled, dark shadows in the air. They whistled "all clear."

No blackwings had attempted to approach Mondarath since the dawn attack.

"Is it time, Magister Macal?" a child whispered, her grubby fist pushing at my arm. Her mother gone, her brother still asleep, she stood at my elbow wrapped in a light quilt and the taut stance of constant worry.

I'd disturbed her when I walked by a group of sleeping children, all tossed together like garden leaves after a storm.

"Soon," I whispered, looking at the gray light around us. "Almost time." The child smiled and returned to her bedding. Once I would have replied with certainty; now I was grateful she was too young to hear my hesitation.

I tucked the silk quilts tighter around her against the chill.

"Macal?" The same child again. All Magisters know the rule: answer one question and you are rewarded with a thousand more.

"What is it . . ." I struggled to remember this youngster's name. "Maili?"

"Will they come?"

I tensed again, worried she meant blackwings. Maili was from a tower that had already been attacked.

But she continued, "The buyers?" She held in a fist a multi-colored set of silk cords, braided. I knew they'd been her mothers'. Her chin was set. Determined.

"They'll come. I'll help you trade." Across the tier, I saw Sidra rise, then begin to roll her sleeping mat and tuck it away, making room for the vendors who would arrive on the balcony. The young girl shook her head and gripped her braided silk cords tight.

"These are mine to trade by myself," Maili said, stubborn.

In the near distance, Viit and Densira began to wake: oil lamps sparkled in the soft blue light. But the space between towers stayed empty. No one crossed the sky on colored wings to come to Mondarath yet. The smell of smoke grew. And the young girl, her parents missing, made ready for the market.

For moons, we'd waited, barricaded tight in the towers of the northeast, holding fast to our laws, our songs. We'd waited for order to return, and we'd grown thin doing so. Our stores had dwindled to what our few towers could produce in the garden tiers and what our hunters could catch. There was danger in that. We couldn't wait, couldn't be afraid any longer.

Maili found a tolerant vendor who'd slept on our tier the night before. The man held three whipperling chicks in a basket. Maili knelt beside him and spread her silk cords on a small piece of woven fiber.

The vendor looked to me and called, "Macal, what if no one comes?" Maili watched the two of us to see if my answer would be different.

"If no one comes," Sidra said, coming to stand beside me, her dark hair unbraided still and shining with oil, "I'll buy your cords, Maili. Or trade you for this." She held up one of the last of our apples, and the child's eyes grew wide with delight.

To me, Sidra whispered, "Did you sleep?" She looked doubt-
fully at the blanket, at my wings.

"Of course," I lied.

She ran fingers through my hair. "You are as cold as a dawn
wind, Macal."

At her look, I raised my chin. "We foiled an attack. Six blackwings. The seventh is bound on the balcony."

Sidra, daughter of one councilor, partner of another, drew a
sharp breath and raised her own chin to match. Whispered,
"You flew in battle?"

"And won. The market is safe."

She nodded, but her brow furrowed. "Dangerous times.
Should we change course for safety's sake?"

"I believe we need a market more." I hoped she would too.

Nearby, vendors who'd slept at Mondarath overnight set out
their wares: local vegetables, seeds, a few long-held jars of honey
and muzz. Not nearly enough. Scourweed and small scraps of
silk for patching wings. Oh, how we needed the silk.

I tried to relax. Our guards were strong in the air. We'd
caught a blackwing. We'd stopped more. The market would
happen. All would be well.

But the sky remained empty. And the wares on display
looked sparse to my eye. No tea, no bone cutters, no long
swaths of wingsilk. Those were from the southern towers. What
we offered today was a lack of things, not a surfeit.

Still, I nodded to each vendor and clasped their hands. Markets were a chance to start again.

Would this be enough?

Waiting turned to wondering, our balcony growing warmer
as the sun climbed higher.

"Sometimes vendors are late. Buyers sleep in." Sidra frowned
as she looked across the empty sky. "We agreed on midmorning. But people might wait to see if it is safe. No one likes to be

first across a new bridge." She did not mention what I'd told her of the attack.

I hesitated. "There is always risk."

Even as we spoke, the rope ladders to our tier shook and tightened. Another vendor climbed up from below. Dojha Viit grinned and shook out a small silk mat as she bowed. "Greetings, Risen. Magister Macal. Sidra."

I exchanged my bow for hers. "Greetings, Dojha. You are welcome here."

Sidra embraced her old friend tightly, then let her go, looking closely at her dark brown eyes. "You haven't been eating."

"The fledges eat first." Four fierce words, each carefully knotted with no room between them for argument.

In the distance, figures began to gather on the bridge from Viit. I pointed at them. "Just late indeed." There would be a market today, after all.

But Sidra's frown lingered. I saw her slip an apple from her pocket and press it into Dojha's hand.

Around me, most Mondarath citizens had risen and put their mats away. Fledges and adults circled the few vendors warily, looking through the wares available, buying little.

Sidra left my side. "I have an idea." Moments later, she returned carrying a basket of teas from two Allsuns ago. We'd been saving them for my brother Wik's return. For the homecoming of our friends, Kirit and Nat.

"There's no reason to hold back any longer," she said, practical as always, but her voice broke on "hold." I pressed my hand to her cheek, then touched my fingertip to my eye and looked up. I felt as if I was choking, but not from sadness. A tension rose up between Sidra and me—two towers, separated for a moment.

"No reason, especially if you've given up hope," I said.

She looked at me, surprised. "On the contrary. I have hope for this market." She pulled away, turned, and did not explain further. She spread the tea out on Maili's mat—a faded silk square with a map of towers marked on it. When Sidra stepped back, murmuring, "Best get a fair price, little one," Maili's expression spread into a wide grin. Several of Mondarath's, Viit's, and Densira's hightower families gathered round to grab up the bounty.

"What if the blackwings come?" the bird vendor said.

Sidra pressed a hand to her chest, but then stepped back, into the slowly growing rows of vendors and buyers, who had all stilled, watching us intently.

Is a market a market when few come to buy and even fewer have things to sell? Even if it's the only one of its kind left? My shoulders sagged with the weight of our responsibility to the community. A normal market was crowded.

I lost sight of Sidra among the sparse sellers and buyers. Then I heard her.

"Ridiculous!" Sidra's irritated laughter rippled across the tier. "That's far too much."

"Times are hard, Risen." The vendor, Sarai Densira, waved her hand over several items we already had plenty of. "Perhaps later, if I haven't sold the lot."

Was Sidra mocking us by playing at markets when she knew the risk? I readied to scold her, and the Densira vendor too, when I realized their words had caused the entire tier to relax. Children once more ran through the rough stallways, and three new shoppers crossed the bridge from Viit.

The pattern of barter had offered the day a familiar rhythm, and people knew the words to this song. Soon more haggling echoed across the tier.

Sidra came to stand by my side. "A little early for haggling?" I teased, but I was proud. This was the city as I knew it best: hard won and ready to rise to any challenge. This was my partner, who could shift tension into victory.

"It's the one joy remaining to me, love," she said. "We cannot survive on muzz and scourweed."

Another vendor waved for her attention, pulling a small basket from a pannier. "Why worry over scourweed when you could be feasting on stone fruit?"

At the words, many heads turned. Stone fruit was growing rarer, as much of it was in the south. Stomachs, including mine, growled.

"Trade or markers," the vendor said. But he slipped two small fruits to the waiting children.

"Save the pits," Sidra called. "You can plant them." New hope in her voice.

The children, each clutching a nearly ripe stone fruit, had cleared the balcony and entered the market.

It was gone all too quickly, but it had done the trick. My anger faded. Others began to buy and sell.

All around, families brought from their stores things they'd held dear during the fortifications. Even Sidra crowed with delight on seeing the perfect yellow thread she needed to mend her wings.

Across the empty sky marked by too few birds, I saw one flier, then two, approaching on the morning breeze from the southwest. They came faster and more directly than anyone had a right to do when towers were on such alert during Fortify.

More blackwings? I whistled for my guards. Reached for my wingset again.

The hunters circling Mondarath formed a claw in the air and surrounded them, threatening to drop them from the sky.

"Let them land," I called. "Guard them close." I stayed wary, my fingers touching the grip of the glass-tooth knife at my belt.

Guards, two of them. One very young. Neither wore black wings. *Relax, Macal.* Neither spared a glance for Urie.

"Sidra." I drew her aside, away from the vendors and shoppers, and we went together to greet the guards. On the way, she lifted a cupful of chicory from over our small guano stove and held it, waiting, while the guards landed and furled their wings.

She passed it to me and our fingertips brushed. For a moment, I held her hands in mine, and the cup too. She held my gaze, and I was caught there, connected to her and strengthened by her. The half smile, the dimple in her cheek. The wink and the sideways glance at the young guard she thought should receive the cup first. Then she slid her hands from beneath mine and stepped forward with me.

"Strength to your wings," I said softly. I offered the cup to the new arrival Sidra had selected.

The first guard bowed, her hair falling loose from her braids and sweeping past a scabbed-over knife scar, red at the edges. She'd come from the southeast a fortnight ago and had been staying at Amrath. I'd last seen her when their tower council had agreed to the market days.

"Thank you, Risen," she said, taking the cup and sipping enough to wet her lips and no more. Minlin from Grigrit, now Amrath. Minlin, who passed the cup back to me to share again, rather than passing it herself. Sidra had chosen well.

"Our honor to serve the city of the north and west," the second murmured, bowing, then taking the cup from my hand. A stranger's face, but the markers tied to his wings and in his hair were from Grigrit. For a moment my heart rose. Perhaps they were here to trade.

Then I saw their empty satchels, their hard looks. Had I been mistaken? I touched my knife, but left it sheathed. The Mondarath guards who'd landed with the travelers drew closer.

Sidra, retrieving the bone cup from the second guard, was closest, and in most danger—and one of the visiting guards had closed his hand around the space above his arm sheath. The wind rushed in my ears. Sidra—I had to warn her. To shout.

But instead of a knife, the guard withdrew a message chip. This was no attack after all, but news. "From Amrath," she said slowly. Our messengers had passed in the sky. "Blackwings raided in the middle of the night. They also infiltrated Naza at dawn. Mondarath holds the only market in the northwest now."

I bit back a groan. My warning hadn't come in time. We'd been defeated before we even began.

Urie, tethered on the balcony, was trying to make himself look as small as possible.

No. We were not fully defeated. We'd captured their first attacker and stopped a blackwing attack. One of three. That wasn't enough.

The bone horns began to sound long and low at Wirra and Varu. *Defend. Fortify. Attackers.* Again.

We had saved our own tower, but the quadrant was still in danger.

"Clouds." The message chip I held dropped from my fingers and hit the floor with a crack. A gray pall thickened in the distance above Varu as smoke spilled from the side of the bone-white tower.

The guards turned and watched. "More attacks," said the one with the scar. "We should go."

I helped them lift wingsets to shoulders and tighten their straps. Sidra brought another bone cup of water. Each sipped. "On your wings," she said.

"On your wings, Risen," the youngest responded, and spread hers. But she stopped, frozen, watching a new figure, trailing smoke on the wind, approach Mondarath. The flier passed through a building line of guards that stretched to Viit, Densira, and Wirra. I heard faint windsigns: "known" and "friend."

I'd sent a refugee guard from Laria back to the southwest in hopes of trading. Raq, one of few among those who could still locate supplies. Brown wings, a particularly hesitant dip to her glide path from having grown a little too big for the wingset.

The Amrath messengers recognized her too. "You sent Raq to the southwest on her own?"

I hadn't thought they'd know each other, but I realized that was foolish. Raq traded with many towers. "I sent her south to broker better trade. She seemed capable and willing."

The young guards turned and looked at me, eyes wide, and I cleared my throat. "She wanted to go. Said she knew just who to talk to."

By now, Raq was closer. Her wings wobbled and failed, then caught the wind again as she struggled to take the most direct path.

"Go help her," I ordered. The guards launched, their wings locked. I prepared to join them. Another battle was the last thing we needed, but I would not sacrifice my tower. "Stay close," I shouted, then whistled for arrow formation.

Sidra put her hand on my arm. "You are needed here more, Macal."

As she spoke, my order was relayed through the air. I closed my eyes against the wind for a heartbeat's time, my feet still firmly planted on the tier. Around me, quieter sounds of agreement, whispers of fear. A vendor far to the back still hawked their wares.

Sidra was right. I paced the length of the balcony. When I approached him, Urie stood eagerly, bound hands extended. "Let me help too. As a show of goodwill."

Thanks to Urie, we knew danger threatened the northwest again.

We'd known already that the trouble Dix had brewed in the southwest—trying to grasp control of the city for herself through lies and betrayals—would spread. But I had hoped for a respite now that she was gone, and a chance to restock before more trouble came.

I'd hoped we could change the wind's direction. Instead, we'd just strengthened it.

More smoke poured now from Varu, and then from farther away, near Bissel. "They're attacking in broad daylight." How could I stay?

"There is no council left, and no Singers, to enforce Laws beyond your own tower," Sidra said gently, pulling my fingers from the straps. "You are the last of both. And the unrest is spreading too fast to be chance. We need you to stay safe. Talk to the captive blackwing again."

She was right. We were too few, and the blackwings were still too many in the southwest to be safe. Urie was our best source of information. If we could trust him.

Raq, her tailskirts and footsling smoldering, finally careened close enough to the guards for them to bring her in. She dropped to the balcony, and we beat at her robes while she whispered through a smoke-hoarse voice.

"They shot fire arrows at me! From Varu! I'd stopped to rest. They wove through the tiers like they lived there. Amrath, Varu, even Haim. And no one in the southwest would talk to me. They're too afraid of the blackwings."

Those who had come to Mondarath to shop pressed close to the balcony once more, and this time nothing could distract them from watching and listening. Remaining vendors began stowing their wares. Maili put her silk cords back in her pocket and clutched Sidra's tea. Raq raised an eyebrow at our captive blackwing.

"Fortify," I told my guards. Our quadrant was not yet entirely on fire, we still had a chance. But for how long? Had Viit been infiltrated? I glanced at the people still on the bridge. Did we know them well enough? I turned to the boy.

Urie shrank from my gaze. His guards moved closer to him. Tower against tower. The songs had come true.

"Tell me the rest of what you know," I ordered our captive blackwing.

There would be no bridges built from trade. And no more markets today.

# 5

## NAT, BELOW

*⌐ All that shook, all that fell was sky and bone, ⌐*

When Nimru attacked, I wanted to rise above the desert's red dust, to fly away, and up. To get out fast.

My feet remained firmly planted on the ground. I would fight instead.

The bone eaters ringing Nimru dove and swooped. Their shadows huge and black; their wings blocked the sun. A dust cloud built around them, around Nimru as that city increased speed. More bone eaters launched from Corat's husk to cruise languidly in Nimru's wake.

But our bone eaters, the ones who'd done nothing in days? They rose on their haunches and shrieked as if they knew what was coming.

"We should run," Kirit said. "Right at it."

The idea of running right at a creature whose pores were bigger than me was laughable. "Nimru would barely notice even as its foot pressed your wings into the dust," I said. "Your shoulders, I mean."

Kirit looked at me, her chin set. The setting sun caught her scars, the few beads remaining in her hair. "We'll chase it away anyway."

"You can't chase it away, Kirit. You saw what it did to Corat. Kill it or be killed by it."

She looked hard at our own city's brow, at the sores on its hide. At giant battle scuffs in the dirt all around its resting place. "We'll find its weakness. Chase it off, if we can."

Cities. I was done with them. I didn't want to leave the other city standing. I wanted to end it, get my family, and move to safety.

Wherever safety was.

Nimru put its head down to smell the ground, stuck a nose in the awful runoff from our city, still some ways off. Then it lifted its gaze to us again and kept moving.

Wik lifted his hand again. Thumb aligned with the horizon. He rose to his feet.

"How much longer do we have?" Ciel asked. Her pile of arrows had grown.

"Go for the eyes if Nimru lowers its head like that again," Wik ordered. "All of us. The left eye. Hook it and try to pull." He looked at Ciel. "Not long now."

The eye was one of the most tender spots on any creature. If we could alter Nimru's inexorable path away from our city, we might—not turn it exactly, but keep it from gaining a direct hit.

An oncoming city, even a small one in the distance, would not be in the distance for long. And we were not prepared.

We should have climbed. We should have gone up instead of remaining here. We should have tried to reach the clouds and never stopped.

Nimru took up the entire horizon while still far away. Though it moved slowly, it did not stop. The momentum it built up while first trundling, then pounding, then barreling right at its prey was a tattoo of hunger against the ground.

Once, I would have given my wings to know this truth about the cities.

Nimru—how I regretted giving it a name—had set its sights

on our immobilized, dying city, and us. I would forgo any chance at wings to make it go away.

Wik's and Kirit's feet pounded the city's hide, beating fast patterns.

"It cannot die, it must not die," Kirit whispered as she ran past. Her eyes were focused on the monster in the distance. She didn't know I'd heard.

I rose to the balls of my feet, grabbed arrows from Ciel, and raced behind her to our city's far side.

"We'll try to divert it!" Wik called over his shoulder.

Four tiny people. Only ten bone eaters. Not near enough to turn anything.

As Nimru closed on our flank, its own bone eaters, starved-looking in comparison to the sleek, fat bone eaters of our city, began to attack. They dove at us. Ciel fired arrows until Wik yelled, "Save those!"

She ran to grab bones from the midden to throw instead. Wik joined her.

Large pieces of white bone arced into the sunset-reddened sky.

All but one bone eater chased the delicacies.

The last bird swooped low, casting a dark shadow as it reached out its claws to catch live prey: me. It tried to grab my hair and lift me by it. I ducked, barely. "Watch out!"

"Ciel, get back on the city! Stay with us," Wik yelled. But Ciel had already slid down a flank and was out front, waving a bone hook at the last, diving bone eater.

While we were distracted, Nimru moved faster and dust billowed, blinding us.

I could hear it roaring. Our own city bellowed but did not move. Nimru turned slightly at the last moment and slipped in the fetid runoff from our city's side. The giant head bent once more to the ground.

"Now!" Wik said, running as fast as he could at the monster's head.

"No! Get back!" Kirit yelled. Her voice strong as a knife, cracked with worry.

"If we don't stop it, there'll be nothing to get back to," Wik yelled over his shoulder.

He was right. I chased the tattooed Singer into the cloud of dust, choking as it clogged my throat and blew into my eyes.

The city's head was still low when we reached it. Wik threw his line, caught a sharp ridge above Nimru's brow, and hauled himself up. I climbed up behind him, missing the city's gnashing teeth, the hot hiss of its breath too close.

A black carcass crashed to the ground below us. One of the derelict bone eaters, its throat ripped by a cousin's claw. Our own bone eaters finally dove in force.

All ten circled Nimru now. And Nimru, with all of its momentum, slid uncontrollably towards our own city, its legs scrambling for purchase on the red mud.

Wik and I rode Nimru as it wobbled and swayed. We clung to the enormous bulk of it and tried to keep climbing. I lost my grip and slid down the rope. Began climbing again. Below us, Kirit fired arrows at the creature's right eye. I couldn't see Ciel.

Finally, Wik dangled above Nimru's left eye, half his robe tied over a bone spur on its forehead. He swung himself back and forth until he had enough force to drive his bone hook into the corner of the creature's eye. On the next swing, he drew his knife and stabbed at its lower lid.

I dug my own knife into the city's broad foot as it passed and hauled myself up on a ridge of fat, then began stabbing and digging at the tender spots between its claws, where the nail met the skin. Blood tinted the air crimson. Far above, I could barely make out Wik. I couldn't see the others. I kept stabbing, and the creature roared in pain, a sound that shook the world and left me nearly deaf.

Nimru thrashed, the motion creating wind vortexes, and tried to bite at us and peel us from its skin. Kirit and Ciel—they'd made it out alive—shot arrows past my line of sight, striking the eye, the delicate inner nostrils, everywhere that seemed the least bit tender. Ciel ran forward, trying for a better shot.

Meantime the flock of bone eaters grew to twenty, then thirty. The hungry birds swooped at the city's injured eye in twos and threes, and Nimru began to slow.

"Get me more hooks!" Wik bellowed. I tried to scramble up closer to him, but Kirit was on the rope now, and much faster. She drove the next hook into the city's seeping eye and loosed the strip of silk tying Wik to the creature's head. Then he swung all his weight against the hook and Nimru roared, shaking its head hard, as if a stinger had caused it great pain.

Slowly, Nimru began to turn, rumbling and gnashing at us. At the bone eaters.

This time, momentum worked with the smaller city's bulk and with gravity to pull it off balance. Nimru slid once more on the slippery ground and runoff from our larger city. It tilted and wobbled. Struggled to regain its footing. Blood gushed black from its wounds, adding to the mess on the ground. Thick yellow claws dug into the dirt, and the earth cracked, quaked, and lifted.

In the dust and confusion, our own city watched through a slatted yellow eye the size of a tower tier. Jaws slowly opened.

Nimru shuddered. Its foreleg collapsed beneath it.

Clouds, it was going to fall over, and we were on the low side.

"Get off now!" I yelled and dragged Ciel with me, back and closer to the ground, hoping Kirit and Wik would jump.

Wik's robe tangled on the winghook. He struggled and kicked, trying to break free.

I yanked the few grips we had remaining and drove them into

Nimru's flank. Began to climb until I was close enough to throw a grip-anchored rope. Wik caught the rope, barely. He wriggled to the end of the bone hook, dropped, and swung free. He hit the ground hard, just beyond the city's thrashing foot.

Kirit followed. Nimru rolled. We slid down its flank and ran out of the increasing shadow. The ground darkened, the narrowing space between the two cities blocking the sunlight.

Nimru's smaller spires began to break with loud popping and shearing sounds. Bone cracked. Shards hit the ground around us.

"Get clear!" I yelled as the smaller city crashed into our larger one, the tips of its spires connecting with and destroying large chunks of the bone ridge near the cloudline as it came down. We ran clear as a sound like deep thunder echoed over and over again. The sound of Nimru in pain, protesting gravity, pain, and death.

I pushed Kirit away from a falling piece of tower. Bone smashed the ground near where we'd just stood.

"The city above!" Kirit pointed up.

Pieces of smaller tower tiers smashed through layers of bone high above. A cloud of dark wings—birds or bats—erupted overhead, out of the collapsing bone structures. The creatures sped off.

The sick sound of towers cracking began anew.

Nimru's towers dug deep into the larger spires of our own city. They stuck there, at sloping angles.

The earth shook with the force of the blow, and the smaller city crumpled and bled. Our own city wavered, but stayed upright. Both cities groaned and the smaller one breathed in painfully, its sides shuddering. Then its eyes rolled back and a brackish vomit poured from its mouth that ended in foam.

The sounds from above began to cascade, a rumbling and tearing. Unimaginable.

"Run far," Wik yelled as a larger chunk of tower, crusted with filth and debris, crashed to the ground. Then another. Above, a shadow loomed and grew large in the cloud top. I did not move, shocked. The city above was falling on us. Kirit grabbed my arm and pulled.

One struck tower cracked with a wrenching sound. Daylight poured through cracks where smaller spires intersected the tiers. It fell now, ripping through the clouds and trailing streamers of vapor behind it, falling fast and sudden and crashing to earth atop Nimru, crushing its head.

The point of the tower dug a crater in the mud below as it plowed into the earth. Bone drove everything before it, birds and moss and plants and clouds; I could not look to see if there were people inside.

A hundred tiers or more had crashed to the ground. The dust billowed and enveloped us. We could not see.

The world came down around us, and we ran for shelter.

# 6

## MACAL, ABOVE

The city's last day began like any other: tense and angry. For two days after the market attacks, the towers had furled in on themselves. The city was wound as tight as stowed wings. Few messengers arrived at—or left—Mondarath.

We braced for the blackwings to come for the remaining towers in our quadrant. "What are they waiting for?" citizens whispered.

Sidra looked at me with clear eyes. "They are waiting for us to weaken."

We were weak already. Scarcity would do the rest of their job for them.

Within our tiers, fights grew pettier. Many blamed Urie, Raq, or anyone they didn't know. *Blackwings. They could be anywhere.* The air grew charged with fear.

The sky had emptied of birds and fliers both.

Urie, arms still bound, looked out at the sky from the balcony. He'd told us enough to keep the blackwings at bay for now: what heights they flew, how they used the clouds for cover.

We'd strategized: guarded the bridges, hidden the remaining food. We didn't let anyone approach unchallenged. This was a different life than anyone had known on the open tiers.

I was starting to believe that the young blackwing truly

wanted to stay on Mondarath. That it wasn't an act. From what I'd seen out on the wind beyond Mondarath, his tales of black-wing infighting were more than accurate.

I'd decided to allow him a taste of freedom, to see what he'd do, but I couldn't let him feel too comfortable. Sidra helped me come up with a plan.

"It's a bit like training a bird," she'd explained.

Urie wiped his bound hands on his robes and scrubbed at his face with his knuckles, trying to get some of the grime off. Then he bowed his head to Sidra as she approached him. "Risen."

She knelt by him. "You helped our tower. You're welcome to shelter here for as long as you wish to continue to help," she replied. "You do not need to go back." She said this loudly enough for all on the tier to hear. "There are many of you with pasts in the southwest quadrant who shelter here. We do not ask you about this, only that you declare your loyalty to this tower, this quadrant."

"That's premature," I started. We hadn't talked about this.

Sidra gave me a look that said, *Enough. Stop torturing this boy.* She gestured to Urie's hands. "We've welcomed far more dangerous guests to Mondarath in the past," she said.

I wasn't torturing him. I needed his help, but I didn't trust him. I couldn't very well go to the southwest myself. And Raq had failed.

*He was so young still. He'd betrayed his commander to stay here. Could we trust him?*

Seeing my hesitation, Sidra touched my shoulder.

I nodded, finally. Sidra loosed his ties, smiling at the boy.

Urie smiled back and clasped her arm. "Thank you." Then his expression shifted from relief to worry.

The balcony stilled, everyone listening.

"The southwest is lost," he whispered, rubbing his wrists.

"Blackwing factions struggle amongst themselves to control towers—not even quadrants, and I think Rya—one of the leaders—is fighting to ride that out. She's smart. But my aunts can't risk waiting. They are too valuable to some factions. Rya promised to protect them, but she's not strong enough yet."

His aunts were why Urie had agreed to come here. I understood now.

"Rya?" Urie had mentioned her name earlier. I knew that name. Doran's daughter.

After Dix's takeover of Grigrit, when Doran was declared a Lawsbreaker and banished into the clouds, Rya had gone into the wind. "She still lives?"

And if she did, under what possible circumstance would Rya take the wings of the people who killed her father?

Urie bobbed his head. "She's thriving. Her tower—she took back Grigrit—is organized. She's got artifexes under her wing. But she still must follow orders from the quadrant leader. And he's trying to keep her from power."

He pulled back, frowning. "Or, he was. She was supposed to join the raiding party two days ago. She knew it was a trap. She still obeyed orders."

We hadn't told anyone what had happened in the sky beyond Mondarath. "Does Rya have tattoos?"

Urie nodded. Put his fingers to his eyes, like wings.

I put a hand on his shoulder. "Then she lives. We surprised them while another blackwing attacked her. She got away." What that said about infighting among the blackwings was important. But what the raids said about our own weaknesses in the north was more so.

"Which blackwings are which?" I asked. My fingers ached, my shoulders too.

Urie shook his head. "Some factions are making lighter-than-air, as you knew. Others are deciding who can and can't have wings. Or food. The leaders from each tower fight often; only a few blackwings can get everyone's attention. Rya is one of those. That's why the quadrant leader doesn't like her."

I wondered at that. "But she can see reason? She can lead?" Even as I said it, my mind balked. *She's a blackwing!*

And still I'd let her escape.

"She's convinced some of her people that if they work hard enough, they won't need the towers or Laws. Some believe they might not even need wings," Urie said.

"It's cloudtouched, but true," Raq said. She made a face like she'd sucked on a sourfruit, a delicacy we hadn't seen in moons.

"What's her real goal?" I needed to know.

Urie answered Raq. "It doesn't seem cloudtouched when you're around Rya. She's got different ideas about how to do things. Blackwings. Conclaves. She's like a clear sky." Urie's eyes softened at the edges for a moment.

I watched him carefully. "Are you with us, or with her?"

Raq spoke before Urie could respond. "Rya's very compelling. And once a blackwing, always a blackwing."

Urie could not contain his frustration. "Rya had my aunts working on a lighter-than-air project. They're artifexes. They're important." He sighed. "And when a blackwing group from Laria tried to kidnap them, Rya intervened. That angered the blackwing quadrant leader. I trust Rya, but not the others."

We were past the edge of war. Urie's aunts might help us, and he wanted to bring them here, but politics and alliances roiled the southwest. Helping him could bring the blackwings to our balcony again. I hesitated.

But Sidra smiled and held out her hand to him, as she'd do with a skittish bird. "You are welcome to bring them here."

"Would you let me have a visitor kavik to send a message?" Urie asked.

*Visitor kaviks.* A relic from another time. "We don't keep extra, not any longer." The birds couldn't be trusted to fly where they were told, not after Dix's new ones had homed straight for blackwings invaded the roosts. We rarely used our remaining whipperlings either. "Face-to-face is better than message chips, always." Looking people in the eye, questioning them to see their reactions. Flesh couldn't conceal lies as easily as bone. I watched Urie's eyes. Was he concealing anything? He needed to be truthful if he was going to stay in the northwest.

A guard shift landed. Another three guards launched from the towertop and began to fly a Fortify formation around the tower, ready to fight.

While Mondarath watched its guards glide the wind, Urie spoke again. "The southwest says towers should save themselves, raid for what they need. Cut bridges if they have to. And appease the city at all costs. Many of them believe Dix's sacrifice kept the city quiet since council fall but that it will roar soon."

"Rya will never celebrate Dix." Sidra handed him the last stone fruit. "Eat."

"What sacrifice?" Maili asked quietly, drawn to Sidra's side by the fruit. I tried to shoo her away, but she clung like nettles.

Urie finished most of the fruit in three bites, then handed Maili the last bite and the pit. He kept talking while he chewed, his voice matter-of-fact. "Dix pursued the Spirebreaker and Brokenwings below the clouds for their crimes," he said, his voice light. "The sacrifice that cleansed the city. There's a song about it, at least in the south, by that name."

Spirebreaker and Brokenwings. He meant Kirit and Nat. And my brother, Wik, with them. And Ciel and Moc. All fighting below the clouds after Dix betrayed the council. All lost to us now. Perhaps forever. No, I would not let this stand.

I turned on the boy fast enough to make him blink. "That is

what you were taught by your aunts?" My own voice rippled with anger. He'd stayed with us for days as a captive believing this, and I hadn't known. What else didn't I know? "Can you think past this to a different truth?" His time on our tower hung in the balance.

Urie put his hands behind his back, wary now. "Are you challenging history, Risen?"

"I'm challenging blackwing history. I'm challenging the rumors spread by kaviks and songs in the south. I'm challenging what you think you know. Will you listen?" Or will we wake one night to find you gone and our bridge cut?

I rubbed my temples. So much distrust, everywhere.

"No—yes, I can listen." His voice was quiet. "I didn't know there was another side to the story." A look in Urie's eyes told me this was true. He was terrified of his misstep.

"Breathe. I am challenging what you think you know, not *you*." Voice steady, I held my calm. I was a Magister. Singer-born. This kind of teaching was our charge and our trust. *And our moment of greatest betrayal to our community.* I could redeem that, starting now.

"Even after all my years in the sky, understanding why people need someone to blame when they hit rough wind is beyond my patience. Especially this morning." If I'd flown against this boy in the Gyre, fighting for the right to speak, I would have beaten him to clear this truth. The thought made me catch my breath. I a grown man; he, not much more than a child.

But those, again, were long-gone Singer ways. And the Gyre was long gone too. We could be better. All of us.

To his credit, Urie drew a deep breath and nodded. "There are many ways to sing a song, I guess."

The tension ebbed. The echo of the Gyre's songs faded.

"There are." The version of The Rise I'd learned as a child

in the Spire was a good example. The towers had different words, and I'd had to relearn.

Urie ducked his head. He could relearn too.

Perhaps one day, he could teach others. But first he needed to teach me what he knew.

I nodded to him. "You are welcome here as long as you are willing to look past convenient truths and renounce the southwest's lies."

"I will." Again, earnest voice, clear eyes.

I had few other options. I decided to trust him. Clapped him on the shoulder. He drew a shuddering breath.

"You mentioned your aunts. What about more artifexes? All of them?" I'd take any opportunity to find out more about the lighter-than-air he'd been working on. We needed that now more than ever, with the towers so crowded. But everyone in the north who'd known about it was dead or had disappeared.

Urie tilted his head, thinking. "My aunts are at Grigrit with several others. They've got schematics and the stills that were taken from Laria during the battle. They're figuring out how they work. It's slow going. But, Macal? They're always watched because of the kidnappings."

Raq sucked her teeth and nodded agreement. "He's telling the truth. I barely saw them."

If we couldn't get to the artifexes, we couldn't get the lighter-than-air either.

"Barely is better than not at all," Sidra said. "We'll find them."

"Would they come here willingly, if we could get them out of Grigrit?" Sidra asked Urie.

He nodded. "They want to leave. I want them safe."

Sidra was right, barely was better than not at all. "We'll make plans to fly tonight," I said to the nearest guard. "Tell Viit and the towers." It was a chance at change. We had to try.

As the guard unfurled his wings at the balcony's edge, preparing to follow my orders, he stumbled.

A moment later, the tier jerked from beneath my feet, then slammed back.

Mondarath shook. All the towers shook.

"What is it?" Maili cried. I gathered her in my arms and held tight.

Below us, shouting and terror. An enormous cloud of bone dust began to billow around Mondarath.

Trying to calm my own jagged breaths, I remembered my long-ago Spire training, the promises my Magisters had made. The shaking would end. The roars would quiet. They always did.

But Mondarath kept shaking. The very air seemed to quiver as the towers jerked and tumbled. With my free hand, I grabbed for Sidra's arm and held on. Sidra clung to Dojha.

The sounds were the worst. They were unlike any roar I'd ever heard, even during my time in the Spire. Much worse.

Urie lost his balance and wobbled at the balcony edge, still wingless. Sidra and I stumbled to catch him and pull him back without me losing my grip on Maili.

Raq, wings half unfurled, fell off the ledge, then righted and fought her way up through the turbulent air.

All around us, roosting birds tumbled still half asleep. They hadn't time to spread their wings. Feathers spilled into the bone dust clouds, while dark bodies spun into the depths. Wings struggled to pull against the tide of gravity and surprise.

The towers kept shaking.

Below, the clouds seemed to bubble and bulge. Holes opened like eyes in the mist. Snapped shut again. The roaring all around grew louder, and I saw more birds fall into the clouds.

Sidra stumbled and fell to her hands and knees, her eyes on

the tumbling figures, which were not birds at all, but people. I reached for her, steadied her.

People fought to spread their wings. The clouds reached up to swallow them.

I tried to join those already in the air, but the tower jolted and rolled too much for anyone on it to gain footing. I couldn't fly.

"Get them!" I yelled to my guards already in the air, and I was not the only one. Everyone still on the tower yelled and pointed for someone.

Guards dove and hooked as many as they could, then swooped and circled, unsure of where to put their rescues. I tried to rise, to help, but my neighbors pressed me against the balcony edge while the towers kept shaking, and all we could do was watch.

With a terrible crack that we could hear clear out at Mondarath, the Spire listed and shattered. In slow time, the distance making it seem even less real, a great sheath of its bone wall swung up into the air and spun outward, striking Varu, then Bissel. Bissel buckled and slid into the clouds. Nearer to us, Wirra cracked and toppled with a terrible roar.

The wind's soft passage turned to screams and terror. My heartbeat drowned out all sound; Sidra's hand clutched mine. Bodies pressed against us. Maili's mouth opened in a silent scream.

Then sound returned as the noise built with the shaking to a maelstrom roar. The wind swirled. Raq and the guards fought to stay aloft. Neither air nor tower was safe.

As the city bucked, we wrapped arms tight against a bone spur and braced several guards who were sliding down the bone tier. Across the sky, others on Densira and Viit held on to anything they could.

Gravity tugged at us, and we formed nets with our bodies,

wrists locked around forearms, elbows hooked at angles. My shoulders rubbed hard against my neighbors', and I smelled fear thick as smoke.

Together, we resisted the pull of everything that wanted to swallow us, and all we held.

Between Densira and Viit, the bridge Kirit and the Singers had built three Allmoons prior tossed and flipped. Sinew and fiber squealed in the wind as the towers that pillared the bridge jumped in the shake.

"It's going to break!" Sidra said, her voice loud against the roaring in my ears. More screams and shouts filled the air and then the city jolted.

The shaking turned into a rolling wave that jarred my muscles from my bones, then jerked them taut. The bridge between Densira and Viit snapped and swung loose. "No." The word tore from my lips, aimed at everything: my neighbors, the people clinging to the bridge's remains, the city. I lunged for the edge to help. "Hold on!"

"Macal!" Sidra said, her voice shaking. Her arms strained, and she tightened her grip on our neighbors, even as they also tried to pull away to go to Densira's aid. "You cannot. You must stay and lead."

My grip on my towermates, and their grip on me, meant we couldn't do more than shout anyway. So we watched, hearts railing against the fact that we weren't in the air, helping.

When Densira's core wall began to crack at the point where the bridge had been, the noise rose to incomprehensible levels. A new dark line grew visible even from a distance. The air filled with more dust and a rich smell of heartbone that caused Sidra to vomit and me to feel dizzy.

Sounds of bone cracking, sounds of fliers taking to the air, young children in their arms, sounds of shrieking from those who hadn't donned their wings in time. Sounds of gravity, embodied, as the tiers above the crack tilted and began to twist, then fell away into the clouds, tumbling end over end. Densira's pieces of daily life erupted from the tiers—mats and shutters, wingsets and cookpots. People. The broken tower spun, batting these from the air as it tumbled, breaking bodies and silencing screams until the bone dust silted red in the afternoon light.

A guard lifted Maili and took her away from the balcony.

As the survivors hung unbelieving in the suddenly quiet air, the city stilled. The fingers that bruised my arm from holding on so long peeled away, and I unhooked my elbows from my neighbors'. Sidra, pale and ill, would not release my hand.

The first thought I had horrified me. *Safe!* I was safe, and those I loved best were too. Among all of my city, we had survived.

But then the dust cleared from my thoughts. It was up to us to save the city now.

Bile choked my throat. All of the city. Save us.

Turning to Sidra, I gestured into the dust-filled sky. "We'll gather survivors."

Guards lifted more citizens to safety, while other residents circled, shocked.

"And check in on other quadrants," Sidra said. She peered out through the dusty air. "I can't see farther than the northwest quadrant." Her voice quavered. "I must find Dojha." Her childhood friend. Her wingmate.

"We'll find her." My mind, attempting to encompass the scale of what had just happened to us, fed me songs, Laws. Tradition. Luck.

*We were unlucky!* Panic swirled, and I fought it.

*Think of what's needed, Macal.* Shelter, safety. Those first. We would find out what happened, stabilize, rebuild. To do that, we'd need lighter-than-air. A truce with the blackwings. My mind spun with needs.

"Macal? Your orders?" Raq called.

So many answers to that question, and so many people looking to me for those answers. "Survivors. Find them now. Bring them here or to the closest stable tower." We'd deal with the blackwings later.

"Your wings? Can you fly?" I asked Sidra.

"I think so, with repairs." The press of bodies on the balcony had crumpled Sidra's right wing. She smoothed the silk with shaking hands, then removed a broken batten and looked around for a replacement.

The dust in the air made everything feel tightly constrained, as if we were trapped within bone. We heard the sounds of our own breathing, close.

Farther away, shouts and cries echoed.

I pulled the winghooks from over my shoulder and looked at them. They wouldn't help replace Sidra's batten. My breath caught. What if the city shook again while she was fixing her wings? "Hurry, Sidra."

The jolt had been severe enough that many had crumpled wings, some beyond repair. Sidra traded out battens with a neighbor until she had full support, though not full power. "This will have to do." Raq found Urie an extra pair of wings, green with whorls of gold, slightly damaged but still flyable.

We were ready to fly when, with a rumble, the light's angle shifted.

Shadows grew in new places. The birds lifted from the towers and flew off. The entire city listed slightly east, and citizens locked arms and grabbed on to bone spurs again. I smelled spilled chicory, heard someone sobbing.

Sidra knotted her fingers in my robe. "Macal," she whispered.

"We're still here." For now, that was all I knew. That was all that mattered.

"Still here," she echoed. Her fingers tightened, holding on to me, rather than the tower.

As quickly as it had started, the motion stopped, and we looked around, shocked at the difference a few moments made.

Densira's top six tiers were gone. While Viit looked steady enough, many of its residents clung to its high side. Five citizens still swung from the bridge's remains, their wings missing or damaged. Several guards swooped to their aid.

From this distance, I could not tell friends from strangers, but it did not matter.

I launched into the dusty air and aimed for the bridge. Behind me, Sidra shouted for others to do the same. The city I'd known and loved since I left the Spire was gone. In its place was a mass of broken bone towers and red dust. Through the haze, I could see a handful of mostly intact tiers. Others, like Bissel, had disappeared completely.

In twos and threes, we moved the people on the bridge to the safety of our tiers and returned to the sky.

Sounds of crying. Trapped sounds. Singer training had sharpened my ears, and I could hear what other rescuers could not. In Densira's broken topmost tiers, I heard wailing.

After frantic searching, I saw a tiny foot, toes moving with every cry. A child's leg pinned beneath a bone column. Gently, I lifted the column away and raised the small boy—for it was a boy, dusted like a ghost—to my chest. "We'll fly to Mondarath," I said. The boy looked at me, mute from fear.

"You'll be safe there," Sidra promised, another child in her arms.

Moments ago, what was wrong with the city had been a topic of open debate. Now what was wrong was obvious.

We flew through clearing dust to Mondarath and gave the children to a family who had set up healer stations in their tier.

Their floors were filled with bodies, the air with moans. I saw Dojha there, tending a young woman.

When I returned to the sky, the dust had cleared, and I could count towers nearby, including Mondarath—eleven within my line of sight here and in the south.

Eleven.

Out of more than twenty north of the Spire and several dozen more south of it.

Another set of cracks, like thunder from below, crossed the sky. A balcony tier on Viit rippled.

"Get your people out of there," I heard Urie yell. He'd been flying citizens to safety, like the rest of our tower guard. But his warning came too late.

The cracking sounds continued until the tier sheared down the side of Viit, taking the balconies below with it. Screams ruptured the air again.

"We are so tiny here, so few against a city coming apart. How do we recover?" Another guard panicked.

"We're together in this," Sidra said. "We're not few." Her voice, a calming breeze. The guard settled. I knew what it cost her, and I wished I could hold her hand for strength.

"Bring everyone you can to Mondarath, then Varu," I said. I hoped the blackwings would stand down in light of the disaster. "Those seem to be the most secure towers in the north." Somehow our tower had stood firm. It had no bridges to pull and sway against the shaking. Amrath also stood, damaged but still upright. Naza, close by, was cracked in half, its core wall exposed and several tiers to the south completely gone.

Rich smells soured the wind throughout the morning. When the shaking began, sharp undernotes of brass and blood had mixed with heartbone. Now those scents turned to rot and spoilage.

I drew closer to Mondarath, taller now than its neighbors.

Those other once-proud towers had broken off at the higher tiers, or fallen into the clouds. The sight made my breath catch, and my next words, spoken to the still-circling guards, came as a rush of emotion. "Get everyone as low as you can. Get down to the lower tiers."

The upper tiers were no longer safe. The cracked towers were no longer safe. A rotten smell permeated the air. The city's quake was one part of a puzzle. The rotten smell another. But how far down did the cracks go? What had caused the quake? We would need to know.

Coming from the east, Urie appeared, flying roughly, and burdened. When he landed beside me, I saw he carried two smaller fledges, both uninjured, both crying. The children's weeping father stumbled through the air behind him, looking for a place to land safely on the balcony. There was none. "Don't land. Go down," I waved him off and pointed. "We'll bring the children to you."

But the man wouldn't listen. Instead he furled his wings in the air and crashed to the balcony, stepping hard on an injured woman. Her companions rushed the man and dragged him towards the edge.

"Stop!" I put the full force of command into my voice. "Let him go. He only wants his family, as you do." And, miraculously, they stopped. Let go his robe and returned to tend to their own.

Urie had stayed and helped us. He hadn't needed to. I clasped his arm in the tumult. "Thank you, Urie Mondarath. You are welcome here."

But even as I did so, a song echoed in my mind. I recognized it as an old Singer's tune, but nothing more, and pushed it away. Not now. I bent to help the wounded. To wonder who among the survivors would help me lead this group, with no signs of safety around us.

Later, I would remember the song. It was the kind of song

taught to very young Singers in times of emergency and grief, one that had no real meaning when the city was safe. A singsong rhythm. A Law, really, something old that dug deep into memory and remained there until it was needed:

*Gather in safety and remove*
*To highest of towers, away from cloud and fear.*

Abandon. The song for evacuating a tower. And it could not help us now.

# 7

## KIRIT, BELOW

*⌒ Then two went far and two climbed home ⌒*

My city fell around me, and I could not save it.

Bone shards struck the cities' hides and the dusty ground.
The earth shook. That was frightening enough. Worse, familiar objects—broken wings, parts of a loom, small treasures long
carried up from tier to tier—now plummeted, their value rendered false and surreal by the drop.

I choked on dust and bone, stunned. Saw a cup, flattened; a
spoon, bent. I focused on those so that I did not have to see
what else fell.

But I heard it fall. I heard it until I could not listen, until the
sound of now blended with the sound of the council falling long
ago, falling around me in the clouds. I could not close my ears,
no matter how much I wanted to.

Wik dragged me away from the city's side. Nat and Ciel
scrambled after us. We huddled in the open, waiting out the
shaking and shattering, for what seemed whole lifetimes.

*Are you all right?* they asked each other. Each time someone
asked me, I lied mutely, nodding, *Yes, I'm all right.* I was not all
right. None of us were.

When it grew quiet, Ciel whispered, "Which tower fell? What
quadrant?"

"No telling," Wik said. He didn't correct tower to *towers,* though I knew it had to be more than one. "From that far up and us so turned around? No knowing until we can see the wreckage."

I'd opened my eyes, now I shut them again. Nat, gray as bone, knelt beside me. "It cannot die." Why speak of it. Why say anything.

We tried not to talk too much. Closed mouths, eyes, noses. Drowned in the torrential smashed air of our city.

"Let it be a tower long abandoned," a voice murmured, strange and hollow. My voice. I tried to stop speaking, but couldn't. My mouth filled with grit. "Let it have been empty and so far gone already."

But we all knew that was unlikely. A broken cup, a bent spoon, shattered wings told us otherwise.

Finally, the dust cleared. The clouds, when we could see them again, glowed with a hint of sunrise. The silence was broken now and then by more small pieces of bone hitting the ground, but no more towers fell near us.

The wreckage spread so far, it seemed to touch the horizon. The city cast a strange shadow as the sun came up: its spires were tangled and bent. Two giant bodies lay low and close.

What was left of Nimru leaned against our former home. Its spires jammed against our city's bone ridge below the cloudline at sharp, jagged angles. The fall of debris continued, a soft patter on the ground.

That sound, like a heavy rain, was the loudest in the world.

Debris littered the desert around the city. We were painted pale with the dust of it. In the distance, the air swirled and lifted, reaching for the sky.

Had skymouths been brought to the ground by the disaster? Was that a dust-limned tentacle out there on the ground? I rubbed my eyes, and the vision disappeared.

When the birds returned, they circled to the ground to inspect the wreckage. They avoided the towers. Large birds first, then the smaller ones. The bone eaters loomed, then began lifting pieces of bone away.

To eat them. To feed the remains to the city.

*No.*

Though I'd known the bone eaters were coming and what they would do, my stomach flipped over, then hung there. I fought my own memories of driving away the birds from my mother's body, even as I realized this horror had bought us a chance.

"Wik," I whispered. He'd moved from our shelter. Stood looking at our dying city, and at Nimru, the city we'd tried to turn. I was not loud enough. "Wik!" I scrambled to join him.

When our city breathed its last, which might be soon, the towers above would not survive. But for the moment, the bulk of our city rested upright, propped by the fallen spires of its sibling.

We stared at the wreckage. Wik began collecting things from the rubble: a brass spear, arrows, bone hooks, grips. He did not speak.

"We have food, both for us and the city," I said. "Carrion and vegetation, both. We can sift through the wreckage for supplies."

"We can also climb Nimru's remaining spires," Nat added. "And go back up."

He saw it too.

"And then what?" Wik asked quietly. "We'll have to convince an entire city we speak an impossible truth."

"How long do we have?" I tried to judge the angle of the city as it rested against Nimru. Would it collapse first, or roll on its side, like Corat had? *How much time?*

The city opened a huge eye. Heaved a breath. *Still alive.*

Wik cleared his throat. "With the food supply and what the city eats, we might have a couple of moons. Fourteen or fifteen days." His voice sounded sure. His eyes, though. Those hawk eyes, normally so focused. His eyes darted everywhere.

Even as I hesitated, calculating, Nat and Ciel rushed forward.

"Fourteen days!" Ciel said, already scrambling up Nimru's lower limb.

"Come *on,* Kirit!" Nat yelled.

My legs wouldn't move.

"We need to find a place to take them when they come down!" As I said it, I knew I was right. Here, at the bottom of the city, they would be exposed to heat and damp, to predators. They would not be able to fly away. "We have to find them refuge, sanctuary."

I sounded brave, but I was afraid. I couldn't face the wreckage of the city above.

A city I'd helped destroy when I broke the Spire so many Allsuns ago.

"Do that later, Kirit! We go up and get them down now!" Nat climbed on the first chunks of bone spires. Ciel yelled, and he hauled her up too.

My knees locked. My chest constricted. I couldn't go back up.

Wik, his eyebrows drawn together in concern, turned to stare at me. "I didn't know Nimru would slip. That it would fall like this. How could I not know?" His words were so quiet.

He took a breath and coughed. Covered his tattooed face with a scarred hand.

When he straightened, he turned back to our companions, stronger now. "Think for a moment! Going back up now is like throwing yourself to the clouds. It's not safe. Where will you be if the city rolls and the towers collapse?" He gestured to the spires of both cities, so precariously intersected.

"We *have* to go up now. It's their last chance," Ciel protested.

"It will be mayhem up there. Who will believe you? What

will you tell them? That we've been living on this"—Wik pointed to the city—"like fleas on a bird? They'll throw you right back down again."

"We still need to find a new place to shelter," I added. "Now more than ever." My stomach curdled, unhappy with my choices.

Ciel straightened, fingers clutching the bone tower, the set of her chin fierce. "*I* will tell them that if they stay above the clouds, they'll fall and die. And *I* have to go back up *because* there will be mayhem. And Moc is there in the middle of it. There's a little time now. And there is a way up. *I* must try." She was shouting. Tears ran tracks through the dirt on her cheeks.

Wik put his hands up in defeat, but his face was resolute. "You're right. Kirit is too." His eyes still darted up and down, studying the wreckage. The horizon. "We split up. You get them, we'll find a place for them."

High on the ridgeline, my wing-brother, Nat, watched me, saying nothing. The look in his eyes was one that would stay with me longer than any Lawsmark. *Betrayal. Abandonment.*

In his eyes, I was turning my back on our city.

In my own eyes, I'd already done much more than that.

I'd killed the city long before I knew what it was. I was not Spirebreaker, nor Skyshouter.

I was Citykiller.

Now I had a chance to undo the damage. To step away from what I'd wrought and find a way to begin again.

*No time to hesitate.* How many times had I heard that, from my mother, from my own lips? I turned from the cities and faced my future, just as Nat and Ciel faced theirs. Over my shoulder, I said, "Strength to your wings. We'll meet again, here."

I could not say more. More would mean good-bye.

Nat spoke, finally, his voice thick with emotion. "Maalik will stay with you. Take care of him. Get him strong again, and you can signal us when you find our home."

A whistle by my ear. A wing brush against my cheek, like soft fingers. Small claws pricked my shoulder. A moment's forgiveness? The whipperling nestled in the collar of my robe. I felt lighter with him there, and heavier. His soft breaths became a reminder of my obligation.

I turned for a last look at my friend. Nat might not make it, nor Ciel. Wik and I might not survive either. But we had to try. "A moon. No more. I will signal you. Safe passage."

Nat waved and, without another word, continued his climb. *Up. Up. Up.*

We had a chance. Our last chance, to rescue the city.

# 8

## NAT, BETWEEN

*On birdback, through cloudburst, so close to home*

Three Allsuns ago, what I wanted most was a good hunting bow. A new set of wings. Goose and gryphon for my family, comfort for my mother. That's what mattered.

What I wanted most now was to make it to the top of a fallen tower. To climb into the clouds. To save my friends and family.

Three Allsuns ago, I would have called that cloudtouched.

Now I picked splinters of rotting bone from my fingertips as I climbed.

Ciel scrambled ahead of me. I'd convinced her to use a tether, in case she slipped. "And in case *you* slip," she'd replied. But I couldn't get her to pace herself. She'd scramble a few tiers as fast as she could, then have to stop and rest. Each rest became longer, her breathing shallower. When she slipped, she grazed shins and elbows. She kept going.

When she rested next, I helped pull splinters from her forearms. I didn't lecture her. I understood her momentum; all I wanted to do was keep moving too. One step closer to my family—to my mother, Elna; to Beliak and Ceetcee—was better than where I'd been the moment before. And each stop to rest slowed us more than an even pace would have. My frustration grew.

When I'd seen them last, Beliak lay injured. Ceetcee's belly was growing bigger, and Elna, weakened from her descent into the clouds, had sickened. Now that we were moving towards them, my fears for them grew too.

"You can keep going, Nat," Ciel said at one such stop. She rested in the crook of a bone spur rendered soft and green by moss and rime. "I'll catch up." She returned to sucking on a de-splintered finger, trying to numb the sting. Hiding how fast her breathing was, how her ribs were working like bellows.

"This looked a lot easier from the ground," I said, giving her time. Easier at least than cutting steps in the harsh, unscalable bone ridge. The collapsed spires from Nimru had helped with that. But now the climb had grown repetitive, the clouds loomed, and we were still far away. *Fifteen days to get up and back down.* It felt impossible.

I tossed a bone shard in the air and caught it, thinking. No more throwing things off the towers. Not when I risked hurting someone below.

Above, the gray expanse was lit red by the day's second sunset as the sun descended below the cloud again and pressed upon the horizon. The cloud's underside moved and turned slowly above us, still at least a day away.

I shook myself to stay awake, then shook Ciel. She'd dozed off with her finger still in her mouth. "No time to sleep, not yet. We still have the light for at least one more tier."

We might never make it through the cloud in time if our stops grew longer. Maybe Ciel was right. I could keep going.

"What if you went back down?" I said, worried. "It's not that far, and it's safer than continuing to go up. You could still catch up to Kirit and Wik."

She glared at me. "My brother is up there." She shouldered her pack—a bag we'd filled with a few items from the collapse: grips, some food. No wings, though.

If Ciel would listen, she'd be able to get back down from

where she was, and I wouldn't have to worry about her when the harder vertical climb began. "I'll bring Moc back down to you," I said. "I promise."

I'd saved her twin's life once already. But I'd also nearly lost him in the clouds.

I wanted Ciel to listen to me. I'd saved her life too.

But she shook her head, a slow *no*. I stifled a groan, and my stomach rumbled. Hunger.

"What if you fall?" We'd had this argument before. She made a face at me as she lifted the safety line between us.

"If we climb together, you'll catch me. If I climb alone, I'll tether to the tower." She wouldn't stop climbing.

Her determination made me grin, even as the reality frustrated me. "All right." I came to sit beside her on the bone spur. Ciel was lankier than when I'd first met her and her brother. Her legs swung over the edge of the tower, all knobby knees and ankles. Her silk footwraps had long worn away, but she was skilled at climbing barefoot now. Calluses and sore spots marked her still-small feet. I pulled out my water sack, and she smiled. Her cracked lips began to bleed a little.

"Drink some water," I said.

"It isn't time for that yet."

"Do it anyway. I can't carry you if you pass out."

As she sipped, we watched a large black beetle with crimson markings on its back crawl up the incline and wave its pincers at us.

Since the collapse, we'd seen all sorts of bugs, but none this big. Was it edible? I worried about having enough to eat. "What if one of us got sick? Fell. What would the other do?"

Ciel frowned. "Keep going. That's most important. Stop worrying."

I worried at her because I couldn't worry about anyone else. Not about Kirit and Wik, still below us on the ground. I was too angry to worry about them. Not about Maalik, who I hoped would protect them, or at least might recover from his own fall. Not for my family far above me in the clouds. When I thought about what might have happened to them in the meantime, I couldn't breathe. I needed to breathe. So I worried at Ciel instead.

She waved me away. After a long wait, she finally nodded. "Ready." We began to climb again.

When we drew close to the top of the collapsed tower, the jagged breaks began. We were within reach of the main upright tiers of living bone that would, I hoped, take us to our friends and family and then above the clouds. If any of their tiers were still standing after the collapse.

Ciel panted, sweat plastering her hair to her forehead.

"Slow down," I said. "We're closer to the midgrowth than I thought." Ciel drank a few sips—her allotment and mine too.

The sun sank farther below the cloudline, highlighting telltale dents and ridges in the bone towers where each central core had grown over its tiers. The growth had connected and formed a solid wall below, but now there were more places to grip. How had we climbed so far and not reached the clouds?

I threw the bone chip in the air again. A breeze tumbled it, but it still fell straight down. I caught it, thinking harder.

What if we were closer to the midgrowth because so many of the outer towers had collapsed all around the city? Some of the breaks did look jagged, the bone beneath, white and yellow, rather than brown and gray. If not for the tilted bone spires we'd scrambled up, the route would have been impossible.

Ciel, struggling to stay on her feet, nearly warbled with hope. "We might make it to the cloud before true night tomorrow," she said. "I'd been wishing we could fly, but now we'll be all right."

Even if our wings had been intact, we couldn't have flown

up to this level. Far below, the wind wasn't strong enough. Here, the towers weren't high enough to generate their own updrafts. But I knew how she felt. I longed to fly again too. After I found my family and didn't let them go.

*Tomorrow night.* Ciel could make it from here. If I kept climbing on my own, I might reach the cloud earlier. By tomorrow morning, even. I could feel their arms around me, hear their voices. Ceetcee's laugh, Beliak scolding.

Instead, the heavy, looming cloud above us pressed down, making my skull ache, even as the cloud itself remained stubbornly out of reach.

I wavered on the problem. I could move faster without Ciel, but if I did, she would have to pace herself on her own, remember to drink water. And so I could not—would not—abandon her either. Slowly we crossed the span where the smaller city's broken towers jammed into the thicker, older bone tiers of our own city. The first time I touched one of our towers, my skin prickled. I was finally going home.

But Ciel's arms drooped. "I need to rest again," she finally admitted.

"There's a safe spot here." A small depression in the bone wall was Ciel-sized and sheltered by an outgrowth of core. A ledge beside it would let me sit and keep watch.

In the towers above, the central core pushed out as the tiers rose, moving occupants up, always up. Here, the core looked like so much kept goose fat drippings, solidified and mashed together. The result was a variegated tint, depending on the age and width of the towers, and the lichen that grew on its southern edges.

I withdrew a tether and drove two bone pitons into the thick wall to secure Ciel to the side of the tower, and her eyelids drooped further as she fought sleep. "Rest," I said.

Ciel tossed restlessly in the nook, then slid into a dream. The moon passed between the horizon below and the cloud above. I settled my main water sack and the food satchel beside me and leaned back on the tower wall. We would climb this together.

When she woke, I would still be here.

Yes, a moment to rest would be good. Then we would climb.

When I closed my eyes, I saw Nimru attack again. I saw that often now, dreaming or awake.

❧ ❧ ❧

I woke struggling.

In the distance, Ciel screamed. Below me, I saw only air, and the bone tower receding.

A bone eater's giant black feathers whispered in the passing air. Its purple-black claw edged in more feathers, tightened around me. Above, the bird's barb-encrusted tongue rasped against its beak.

My pack, made of torn robes and braided vines, fell away. It bounced down the tower's outgrowth. Imagining my body bouncing similarly, I stopped struggling. Ciel crawled to grab the pack before it slid farther. She hung on to it while I was lifted higher.

The black grip wrapped me so tightly I couldn't scream. The bone eater took me farther away from the cities and the ground. The bird banked and began to turn towards the east, to a rocky rise.

I knew why: to drop me, then wait to suck the marrow from my bones.

I lay still and tried to breathe in the bone eater's grip. Looked up at the black expanse of feathers above me until my heart began to beat a fast pattern of panic again. Against my better judgment, I looked down.

Below, two tiny cities lay close together. Two more walked

slowly in the distance. Dust whorls might have been Kirit and Wik making their passage across the red desert. From this height, I made out lines and patterns in the ridges. Places cities had fought and died? Perhaps something else. Beyond the stone ridge where I was headed, more ridges appeared, sharp cones of stone and dirt, with clouds or smoke ringing several.

Beyond that, something sparkled. Water? It was so far, and very bright.

There was more to discover beyond our city. The idea would have delighted me, if I weren't busy trying not to die.

No.

I couldn't die. Not with Ciel stuck on the bone spurs. Not with my family stranded in the midcloud.

I hadn't died in the Spire.

I hadn't died by falling through the clouds.

I was not going to die now because a bone eater thought I was a meal.

The claw gripping my waist and shoulders ever tighter said otherwise. It stank, too.

A seeping crack in the claw's cuticle nearest my chest, in particular.

An idea grappled with my fear and panic. *Breathe, Nat. Think. You're a hunter. You've flown the Gyre.* You can use this.

I'd stuffed a skein of tethers in my robe pocket from the wreckage. I could stretch my fingers enough to reach it. Tying it to the bird's claw was hard, but with my teeth and both hands, I managed. I wrapped it as tight as I could near the dewclaw and slipped one wrist through the gap, then I dug at the cracked claw with my other hand.

The giant bird screeched so loud my eardrums ached. Then I was tumbling nearly free, save for my wrist, caught painfully in the tether. I pulled myself up arm over arm as the bird wheeled to look for me.

Before it realized I was not falling through the air, I'd reached the top of the claws and scrambled upright, braced against its leg.

When I drew my knife and stuck it through feathers into the bony cartilage there, the leg pulled in close to the bird's body. Pressed me into suffocating, dandruff-filled down. Feathers' greased edges and sharp points scratched my skin. I sneezed again and again as I scrambled higher on the bird's flank, then to its back.

The world spun beneath me. My fingers dug deep into the bird's skin, and it screeched. Bucked. Tried to rid itself of me.

Wingless, with one last chance. I was not going to fall, not going to disappear from this world.

One tether left. Spidersilk, strong and elastic. A legacy from home. I looped it as we flew, the line blowing against my arm in the wind, and tied a knot in one end. Then I tossed it in front of the bird and hoped the ruse would work.

The motion caught the bone eater's eye. The bird dove for the knot, catching the line in its beak. I pulled hard, hoping it wouldn't break. With a guttural choking noise, the giant bird twisted, tried to shake me off, then shifted to ease the pressure on its beak. The cities came back into view, very far away. The cloud edge was closer.

I could fly up from here. I could push the bone eater higher and reach the towers. I adjusted my crouch on the bird's back, trying to hang on as it flew closer to home than I'd been in moons. Fear was as sharp in my mouth as the wind beating at my face. This was not exhilarating flight; this was pure, unleashed terror that I held by the beak.

We flew for a long time, until suddenly, the giant bird wasn't turning any longer. It had ducked its head low. I drew back on my improvised harness to keep the line taut.

A wall of solid bone lay directly ahead of us. The bone eater had ducked in order to run headfirst into the tower. At full speed. The carrion bird might have hoped to fly between a series of holes broken in the towers and decapitate me, but its aim was terrible. Especially with me yanking on its beak.

The beast's tongue clacked hard and dark against its beak. A high-pitched keen echoed from its throat as it rippled past the bone lattice and through it. Fast enough to scrape at me, but not slow enough for me to safely jump away from the bird.

So I jumped off anyway.

I careened right into the core wall, curling myself into a ball as I rolled across the tier, letting the precious tether go and crashing hard enough to knock all breath from my lungs. I coughed desperately, waiting for a claw to descend. But the bone eater's broad back retreated, and for a moment I saw blue sky and the trailing edge of a cloud.

Then the thing turned and came back, beak first, tongue extended, reaching for me. There was nowhere else for me to hide.

*What if one of us couldn't continue?*

I'd been worrying about Ciel then. Now her answer was my only hope for my family.

*The other would go on for both of us.* But I had to keep fighting too.

I shut my eyes and thought hard about living. Then I charged. I scrambled, dizzy, right at the beak, the head behind it, and the dark eyeballs set in that head, which were glaring at me.

The bird squawked in rage, blasting me with a shower of acrid spit and foul air that made me retch. I stood once more, wobbling on my feet. Kirit's strategy came to mind: *Just run right at it.* So I charged, shouting, nearly falling into it.

The bone eater gave another squawk, louder this time, and tried to pull itself out of the tier. It smacked its head on the bone floor, then thrashed and gave a horrible rattle in its throat.

A river of bile poured from its mouth, followed by red-purple blood, and as I watched, amazed, the bone eater died on the floor in front of me.

I carefully picked my way past its neck and upper body to find the other half of it hanging over the edge, skewered by a spear through its belly. Beside the gushing wound, and completely covered in filth, was Ciel, up to her arms in gore, triumphant.

"You won't believe this." She pulled two bone tablets, a brass plaque, and a grimy flint from its belly. She wobbled on her feet and her arms shook, but she held up a hand when I tried to help her. "I helped the windbeaters skin birds when I was a fledge. We can use a lot of it when we climb. Here—" Ciel handed me a bone knife. "Get its feathers."

"How did you get up here so fast?" I asked her. *Why didn't you keep climbing?*

She chuckled. "You left your grips down below. I put your pair on my feet, and mine on my hands." She wiggled her bare toes, then pointed to a pair of grips discarded nearby.

Slowly, to the sound of ripping and tearing, we took the bone eater apart. The guts went in one pile, the belly contents in another. Feathers and the strangely dark bones, we set aside.

Ciel cleaned the skull and offered it to me. I pushed it back to her. "That's yours—you earned it."

"I can't carry it up, it's too big." She looked at the heavy thing sadly, then pushed it to the edge of the tier along with the rest of the bird's entrails. Shoved hard. "Let it feed the city," she said. Then she looked at her arms and her robe. "This is never going to scrub off." Her brass-colored hair was matted thickly with gore.

If we'd had scourweed, she might have had a chance. As it was, she stank, and I did too. "When we get to the midcloud," I promised, "there will be water to wash with." I dried the flint and used it to start a small fire out of brush in the tier. "Hard to believe anything would eat flint."

I hooked a chunk of bone eater's thigh meat over the fire. It sizzled and popped, rich with fat. The result was gamey, but delicious.

Concealed between bone spurs, we rested for a few hours on full stomachs. When morning came, we stepped from the tier and looked up. We were far above where we'd been, right at the cloud's edge. Moisture prickled my skin, wind tugged at me. Soon, maybe, I could see stars again.

"Best start now," Ciel said. Her voice was calm; she sounded surer of herself.

"You did well back there," I whispered.

She beamed. "I know."

Using our handmade grips and pitons, plus the tether lines we'd brought from below, we set off. We began our spiderlike crawl up the bone towers.

# 9

## KIRIT, BELOW

*⌒ Across desert, through illness, in search of home ⌒*

Walking away from the city was like flying into a storm: fast, my heart pounding the risk, the distance, the losses. But we weren't flying. There was no storm. Just our footsteps in the dust.

We walked away from everything we knew. Our friends, our pasts. We walked away from the broken Spire; away from Laws.

My feet—callused beyond any tower dweller's, save my companions'—scuffed the ground and raised small clouds of red dust. Cruel imitations of wind, at ankle level. These hung behind me and then pulled back to the ground as I walked away.

With the desert open before us, for a moment, it felt like a new start, a new chance to right everything wrong.

❧ ❧ ❧

"Tower and Spire no more," I whispered, thinking of The Rise, but also of our names. *No more Densira, no more Skyshouter.* "But still Spirebreaker."

"And Citykiller," Wik whispered beside me.

I stopped, dust coating my feet. Stared at him. My worst name for myself on his lips. The very air weighed me down. "Why would you walk with me, then?"

He turned back towards the two intertwined cities and said, very quietly, "I meant me." He pointed at Nimru. "I did that."

At that moment, I wanted to wrap my arms around him for comfort, for both of us. But he held up a hand, determined to continue. "It gives them—and us—time. Time enough to reach my brother, time to convince the city to move. If anyone can guide them down, it's Macal."

My arms hung by my sides, useless as wings. I couldn't speak. He was *proud*.

Wik stared at the cities, piled side by side in the distance. Swallowed and bit his lip. "That doesn't make up for what Nimru did to the city, I know. But we gave the towers more time."

I clenched my fists. "This is Singer logic? The ends justify the means? Do you feel the same about what I did to the city?"

He bent his head. The silver tattoos on his cheeks caught the light. He'd thought about it, as had I. "The Spire would have cracked without your shouts. With enough time. The city was already crushed by its own weight. You just . . ."

"Sped up the process." That's what he was trying to say. "A process our ancestors began by climbing the towers, by forcing them to grow higher. By thinking we were all there was. Now we know differently." So many were trapped above, on the city I'd killed.

Wik's charge at Nimru had bought them more time.

Wik's face was fierce, his skymouth-ink tattoos stark against his skin. "You didn't—"

But I saw a flicker of conflict cross his face. He *did* see the two actions differently. One was in service to the city. To keep it safe. Our trust. One sped our downfall.

"I did. As much as anyone." But I was finished. Too many had died.

Wik stayed where he was. Would he follow a citykiller? Or

would he return to climb with Nat and Ciel? He'd wanted to, once. To find his brother.

Finally, his words came fast. "Let's find them a good home." He turned away, thinking I didn't see the moisture rimming his eyes. And I didn't let him see mine. We began trudging into the desert together, but separate.

Behind us, the noise of the city—its groans from its injuries, the rumble of its breath, the sound of chewing, diminished as we walked. The smell of it: breath and broken skin curdling the air, faded too.

"Given what we know, we can't have blue sky and towers above the clouds without killing the city below," I finally said, trudging again. *If we found a new city.*

Wik sighed and stopped walking. "We could be more aware of the risks, make Laws about raising the towers."

"You know that wouldn't be enough, not after a few generations." Going higher was what we knew. People's self-interest would win out. Our presence had changed the city's life, altered its natural course. Now we walked away from it. I tugged Wik along.

With us gone, several bone eaters had already returned and resumed feeding our former city. We could see them swooping, small dark spots, as we walked away. They fought over the scraps again.

We weren't needed on the ground.

Maalik left my shoulder and circled above, testing his wings. After a few moments, I whistled and he returned. His claws gently pinched my shoulder.

"If we could fly," I began. If there was a place high enough and windy enough, I'd find wings and launch myself from it into the sky once again.

Wik snorted. "On what wind?" Flying was not possible where we were.

"Maybe there's something across the desert? Maybe we'll find a city—"

A city that rose up and into the clouds, where we *could* fly, just as before? We'd have the same problems, the same destruction for the city.

"Come on," I said. The worry must wait. "Let's find out."

We knew now that the world was vast, that the clouds ended, and the wind too. We knew more, and less, than before. I knew, too—in my gut—that we couldn't survive here.

For now, we walked, and my legs and ankles ached. My steps were no longer as sure as they'd been.

As the city receded behind us, Wik took my hand and squeezed it tight.

"No more deaths. Not by my doing," I whispered. It was a vow I'd been turning over in my mind since before the black-wings had come to the meadow in the midcloud. Since before we fell. I couldn't keep the promise then. Now? I would try harder. I would walk away from Kirit Citykiller too.

"That's an impossible vow to keep. You're not a Singer any longer. You're a hero of the city." Wik frowned. "What if you need to defend the community?"

"I would defend it." I knew that much. All of the community. Not just some of it.

Wik chewed his lip. The sun rose higher. It was nearing time to stop and find shade. "What if you had to choose between my life and your promise?"

Sounds of our feet scuffing the dirt, sounds of the weak breeze, the dirt husking our breaths, a hollow space that I could not fill with an answer. Finally, "I don't know yet," tumbled from my lips, a confession of sorts.

I waited for him to storm at me—to tell me I was neither a good Nightwing nor a good companion on a journey. I waited for him to fear all that he risked in my company.

His shoulders did dip a little. His eyes, when he looked at me, were hooded at first. He was Singer-trained, a hunter, a fighter. Together, we'd fought and killed for the city. How could I betray him like this? I tried to speak again, to explain. To let my words tumble from me so that we could trip on them as we walked. But only silence came. And Wik's silence matched mine.

I waited for him to turn and walk away.

But he kept pace with me. His strides were longer than mine, but taken slower.

Then, quietly, "It's all right," he said. "You don't need to know until you know."

He squeezed my hand again, and something deep inside my lungs shifted. I could breathe easier. I pressed his fingers between mine. That seemed to be enough for him to know I heard him, because the air eased around us, and we passed through it faster.

"I won't leave," he said even more quietly.

"That's a hard vow to keep," I answered. We trudged ahead anyway.

The ground hurt our feet; our shins and knees ached and creaked and refused to grow stronger. We walked across a dirt-filled plain rough with an unfamiliarity of rocks and small scrub plants.

Once I felt something brush my foot and slide away, but when I looked, I saw nothing.

As our pace across the warming desert slowed, two bone eaters came to investigate. "We're not dead yet," I scolded. The bigger bone eater screeched at me, then flew back to the city. The smaller one dove slow and sure, talons out, but still too high.

Wik knelt for a rock, but I just stared the enormous bird

down. I curled my hands into fists. It veered away at the last minute and headed home.

"You didn't blink," Wik said. "You weren't afraid."

No. Not for myself, I wasn't. "I was less afraid than it was. That's all that counts."

❧ ❧ ❧

In a morning's walk, we found a patch of broad, spike-leaved ground plants with purple flowers. They turned out to be filled with a sweet liquid that smelled somewhat like muzz. I put a dab on my arm. When it did not burn or give me a rash, we tasted some on our tongues. After a half day in the shade of the plants, when we didn't feel ill, we each took a sip and kept walking.

"We were already cloudbound and worse, already commit-ted to the ground," Wik said.

"But not dead after all," I reminded both of us. That was hopeful.

Over a small ridge, we glimpsed a new city in the distance. Smaller than Corat and Nimru. Smaller by far than our own city. Slowly, it crossed the hot reddish plain. Between us and that city lay more ground plants and a bumpy terrain.

"What will we do when we get close to it?" I asked, scuffing the ground with my foot while we sipped again at the broadleaf plant. The city wasn't one we'd seen and named. It wasn't the city Dix had been trying to drag Ciel towards all those moons ago either. That one had several broken spires. This one looked young; its towers spiraled upwards, but didn't reach the clouds. Bone eaters circled, a black cloud seen from a distance.

"We'll climb it. See if it's safe enough to stay." Wik sounded so confident.

"We have to get there first," I said. "Then climb it."

"Our ancestors managed."

"There aren't any songs about climbing onto a city," I said.

Wik's face stuck halfway between doubt and negation.

"There are songs about that?"

He nodded. "We learned the really old songs as fledges. About how to abandon a tower. What bad heartbone smelled like. I don't remember them all, but there have to be songs about climbing cities."

Singers. They'd kept so much knowledge to themselves. "What does bad heartbone smell like?"

"Like smoke." He looked up, and the light hit his cheekbones and jawline. "How long, do you think?"

"Until Nat and Ciel make it above the clouds? Or until they bring the citizens down to us? Those are two very different questions."

Wik turned to walk backwards, looking behind us at the distant, hazy shape that was our fallen city and its nemesis, Nimru. "Both. How long?"

"If they're lucky, I think they can reach the midcloud in a few days. If we're lucky, the city has at least a couple of moons left."

"A couple moons, more or less. At worst, ten days."

We couldn't keep moving. The sun was too hot on the sand. We pulled our tattered, sweat-drenched robes over us. The heat beat at us, and we leaned against each other to wait. The heat made it to hard to speak, to think.

"Kirit," Wik whispered after a long time staring at the sand where we'd dug. "I'd understand. If you wouldn't kill a bone eater, or even anything else."

*What if you had to chose between my life and your promise?* I hadn't answered his question. But I knew now that I'd break my promise. His was one death I could not accept.

I took his hand again. Squeezed hard.

Our steps took on a familiar, jarring rhythm. Our bones echoed with the ground's opinion of us. We did not belong here. The ground let us know that with every step. No plants offered themselves this far out as food. We survived by hunting the small rats that skittered from the smallest of shadows into narrow tunnels. Maalik took to the sky more than once to chase the black bugs that raced across the sand, but the whipperling quickly returned to my shoulder each time.

Life on the ground was a surprise. How small it was. How it darted and flashed before us, then disappeared.

We were nearing a small hill when something dark lifted from the ground and then sank out of sight. Wik and I both froze. Maalik stuck his head into my robe and hid.

"What is it?" I asked.

We drew closer and found a span of silk, a piece of a dark footsling, half buried in the dirt.

"Blackwing," Wik muttered under his breath. "This far out." He looked around, but we could find nothing more of it.

We kept walking, crossing the desert, but more tense and alert now.

If a blackwing had survived this far out here, we could be closing in on an enemy, as well as the closest city and its ring of circling bone eaters.

Even with the footsling suggesting others had fared poorly in the desert, we let it lull us into its slow beats.

We knew the cities were deadly, and the clouds were dangerous. We didn't know anything about this dry expanse or that the ground itself was the least safe of all.

A full day and a half from our former, dying city, we discovered the first of the big hills, the size of a small city, that mounded the ground.

As we neared them, my calves worked harder to crest a rise in the ground. Muscles pulled at the backs of my knees, drew a slow ache from my shins. I was used to aches from my arms after long flights. In my legs, this feeling was especially strange.

The earthen rise we climbed wasn't big at first. Then suddenly we felt a little cooler. The heat from the ground no longer pushed so hard at our newly callused feet.

"What an odd place," Wik said. "This is a nearly perfect curve." We hadn't seen anything close to geometry since leaving the city above.

Now, after days of walking the desert, this oddity, plus the sound of Wik's curiosity, shook me from my catalogue of aches.

We skirted the edge of the mound, tapping at it with our bone hooks. Dirt slid away from the surface, revealing a dark, mottled hide, thick like that of our city.

Wik dug into the dirt below the skin with his bone hook, still gory from the run-in with Nimru. He cleared a hole below big enough for a child. Then he hit something soft. "Huh."

The hole was filled with an immense egg, dormant. It didn't look like a silkspider hatch, or a whipperling clutch.

"Did you bring the brass plates?" Wik said. He reached a hand back and pulled me forward, up the hill.

I'd brought several and given Ciel the rest to help convince the towers. "Which one do you want?"

"The one with the moons and stars on it."

I dug in my satchel until I felt the piece of brass. When I passed it over to Wik, he held up the plate to the strangely marked skin of the thing beneath the mound.

The etching wasn't a match, but it was similar.

"Maybe these things were smaller once. And this place . . ." He looked closely at the reversed drawing and then flipped it upside down.

The moons and stars became pits and gaps in the desert floor.

The plate became a map, not of the sky, as we'd thought, but of the ground, with several city hatchlings marked.

"All this time, we didn't know what we knew." *How many of our assumptions have been upside down?* "How much has been lost?"

Other symbols on the brass surface, even flipped—even when I tried to imagine them reversed, as if they'd been pressed into silk—still did not make sense. But the markings for what lived under the cities, which we'd thought were moons in the sky, now meant so much more.

"They lay eggs," Wik said in wonder. "And the eggs get drawn down into the earth somehow, and kept the right temperature. This one looks like it got too hot."

My feet pressed the leathery shell. It crackled like dried leaves. He was right. Dead. We stood on the grave of a city that never was.

"Could people have lived on the ground before the cities— arrived? Appeared?" I wasn't sure if those were the right words. I rubbed the square marks on the plates. "Could people still be here?" I looked around. Saw nothing but more hills. That made me shiver.

Wik pointed to a small etching on the side of the plate— a nascent city pulling itself from the ground, and another, a city lying in a hole it had dug for an egg. The drawing was rough, which was why we'd mistaken it for moonrise.

There were measurements, markings along the side. "How many moons is that?"

"Many," I said. I swallowed dryly. Generations or more.

"The cities look like they erupted from the ground," Wik said. "Look at the crushed pieces of mechanicals," he pointed at the dirt he'd cleared out of the hole. "Look at all the metal." This last he breathed out. What we'd considered riches in the clouds was nothing to what seemed buried deep in the ground here. Still, Wik couldn't keep himself from picking up and pocketing a small piece of the unfamiliar gray metal.

"Perhaps there's more beneath the dirt," I said. "I wish we had a guide." The land around us was so strange, more so than even the midcloud. There, we'd had Aliati and her scavenger knowledge to fall back on. Now we were on our own. "If the blackwing got this far, I don't know how they'd miss this."

"Would that the scavengers had ever come this low," Wik said, shaking his head. "We'd have had so much more to work with."

"At some point, some might have, but not for generations. Maybe when the cities were small." And if they had, they wouldn't have been able to get back above the clouds any better than us. Wik's excitement at discovery was distracting him. I cleared my throat.

Wik executed a slow turn. "I don't think we're going to come across any small cities, not right now."

"Unless one hatches." That made me look at the hills and mounds around us with new eyes. A newborn, hungry city was likely as dangerous as a bone eater hatchling. All sharp teeth and ravenous stomach. We had new fears to reckon with. New reasons to hurry.

Around us the desert mounds, interspersed with smaller rises, revealed more eggs, each overheated and leathery. The ridge on the horizon rose higher, and we climbed that, away from the ruined hatchery.

Here, it smelled like stagnant water and something else: sharp and green. Vegetation grew nearby, and I was hungry enough to sniff it out. Wik's nose wrinkled too.

"I'll forage," Wik said. "If we find a city, we'll need strength." He limped towards the green smells.

A thin breeze brushed my cheek, and I wanted to believe—

for there were breezes, they were just tiny things—that we would fly again. That we'd rise up in the air, the wind full against the silk spans of our wings, a city thriving beneath us. That we could do it without killing another city. Without harming another being, now that we knew what the cost was.

Wik, even when our council had draped him in Lawsmarkers for being a Singer, didn't quit easily. I wanted to believe we would find what we sought, together. That this one person who shared so much of my history, so much of what I knew, would be the one who finished this journey with me, no matter my answer to his question, no matter how the ground tested us.

Instead, we walked, separately again. My eyes and mouth caked with grit that even the liquid from the broadleaf plant couldn't clear. My feet ached. When we rested, Wik relented, and we sheltered beneath the same cloak.

❧ ❧ ❧

Finally after many days with the young city in sight, we were no longer walking away from our home: we could not see its body any longer, and could only see the glimpses of towers on its back, raking through the cloud, in shadow and haze.

We had only the new city to walk towards.

Wik returned, long stalks of a spiky silver plant in his hand. Different than the broadleaf we'd been sucking dry of moisture.

"What if a city won't have us?" I asked as I looked at the stalks. Only one way to find out if it was dangerous. I broke a section off and rubbed it on my arm.

"What kind of question is that? Cities don't get a choice."

"They should," I said.

"You figure out how to talk to a city, then. It doesn't look like our ancestors ever figured it out."

"If we can't figure it out," I echoed his words, "we might keep walking until we are out of range of the cities and find a place on high ground."

When the stalks didn't raise any reaction on my skin, I took a tiny bite and waited.

I looked once more to the distant ridges, the smoke on the horizon. Between the ridge and the hills where we walked, the city we were trying to reach had turned suddenly and moved towards a dip in the ground. It bent its head low and tore at something in the dirt, then shook wildly. I could see nothing. Then a spray of silver-blue. Then only loud sounds of the city chewing as we drew closer.

"What is that city eating?" Its jaws gaped as if something large and gristly hung there, but we saw nothing. As it chewed, I thought I saw silver glints in the red dust. The color of my tattoos, and Wik's.

"Don't." Wik put out a steadying hand just as I picked up the pace. "Look." Another divot just before us had shifted. Red sand poured into a newly formed hole. The sand ran in rivulets, some packed hard against the ground, some moving in the other direction.

"What is that? Another egg?" I moved forward to investigate. I should have stepped back, as Wik had.

The slick feel of a tentacle wrapping my ankle was my only warning. The rough grip yanked me off my feet and dragged me several lengths through the dust. I scrambled, clutching at the still air, the shifting ground.

Maalik squawked and flew into the air. The terrain scratched my back raw and cut at my elbows. I kicked at what I could not see. I tried to hack at what was pulling me, but that only got my arm entangled too, and lost me my bow.

Behind me, Wik stopped yelling. *Has he been grabbed too?*

His echoing clicks from above and to my left told me he was still free.

I planted the bone hook I'd been carrying in the ground and hung on to it. I would not make this easy. The tentacle pulled tighter at my ankle. I closed my eyes and echoed as Wik did.

There was too much dust. All I could sense was confusion. An indistinct shape rising from the hole in the ground several lengths away. Curling tentacles waving in the air.

Another tentacle wrapped my leg, this one higher on my calf. My grip on the grounded hook began to slip.

"A skymouth. Here!" I yelled hoarsely.

No response.

"Wik!"

*Where has he gone?* He wouldn't flee. But would he fight for me when I hadn't been sure I could kill, even for him? When I'd disdained his return as citykiller because I hated my own role in the same crime?

The grinding sound of rough dirt sliding beneath me. I was dragged again, closer this time, and more slowly, against the anchor I'd planted. My leg felt as if it was being pulled from my body, but my fingertips clung to the bone hook.

"Wik!" I tried to pry it loose from the dirt while kicking, but that only made the tentacle in the ground pull harder. I couldn't feel my foot any longer. Where was Wik?

I lost my grip on the bone hook, and it sprang back upright in the dirt as I was dragged again. I flipped facedown, then scrabbled at the ground with my fingers. Dirt filled my mouth, my nose, as I fought to turn over again. I barely managed to roll just as Wik took a running leap and landed directly over the hole in the ground.

He stumbled, then grabbed at something I couldn't see. He cut and slashed at the air with his knife.

Maalik dove too, screeching. His small body jerked from the air and tumbled, all feathers and rage, before he fought his way free. Then he circled back, uncontested.

The tentacles released my leg. Maalik flew to me, and I scrambled upright, my skin throbbing, fingers and face bloodied, my shin a bees' nest of tingle and ache.

Wik had circled to one side of what had attacked us and crouched cautiously, ready to fight. He dug in the ground beside it. Slowly, as he shoved the sand away, a carapace emerged, coiled in on itself and the same shade as the dirt, but mottled. Hard. Silver fluid ran from it.

"Not a skymouth. Something near to it, though," Wik muttered. He paced a length of dirt, then kicked dust into the air and let it drop. I saw the tentacles. Long ones, several more stretching almost to me. "Big. Thing's shell is the size of a tower core."

Together, we looked across the desert we'd crossed. Noticed just how many mounds of different sizes there were in the earth here. Just how many places the invisible predators could have been hiding.

"What are they?" My voice was a rasp.

"Call them groundmouths, until we know better," Wik answered. He said it as if we were the first here. As if we had any right to name things here.

The broken metal in the ground said we were not the first, by far. The ground hid layers upon layers of evidence that this world had many names for things. Names we could never know.

But now we knew one new thing about the ground. An invisible *groundmouth* could lurk, and grasp. We could guess from the city in the distance that cities liked to eat these creatures.

No wonder our ancestors wanted to get as high as they could away from this. No wonder they had cautioned us that below the clouds was dangerous. It was safer to never, ever come back down.

My leg throbbed. When I examined it, pushing my tattered robe aside and pulling at the torn legging beneath, I saw the skin purpling where the groundmouth had grasped it, near enough to where I'd broken it previously to worry me. I could still put weight on it, so I did, leaning away from the pulse that echoed up through my leg and hip with every step.

"All right?" Wik asked. He looked ready to carry me.

"I'm fine," I said, smiling for emphasis. *Absolutely fine.* And I would stay fine. I had to. Wik could walk by my side, he could wait for me if he wanted, but I would carry myself as long as I could walk.

Maalik spread his wings while clinging to my shoulder. The shade and small breeze from the motion was a cooling relief. The blood on my face began to dry. Then the whipperling furled his wings again and began to smooth his feathers.

I began to move again, going out ahead of Wik's doubtful gaze. If he could continue on, I could also. As a distraction from the pain, I held the image of the brass plate in my mind. It had to contain a clue about the groundmouths. I thought of the other plates Nat had carried through the clouds to help prove to the towers that everyone must come down. And about those plates I'd gathered from where Dix had fallen, from the ruins of the city. How they showed weapons and flying mechanisms and life cycles. Maybe not all of our great-great-great-dependents had wanted to stay far from the dangers. Perhaps they'd been planning to artifex their way home, but had forgotten as more life-and-death needs took over.

Wik caught up with me. He brushed at his robes, looking anywhere but at me or my leg. "I won't worry until you tell me to."

*Good choice.*

Wik's robes were wet and flecked with silver-blue ink. So was his face.

"What is that?" It didn't look like skymouth guts, or skymouth ink at all. That would have burned.

"Before it died, it sprayed a lot of ink in the air." Wik wiped at his ear with a dust-fouled corner of his sleeve.

"Did you breathe any of that in?" I tried to think of what Elna would do for aspiration of a skymouth's defensive spray, but I had no idea.

"Tried not to." Wik shrugged. "I'm sure it will be fine." He smiled at me. "And," he added as he brushed his face again with his robe, "now we know."

We did know. And we would be more careful in the future.

# 10

## MACAL, ABOVE

*⁓ Above the clouds, destruction vast, the Magister
flew alone ⁓*

Gruff voiced and dirty with tower dust and blood, the northwest councilors—most so new as tower leaders I didn't yet know their names—gathered warily around me in the shelter of Mondarath's lowtower. Sidra and I had bargained and begged for enough stools and cushions to seat all who'd come. We crowded against the core wall, trying to stay quiet enough that few nearby would overhear.

When I had their attention, I didn't waste time.

"All of us have to move lower. The towertops aren't safe anymore." I let that sink in. "Ginth and Amrath, your towers are showing cracks too near their cores. You must move immediately. We will assist you."

The councilor from Amrath—the youngest among us—stared at me. She was working the ragged cuticle of her thumb with her teeth. The skin puckered and bled as she spoke.

"The blackwings took everything we had. What about supplies?" the councilor said. "We need medicine, spidersilk for bandages."

"We need hang-sacks so that our people can sleep in the lowtower," the councilor from Varu added. "Our core is too wide for more than a few tiers from other towers to shelter there."

"Would you crowd all of us on fewer towers, with few supplies?" one councilor from Laria protested. "Why not separate the Lawsbreakers from each tower and use them to appease the city? It obviously needs it."

"We will not have another Conclave," I said. "Enough citizens have died on that account." I paused. "Going into the clouds, however—"

Another councilor jumped in, almost as young as the woman from Amrath. Fear etched his eyes. "Would you send us to explore the clouds, never to return?"

"Careful excursions. That will return. We need to find out what caused the quake. That starts in the clouds. And I'm saying if we don't expand the area of the city that is livable, by one means or another, people will begin to attack each other."

"They already are," murmured the Varu councilor. "Stealing too."

I knew this was true. Already, several on Mondarath had been caught. Fear drove discord. So did hunger.

"You say we must abandon all tiers that look unsteady, all at once. That we must crowd together and sacrifice," the councilor from Varu said. "When people grow angry and want to live on their damaged tiers, what then?"

The tower council had always been a slow vortex of ideas, a community coming together to agree on purpose. Questions were natural. Arguments too. We had no time for either.

"We are back to Singer laws, for the moment. They try it, they go against Laws."

No one spoke for a moment.

"Singer laws, from a Singer." The new towerman from Viit spat every word. She'd been the oldest person on what remained of that tower.

"Hush," Varu silenced her. "We are working together for now."

But the man's look said that "now" would last only until my first big mistake.

I could make no mistakes. There were too many lives in the balance. We had to get everyone housed, and safely, either on tiers or elsewhere. I had to lead, so that the surviving city could benefit from what each tower had. It turned out that several of the towers closest to the Spire had their own small stashes of lighter-than-air. Varu, for instance, had squirreled away several large sacks of the stuff. While the gas would eventually run out, for now it kept a small group of brave souls housed on a tarp just outside of the tower proper.

*Abandon.* The Law wove through my mind, through everything I did. It tinged every possible mistake. What didn't I yet understand?

Not for the first time, I wished Kirit and Nat were here to tell me what they knew about the city, about the undercloud. Instead, all I had to rely on in front of the new group of councilors was Laws, and Singer knowledge. The tower abandonment song.

"The law says *gather in safety and remove,*" I sang, remembering. "*To highest of towers, away from cloud and fear.* But we cannot move high. It's not safe. We have to go low."

"Into the clouds?" The young woman's voice cracked.

"If we must." I was again thinking of Wik, Kirit, and Nat, of the glowing lights from long ago. Perhaps we could hide in the clouds too. At least temporarily.

"If we could discover why the city shook, we could call on all quadrants to work together again to fix it," I proposed. "We won't have to leave people behind."

As I spoke, I thought about the city and its bridges that had broken. "The bridges," I realized. "The towers that fell all had bridges. When the city shook, they couldn't compensate. Their neighbors dragged them down."

My fellow tower leaders looked as shaken as the city. Truth be told, I was too.

"You say we should work together," Varu said. "But if bridges and connections brought down the towers, why should we follow you?"

"If risking connections keeps us from remaining isolated until the city dies around us, tower by tower? I'll do it," Sidra argued. She'd lost her father in council fall, her mother to the bone dust fevers the year following the Spire's destruction. She had no one else but me, and the fear in her voice was vivid. The anger too. It caught like a market fire. I watched it spread from face to face.

"She's right," I said. To let Varu take the lead was tempting. But I knew I couldn't cede yet. "We cannot forge strong ties unless we risk collapse too."

Around us, Mondarath's residents squabbled for room, trying to get as close to what they thought of as the most stable parts of the lowtower as possible: the cores, where the council was trying to meet. Despite our best efforts, many listened carefully.

Sidra spoke again. "We'll work to keep the community together as much as we can. We'll find more room. And we'll figure out what has happened to our city."

A few councilors nodded. Then one harried guard carried a half-full sack of what looked like dirgeons past, towards what Sidra had designated a general commissary. The tip of his half-furled green silk wings bumped the young Amrath councilor in the shoulder. Dust shook from the councilor's hair when she jumped.

"Watch yourself!"

For a moment, tensions flared anew. Some looked at the sack of dirgeons hungrily.

"I will try to help you," I said after letting them go on for a moment. "But we have to pool our resources so that everyone can manage."

The councilor from Amrath shook her head. "We need food, no matter where we rest. We need stability. Going near the clouds means disaster."

I waved Urie and Raq over. "It means survival too," I said as calmly as I could.

Urie carried a blank bone slate and a sharp stylus. "Tell Raq what you have, and we'll help distribute."

No one volunteered to go first. They shifted on their stools and looked at each other, waiting. "We're not telling your pet blackwing and scavenger anything."

"Urie is with us. And Raq's a guard, not a scavenger." I kept myself from sighing, which would only anger them more. "Mondarath has herbs, rope, and muzz." Urie wrote it all down. Then I turned to the young councilor from Amrath. It wasn't fair to pick on her, as she was the youngest, but it was expedient.

"Hang-sacks, about twenty. Cushions, silk, five council plinths in various states of repair . . ." She kept speaking until she reached the food stores. She paled. "The blackwings took most of our food."

"We'll get you some, Risen," the councilor from Varu said. "We could trade for the hang-sacks." He was an older councilman who'd lived through the blackwing attack and had refused to fight at Laria. Now he drew a deep breath as if the thought was costing him dearly and named a ridiculously low weight of dried fruit for the trade.

"We will gather all of your resources." I stared at Councilor Varu especially hard. "Here. And distribute them fairly."

"After the disaster of your market, I'm not sure I like this," the councilor said.

I held up a hand. "Enough. No more tower by tower. You will

have hang-sacks." I nodded at the elder councilman. "And she will have food."

"Here," Sidra added, "we need catchments, as several of ours fell during the quake." We were running out of water rapidly. If we could get catchments set before sunset, we had hope of starting the condensation and collection process again.

"Ours are gone," said Naza. Two other tower councilors nodded. All but one of the unstable towers.

"We'll find more. And we'll use the remaining lighter-than-air to help float hang-sacks from the towers," I said, though I despaired ever having enough lighter-than-air to float more than a few tiers' worth.

"If we can find an artifex with experience making the gas, we can try to tap the damaged towers for more," Councilor Amrath suggested.

*Away from cloud and fear—*

She was right. I thought of who, in this new landscape, we could get to help us. If only we had Urie's aunts. I turned to the boy. "We need the artifexes. I don't care how we get them."

He nodded. Made another note about Grigrit.

*Gather in safety and remove—*

The point of the Law wasn't going up, it was getting out. The point was doing whatever it took to survive. We needed those artifexes.

The councilor from Varu jumped up. He motioned to the four tower guards who'd come with him. "Maybe we don't give Grigrit a choice. Gather hunters from the other standing towers and go get the artifexes, and as much lighter-than-air as you can."

"Wait!" Sidra stared at us. She spoke low and carefully. "That is advocating War. How can you consider that?" Her gaze pried at mine as if she were trying to prize loose a knot.

"It isn't War," Varu said. "We're offering citizens a different tower to live on. And *they* attacked our markets. How am I breaking Laws?"

"Blackwings attacked us. We are unsure about which ones," Sidra countered. "There are factions. Urie's confirmed it."

And I'd seen evidence of it. Still, I came down in the middle. "Urie said messages went through Grigrit. We have a right to defend ourselves. But not to attack."

Sidra nodded, acknowledging the point. "But this isn't defense. You, Macal, lead by example. I've seen you. People follow you because of it. Will your example be Singer strategies now? Will you side with Varu to take us to War?"

Her voice, cast low as it was, caught the attention of other tower representatives, of citizens trying to sleep in the tier. Many people turned towards me, eyes filled with questions.

*Singer.*

Their mistrust always came back to the tower I was born to. Was I what they thought? Singer-born, always sworn? Was Sidra starting to believe that?

"We won't lead from fear," I whispered. "We're better than that."

Beyond the tier where the council met, beside broken tiers and the few standing towers, broad spans of sky hurt like lost limbs. Markets and bridges were for peacetime. I had to face the truth: I'd turned away from the Singers young, I'd promised to lead by example, but in times of great stress, I'd fallen back on Singer strategies.

I'd miscalculated and let Varu push the council in the wrong direction. Sidra was correct, and once again I was grateful for her advice. But even if we couldn't float the city, the citizens also needed to know what could befall them. "The towers are unstable. I would rather turn us into a community that can live beyond the towers than turn to War," I said quietly. The gasps spread around the tier. "To do that, we need artifexes. Even if we don't go into the southwest, which I concede is a bad idea. The southwest has no interest in helping us."

"You're skytouched," said Councilor Varu, my once-ally, now opponent. I'd made my mistake for sure.

There were murmurs of "he's not wrong" among the group.

"War is out of the question. Abandonment is different now. We cannot go up. And in going down," Sidra said, "we'd leave too many people stranded, unable to fly or climb. I won't leave people behind. And we do not even know what has happened, or why the city roared the way it did."

*Like no roar I can recall.*

ϟ ϟ ϟ

As the council meeting ended, a shadow crossed the sun, dark and regular. Except it wasn't a shadow. I looked up the side of the tower. The edge of War had come to us first.

Urie rushed past me to the balcony, trying to avoid the gathered refugees.

Blackwings rode a platform suspended from skymouth husks filled with lighter-than-air. They guided its passage on the wind using windbeaters' wings, some that looked old enough to be from the Spire itself.

My fists clenched as I remembered the last time I'd seen something like this platform. When the city council was attacked—and some had blamed Singers. Now we knew that wasn't true. But the shadow was the same. So many had died then. So much of the collapse of the city's connections could be traced to that dark moment.

Memories of the council attack continued to flood in. Of Nat, Beliak, and Ceetcee, of my niece and nephew all fighting to survive that moment. Of Kirit and Ezarit lost to the clouds.

Though these blackwings weren't attacking, and they stayed

well away from the still-populated towers. This time, I flew from the balcony with our guards and Sidra by my side to meet them.

The wind whistled in my ears as we flew a circuit. The black-wings drew down on us with their bows. We halted our approach once I was within shouting range, and they did not fire.

Several blackwings seemed to be sketching on large bone tablets. Making a map? It could be more than that, I realized with a jolt. The blackwings might be coldly surveying the north, as a way to determine their next move.

I hailed them. "We'll trade able hands to your towers in return for medicine for ours."

Laughter, brief and sharp. The first I'd heard since before the quake, peppered the sky. "Your help is not wanted here. Any medicine, we'll keep with us." Their weapons glittered in the dust and sun.

"We're still one city," I said. "We can help each other."

"Save yourselves," said a blackwing on the platform. His wings were edged with glass.

They didn't speak to us further or look our way; instead, they finished their survey and returned to the south.

Sidra and I turned back to Mondarath, shaken by the encounter. "What could they want?" she asked. "What about their people who need help?"

How could the blackwings not see we were weaker working at cross purposes? We needed a bridge. "What about supplies we need that they have?" I thought about those two precious jars of honey and the packet of medicine at the market. There wasn't much left here. And about the artifexes and the lighter-than-air. "How will we last with only the goods the northwest can make on its own?"

Whatever they were up to, it was an incursion. I turned to Sidra. "Now, see?" I said. "That *is* an act of war. Or at least provocation. They were assessing what was worth taking and what was best left to rot." We had no way of knowing, but it was safe to prepare for the worst. "We need to get our hands on more of the lighter-than-air immediately."

We landed on Mondarath. Sidra, still shaken and pale, nodded instead of arguing.

"The southwest's artifexes have obviously figured out more of the formula if they're using gas for excursions." Urie sounded worried that I wouldn't believe him.

I wasn't sure I did.

But he kept speaking. "We'll find my aunts. I don't care if we have to kidnap them from the southwest. If they've done it, and showed others how—" He didn't finish the sentence.

*Kidnap.* The whisper went through the tower. I looked around. I didn't kidnap or steal any more than I advocated for war. But I had come close. Again, I questioned my motives, my approach. I sounded too much like a Singer for my own ears. Who knew what I sounded like to the others. The councilors returned to their towers with few decisions made; the council ended in disarray.

I had to do better. We had to work together, or we would fall apart completely. *Fear serves no one, Macal.*

❧ ❧ ❧

Over the next days, Mondarath and the remaining towers struggled to pull together. We marked tremendous losses on bone tablets and gathered for Allsuns.

The new council, nine of us, looked up at the briefly starlit sky and promised those who'd been lost we would save the city for those who survived.

We sang Remembrances, my voice lifted and twined with Sidra's, with the council's, with those we'd accepted into our community as refugees from the south. Their words were slightly different, and we heard the off notes, the extra syllables in the song that lifted from our tower. We kept singing anyway. I clasped Sidra's hand, Urie's shoulder. We sang together, even if we sang differently.

When we finished Remembrances, most gathered on a single tower, the councilor from Amrath turned to me, her robe torn, a bandage on her arm. "How will you choose, Macal?"

"Choose?" The wind was blowing in the wrong direction, and Urie was having a hard time getting to the southern towers.

"We know once you have enough lighter-than-air, you'll leave. How will you choose who goes on the floats, who gets to leave the city?" Councilor Varu looked at me, bone-faced.

"No one is leaving unless we all go together," I said. The thought of leaving the city on floats, to be blown in whatever direction without anchors, terrified me. A float would have some direction, but eventually the gas would run out and we would sink into the clouds, never to be heard from again.

Amrath pursed her lips. "That's a lie. What you've already said about the lighter-than-air and the plinths? That proves it."

"You're altering my meaning."

"Towerfolk already say you're drawing up a tier's worth to fly from here. There's not enough lighter-than-air stored, even in the southwest, for more than that. That Doran's plan was similar, before he fell."

How did she hear those rumors? Varu? The blackwings that had infiltrated Amrath's market, had they stayed after the disaster?

"There is some gas left, but if we find artifexes, we can make more." I hoped we could. "And we can do that much more efficiently if we stay near the bone towers, the city." Our birthplace, whether we were Singer or tower. "Eventually, we can rebuild the city, and strengthen it again, if we have enough artifexes working on the problem."

Varu, who'd been quiet so far, spat on the balcony. A fair measure of rudeness when one could easily spit over the edge, into the clouds. "We cannot and will not survive without figuring out what happened. Like you said. Someone has to explore. Who will go?"

The clouds again. "The songs say—"

He held up a hand. "I know what the songs say. They say we rise above the clouds, to safety. That the clouds *are* dangerous. No one returns. Not the cloudbound, not the Skyshouter, nor Brokenwings. Not your Singer brother. The clouds let no one go."

There was a wisp of hope they were still alive down there. "We can use the tiers that are as close to the cloudline as possible," I finally conceded. It was a dangerous thing, but I believed Nat and Kirit had survived that far, just a few tiers into the clouds. Supposedly, they'd been spotted at Laria.

"If we are going to stay near the towers," Sidra said loudly, for she knew that was my plan, "we should also find a scavenger or two. They'll know where the instability lies, if anyone does. Or maybe even how far down this goes." Her words felt dark, as if the city itself had broken Laws.

"A good approach. Find the instability, fix it, and rise," the Varu councilor said.

Scavengers were a good idea. "Who will go?" I asked the group. Volunteers would be making themselves cloudbound, the worst punishment for the city's worst offenders.

A roaring silence. No one stepped forward. One towerman cleared his throat but did not speak.

"No one's heard from the southwest in days," the councilor from Amrath added. "We have family there. But no messages, nothing. My partner wants me to check it out. I'll follow Urie to Grigrit. We'll try to find the artifexes and sneak them out, as well as get my family."

"Then I will go below," I finally said, after no one else volunteered.

I was a Magister. I'd never imagined myself as leader. Sidra had. I'd stepped away from the Spire's desire to control the city when I was young. After that, I taught others. Flight. Laws. I'd sought out talent among the towers for artifexes and leaders. I'd been a connector, a bridge. Not a hero.

Now I was making life-or-death decisions for my neighbors and their families. It didn't sit well with me at all.

To my left, my partner stared at me, whispering, "Cloud-bound." Her voice shook new cadence into that one word. The idea didn't sit well with her either.

"Leading by example," I whispered.

"You can't. We need you here."

I said it quietly, for her ears only. "This time, I will go. I am the one who must."

She shook her head, brushed off her sleeves, and said, "Then I'll join you there."

On the towertop, with light already breaking Allsuns' next dawn, I studied her face, determined to remember her eyes, her cheekbones, every wind line.

"No." I wished I could have said anything else. "I need you to stay and guide the city. Both of us cannot go."

She closed her eyes, drawing shutters over her thoughts. Then opened them again. Looked hard at me, tracing the line of my chin with a finger. "I will help guide the city, and you will return." It was not a question.

"I will." Mine was a promise.

Sidra would work with the council to hold the towers together. And I would find the instability in the city below and help repair it if I could.

# 11

## KIRIT, BELOW

*⤳ Skyshouter and Nightwing climbed new cities formed of bone ⤳*

In the time it took to fight off the groundmouth, the young city had moved again.

Wik and I walked on, lying to each other about our injuries, dismayed by how far our goal had traveled away from us.

"We may never catch it," Wik muttered. He scanned the distance, seeking other cities.

Our world was parceled out in painful steps. The red soil crunched and slid beneath our feet; the strip of blue sky taunted us before it disappeared above the thick cloud above. The sun beat down hard. The very ground reached out for us. I refused to disappear into this landscape without a fight. I also refused to destroy it.

The new city had begun to turn again and seemed to keep to a looping path. As we walked, I realized there was a deep track running near us. I pointed it out to Wik. "Looks like regular passage here. Like a family would wear in bone after years in the same tier."

He nodded. "Might not be smart, but they seem pretty territorial."

Were cities as territorial as towers? Our own towers had been on the verge of tearing each other apart. But we'd also spent many years weaving a city together with bridges and songs. We could do it again. What kinds of songs might our community have made out of a landscape like this one?

"Having seen them fight, I'm not surprised at the territory keeping," Wik continued, breaking my train of thought. He held up his hands to make a frame and watched the city cross the horizon from his left hand to his right. "These are slow, though. We could find a way to climb them." His words were cautious.

We'd already seen one build up speed and attack.

The deep track traced a path from water source—a stream running through the red dirt, and disappearing at intervals—to a thick group of groundmouths, and back. The city was too big to fear the groundmouths, or to think about them as anything other than a snack.

"Look." Wik knelt. Pulled another strip of black silk from the sand. This one smaller and crisp with dried blood. "The blackwing made it this far."

Had they reached the new city before us? Probably not if they were wounded. I tried to determine how far they might have had to walk, hurt. Wondered if they could have made it. "Probably not much farther."

Wik set his jaw and said nothing.

\ \ \

If we survived, our songs would have to change. Our old songs gave us a bone forest, The Rise—when we'd been on a city's back the whole time. What new songs would come now? How would our community adjust? *Would* we be able to change?

We had to catch a city to find out.

"What should we call this one? In case we catch it?" Though that seemed increasingly impossible. I gritted my teeth against the fire that was coursing across my leg with every step. "How about Varat, after the tower Varu?" The tower where my mother had made her final home.

Wik nodded, looking ahead again. "Cities in motion are far different than a city trapped under its own weight. You were right to be worried earlier." He'd been thinking ahead after all. "What if Varat's smart? As smart as the bone eaters?"

The bone eaters had adjusted their lives to our presence. Could an active city do the same?

The other cities distantly visible on the horizon seemed to have similar loops, ones that crisscrossed in places and left tracks with stops and starts across the broad, dry stretch of land.

Once we'd sheltered in a cloudbound cave. My own city had pronounced me a traitor; blackwings had killed my mother, my friends. The scavenger Aliati had shown me how to gauge distance with string and a game-board map. Not knowing whether I'd see Aliati again was a dull ache. But what she'd taught me, and all of us sheltering in that cave, was how to plan based on known routes and measurements. I measured the distance against my thumb and forefinger, as Wik had done.

"If that city takes the same route," I said, pointing, "we can catch it." I tried to judge how long it would take to reach a certain point on the loop it walked. Maybe soon. "It doesn't need to stop if we're ahead of it. We can try to climb up one of its legs, use the grips if we have to." How had our ancestors done it? Likely when the cities were much smaller.

"If we use our grips, it might try to bite us." Wik sounded dubious. "Better to wait for it to stop and feed."

I wouldn't wait. Our friends counted on us finding a new home. "Who knows when it will stop again?" Would I be able to climb at all? I brushed that worry away. I had to climb. "Let's try."

We'd made rudimentary claws and gathered bone- and metal-tipped arrows before leaving the city. We'd sorted through tiers of rubble looking for more finds. Much of it had been gross and ruined, but there were a few items, including metal I couldn't recognize—not brass, but heavier—that we left behind as too much to carry with us. We took the knives and spears, and a smashed pair of lenses that reminded me very much of my mother's.

In the rubble, Wik had found the remains of a small windup toy, a tiny city that walked a few noisy paces in the dust when a metal knob at its side was twisted. It had no towers, just a plate ridge on its back. Its head snapped back and forth at the air. It walked a circle, clacking, its metal parts whining, and then fell over. He held it in his palm now. Our past hadn't forgotten the cities. The memories had just fallen away, or been discarded as we rose.

"What would Djonn make of all of this?" I wondered aloud to calm my nerves about climbing the new city.

Wik shook his head. "He'd probably take measurements for a harness or a weapon."

That was true. "Though he might approach tasks differently on the ground." As I was.

Once I would have rushed in. Once I'd have claimed this city as my birthright. The ground an adventure I deserved to have. I knew so much more now. I knew that the cities didn't care who was deserving and who wasn't. To a city, we were food and brief flickers of movement in the sky. We barely registered.

Our songs would have to change to reflect that change. If we survived.

The only person I could share this new realization with was Wik.

But he already knew how much destruction I'd caused, and the lessons I'd learned on the way down to the ground.

"Being on the ground changes all of us," he added.

"Would you kill another city now that you know more?" I asked. Would those who came after us do so?

He didn't look at me. "I might." Less sure than before.

How would the others change when they came down to the ground? Would they elect to come?

I imagined that life in the city was trying to return to normal, everyone keeping pace, going about their business, pretending all was well, while maneuvering around the unlucky. The thought made me shiver with cold and sorrow. They would know soon.

We had to help them, even if we could not get to them.

"When Nat brings Djonn down from the clouds and we find a safe place that's out of biting range of cities and groundmouths, you should ask them what they'd do differently down here," Wik said. He glanced at my leg, then looked away, jaw clenched. "If it's not too late."

"How much time do we have to find a home for them? Not much." I spoke forcefully, angry again with him, with everything. We wouldn't stop until we'd found home. "We won't give up."

"On your wings, Risen," he said, then bit his lip. His sense of humor was as broken as the city.

My voice rose again. "Wik! No one is 'Risen' now, nor once the city falls." No one alive, in any case. Only the ghosts we left above. Ezarit. Doran. So many ghosts.

Wik stared into the distance, at nothing. At his own ghosts.

I tugged at his hand, distracting him, apologizing without words. "Help me catch Varat. Then we'll see."

For the first time in a long time, the curve of his mouth shifted, ticking up into his cheek. I saw his eyes gleam, but that could have been the sunlight.

"Yes," he said. "Let's go."

And we headed to the point where we'd meet and trap a new city.

༺ ༺ ༺

When the city stopped and dipped its head to eat one of the groundmouths we'd skirted, we grappled it around its toes. Above us, the bone spires on its back rose in graceful twists, gray and green near the bottom, stark white above. None neared the clouds. Instead a thick ridge of bone connected each tower, the fused plate growing much broader and thicker than the one on the city we'd left.

While Varat was relatively still, Wik shimmied up its calloused, bulbous ankle. He set a grip in one of the wrinkles and tested it. It held.

A trio of bone eaters circled high. One dropped a chunk of carrion in front of the city and then disappeared again.

The city abandoned its invisible meal and began to devour the meat. It kept walking.

"See those follicles in the skin?" Wik pointed. "I don't think they're that sensitive. Drive your grips in there, and the city won't even notice." I looked up at him and hoped my upper arm strength was going to be enough. My leg had buckled once already, though I'd covered for myself pretty well, by pointing out the groundmouth ridges ahead. Wik hadn't noticed my limp.

As we pulled ourselves up the city's ankle, I was having a harder time concealing my pain. I set a grip where he'd suggested. The flank jerked slightly, like a bird would if a gnat was bothering it. Then I set a second one.

*You can do this, Kirit.* I reached up and pulled with both hands, lifting the rest of me as deadweight. It hurt like anything. I thought back to the Spire, so many Allsuns ago, to my climb from the oubliette and Wik at the top, looking down at me as I struggled.

"You want a tether?" Wik asked.

*No.* I had never felt anger swell so fast. I was trying to concentrate. "I've got it."

But I didn't. I slipped and nearly fell back on my bad leg. The pain hurt all the way to my teeth.

"I'll take the tether." I hated every word. I didn't want to need help. But I wasn't going to get atop this city without it.

Wik braced himself on a ridge near the city's elbow, put in a grip, and tied the line to it. We both worked to haul me up. When I reached his level, I was drenched with sweat and gasping.

The pain in my leg, however? Nearly completely gone.

"You look pale," Wik said. He touched my cheek with his palm. "Cold too." His hand was warm against my skin.

I looked away, searching for something to say to distract him. He was not going to make me go back down. We were here. We would climb.

But I didn't need to worry. Wik hoisted himself up higher. When he'd reached the city's shoulder, he dropped the rope again. I'd closed my eyes to rest, but the rope hit me on the head and woke me. "Tie on and climb!"

My fingers fumbled with the knot, but I finally wrapped the line around my chest, under my arms, and then made a loop with the right hand side of the line. Doing so, as tired as I was, relied on many years of practice tying knots. Otherwise, my current lack of coordination would have caught Wik's attention for sure. I drove the head of the line up through the loop, down and around the feeder line and back up and into the loop again. When tight with pressure on each end, the knot wouldn't pull apart. *Keep going, Kirit.*

That climb grew stranger still. The city's hide seemed to ripple. I heard voices—my mother's whispering *faster, no time.* Elna's *don't fall,* Doran and Rumul chiding me, Nat egging me on. Even Dix, laughing at me.

My mother's voice. I'd longed to hear it again. Ezarit. *No time to be afraid.*

But the others crowded in. Talked over her. They asked me questions too. *How can you get people up on a city without getting trampled? How do you choose who to save?*

The second question I waved away. *Everyone. You save everyone. You save the city.*

The first question I repeated aloud. "I don't know, how *do* you think we'll get everyone up here without getting trampled?" The idea of bringing a tower full of people onto this city appealed, but the mechanics of raising everyone up gave me pause, even as we climbed the thick hide.

As if in answer, the city gave a low growl. Our world shook. We held on.

The hide here was as thick as our own city, but more supple. The give of it as we crawled across a stretch of skin and the bone ridges came into sight far above. It made me a little dizzy. "This is a very young city."

"Young and hungry," Wik whispered back. "Look." Already the city's head had dipped towards more of the divots in the ground without stopping its walk. It ripped the invisible ground-mouths from their holes, at once scattering dirt and releasing a nearly invisible spray of the same liquid that had struck Wik. Some dropped back down to the ground, but most of the spray spiraled up into the air, catching the sunlight as it went, until it seemed to disappear into the clouds.

"What is that?" Wik batted absently at his hair, as if waving away bugs. There wasn't anything near him that I could see. His hair looked wet instead of dusty.

Again, the scent of smoke and cooked vegetation wafted towards us and I felt for the direction of the breeze.

I couldn't help myself, I imagined bodies dropping from the cloud in order to feed this city. "Wik, what if there are people living here already?" I asked as if he was right beside me, not trying to haul me up from above. He didn't answer, but I continued. "I mean, many fliers who went out exploring didn't return. And it is ridiculous to think that our ancestors were the only ones who had ever climbed a city."

I was babbling now. And Wik was too high to stop me when I thought I saw my mother circling nearby. I stepped from my perch to reach her. And the rope caught me and I swung, nearly limp, facing out towards the dry plain. My vision blurred.

Wik grunted. The rope line tensed. I began moving up the hide of the city in jerks and starts. The city's skin scraped at my back, the rope dug into my armpits and hurt. I tried to scramble and help, but I could barely lift my arms. "Do you think they can fly?"

"Who?" Wik said as he lifted me off the tether line and helped me sit on the city's flat hide. He smiled the kind of smile that melted my heart.

"The people who live on this city! I've been telling you about them. We might not look like them. We might not talk like them at all. We couldn't even read the plates in the midcloud. How do we talk to anyone down here—if there is anyone?" We'd seen signs of civilizations long gone, broken metal, outlines in the dirt that spoke of human-built structures buried deep.

Wik's face changed as he considered my behavior. "Perhaps they'll have songs, just like us. You should lie down."

"Perhaps they'll eat us, or worse."

"What could be worse than being eaten? Being eaten alive." Wik's eyes shone. He wasn't laughing. "Lie down."

"It's not funny."

Wik started humming a passage from The Rise.

"Shhhhh," I said. But my eyes closed.

"Rest," I heard him say. I felt a tug at my leg. Heard him hiss. He touched the break, and I saw stars behind my eyes. I might have cried out.

I saw Maalik flying away, into the star-filled, daytime sky.

# 12

## NAT, BETWEEN

*⌒ And Brokenwings returned to find his mates. ⌒*

My family waited for me within the clouds. Between them and me, calcified bridges draped moss across towers. Trunks that had grown together below began to fork and diverge. Damp bone and dark twists made passages dangerous.

None of these obstacles could stop me.

Ciel and I climbed to the short, creaking span of an ancient bridge. The calcified expanse crackled beneath us as we scrambled to the next tower. We rested in a narrow cave and on spare ledges. We inched our way higher, trying to track the time but growing confused in the clouds. Then in the half-light of day, we found ourselves standing on a terminated bone trunk, far beneath a bone-white bridge and the dark shadow of a structure above it.

"There." Ciel pointed. "The meadow." Far above, a bit of moss-covered plinth hung from a neatly cut hole in the shadow. We were so very close.

"Finally." I pictured my friends and family as I'd last seen them, being taken inside the towers by Dix's guards. I hoped they'd survived. The thought of being able to finally know tied a knot of relief and worry in my stomach. But my relief was brief.

We were unattainably close. The next bridge between the

towers was a much thinner span of calcified rope and bone. Below us on each side of the tower, the mist rippled. The depths were filled with gravity's hunger, ready to throw two wingless climbers down to the distant ground.

"If we could fly," Ciel said.

"Unless scavengers have stashed wings here, we can't." We would need to cross the bridge one at a time. The span creaked softly in the midcloud wind.

"Maybe there's something more stable below." Ciel peered over the edge, then got on her stomach to look closer. Then she gave a small screech and scooted backwards, scraping her hands on the towertop. "Skymouth," she whispered. "Resting just there."

"Littlemouths, you mean?" Skymouths didn't often lurk close to towers, except in the Spire, or if they were hunting. In the midcloud, they preferred coasting breezes in order to hunt. I'd once seen one seek out a bone eater and squeeze it to death. I hoped these weren't hunting.

Ciel shook her head, cautiously peering over the edge. "Small skymouths. Three of them. On the tower."

My ragged robe snagged the rough towertop as I knelt beside her. I held myself still, though the damp moss and a sharp lightning-strike smell made me want to sneeze. The glimmer of phosphorescence on the tower side looked layered, interleaved. Three bodies breathed rhythmically, almost as one.

As we watched, one of the skymouths gently peeled away and faded into the depths, its glowing outline disappearing as it sank into the clouds. The others followed.

The damp air made Ciel's voice hoarse. "Come on, we need to go too."

"You first." If the bridge broke under my weight, at least she would get there.

Ciel dug in her pack for spidersilk. She tied a tether around her waist and tossed me the other end. I secured it to an edge of the bone tower and held on as she scaled the last bit of tower to the calcified bridge.

She began to cross, and the bridge creaked again. When she was halfway, she untied the tether and scrambled to the other side. Waved from a perch there. With my heart thudding in my ears, I gathered up the tether and prepared to follow her across.

With each step, the bridge's creaks and groans grew louder. The bridge was old, but its three-line design was familiar—one broader span of sinew and fiber for the feet, two guide rail spans above. The rough grind of bone against my hands, the crackling beneath my feet, was not a normal bridge crossing. But I was almost to the other side.

After the first guide rope snapped, the bridge tipped, and I leaned hard against the sway. The guide was still attached to the triple tower where Ciel crouched, and I pulled my way forward. As I drew close enough, I tossed the tether line and she tied it to the tower. Ciel pointed to one of the almost-overgrown grips carved in the tower side. "Jump for those!"

I didn't hesitate. I landed in a heap on a moss-encrusted bone spur. The impact knocked the wind right out of me. Ciel scrambled to my side. The bridge swung, tangled and broken, just behind us.

The crossing had taken moments. I looked up, my vision sparked with stars from the impact. I looked down, over the bone spur's side. Whispered, "Ciel, look."

The skymouths had made the same crossing. Two clung to the tower wall, resting, curled up like a mated pair. Overlapping layers of glow and sparkle cast the rest of the tower in darkness. In the distance, the third one detached and began to undulate through the air towards the other two.

I'd never fallen for superstition, but three skymouths,

clustering as if for comfort? Made me wonder if they knew already what the people above did not: that the towers were dying.

"Flee," I whispered. "Go somewhere safe."

The small community of skymouths huddled closer to each other.

As we watched them resting, my heart calmed its desperate beat. My breathing slowed, and hope bloomed in my chest. We'd come far in our desperate climb.

Not too far overhead was the cave I'd been desperate to reach for so long. Ciel and I began to climb again.

\ \ \

When we finally neared the cave, my ribs no longer hurt; my hands did not ache in the grips. I felt nothing but the heavy pull of anticipation.

*Where are they?* Every part of me wanted to see my family alive and well.

Suddenly, the cave mouth appeared, a dark outline framing a flicker of fire. The sharp smell of cooking lichen. Ceetcee, Beliak, Djonn, and Moc gathered around the cookfire, talking.

*Where is Elna?* I couldn't see her.

*Is she all right?* I wasn't sure I could stand knowing if she wasn't, not yet.

I stopped climbing and looked up at the flame dancing with the shadows in the cave. I couldn't move.

Below, days ago, Kirit had stood unmoving before the fallen tower. Had refused to climb. I'd been furious. Now I realized she'd been afraid, trapped between the past and the future.

Now I understood.

Ciel sped up the lichen-soft tower ahead of me. She pulled herself up to the cave mouth and climbed into the cave. Shouts of joy and a baby's cry drifted down to me before her feet disappeared over the ledge.

My heart felt like it stopped and then restarted with a new rhythm. A baby's cry.

I'd imagined this reunion for so many nights. Now it was real. They were right there. I could hear them laughing. They were well. I knew that now.

But if Elna was gone? I would learn that too, and I wasn't sure I wanted to know. Worse, I bore knowledge that would change their world. Not for the better. I had to tell them.

But I couldn't make my feet move. I stared up, trapped by fear. It was a sour taste in my mouth and a weight in my belly.

A shadow detached itself from the group around the fire and emerged into the mist.

"Nat!" Beliak slid and stumbled from the cave mouth and down tower's slope, joyous. Ceetcee right behind him.

Our lives had been split apart by wind and gravity. By black-wing attack. I felt like we were meeting again for the first time, but at breakneck, crushing speed. I wanted to tell him everything I had become. To know everything that had happened to him and to Ceetcee. I wanted everyone else to disappear and leave the three of us—the four of us now—alone.

Instead, "Are you all right? Is everyone—" emerged from my mouth instead. A pale shadow of what I felt. Beliak's robe, torn at the knee, revealed a well-healed wound. His face was thin, and there were rings around his eyes. I felt a sudden jolt of jealousy that Djonn and Ceetcee had been here to help him, then we were embracing and I was crushed in his and Ceet-cee's arms.

Another thin wail tore at us. "The baby's all right," she whispered at my look of alarm.

*The baby.* Ceetcee turned, a shy smile on her face. Strapped on her back, because she wasn't riding the wind yet, was a tiny, bald miniature of Ceetcee. Piercing dark eyes, skin the color of brass. The baby looked wan, but alive. So did Ceetcee.

I reached out a hand to touch the tiny head. Saw again the scars on my fingers, the dirt beneath my fingernails. My hand hovered in the air. "So beautiful. Healthy? What is her name?" I was afraid of the answer, as much as I was about Elna.

"We're all right. We can't spend too much longer beneath the clouds, but for now, she's fine . . ." Ceetcee trailed off. "What is it?"

Above us, Ciel and Moc were already arguing. Djonn tried to get them to calm down. "Ciel, slow down," Moc cautioned. "You're making no sense."

"It's true!" Ciel said. "Nat!" She waved me up.

Pulling Beliak and Ceetcee along with me, I climbed to the cave where last we'd made a stand against the blackwings, and the city above had tried to kill us.

"Where is Elna?" I finally managed.

"Your mother's all right," Ceetcee began. I could breathe again. "Just weak."

Moc pointed at Ciel, who was now a head taller than her twin. "She says the city's alive, but it's dying!"

They all turned to look at me, and Ciel raged, "You'd believe him but not me? Why? We've both seen it!"

I held up both hands, forcing Beliak and Ceetcee to let me go, and forcing myself to let them go. "Listen to Ciel. She's right."

I looked for Elna but didn't see her in the dim cave. My heart sank. But with everyone focused on Ciel, I couldn't risk distracting them from her story. This was why we were here. To convince them to leave the towers. We had to make them listen. I could wait a few moments more to see Elna, so long as she was alive.

Ciel began by describing the fall and our first sighting of the city. "It is so big, this whole cave could fit in one of its eyes," she said. "And it eats people! It ate Hiroli!"

Some concerned blinking among the adults in the room turned into throat clearing and a raised eyebrow at me, but then Moc said, "Really?"

I nodded. "Ciel tells the truth."

"What about Dix?" Beliak asked. "Did Dix chase you below? Is she still down there?"

He sounded as if he hoped the city had eaten Dix too.

"We found her hanging on a bone spur near the ground," I said. "It was a difficult landing."

"Her blackwing guards are gone too," Ciel added. "But right now, what you need to know is that there are other cities, just like this one but much smaller. They can walk around, and . . ." She paused, and I gestured with my chin, *Go on, say it.* "And attack things. They move pretty slow, but they're really hard to stop." She shuddered.

"How big?" Moc said. "The towers take days to fly across."

"Longer on the ground. The towers all grow together into a ridge, and if they hadn't grown so high . . ." I stopped, thinking of all the times I'd helped scrub at a towertop with scourweed, in hopes of raising a new tier so that my tower might rise higher, and my fortunes with it. "The weight of the towers has kept this city immobile for a long time."

I knelt down to draw what we'd been able to see of the city from the ground, to show them the elevations, the middens, the places where the bone eaters roosted, and what they did as part of the city's life cycle.

"Next you'll be saying that you found an ancient city," Beliak said, his voice half joking. His disbelief stung.

I shook my head. "We haven't had time. We've been too busy trying to keep the city alive until we could find a way to signal you and to get you to safety."

"To signal the whole city," Ciel added.

I bit my lip. *You were all I thought of.* If convincing these four was taking so long, how long would it take to tell the entire city the truth? We didn't have much time at all.

"The thing is," I finally said, "you must be off the towers and somewhere safe very soon."

Just then, a figure limped through the back tunnel, tracing confident fingers along a wall. "You all are disturbing the little-mouths," Elna said. She looked healthy, if frail. Her hair had been cloud and bone colored for as long as I could remember. Her eyes—formerly a very pale blue—were now fully clouded over. Skyblind.

My mother. I ran to her and touched her shoulder. Real. She was here and all right, like Ceetcee had said. "It's me, Nat."

The embrace Elna pulled me into wasn't a strong one. "You came back," she whispered. "You're here."

We stood there for a long moment. I did not want to shatter it. But I had to.

"I came back, and now we have to leave, fast," I whispered. Her eyes widened with surprise. "We have to go down through the clouds—now."

# 13

## MACAL, BETWEEN

*~ A midcloud discovery, as the world quaked ~*

Before Allsuns, I'd wanted to take wing to help warn the city. Now, flying close to the clouds, searching for reasons for the disaster, I passed the shattered base of a tower, the rough bone core still seeping and the smell of rot everywhere.

I peered through the mist, looking for any scavengers working the cloudline for the wealth that had fallen from the tiers so very recently. For anyone who might help guide me.

Which is how, when the southern towers began their Conclave, I'd glided low enough that I nearly became one of their sacrifices.

A shadow spun through the light above, and I pulled hard on my wing grips to dodge. Gravity and wind fought me for control as a Lawsbreaker's body plummeted past.

"Below you!" I shouted as if flight students were still with me. But I flew alone in the midst of a Conclave.

I remained aloft. The body fell. An old woman, her mouth open, shocked. The trail of blood in the air indicated she did not go peaceably.

Above, shadows, spinning arms and legs, wingless. More cloudbound, being sent to placate the city.

*Save someone, Macal.* I followed, trying to catch each, until the bodies were lost in the clouds and mist. I circled, no longer looking up. *Clouds.* The mist made my vision waver. I was certain it was the mist. The mist was in my throat too, choking me with anger.

*Lawsbreakers?* The bodies I'd seen bore few markers.

I searched for grip hooks on the side of a nearby tower, one that had not cracked. Held on so I could breathe. I had to stay calm down here.

Sidra, if she were here, would likely frown, and say, *What could they have possibly done in the wreckage of the city? The old woman wore no Lawsmarkers.* The reason I'd called them Lawsbreakers in my mind was because they were cloudbound. *The one does not inherently follow the other.*

What were the towers doing? The city hadn't quaked again, nor had it shifted its canted angle further. My search for scavengers to accompany me below could wait.

I circled up to the high tower of Grigrit, where two rings of blackwings stood, one at guard and one group trying to push their way in. Three prisoners, bound and wingless, waited on the towertop.

"You are making a desperate mistake," a woman's voice said, high and clear in the wind. "The city does not want your offerings any longer. Stop this."

Laughter from the inner circle. "How do you know this, Rya? Have you asked the city?"

"Perhaps I have. Tell your blackwings to release their Lawsbreakers to me." Once close enough, I could see several Lawsbreakers shivering in the wind, their thin robes not enough for the cold. The woman speaking stood nose to nose with a tall blackwing. He'd called her Rya.

*Rya.* I'd found her again. And she was trying to stop the Conclave.

Wishing Urie—or someone already known here—had accompanied me, I approached the tower. The assembled group stepped back without a word. Their furled dark wings rustled as they made room for me—a councilman and Singer—before the two leaders.

They did not bow when I furled my own wings and dropped to the towertop.

For a moment, our robes flapping in the wind were the only sound on the tower. The leaders gave no words of welcome. Then Rya approached me.

When our eyes met, I saw recognition. She knew me from the clouds beyond Mondarath, but she didn't speak of it. Nor did I.

She wore dark feathers now across her shoulders and on her wings. "You've come to offer your loyalty? What tower?" she asked.

I shook my head. "I've come to find out what you do here."

"What *they* do"—she gestured behind her—"is wrong. I am trying to right it. Your loyalty would help."

I would give no one my loyalty that easily, no matter how much I wanted to unite the city. Especially not when three more citizens stood at the edges of a tower awaiting their fate. But I knew, from what I'd seen, that Rya's blackwing alliances balanced on a knife's edge.

Rya turned back to the other blackwing leader, bracing for confrontation. More feathers decorated the back of her robes. They rustled with her movement. Hunger and determination had sharpened her face to edges and points. She'd painted the hollows near her eyes with a dye used for wingsets, creating colorful angles and small hash marks. She was the most beautiful blackwing I had ever seen.

And she was challenging the others, in defense of the cloudbound.

I could not offer loyalty, but I could still strengthen her case.

"I wait to hear from you, Risen," I addressed her as leader, and bowed, ignoring the other blackwing. "As an emissary from the northwest. What happens here?"

The challenged blackwing's lips parted slightly. Rya's attendants and the assembled wingless prisoners watched her, and him.

The other blackwing leader spoke first and quickly. "We keep the city alive here, Risen. That is what we do. These are Lawsbreakers. Join us, or join them." His voice grew thick with disdain. "You too, Rya."

I looked at the blackwings, then at the assembled Lawsbreakers. Recognized one: the wingfighter Aliati. The others were children. All were bound.

Pressing my hand to my robe, as if preparing to make a speech, I palmed my knife and nodded. "I understand your need to appease the city." I saw Rya watching. "This is leadership in hard times. I understand that too. But what have these children done? What laws have they broken?" None of the prisoners wore Lawsmarkers. They just looked thin and hungry.

"Tower laws," the blackwing growled. "Insurrection," he added, looking hard at Rya and then at me. "Both of you."

His companions moved forward, while Rya stayed completely still.

I was faster.

Singer training had prepared me, though I rarely used it. Wingfighting, on the other hand, had been my joy. I ducked under their reach and came up behind one of the guards, then spun to the left, near the tower's edge.

Leaping in the air, I grabbed the three "Lawsbreakers," though I didn't know how I would carry them all. Aliati felt very light, even with the two children who clung to her.

The two guards still on the tower shouted for help and began to pursue us, but as we dove through the clouds, I heard Rya shout, "Let him go! He'll do your work for you twice over."

The guards did not follow us past the clouds. Rya had bought me time.

Aliati shifted in my grasp and tried to reach for my knife. "Careful!" I shouted in the whistling air as we plunged. "You'll end us all." The children clung and whimpered.

Aliati growled, her dark hair blowing in the wind.

"I'm as good as dead anyway. I came back up here for supplies and help. Now I have nothing. Not even wings."

"That's not true. You'll find shelter, more supplies." *Supplies for what?* I wondered. "You'll get new wings." *For now, at least.*

"The last tower that offered me shelter tricked me and traded me to Grigrit for appeasement. What would you trade me for?"

The wind whistled around us as I absorbed the news. "I wouldn't do that."

"Everyone always says they won't, until they do," Aliati whispered. But she stopped trying to grab my knife.

ᘏ  ᘏ  ᘏ

We flew until Aliati spotted a pale shadow in the clouds, a ledge far below Grigrit and its guards.

"Set me down here," the young woman instructed me. "It's safe."

"What is it?" I called. I couldn't see the tower clearly.

Aliati laughed. "It's the ghost tower." She was so matter-of-fact about it, I guessed she'd been here before.

"What tower sold you to Grigrit? What Laws did you break?" I finally asked as we set down on the rough top of the truncated tower.

Aliati looked at me a long time, then took the children from her back and brushed their hair with her fingers, soothing them. "Scavenging. You know, how most towers get their metal? When they don't want to pay for what we find for them, they call us Lawsbreakers." She hadn't told me what tower, I noticed.

It wasn't just that, I knew. "The southwestern towers are strict about that."

She snorted. "The northern towers aren't any better. You think you're so enlightened up there, but you dislike scavengers just as much, even though you use them." Aliati's face was bruised, and she looked unsteady on her feet. "We've traded before. Raq found you things others couldn't. It was useful. For the market."

Raq. I should have guessed. But I'd never asked.

Aliati looked at me, and at the fledges. "You should be on your way. You've tumbled into a blackwing power struggle, and none of them will be happy with you. Except maybe Rya. Take these two with you when you go. Fly them out of here. Back to the northwest."

I had to think fast. Aliati was, like Raq, a scavenger. The metal beads in her hair, her talent with wingfighting, her resourcefulness at Mondarath. How had I not seen it before? The answer was my own assumptions. Because it wasn't obvious up above the clouds. The beads didn't sparkle like glass ones did. But down here, Aliati seemed relaxed and very much at home.

"I need a scavenger now, and I'll pay proper respect," I said.

Aliati laughed again. "The city's finally shaken so hard you're willing to come below the clouds and ask politely for help? What took you so long?"

"You know the undercloud. Help us find out what's wrong with the city. We need to know so we can prepare the citizens."

She waved me towards the edge of the tower. "I've been down twice since the shake, and I have to tell you, there's nothing here. A few breaks, some torn bridgework. Nothing that would cause a quake."

"How low have you gone?" I asked.

Aliati shrugged, but her eyes were guarded. "Low enough. Go too low, you can get sick."

I boggled at this, and then, peering through the mist, I shivered. There was too much. "We can't find anything in this fog, but I need to keep looking," I said. "I can pay," I added when Aliati looked disinterested, staring into the depths as if she wanted to leap. "I have marks and trade goods. Back uptower."

Aliati snorted. "I can find everything I need down here."

"Except wings." She had none. Nor did the fledges.

The scavenger acknowledged this with a nod. "Except wings." She frowned, but it quickly turned into one of her slanted grins. "But going down? I don't need wings. And I can always climb back up."

No wings. Outside of the towers. The idea shocked me. No, it horrified me. Then it intrigued me. "How do you do this?"

Aliati pulled out bone claw grips tipped with metal from deep within her satchel. She put them on her hands and grasped the tower with them. The two children hopped on Aliati's back, and she began to climb. The grips dug into the bone and left small marks as she passed.

Aliati skittered up the wall, fast as a silkspider, even carrying two fledges.

But Aliati had disappeared into the clouds and left me alone.

The mist closed in on me again, the quiet. How could she be at home down here?

I tried to leave the ghost tower, tried to fly in a direction that made sense, but without a guide, in the strange gray shadows of the undercloud, I was reluctant to go far. The dim light faded too soon and then it was too late for me to move. I would have to spend the night on the tower, alone.

I curled up in my robe and tried to keep warm as best I could, but the damp and the darkness leached everything: warmth, hope. I shivered in my cloak. "Tomorrow morning, I'll try one more time to find out what happened, then I'll go back up," I promised myself, and Sidra.

Discomfort woke me much later, a poke at my side with a sharp point. Aliati sat before me, head cocked, waiting for me to wake.

"I have what you want," she said in a hoarse whisper. "How much are you willing to pay?" Her claw fingers glittered in the darkness.

"Anything," I said recklessly. "Anything to save the city."

# PART TWO

## THE GATHERING

# 14

## MACAL, MIDCLOUD

*⁓ Within the cloud, the rescue started ⁓*

All my weapons and my dreams—this was the price Aliati collected.

Dreams for the city above, dreams for the future. They all dissipated as we flew into the midcloud.

My weapons, Aliati said she took as a precaution.

In the mist, Aliati's wings disappeared often, and I struggled to follow. The buffeting wind, the damp—these became familiar quickly. So too, the fear of being lost in the cloud. I tried to fly more daring angles, as she would not slow for me.

But the unease I felt below the clouds? That I couldn't get used to.

"Keep up, Macal," she shouted behind her, into the dimming cloudlight.

❧ ❧ ❧

As we flew, we passed the towers growing together. The cracked and broken trunks. I realized somewhere far below, each tower depended on the others to rise above the clouds. None was unaffected by the quake.

We could not bind the towers together. We could not save them with bridges.

There was no market barter, no song that could save them.

Aliati stopped to rest on a ledge and brush the moisture from her wings. I landed beside her.

"Where are you taking me?" I asked, breathless. Above, the remaining towers rose into the brighter cloud.

She sat on the towertop and pulled her knees to her chest for warmth. "Home. But we have to stop for a while. You need to adjust to the air here." She would say no more than that. She closed her eyes and hummed an old song. "Corwin and The Nest of Thieves." She passed me a water sack and made me drink. I curled up and slept on the towertop, beneath my wings.

When we were rested, we descended again, but this time Aliati flew by my side, our pinions wobbling on the wind, just far enough to avoid an accident, but close enough not to lose sight of one another. When she dove deeper into the midcloud, passing a bone-encrusted bridge, I followed. Wind battering the edges of our wings, the only sound in my ears.

I couldn't imagine anyone living at these depths. Yet Aliati had called it home.

She whistled a complex windsign. I looked around, saw only more towers, a broad gap of cloud. Then a whistle returned on the wind, out of nowhere.

Below us, a cloud seemed to part, and with a shout, Aliati dove for it. I adjusted my wing grips and dove to follow, stunned by the widening expanse of green below.

We flew beneath a netting of skymouth skins, and I gasped. "Hidden in plain sight!"

"Not so plain." Aliati laughed. "We're pretty far down."

She was right about that. When we landed beside the closest of the three towers, I knelt by a large fern, dizzy from the rich air.

Aliati, her wings half furled, had run to thrown her arms around a young, wingless man. He walked crookedly, and she nearly knocked him over. She released him and led him my way.

Others followed. In the mist, I could see large structures—mechanicals—and several blackwings working on them.

I tensed. *More blackwings.* What had Aliati led me into? She approached, and I reached for my knife. Found the sheath empty. *Taken as a precaution.* "Blackwings? How could you lead me here?"

The young man dipped his head to me. "You are welcome, Risen. And you have nothing to fear from us. Nor do the blackwings who chose to stay when Dix was chased from this meadow by Kirit and Nat and your brother, Wik."

My brother. This man had seen him alive. Knew what had happened. Aliati's face cracked a faint smile. "You are welcome here, Risen."

That word, *Risen.* I frowned. "There are no Risen anymore. No hightower. A quake has taken out so many towers, and all are racing to see how low they can live."

The young man groaned. "My apologies. We didn't know the destruction's extent. We felt only a few shakes here." He pointed to the shards of bone in the meadow. "How much damage above?"

"Many edge towers and tiers are gone or damaged," I replied. My heart pounded out the details of the quake, the number dead, but I held my tongue. "Wirra and Densira included. Viit took damage."

Aliati gasped. "All gone?" She hadn't seen the northwest. Only the south.

I let it sink in. All gone. So much loss.

The moment of greeting, of seeing familiar faces, shredded into sounds of grief. Even as more approached, word spread about the towers. Ceetcee and Beliak joined us to listen. Tears ran down their cheeks.

Moc approached. My nephew. Safe. Who else was? No one had told me yet.

But they were safe. The midcloud was safer than the towers. "We need to bring as many as we can to safety." If Moc and Ceetcee were here, unharmed, I was willing to trust Aliati on the blackwings. For now.

"But we'll not be here for very long," Moc said, patting me on the arm. "We're readying to leave."

*Why would they come back up above the clouds when this meadow is already safer than the towers above?* "I don't understand," I said.

In answer, they led me inside one of the towers, towards an alcove that glowed blue with littlemouths, and I understood even less.

At the alcove's threshold, a frail older woman spoke softly to a barefoot man in a ragged hunter cloak, his back turned to me. "Up is safer," she said. Her voice was calm, quiet. A voice I knew. "Djonn's artifexing a climber to take us back above the clouds."

"You don't understand," the young man said. "We have to go somewhere safer. We don't have long at all."

Moc had said a similar thing.

"Where would we go? Lower than here? How will your daughter make the trip?" the old woman said. She touched his arm gently. I coughed, and her pale face turned towards me. Elna. The young man turned too. His face was scarred and filthy, but I knew those eyes, that stubborn chin.

"Nat! Elna!" Aliati had helped me find them, after so much time. She'd made good on her bargain. I could return and help the people above with the knowledge. "What has happened? Do you know why the city roared?"

They turned to me, faces tense.

"It's dying," Nat said, as if he'd said it many times, and as if he never wished to say these words again. "If not already dead. We have ten days, or less, to flee."

↘ ↘ ↘

We gathered in the alcove where littlemouths nested. Brass plates engraved with artifex schematics from long ago lined the walls of this space, holding open a gap of bone as the tower grew.

The resulting cave had become a refuge for the skymouths' younger cousins long ago. It was a good place to plan. It was beautiful. I wished Sidra were with me to see it. And to help me phrase my questions. I had so many questions about it, about everything.

Nat had pulled me aside to tell me news of my brother. "He lives. He is searching for a new home for us, with Kirit." He'd described the city to me also, and how it was dying. For that, I was grateful, but I wanted to know much more. *After.* I knew the important thing about Wik: that he was alive, or had been the last time Nat and Ciel had seen him. The rest would wait until I knew how to best save the city above.

Now I sat next to Nat and Ceetcee, while Moc and Aliati helped Djonn lower himself stiffly to the floor. The artifex was in pain, that was clear.

While everyone arrived, Ciel began to hum.

All around us, littlemouths glowed, first soft, then bright. The room's walls gleamed with brass.

It took me a moment to realize Ciel hummed The Rise. A moment of jarring recognition: the melody was the same for tower as it was for Singers, but the words were different. I'd learned both versions, had loved both versions. Hearing it stripped down to notes made me love the heart of it even more. The song that my mother had sung to me and to Wik to calm us. The song that our ancestors had used to tell their history.

"How will we tell everyone?" Ceetcee spoke first. The baby slept in a sling on her back, backlit by littlemouth light. Ceetcee crossed her arms and swayed side to side, gently. "We can't leave people up there. Not a single one."

The cave quieted until we could hear rain spatter the lichen and ferns in the meadow just outside: fat drops on tiny leaves. Someone in the meadow cursed. Several blackwings who had once attacked the midcloud were camped outside. Aliati had taken their wings, rather than risk them revealing the cave's location to the clouds above. She still had my weapons too.

"Would *those above* save *us*?" Djonn asked after a long stretch. He didn't look at me.

Ceetcee turned and looked him full in the eyes, then looked at me. "*I would* if I were them," she said.

Beliak shifted his feet as if he were caught between two opposing gusts. Elna coughed softly into her hand.

I breathed deep. Smoke from the cookfire in the larger cave and the greenery's thick scent and mist in the meadow outside wove their way into this alcove.

So many remained above.

Nat spoke first. "How do you propose we get them all down? There aren't nearly enough of us, and we're Lawsbreakers above the clouds. We'll be thrown right down again. The rest of the city can wait until you all are safe."

The group was quiet.

I grappled with anger, with frustration. "Those are people you're talking about. You cannot leave them."

Djonn looked at me from where he lay on the cave floor. He looked at Nat too. Instead of answering, he began to draw on the bone with a piece of charcoal. "We've been building climbers, and more propellers for controlling the wind," he said. "So that Elna, Ceetcee, the baby, and I wouldn't have to be carried up in nets." His sketch showed a basket ringed by eight articulated legs. "They're tipped with metal, like grips."

The basket looked as if it could carry five. "We'll need more than that for our group. Especially if Ceetcee wants to include the blackwings in the meadow."

"The climber is meant to go up," Beliak said.

Ciel, still humming, studied the design. She'd helped Djonn build tools and weapons before we fell through the clouds. "It will have to be modified. And we *can* build more of them." When she stopped humming, the littlemouths took a long time to dim.

"In ten days?" Nat sounded doubtful.

My frustration simmered. "There are people above who can help." I wanted him to hear that phrase: *There are people above.*

"If we have more help, we can build a lot of things," Elna said. She smiled in my direction.

"We need *something*," Ciel agreed. "We can't exactly ride a skymouth out of here, or a bone eater. We need a way to carry a lot of people, or lower them down safely." She was talking about more than just the midcloud cave's population, I could tell. Hope wrestled with my anger. Ciel looked at me and began humming The Rise again.

Littlemouths brightened the cave.

"How will you convince the city?" I said. I was compelled to get moving. I knew there would be factions who could not believe what Nat had said. I barely believed it.

Nat tossed a piece of bone in the air and caught it. "We'd have to get the blackwings to help us." He made it sound difficult. Impossible. He was trying to sway the group towards an easier decision.

But Beliak peered at the brass plates. "That could be a good idea."

Nat stifled a groan. "One that's impossible."

Next to the climber sketch, Djonn drew a box kite on the bone floor of the alcove that had been a refuge for them while the towers above hunted them. I tried to understand their reluctance, but now that I knew, I wanted them to agree immediately to help the towers too.

Djonn said slowly, "Not impossible. This is a fairly sturdy structure, and quick to build, if we can make it big enough." He added an inner frame and basket, then he and Ciel began to draw even more elaborate kites and mechanicals than the ones outside, many buoyed by lighter-than-air.

"Do you have lighter-than-air?" Nat asked. "If you don't, this is just another delay."

"We have a little. We might be able to ask a scavenger to find us more," Djonn replied, a shy grin crossing his face. *Aliati.* Of course.

"We have sources too," I said quickly. It wasn't far from the truth.

Djonn continued to draw. Tiers of kites, bound together in wings supported by lighter-than-air. Pulleys and lowering cables that could be secured on climbing spiders or on towers. Nets of all kinds, for catching, rescue. Things we could build out of what we had, in as much time as we had.

"We'll lower the kites with pulleys, for as long as we can," Djonn added. "Once we're at the end of the tethers, the lighter-than-air should help as well. The gas seems to get stronger the lower it goes."

Our means of escape took shape on the bone floor. "But you'll still need more help to build these," I said. "Otherwise, there won't be enough time to get the plinths prepared to support everyone, much less to be lowered. And I don't think we have enough lighter-than-air to float an entire city."

Elna eased herself to the floor where we spoke, tears on her face. Nat must have told her the news about the towers. "When will the city sing Remembrances?"

"We sang at Allsuns two days ago," I said. "We gathered, then began making plans to build floating platforms for the survivors near the remaining towers. But I wanted to make sure the bone cores were untroubled below the clouds. So Aliati brought me here."

"Well then, now is the time to ready yourselves," she said. "To say good-bye to the city."

Nat bowed his head, and Ceetcee nodded. As in the past, especially in city council, Elna's words had helped shift the argument.

I knelt then, in gratitude, near Elna, and pulled a stone fruit from my pocket.

Nat's face, beside her, transformed. "I haven't seen anything like it in moons."

The fruit was bruised and mashed, but everyone stared at it. Elna brushed the stone fruit's fuzzy skin with her fingers.

"Your news has crushed my appetite," Elna said.

I continued to hold the fruit out. "I know. I wish I didn't have such news."

She took the fruit from me and took a tiny bite out of courtesy.

The juice ran down her chin. "Thank you," she murmured. Then she made Nat pass the fruit to everyone else, and they all had a taste, or cut a slice for later, right down to the stone.

"Now you've found us." Moc appeared from the shadows to take the stone fruit pit from my hand. "Thanks to Aliati. What if you led more blackwings here?"

Aliati growled at Moc, but then smiled sadly. "They did not follow us. I'm lucky he found me. I think he's trustworthy enough."

"So no one else is following you?" Nat asked, leaning forward, still chewing.

I shook my head. "The blackwings are busy planning

Conclaves and fighting over space on the towers. Everyone's uneasy." I fought back my own rising unease. "Finding answers to what happened will help."

"Until there's another quake," Ceetcee whispered.

Clearing his throat, Nat said, "It will. And this time, the city will fall."

My eyes widened at the harsh words, and my hands balled into fists. "That's not possible. Not again." I couldn't stop hearing the sounds of my city falling apart.

Nat didn't answer. He reached into his robe and held out a handful of something. It was reddish brown and unlike anything I'd ever seen. "I grabbed this when we were building our packs from the wreckage. It's possible. I wish I'd brought more than a handful of dirt with me."

We peered at the handful of ground. The heft of his proof strengthened the rest of his argument.

"Nat." Beliak elbowed him. "Tell Macal everything you know. Tell Aliati."

As Nat spoke about the cities once more, with Ciel chiming in, I felt worse, like I was in a nightmare. I stood up, pacing around the alcove, nearly tripping over Elna.

"Careful!" Ceetcee and Nat said at the same time. How could I be so clumsy? Me, the Magister who'd pulled Nat from a fall into the clouds during his wingtest. A councilor. The leader of a tower, was now trying to find my way in a dim cave, in the clouds.

From Nat's expression, it looked as if he was having the same thoughts. He, the overconfident wingtester with all the answers. He'd been so sure of everything then: his skill, his strength, the city, the wind. Allmoons later, he was still determined. This was not going to be easy, by any measure.

"My apologies." I bowed to Elna. "This is a lot to take in."

"For all of us," Elna said. "I am glad you came, Magister." She held out a thin hand to me, still sticky with stone fruit juice, and I grasped it. "We can do this. We'll save as much of the city as possible."

Aliati leaned on Djonn's shoulder, and he on hers, each supporting the other. Despite his delight earlier, the artifex looked exhausted. His brace, which I could see parts of now, fit him so poorly, chafe marks were visible beneath his robe when he moved.

Even so, Djonn spoke for me. "Macal's right, there isn't enough lighter-than-air here to float the city. Even with the storage above. We need a different strategy. And more hands to do the work."

In this way, we talked through the night.

"We'll need food," Beliak said. "To support everyone who comes down. There's barely enough food within reach to sustain the eight of us, plus the guards. You can't bring more people here without bringing food for them. And you can't bring them to the meadow, or to the first tower and the cave here. We can't support it."

"Where do you suggest we take them? The Spire is unstable," Nat said.

This part of the evacuation was something I hadn't yet thought about. I had been more focused on getting people down.

"We can use hang-sacks off of the nearby towers, and plinths for shelter. It won't be pleasant, but those who can't fit into a cave will have to rough it for a few days until we're ready to move again. If . . ." I stopped before I said what I was thinking.

*If we move fast enough.*

The baby wailed, and Ceetcee began feeding her. Beliak, Nat, and Aliati walked outside to try to find room for the tower populations.

The baby's eyes squeezed shut, and her hands curled to tiny fists. Only a few days old, very small, with a thready cry that set nerves on edge. After a long moment, Ceetcee gave up trying to nurse. She sighed in frustration.

"Too quick," Elna muttered, but didn't push. "It's harder down here." The baby's wails echoed against the cave walls as Ceetcee let out another sigh. She began to whisper to the infant: nonsense words that sounded like the wind. The child calmed and slept against her chest, and she walked over to me, swaying slightly.

She'd never been one of my flight students, but I remembered her from wingtest. I'd seen her frequently in the air after she moved to Densira. She'd flown with shy grace, making room for others, taking care not to foul anyone's wind. And she'd become a bridge artifex when many had failed the training.

Now Ceetcee looked like the very air weighed her down. But she hadn't hesitated to wrap the child to her chest and head into the meadow to help Djonn make tools. She was heading out to do it again now. As she passed me, she asked, "What did the quake feel like?"

"Like the world rolled beneath us. The cracking was the worst part. You?"

Ceetcee sighed. "We were distracted. But I remember hearing loud crashes, and when I went out to the meadow a few days ago, I saw that pieces of bone had fallen from the Spire and broken against the other towers."

I reached out to touch the infant's head. "You've survived so much already down here." I wished I could take them home, back up to the towers. To Densira, which was no longer there. Or to Mondarath. To help give the child a name and a home.

Ceetcee pressed her lips together. "Elna helped me through the worst of it. She knew what to do."

Elna often did know exactly what to do. But down here? Without healers to help? "It was very brave."

That made Ceetcee laugh, which caught me by surprise. "What else was there to do? We'd been chased below the clouds. I couldn't fly any longer." Her chin lifted a fraction then. "Djonn's climber took a little longer than he planned. He's still working on it. And we were waiting for Nat to return." She smiled at him. "And he did. Now we can all fly down together."

I thought Nat would smile at her words, but instead he paled and swallowed. "You shouldn't have waited for me. I took too long," he finally said.

I heard that strange halt to his words again. He was holding back something. I added that to my worries, and gave the grip I was carving another whack with the knife. The blade, a now-rare skymouth tooth, shaved bone away from one of the points, making it sharp enough to dig bone blade into bone tower.

↖ ↖ ↖

When we returned to the front cave, Beliak took the large gryphon bladder off the tri-stand spread above the fire. Opened it and let the steam run out. I smelled a strange scent.

Nat groaned. "I thought I'd never miss lichen."

I staunched my irritation. The food had been gathered and prepared for us. Above the clouds, we'd hungered for greens, for fruit. But the green vegetation looked much less appealing than the bruised stone fruit, and, after this discussion, I wasn't sure I wanted food either.

"We need to eat, no matter what. I've improved the recipe," Beliak said, winking at me and Nat both. His enthusiasm made me wary.

I found a bone bowl and scooped myself some after the others had taken their share. I *was* starving. The sliver of stone fruit had shaken my appetite, despite my worries. As I chewed, I thought over the losses above, and how to keep from losing more. The problem below. "We can't wait for the towers to work out who goes and who stays, or whether to go at all. There's not enough time."

Nat had been right before, despite himself. We needed the blackwings.

"Going down would be easier in small groups in the climbers, and the kites," Ciel suggested. I remembered the uncertainty of my descent into the clouds and shivered, despite the warmth from the fire.

The others shook their heads. "I agree with what Nat said earlier. We should go down now," Moc said. "We can send Maalik back up with messages. Let them decide to make the journey and follow us as best they can." My nephew paused. "Where *is* your whipperling?"

"I left Maalik with Kirit. So she and Wik can signal when they find a safe place for us to shelter below," Nat said. He shoveled a mouthful of greens into his mouth.

The boiled lichen soured on my tongue. "You can't just *leave* when they signal. We have to work together. You need supplies that we have above the clouds. We need your"—I inclined my head towards Ciel and Nat then—"guidance. Your knowledge. You can't just tell the towers to follow you down and hope for the best. What if we get lost?"

"Some towers don't seem to care about losing others," Aliati muttered.

I choked on the greens. She had a point.

Ceetcee turned to say something sharp, but Elna shook her head. She moved to stand next to Nat. The baby kicked in the sling and began to cry.

"They will care," I said. "There aren't enough of us left to not care any longer, or to decide who is worth keeping and who isn't. Already we've spotted the blackwings aloft making counts of the city. We've tried to do the same."

"How many, do you think?" Djonn asked the question we

wanted to know. How many would need our help? How much chaos would that cause? The undercloud cave fell silent, waiting to hear the answer.

"I cannot say. We haven't been able to survey the southern quadrants. Several hundred in the north. No more." It was not enough. It was too many.

If Wik and Kirit were wrong about the number of days remaining . . . if my own head count was wrong.

Ciel slammed her bowl on the floor. "There's no time," she said, staring into the firelight. "We save everyone, now. We tell them all."

"How will you go about saving everyone, Ciel? It will be madness. People will panic and get hurt." Beliak's voice was tense with worry.

Ceetcee cradled the infant to her chest, then touched Ciel's shoulder. "We have to be careful even about who we tell and what we tell them, or there can be more riots."

"I couldn't agree more," Nat said. "The *less* we tell people, the fewer arguments."

Ciel glared at Nat with startling fierceness. I felt the same way.

"These are people! They are not fledges." I found myself pacing again, dangerously close to Elna. The mood in the alcove darkened.

Ciel's voice rose in pitch, frantic. "Doesn't everyone need to know, don't they deserve to make their own plans even if they can't get enough lighter-than-air? Don't they get a chance?"

Nat spoke quickly to calm her. "They abandoned you, Ciel. They abandoned all of us to the clouds." Too quickly. He sounded as angry as I was. "The city weighed our crimes and let us fall away."

As if I were soothing a concerned councilor, I said, "You found a way to climb back up the city's ridged back, its broken towers, anyway. You came to rescue your family."

Nat nodded, silent.

"You know others would want the same chance."

"I have an idea," Ceetcee said, but the baby continued to cry. She turned to Nat. "Hold her?" and put the tiny creature in his arms. His eyes widened. He held the child like she would slip from his grasp.

Ceetcee knelt on the floor and began to draw next to Djonn's sketches. "We anchor pulleys as low as possible on the low side of the city. Then we can send down successive groups even as we build more kites. We'll tether them below after the last trip, so they can stay aloft." Djonn nodded at her plan.

Nat was transfixed by the baby in his arms. He gripped too tight, and she squalled. "I don't want to drop her," he murmured.

"You won't," Ceetcee whispered and kept drawing schematics. Nat settled the baby in the crook of his elbow, and she quieted.

"How could I not try to save her first?" Nat murmured, looking at the baby.

"There are many fledges above the clouds too," I said quietly. *Who will save them?*

The baby's tiny fingers curled over Nat's thumb. She squalled. He rocked her quiet again, his face rapt.

"Everyone deserves a chance as much as we do," Ceetcee said. "The remaining Singers and the blackwings, the quadrants. The scavengers too." She looked at Aliati, who spread her arms wide. "The whole city. All of us."

The cave fell quiet for several moments. Wind beat its way inside, as a new storm spun clouds into twists beyond the walls and tossed the meadow. Blackwings hurried to cover and tie down the crawler.

A storm brewed inside the bone walls too.

Aliati moved to sit beside Ciel.

"Our community, here—this group," Nat began, still rock-

ing the baby, "is more important to me than the city itself." The
cave amplified his voice and made it ring. "We could all die trying to save the very people who don't want us."

Elna winced as her bones cracked and popped. Her clouded
eyes reflected the firelight. She put a hand on my shoulder. "Our
community is *all* of us. Everyone here," she argued, holding up
a hand to stop protests. "Everyone above. And below: Kirit and
Wik. Those above who are innocent, as well as those who were
complicit in the blackwings' and in the Singers' crimes. We all
rose with the city. We're part of what is happening now. We'll
find a solution together." Her voice lifted and cracked.

Everyone above. Sidra. Rya. Dojha. Urie. The councilors. The
fledges. Nat might have few ties left in the towers, but this
wasn't about friends. This was about holding our community
together. Ten days. So much to do. We needed a decision.

But I waited and watched. I held back from pressing the
cloudbound group to agree with me. It was the hardest thing
I'd ever done.

Elna squeezed Nat's arm, the way a mother sometimes greets
a child returning from a cold flight. "Remember who you were
before the fall, Nat. Who you wanted to be."

A *leader*. He'd wanted to be one once. He'd flown against
Dix. Did he still wish to lead? Did anyone have a choice any
longer?

But. Two Allsuns ago, Nat had been unable to see Dix's
machinations until it was too late. He'd missed turmoil in the
air during his wingtest. *How can someone lead well if they don't
know where they're going?*

"Nothing will keep me from wanting to save my friends first,"
Nat began. "But I'll—we will get everyone down safely."

Djonn watched Nat make this promise and dipped his head
once. "We will. I'll find a way." He scratched his head. "The
more information and help I have, the better."

"Some of us will have to scale the towers, go back up through the clouds, and get the blackwings to see sense," Aliati said. "Others need to begin building. All before the city falls." Two moons—less than that now.

"We'll need food and water for the journey, silkspiders, lots of plinths, lighter-than-air," Ciel began.

"What about wings?" I said. "We'll need spares."

One heartbeat. Two. Djonn added them to the list on the cave floor. "All the wings we can, even if we need to use some for kite silk."

I was so focused on his list, I nearly missed how Nat looked at Ciel, then shook his head. But I saw clearly how Ciel narrowed her eyes. *What was that about?*

She put her bowl of uneaten greens down.

Nat spoke quickly. "Wings too. For everyone descending. But if we bring silkspiders, we won't need extra."

Ciel stayed quiet.

"Tell me more about the predators?" Djonn finally asked in the lull. Ciel described the bone eaters again, and the cities more thoroughly. She drew the giant birds on the floor. Explained how cities fought, stayed alive.

As she spoke, Nat rocked the infant, who cooed softly. "What did you name her?" he whispered, looking at Ceetcee. With the list nearly complete, I admit I was curious too.

"We haven't," Ceetcee whispered back. "It's unlucky, you know that. Naming without a tower is bad luck."

I hadn't known that—a tower superstition, not a Singer one—but Nat nodded as if he was familiar. Elna too. "Shouldn't tempt bad luck. Especially now."

"We'll name her on the ground." Ceetcee gave a little smile when she said it. She took the baby back from Nat.

Ciel paused in her descriptions, her drawings. "Macal, what if the blackwings won't listen? What if they don't believe us?"

"I listened to you," I said. "I believed you. If we can convince Rya, they might still listen to her."

Djonn bowed his head, then shook it, as if he was dislodging something unpleasant. "I worry about blackwings coming here. Working with us. Even if it speeds the work up. They were very demanding last time I worked for them."

I remembered the scene at the city council plinth when Dix and Nat fought. Nat had revealed that fledges—including Ciel and Moc—had been trapped by Dix's blackwings and forced along with Djonn to mine heartbone.

*Demanding* was one word for what the blackwings had done. I had many other words: *cloudnapping, deceit, cruelty.* But perhaps Rya would be different. Urie thought so. I hoped he was right.

In the mist outside, shadows swooped and dove. Skymouths hunted prey in the rain. I peered hard enough at the gray shadows that I saw stars.

"We will keep them in line," Aliati said, frowning.

Djonn looked at me, and I agreed vigorously. "We promise."

Ceetcee drew a long breath. "I'll go with Djonn and Ciel into the meadow and look at how we can speed up the work. We'll look at the plates in the littlemouth cave too, to see if there's anything we can repurpose. They've come in handy before. Maybe there are more machines we can use."

"I'll go back up," I said. "Enlist Sidra and the northwest's council to help motivate the towers." I had what I'd come for now: answers. That these led to more questions and fears was something I could work with. Sidra would help. Soon.

Beliak elbowed Nat hard enough to make him grunt softly. Then jutted his chin at me. "You know the ground," Beliak said sadly to Nat. "We don't."

Oh. I'd been hoping Ciel would accompany me to help me sway the towers.

Nat wavered also. He tossed the piece of bone and caught it once, twice. The third time he put the shard in his pocket. "I'll go," he said to the rain, the cave, and to me.

Even as he spoke the words, I dreaded the possibilities. Did I still think of him as the one who made mistakes, who flew too fast? I did. Was he keeping secrets? Yes, almost certainly. Would he argue with me? Probably. More delays.

We had two moons, no more. I needed his help. I couldn't go back up alone.

"This plan requires everyone to cooperate, on short notice," Ceetcee said. She looked at Nat. "You must make sure they do."

The baby cooed in the dim cave. Ceetcee turned to me, concerned. "Can you and Nat work together?"

"Do you mean whether we can cooperate? Or whether we can get *everyone* to cooperate?" I wasn't sure I was going to like her answer. Or be able to live up to it.

"Both."

Everyone watched me for my answer. "I will."

She looked at Nat. "What about you?"

He straightened. Took the baby in his arms. Put his hand on the baby's down-soft hair. "I'll do everything I can, both here and when we return above the clouds. But if it doesn't work, I'm coming right back down to get you all, and we're leaving. Before the city cracks any farther. Before it falls."

Ceetcee smiled grimly. Nat passed the baby to Beliak. They exchanged a long look, and then Ceetcee put one hand on my shoulder, one hand on Nat's. "That's fair. Time to get to work."

# 15

## KIRIT, BELOW

*⁓ While Skyshouter found a city's heart ⁓*

In my dreams, the ground rose up to meet me and swallowed me whole. The earth crushed my leg. The dirt whispered and screamed.

A firm grip caught my shoulders, held me still. Voices spoke in what might have been soothing tones, but I heard them as shouts and threats. I was trapped in walls of bone. My tears felt hot when they came at all, and like sandpaper when they didn't come. Why had Wik left me alone? I smelled something sharp and astringent moments before it was pushed against my nose, before I fought my way free and upright, and was dizzy but sitting up. Someone spoke, and in the dim light, a hand moved from my arm to touch my face.

The hand was the color of very old bone, brown and speckled. But there was nothing old about my visitor: no wrinkles on their neck or face, or across their shorn head. Above the mask they wore, their eyes were dark, and so much like Ezarit's I gasped and looked again. But similarities stopped there. Small in stature, narrow chested, with thin arms, the stranger tilted their chin and the skin at the corners of their eyes crinkled.

Smiling? At me? I felt dizzy again.

Their head seemed too big to be held up by such a tiny upper body. Their legs looked sturdy enough, though much thicker than mine.

"Where is Wik?" I asked. He'd left me here.

They weren't as tall as me, nor as broad. They looked oddly upside down. I thought I could take them in a fight. They spoke, their words like sand slipping over desert hills, like the clack of a bone eater's beak. What did our words sound like to them, I wondered?

I asked, over and over again, "Where is Wik?"

My visitor's eyes narrowed, trying to comprehend. The individual—I couldn't tell he or she—patted me on the shoulder and pressed me back down to sleep. I leaned back, weak and dizzy, but elated.

There were others, living outside of the city.

The way they spoke, or sang in response to my questions. So many beautiful sounds. But if they told me where Wik was, or where he had been, I couldn't understand.

We couldn't understand each other. But what mattered most was that in this new city, there were other people. We weren't alone.

Oh, how our songs would have to change.

They didn't whistle as much as murmur a language of long, low, whirring sounds. Each was a touch to the ear like silk, like a gentle wind. When the sounds stopped, I wanted them to start again, as a distraction from the pain I felt, the heat in my ears, my skin.

We weren't alone.

The stranger's words shaped an urgency now. Phrases repeated, pitched low, sounds like *kip* and *serra* and something I couldn't make out. I protested, and the voice became more insistent. Then a hand pressed something hot to my leg. I screamed again. This time, another hand stuck something in my mouth. It was too hard to shove out with my tongue; it pushed so far

back I bit down. Suddenly—oh, the pain—I could not feel the
bed beneath me, only the searing pain in my leg and the lack
of space to breathe. The bone walls closed in. Panic closed
in. I could not stay up in the air I could not stay aloft I dreamed
I was falling and the ground caught me and I fell back into
darkness.

\ \ \

I slept in a hammock.

The city swayed beneath me.

I knew these two things.

The third thing I knew was that my leg no longer hurt, and
I could wiggle my toes beneath the rough sheet. That there was
a sheet, a clean one, was another remarkable thing. I'd become
accustomed to dirt and ground.

And the light was a lantern, not the sun.

We weren't alone.

There were other cities, other people.

The realization shocked me awake.

Tired and dizzy, I fought to sit up. A stranger standing by
my hammock made a slicing gesture with their hands, then
pressed my shoulders down. I struggled before falling back on
the hammock.

Across from where I lay, Wik paced. *Wik. Here.*

He caught my gaze. "You're awake. Don't try to move."

*Too late.* I swallowed dryly against nausea as he drew closer.
Handed me a water sack. The room where we were was circular, like a chamber we'd known once, a lifetime ago, lit by the
soft glow of littlemouths.

"Where?" I rasped. "How long?" I looked for my satchel, for
the plates. For Maalik.

He shook his head. "We're on Varat, though of course that's
not what they call it. I don't know how long. A few days?"

*They? A few days?* My satchel, with the brass plates in it, was missing.

The revelations battled through my vertigo. They. There were others here. *That's not what they call it . . .* The sounds of their words in my memory. Words I couldn't understand.

If I couldn't understand, and Wik couldn't, how would we tell them what had happened?

What if they were so different from us, we couldn't ever communicate with them?

Outside, a boom and the sounds of bone creaking were as loud as thunder in the clouds. Then the sway began again, in the opposite direction. The rhythm had permeated my dreams, *boom,* sway . . . *boom,* sway. Bone clattered against bone, and metal clanked.

From down the passage came footsteps. A rough voice with a lilt at the end of it. A softer voice. Words that sounded like water and dust. Though the speakers were nearby, I couldn't make out more.

A flutter within a fold of robe against my chest. A ruffle of feathers. I breathed easier. Maalik, still with me. Still hiding.

Two strangers entered the alcove, their mouths and noses behind woven masks, their hair shorn. They conferred with the person who'd pressed me back into the hammock. All were dressed the same way. One of the strangers had a spiral tattoo on their neck.

Wik stood when they entered. "They've been healing your leg," he said quietly to me. "They saved your life." His voice said more than his words: *Be calm, don't panic.*

I understood why in a moment. They were more than strangers; their language was as mysterious as a bird's, their gestures unfamiliar, and their bodies—thin shoulders and narrow chests, strong hips and legs that I remembered from my illness—still looked upside down to me now that I'd recovered.

*No. They were not different.* We *were. Would they accept us? Did we belong?*

After staring at me, the strangers said something to the healer and left.

The healer's dark brown, hazel-flecked eyes peering at me over their mask were as kind as Ezarit's. Gentle hands pulled the bandage back, instead of the mottled purple I expected, I saw nearly healed skin.

"Only a few days?" Memories of my months of recovery at Grigrit after the bone dust fever set in gave me chills.

I couldn't speak with them. But they seemed to understand my needs. They shared water and food, had healed my leg. Hope, maybe, for more. My mind's map of our city, with each tower and what they traded, had to expand. I tucked the graincake the healer handed me into my robe. Maalik took a bite of it.

"Wik? Do you know what they're saying?" It was a dizzying change to everything we'd known. *We weren't alone.*

"Not yet. Just a few gestures." He sounded frustrated. Understandable.

As the healer chattered at us while changing my bandages, I tried to make sense of where I was. I rested in a stiff hammock, not on a mat. Luminous walls seemed to hold the room close. We were inside the bone, not on a tier.

Long years of work had shaped this city's bone ridge to form this room. The kind of work I'd seen in the midcloud. The walls' light and dark patterns were beautifully carved. Some were newer, and some had soot stains that indicated long wear. More differences from our own city. This community wasn't engaged in constant upward movement. It had a different focus.

I reached for Wik. His hand grasped mine. "This place is so different." Even in the ways its people treated strangers. In the towers an unexpected visitor would have been held and watched. Here, they nursed me back to health.

"We're different too." Wik echoed my thoughts. "They've taken me for a walk along the city. Inside the towers. This is nothing like our city. It's a bit of a drop outside. And—" He hesitated.

*What?* I was woozy again, and fading. *Where is my satchel?*

"Sleep. You'll see."

Intensely frustrated, I fought sleep. But I lost again.

❧ ❧ ❧

"You'll never heal if you keep fighting." My mother's hand on my cheek. Her smell: chicory and spices. The click of glass beads in her hair as she bent over me. Her eyes, smiling. A memory? A fever dream? Even trapped within it, I knew it couldn't last. I leaned into her touch anyway, felt her worry. She'd cared for me during the bone fever, after I broke my leg. She'd been at my side.

Ezarit's hand withdrew, and the dream brightened. I cried out in pain.

Dappled light filtered through carved bone walls. Soft voices rose and fell, tugging me from sleep's last grip. At a healer's touch on my leg, I jumped, causing the hammock to swing.

The healer murmured and gestured, hands up and out, an expulsion of breath from behind their mask. *Calm?*

My heart beat too fast for calm. Where was Wik? My leg throbbed less, but I was missing pieces of myself. Wik, my satchel. My home. My mother.

I rushed to sit up, and instead of making me lie back, the healer helped me. Supported my arm, my back. Cool hands pressed against my quilted silk robe. They hadn't taken that from me, though the fabric was stained beyond recognition.

The healer patted my shoulder. Smiled with their eyes again. I smiled back. The corners of my mouth ached when I did it, the muscles long unused.

The healer gestured at a seat, one with bone wheels. Raised

eyebrows in question. Wik appeared behind them. "Would you like to see the city?"

"Where have you been?" I wanted to clasp his steadying hand again and to prod his shoulder, both. How could he leave me here unguarded?

He grimaced. "You were safe. They wanted to try to talk with me. They have many questions about us, I think." His brow wrinkled. "At least, I'd have questions if I were them. Difficult to tell what the people I've met want so far. Except for one thing. They want to see you."

Once again the healer gestured to the seat. Colored bone eater hide and a bone and brass frame looked like it would be comfortable.

I didn't want comfort. "I'll walk."

Wik frowned, offered a hand to brace me as I slid off the hammock. His grip was firm. His eyes filled with worry. The healer stepped back. Followed us with the seat.

"I'm fine." My leg held my weight, though I wasn't sure for how long. I'd do it anyway. They wanted to see me? They would see me standing.

Besides, I wanted to see the city. I had questions too.

We left the alcove and ducked under a carved bone ramp. Two more Varat citizens flanked us and kept pace.

A maze of corridors split left and right, all shaped with metal partitions. "The city is a warren, from what I can tell," Wik murmured. "Many connections through different tower bases, no real separations. Different distances to the front of the city."

"You've been exploring." He'd left me unguarded while I slept. My satchel had disappeared.

He looked chastened by my tone as much as my words. "As much as I could. Always with an escort. They're very good about steering me away from the ramps, so I haven't been off this tier yet." He wasn't carrying his pack either. Was it missing too?

Our quilted silk robes looked dark and worn among the subtle patterns of our escorts. The healer's shift had subtle metal threads woven through it that sparkled when they walked. Another's tunic featured tiny spiral patterns in pale tones. Tattoos on their dark skin echoed their dress.

Sounds of soft-shod feet walking the many corridors. Quiet conversations. No shouts. No songs that I could hear and begin to understand.

Though our clothes had been laundered, my yellow robe was nearly black from wear; Wik's black robe had turned gray. Our scarred feet looked shocking against the clean bone passage floors. In comparison, our companions' tidy footwraps featured thick soles and elaborate knots.

I caught our escort trying not to stare at us. I stared back anyway, until the walls and floor caught my attention again.

The patterns cut and sanded into the bone walls created light ribbons on our path. The same mark, an ornate spiral, repeated on the path we followed, while others were winnowed away or were replaced with other designs. At one fork, we turned right, and the light-spiral disappeared from the floor. Our escort muttered something, and we stopped, turned back, and took the other fork.

"A map," Wik whispered. "Made of light."

He was right. As we walked, the marks grew brighter, the sanded bone walls thinner in places. Sconces in the walls flickered.

I expected to emerge into a bright space filled with people like those who escorted us. Instead, our passage grew narrower, the intersections fewer. Finally, the only symbol on the path was the spiral. Our escort in the small-patterned shift pushed aside a heavy, woven curtain, and we stepped into darkness.

The other escort spoke. Brief, assertive words. Three voices repeated them. Then the escorts stepped back, pushing Wik and me forward into the dark room.

My eyes adjusted after days of being outdoors and in the dappled light of the healer's alcove. Five figures stood at the front of the room. All were dressed like those who'd escorted us, shorn heads, dark eyes. Their skin, bone, bronze, and dark brown, was marked with small blue spirals on their cheeks or necks.

I shivered. My own tattoos and scars looked silver in the half-light. Wik's hair sparkled blue with groundmouth gore, and his Singer tattoos almost glowed against his skin.

They spoke to us. Words that sounded like rain and wind.

We, not knowing how to answer, remained quiet.

One raised a hand and, from above, a light projected a new pattern on the floor, mottled with color.

In my robe, Maalik's beak poked at my skin. I put a hand to my chest, hoping to calm him. Took a deep breath. Whispered, "Shhhh," so that only Maalik could hear. The whipperling quieted. *Good bird.*

On the floor, light outlined a rough drawing of our city on its knees and Nimru collapsed against its side.

One of the five spoke again. A higher-pitched voice this time. They pointed at the floor. Pointed at us. Then at the floor.

"Yes," Wik said. "Yes. That was our city." He nodded his head, as we'd seen the healer do when voicing approval over my leg.

"They could be asking if we killed it," I whispered. "Killing a city could be a crime here." We had to be careful. Beginnings were tenuous moments.

Wik frowned, not glancing my way. Put a hand on my shoulder to calm me.

Just as I'd done with Maalik. I was no bird.

The tattooed speaker gestured again at the drawing and then

at Wik. Raised their eyebrows and queried once more, with a sound at the end I recognized from the healer's: *serra*. When Wik didn't answer, they repeated the process. Wik swallowed. He put his hand on his own chest, then mimed hooking Nimru's eye. Drove his hands together like two cities crashing. Laid one against the other, then pointed to the image on the floor. "I killed the city."

"Wik!" I grabbed his arm and pulled. Why would he act so stupidly? Why would he risk himself?

He shook me off, whispering, "If it's a crime, they'll take one, not both of us. I will be the citykiller."

I couldn't breathe. How to help him? How to keep him safe?

They asked another question, the interrogative lift at the end so familiar, the words so different. This time, their gestures mimicked how Wik had said he killed the city. I could not speak. Could not disagree. Who would listen?

Wik answered as best he could, repeating his gestures.

They pointed to me, asked the same question. I opened my mouth, and Wik stepped forward, in front of me. Shook his head. Used the healer's slashing gesture. No.

*No.* I would not let him sacrifice himself for me. I grabbed his robe. Pulled. The escorts tugged me back, and I sat down hard on the seat the healer had brought.

From that vantage, I watched as the five stepped forward. They each touched Wik on the shoulder or pressed their forehead to his. One gave Wik a brass bracelet from their own wrist, engraved with symbols we'd seen on the walls. Patted his shoulder and seemed to smile at him.

The healer came forward and gestured at the strange blue glow in Wik's hair. Made a motion, like a spiral, at Wik's ear. Uttered very pleased-sounding words.

One of the five spoke sharply to the healer, who stepped back, chastened.

Killing a strange city was no crime here, it seemed. But speaking out of turn was.

Wik's face shone with surprise.

"A good start," he said, cautiously. He did not look at the healer.

I hoped it was a good start, but I wasn't yet certain.

Behind us, the curtain swung and a cartwheel squealed. Another escort backed through the curtain, moving slowly, pulling a bone cage.

The small cage was large enough for one person, perhaps two. Bone grown from the base had been split and trained into a lattice. Within the cage, draped in black, a figure crouched. I smelled muzz.

The official who'd given Wik the bracelet gestured the cart forward, into the overhead light. The image of the dead cities overlaid the cage until the picture was removed from the light and all that remained was the light itself. A shimmer of silk revealed robes, a black hood. The captive moved slowly, like a drugged Conclave sacrifice. The hood slipped, revealing a face scarred almost beyond recognition in the dim, mottled light.

Almost.

"Kirit, that footsling we found." Wik stared.

I drew a breath that didn't fill my lungs. A blackwing. Here. And not just any blackwing.

For the first time in my life, I was glad I was sitting down.

The officials gestured at the cage. Pointed at Wik's black robe. Said a string of syllables that ended on an up note. A question?

They pointed again at Wik's robe, then at the captive's.

Did we know this person?

Wik looked at me. Did we?

What was the right answer?

I shook my head. We couldn't know the captive. Not if we hoped they'd take us in. I composed my face. "No. I don't know them." Made the "no" gesture my healer had made when I'd first wanted to get up. That Wik had made just a moment ago.

Wik shook his head too. Then turned to the officials. "No. Never seen them before." He repeated the gesture.

Would they accept it? The captive looked like us, dressed like us. This wasn't a good beginning at all.

The five dismissed the cart and the person inside. As the escort wheeled the cart away, the captive began to chuckle.

"You can't kill anyone, can you, Kirit?" she whispered.

I fought to my feet, prepared to speak, and fell back. The five officials walked past us and out, our audience over. On the way out, they put their hands on Wik's shoulders again. Whatever they'd wanted to learn from us, they'd learned. They seemed pleased. They might remain so, until they discovered we'd lied.

A terrible beginning.

Because we did know the captive. We knew her well. We'd left her to die after our fall from the clouds. Now she was here.

Dix.

Fury and fear made me dizzy.

*Dix.*

Our fight to save the city, to find a new home would be much harder now. My failure had arrived here ahead of me.

I had to speak to Wik alone. We had to get a message to our city. To tell them Dix was still alive.

The healer and our escorts chatted at Wik as if he was a hero. Wik, shocked at Dix's reappearance, stared at their attentions. They weren't wrong, though. He was a hero. Just not for this city.

By the time we reached the healer's alcove, I'd begun to doze, not strong enough to fight sleep. At least, I thought over and over, Dix was a captive, while we were still free.

# 16

## NAT, MIDCLOUD

*⁓ The artifex's craft became real in the sky ⁓*

Lies.

Above the clouds, I'd hunted them down. I'd shattered them, like my father had tried to do before me. Lies had cost our city much: time, people, knowledge. I could not stand them.

I hated lying even more. But on my return to the cloudbound cave, I'd barely hesitated.

Ciel glared at me. She hated lies too, even those of omission. "Nat, you could have told them about the wind. You had more than one chance."

Sitting around that fire, I'd said *wings*. I'd said *silkspiders*. I'd said *bring them both*. My only omission: the lack of wind. What awaited us on the ground became a secret monster, one I'd hidden. One that grew as plans became action. It devoured more lies until Ciel stared every time she saw me and hummed new lines of a song instead of talking to me.

And at least five lines in her song were about falling or wind. Hints at what we'd promised not to say. She would drive me skytouched with her verses.

"We chose silence," I whispered to her in the littlemouth cave as she tended them and sang to them. "Stop turning your song into a weapon."

"We must tell them," she said. She lifted a littlemouth to her shoulder and hummed. The creature glowed, growing brighter and dimmer to the rhythm of Ciel's melody.

"If we do, they won't trust us anymore. They'll think I'm holding other information back." I worried at the net of lies, but didn't give it up. Bound by my own words and omissions. I was beginning to understand how my father had felt while working on the Spire long ago. Trapped. Alone. Separate.

"Macal already thinks you're lying," Ciel said.

"He does?" I felt a curl of shame, like a bone shaving, settle in my stomach. Macal had seen me fail and fall before.

She nodded and stopped humming. The littlemouth's light faded. "Moc told me. And Moc *knows* you're lying."

"You told him. Have you told him why?"

Ciel stared me down. Inclined her chin. "Of course I have."

Of course she had. How could she not? "Ciel, if we tell people there's not enough wind to fly, possibly ever again, they might not follow us. They'll waste time trying to float the city or, worse, stay on the towers. Moc can't say anything." I couldn't let that happen. There was no more time. "At least give me time to get my family down to the ground. I can't fix anything unless I know they're all right."

Biting her lip, Ciel sighed. "The baby deserves a chance, a name. A home."

Hope bloomed. She understood. "Yes, yes, she does. Please, Ciel."

Ciel looked at me hard. "Moc won't say anything until I tell him it's all right. But one person absolutely needs to know. Otherwise his designs will fail." She tilted her chin in the direction of the meadow.

She was right. I'd planned to tell Djonn, but hadn't been able to find him alone. I had to try harder.

I escaped the discomfort of Ciel's glare. Walked through the cave tunnels and emerged into the relative brightness of the meadow. Outside, Djonn was adjusting a lever on the climber. "Can you give me a moment?"

He reluctantly pulled his attention from his work. We walked to the far end of the meadow where the box kite rested. I felt the others watching me as I took him aside, but no one followed us.

Djonn said nothing, waiting me out. We'd fought together. He trusted me more than some here. I was about to shatter that. A sour taste rose in my mouth. It had to be done.

"You need to factor in some wind details for your design," I said, pretending like we were looking over the kites. "I'm hoping you'll do it quietly, so no one panics or refuses to descend. Ciel can help."

Djonn's forehead wrinkled. "Why would they refuse? What's down there?"

I spoke quickly, nearly choking on the words. "Not what *is*. It's what's not down there." I met his gaze and didn't flinch. "Wind."

The box kite's frame and half-finished patchwork silk panels flapped in the breeze, mocking me. Djonn was silent, his neck and jaw as rigid as his back.

Finally he said, "That changes my design substantially. You should have told me sooner." Each word clipped with tension. He was very angry. He had every right to be.

Once, it might have felt good to release the lie, but not now. Because the lie wasn't gone. The full truth wasn't known. I'd only wrapped another person in the same trap, a spider caught in a larger web.

Worry seized me. "As I said, Ciel knows and can help you, but . . ." I couldn't finish the sentence.

Djonn watched me carefully. Finally, he spoke. "I think you are right. Too much information, in this case, may be more harmful than good. They will find out soon enough."

Hearing him put it that way made me groan. "When you say it like that, it sounds worse."

Djonn raised his eyebrows. "I am supporting you, though I don't like it. Don't make me make you feel better about this too. That's not who I am. I build things."

He was right. Kirit would have said the same thing. *You won't have to lie or make me feel better.*

"Does Macal know?" Djonn fiddled with a batten in the box kite. His skin was tinged gray from all the work and lack of sleep.

I shook my head. "Can I trust him not to tell more people? He needs to focus on getting everyone down and evacuated." Macal would know I'd failed again.

"He'll do that better with more information."

"But can he keep the secret?" This had been my worry. Macal wasn't a stranger, but he wasn't a friend either. And we'd already disagreed about so much.

Djonn shook his head. "I'll work on the design problem. You work on the towers and the blackwings."

Any relief that Djonn knew was short-lived. "You can't tell anyone either. Not even Aliati." Secrets had a way of bleeding through if enough people knew. I hadn't told Beliak or Ceetcee, although I desperately wanted to. I couldn't tell Elna. She would never make the journey if she knew—she might say our energy was wasted getting her down and we should take someone else. I couldn't bear that.

"I'll wait for you to say something. You know the ground best." Djonn frowned, then looked up.

Overhead, dark shadows flickered in and out of the mist. Gryphons? Bone eaters?

"Blackwings," Djonn said. "Looking for the meadow. They've been at it since Dix came down and didn't come back. Haven't found us yet." Djonn pointed up at the skymouth camouflage.

"We've been hiding in plain sight. Elna helped us turn a sky-mouth skin into netting to hide the meadow."

"Elna did?" I could see her sewing something like that, her deft touch with a needle and sinew.

"We're lucky she's here." Djonn coughed. "Though I don't think it does much for her health, or mine."

Silently, I cursed the cave, the damp.

"Very lucky," Djonn continued, "that she wasn't on Densira when it collapsed."

I let the weight of that mixed luck sink in. Elna was alive because the blackwings had taken her from Densira and brought her here in order to bargain.

For a moment, I couldn't speak.

"When they evacuate, the netting won't matter. Blackwings will finally know where we are," Djonn added, oblivious to my discomfort. "More hands to help with the work. But more risk too." He sounded cautious, at best. His face grew troubled. "Last time we had blackwings here in the meadow, Doran died. We need to be careful."

Doran, Rya's father. He'd fought Dix with us. He'd been my mentor on city council, long ago. He'd maneuvered the truth a lot, omitted information. And he'd paid for it, in the end.

"Agreed," I told Djonn. It was all I could manage.

Blackwings had imprisoned Djonn. They'd fed him heartbone until he couldn't live without it and forced him to artifex for them. He'd escaped, with Aliati's help. They'd kidnapped Elna. Anticipating further contact with blackwings wasn't easy.

"We'll make sure you're all right," I promised. Our hope was that one faction was better than the others. Rya's faction.

"You might have to make sure sooner, rather than later," Djonn said. "Look."

The dark shadows had reappeared in the clouds, passing

between towers, closer this time. The figures flew over the meadow, low enough for wing colors and robes to be visible. Two pairs of blackwings, flanking a set of blue.

"Get everyone inside. Tell Moc," Djonn said.

When I hesitated, Djonn slapped me hard on the arm. "Go! I'll catch up." And I ran, whistling the tower windsign for "danger" as I passed Ciel and Ceetcee on the scaffolding. They grabbed Macal and the guards and pulled them towards the cave. I heard the baby wail in insult as she was jostled, then quiet.

"Do we have arrows?" I asked. I had six left. Ciel had four. "Bows?"

Moc sped past, carrying several very old-looking bows in his hands. They'd been restrung, but they were obviously from one of the cloudbound caches we'd discovered near the meadow, before we fell.

Beliak stuck his head outside. "They landed below the cave and are climbing up."

"I'll go," Moc said, and headed for the tunnels.

"Moc!" Ceetcee called. "Just—hold them off."

Moc grumbled but kept moving.

"I'll go too." Ciel grabbed a bow and sped to catch her brother while the rest of us followed quickly behind them. She'd traded her ragged robes for a fresh set, the quilted green silk not clean exactly, but better than what she'd had. Her hair had been neatly braided. Chasing Moc, she still looked weary.

We made it through the tunnel. Ceil and Moc stood at the cave mouth with Aliati, arrows pointing at three figures pulling their way through the lichen. "Stop there," Aliati shouted.

The blackwings didn't stop. I heard the lichen crunching beneath their feet as they approached, wings half furled. They carried several heavy sacks. No weapons that I could see.

"Hold," I whispered.

"Wait." Macal grabbed my arm. My grip on my own knife grew tighter. "I know them. The one in the middle is Urie Mondarath." He sighed as the blackwings climbed closer. But now I could see the third flier wore green wings, not black, though they were darkened with rainwater.

They climbed to just below the cave, within reach of our ropes.

"He's of your tower? You take responsibility?" I asked.

Macal nodded, but there was a pause before he said, "Yes." Something he was holding back.

Beliak stepped close to the cave edge, still favoring his leg.

"Macal speaks for you," he said. "You are welcome here unless you break his trust and ours."

"We will not!" shouted the blackwing. "Agreed," said the other flier.

The third, Urie, was already in the cave, shaking off the wet from his hair. He was more than bedraggled, though. He had small blisters on his left cheek, chin, and arm. Pieces of his robe were burned away.

"Fire?" Aliati helped Urie with his wings.

He shrugged them off with a mischievous grin. "No! Better." Urie kept smiling while the rest of us waited. "We made it! We've got alembics, Macal!"

Macal leaned close. "Lighter-than-air?"

The boy laughed. "We barely got away from Laria with the supplies and the artifexes but"—and here he stepped back and we saw another line of blackwings approaching, this time carrying burdens—"here they are. My aunts. The alembics."

"On your wings, Urie!" Macal's enthusiasm echoed through the cave. The baby woke at the noise, but Macal kept going. "Now we must set up a steady supply of heartbone." He paused. Clamped a hand over the boy's arm. "But you were supposed to be helping Sidra. What has happened?"

I had bigger concerns. "You brought stolen mechanicals *here*? Are you cloudtouched? Laria and their blackwings will be after both alembics and artifexes." I glared at Macal. This was so dangerous.

Urie smiled even more broadly. "They won't pursue."

Despite his burns, the young hunter's bravado was starting to wear thin. He was barely old enough to have passed his wingtest. How could he understand cross-city politics at this point, when so much was in flux? I was that arrogant, once. Worse for us, what Urie had done now put Macal's and my journey above the clouds in jeopardy. Who would listen now to thieves? To Lawsbreakers?

Ceetcee took one look at my face and stepped between me and the young man. "Tell us why not."

Urie helped the alchemists enter the bone cave as he answered. "Because we set enough hints to blame it on Grigrit. And by the time we left, they were already fighting!" Urie looked around for approval and instead found frowns and looks of concern. "What did I do wrong?"

Macal patted his shoulder. "It's all right."

It had to be all right. But our work had just become more difficult, and there was no changing it. Blackwing factions fighting, when we needed them to agree. Worse and worse.

The second and third fliers dropped their sacks with a clatter in the cave mouth. The bulky bags stank like heartbone. Worse.

Djonn and Aliati moved quickly away from the smell. Ceetcee too, standing as close as she could to the fresh air of the cave opening with the baby's mouth and nose covered by a silk cloth. My course of action was clear. "That has to go outside, now."

Just beyond the cave mouth I saw the silver outlines of several sacks of lighter-than-air, weighted down with bonefall. I grabbed them. "These too."

"I'll show you where to store it," Beliak said. The two artifexes and Urie followed him out the back, turning to get their burdens through the tunnel.

"Won't the alembics rust?" Macal worried as he watched them go. His face, like his brother's, showed little emotion.

I railed at him. "Better they rust than the people in this cave breathe heartbone, don't you think?" He wasn't thinking about the people here. Not about Djonn. Not even about the baby.

When they'd deposited their bags nearer the meadow and the open air, the alchemists joined the blackwings for a midday meal in the meadow. Urie returned with Beliak to the cave, looking hungry and curious. "We've been descending for two days because the scavengers said to take it slow."

"They were right," Aliati said. "Who told you this?"

"Raq," Urie said without hesitation. "She said to look for you."

The flicker of happiness on Aliati's face was quick, but I saw it. Djonn moved to stand beside her. "The whole community will have to come down just as slowly, won't they?"

"Or slower," Aliati said.

Clouds, the time to evacuate had grown even shorter. I hadn't added time for tower citizens to rest along the way, only thought about how long it would take to convince them to come. We'd been here two days already, and it had taken three more to climb up. Two moons at best, and we were nearly halfway through. We couldn't delay. Macal and I had to leave tomorrow.

Macal tensed at the same time, as if he'd had a similar thought. We looked at one another, over the gap of our disagreements. He lifted his chin towards me as if to say, *Go ahead.*

"If we can't bring the whole city down in the next few days," I said quietly, so the alchemists wouldn't hear, "they'll die. We have to start now. Macal wants hundreds to move through the clouds as soon as possible."

Aliati's eyes widened. "There's barely enough time to get

them moving. From what you say, what's propping the city up is holding. But any delay? I don't believe that can last."

I couldn't argue that. It was why I'd hesitated telling anyone about the wind.

The cave echoed with voices as everyone began talking at once.

I put my thumb and my second finger into my mouth and gave the loudest whistle I could. The sound passed through the cave, leaving silence in its wake.

"We're going to move a city full of people, in stages, starting tomorrow, if Macal and I succeed." My voice rose, then caught on the last syllable. "We must check everything. Once the black-wings arrive, organization may become complicated. Know now that Djonn is your leader. His decisions are final."

Urie whispered in surprise, "On your wings."

Macal spoke next. "Most of the city will fly at least part of the way on their own. There must be time given for acclimat-ing to the clouds—Aliati was clear on the risks there. Then, when we reach the lowcloud, everyone will need to descend on the tethered kites that Djonn is working on." He looked at Urie. "They're tiered plinths with buoyancy from lighter-than-air and foils. Those who reach the ground first"—here he gestured at Ceetcee and Beliak—"will help prepare for everyone else."

Ceetcee's face brightened at the prospect. *Clouds,* how could I keep the truth from her?

But Djonn had begun to speak. "The kites can be hooked to tower pulleys at the base of the cloud. We'll have to make sure they're carrying as much lighter-than-air as they can manage, with passengers as ballast."

"Agreed," I said. "Kite crews will be responsible for the safety of their passengers, just like tower leaders. We'll find you the lighter-than-air." Somehow, we would. "When a kite finishes a run, it will offload ballast and rise back up to get another group. Understand so far?"

My companions nodded. *Understood.*

"We'll send down a first crew with the kavik that Urie brought us, so they can let us know they made it safely. That kite will leave tomorrow at the same time Nat and Macal go up. Before we do that"—Djonn looked at me—"we all need to know as much as possible."

I looked at my friends, my family. The people I'd fought to reach. The ones I'd sworn to get away from the city.

The firelight illuminated their faces. All but Ciel returned my gaze, waiting for me to tell them more. Ciel stared at the floor, held her breath. Djonn nodded, eyebrows raised. *Go on,* he seemed to be saying.

The baby, nestled in Beliak's arms, opened her eyes and stared at me.

I struggled to find the words. I had to speak.

# 17

## KIRIT, BELOW

*⌒ An old foe appeared, strange rules they defied ⌒*

When I woke once more in the healer's alcove, Wik's seat was empty. Again.

But beside me, very close, came the sound of ragged breathing.

Groggily, feeling as if I'd had too much muzz, I tried to focus.

A darkly cloaked figure bent near my hammock, rummaging through the healers' medicines. Containers knocked together.

Again, the scent of smoke and cooked vegetation wafted towards me, this time too close.

The hand that reached into my robe was missing two fingers. "You made it all the way here, Kirit," a voice growled.

I understood those words. I'd heard that voice before.

Coarse laughter ricocheted through my shock. Familiar. The hood shadowed the person's features. Another blackwing? I shook my head to clear it. How many of us had walked across the desert? The voice was female. Her tone, bitter. The voice had changed from the one I'd known—deepened, become rougher. But I'd heard it in my nightmares.

The blackwing said, "And you said you didn't know me. I wasn't too grogged to hear." The voice belonged to someone I'd last seen in a cage. I was shocked into alertness. Dix. Freed?

Her fingers rooted in my pockets, between layers of my robe. They pulled and tugged, searching. Maalik chirped. Screeched. Claws scrabbled against my skin, then released.

Dix cackled as I shifted away from her grasp. I wetted my lips, wondering if I was strong enough to fight after the exertions of the day before. I tried to sit up, grew dizzy with the effort.

The best I could do was speak, a protest and a loud alarm, both: "Dix!"

Wik came back in a rush. Looked around, saw nothing. "You're having a nightmare."

"If you'd been here, you would know I'm not."

Wik scanned the room gesturing *sit back, rest,* but I pointed to where Dix had flattened herself on the floor to hide.

"She got out, and she has Maalik." *How could he leave me unguarded? Does he think we were safe here?* I fought to stand. Hung on to the hammock for balance.

Wik grunted, circled the hammock ducking beneath the cables, and yanked the blackwing's robe.

Bone containers of medicine tumbled from her pockets as she struggled to conceal the bird, then to keep Wik's hands away.

"I'll break its neck," she said. "No more whipperling."

Despite myself, I cried out. "No!"

Wik slowed, but was not gentle when he hauled the blackwing up from the floor. "You got out. How?"

Dix did not answer. Once again, I tried to move towards her. This time, I mostly managed. The weakness was frustrating— I'd worked too hard to stand yesterday. But I'd climbed the Spire on a half-healed leg. I could do this too.

"Kirit," Wik cautioned, "you shouldn't—"

"I know I shouldn't, but what choice do we have?" I didn't look at Dix. The urge to hurt her was too strong, and I was still too weak. If I was going to break my vow to not kill anything, it would be with strength. To finish the job I'd thought the fall had done. "She has Maalik!"

I wobbled, and the scar on my leg throbbed. No, it wasn't entirely healed. But I could still fight. I stepped towards Dix. "Give me back the whipperling."

But she stuffed Maalik into her robe. "I'll smother the bird before you can even make a move." Dix looked from me to Wik and back. "If you let me be, I'll let him live."

Broken bones had reset across her face and nose, rendering her almost a stranger, but I recognized her eyes. They were the same as they'd always been: hard and unforgiving. Only now they were ringed with purple bruises and a deadened-seeming fear. The ruin of her hand, her face. Hurt and desperate, she'd do what she said.

We couldn't risk losing Maalik. His small body was too fragile, and Dix still too quick. He was our best hope to contact our cloudbound friends once we found a new city. I signaled Wik to stand down. "How did you get here? How did you get out?"

Dix laughed. "The bone bars weren't very strong, and they don't watch the cage. They think it's solid, think I'm safely muzzed, but they only make sure if the council wants to talk to me. If I don't eat what they give me, I can come and go as I like, and they'll never know I'm gone, until I'm ready to leave the city entirely."

"That figures," Wik said. "From what I gathered, the healer took her in. She stole from them, and others." Wik looked at Dix.

She squirmed. "They gave things to me. Just as they gave you yours." She gestured at the bracelet. "At first, at least," Dix said. "But they have so much! So many things we need to survive." At Wik's ever-darkening look, her tone grew more contrite. "I did ask at first. It was for our city."

That she'd asked for something wasn't the question. That she'd done so in a language they did not understand was a surety.

"They took Dix in. Healed her," Wik said to me. "As they've done for you, Kirit. She repays them by taking things. Just like she did at home."

"Stealing." In the towers it was a serious crime. "Dix, how could you? We need their help."

Here, there were no towers to war against each other. Everyone followed paths within the city. Everything here seemed so orderly, so controlled. When they'd questioned us, they'd seemed merely curious. But curiosity was easily damaged. My unease grew. Would we be welcome here? Not if Dix stayed. Not if they found her here with us.

Yesterday, I'd said I didn't know her because I didn't want to. This city would view my decision in a far less appealing light.

I shook my head. In the best situation, they might have helped us. We were no longer in the best situation.

And that was the least of our worries. Generations ago, we might have had a shared language, but now? I thought back to our interrogation. We could gesture, draw pictures. Misunderstandings could escalate. "We have to get Dix back in the cage. Make her give back what she stole."

Dix said, "I didn't—" before Wik stared at her, hard.

"What did you take?" She'd stolen from the city. She'd stolen Maalik from me. Had she taken more? "My satchel?"

Fear bloomed again. The plates. My wings. The satchel had been with me on the climb. I hadn't dropped it, and Dix obviously had no difficulty sneaking from her cage.

Shoulders and robe caught in Wik's strong hands, Dix struggled, but managed to shrug. "You abandoned me for dead. I walked out from the city and collapsed on the sand. These people from this city found me before the groundmouths did. They have wonders here. They don't need them all. When you pretended I was no one you knew, I figured you wouldn't mind if no one took your medicines." Dix started laughing so hard she coughed. "But I didn't take your satchels. This city's people did."

I saw motion behind one of the alcove's thinned bone panels. Heard shouting.

"They'll find me here, with you." Her lopsided grin showed several broken teeth. "They'll know you lied."

They would hate us then.

Wik growled, "Our first representative here was you." His sour expression said just how bad that was. His newfound status, gone, by association.

We'd both known, upon seeing her. We'd both hoped to hide it from our hosts.

We were guilty too.

This new city wouldn't trust us once they knew we'd lied. Citykiller or no, they'd want us to leave, at best. This was Dix we were talking about. I'd want us to leave too.

"You have to go back to where they're keeping you. You can't be found here." I wanted her to get away from us fast. Better to continue to pretend she didn't know us at all.

Dix chewed on a strand of dirty hair. Her eyes darted to the hallway. "I won't go back into the cage! I'll scream and shake the city with my voice. They're so quiet here, they can't help but hear. They'll find me here with you. They'll cage you too, for colluding with me. And especially for lying about it."

Wik and I looked at each other, eyes widening. Neither of us would ever collude with Dix. But we were in the same room with her. And had no chance of explaining ourselves. Not well. Possibly not at all.

We heard the healer returning. Saw their shadow passing by the thin bone walls.

With her free hand, Dix pulled her robe out of Wik's grasp.

"If you come with me, I'll show you where your satchels are. *And* a way out," Dix said and grabbed my hand with what was left of hers. "If you don't, I'll show them you are liars."

I resisted, for a moment. But I needed the satchel, she had Maalik, and if the healer caught all three of us here, we'd all wind up in that cage.

So we left the healer's room. Me, limping, Wik, with a firm grip on both of us, following Dix's whispered directions.

"Up there," she said. Ahead, a ramp was carved into the ridge wall. We followed a light map shaped like a cloud. "Not far at all."

Wik looked from Dix to me. "Knowing where she's going is probably better than wondering where she's gone."

He had a point.

Dix might break us all. We kept up with her anyway, into the hollowed ridge. *Clouds.* We followed to keep her out of trouble. Because we needed our satchels. We followed because it meant climbing away from any pursuers, into the secrets of a new city.

$$\text{\it ʎ \ ʎ \ ʎ}$$

After many twists and turns, Dix led us to a room filled with mechanisms and treasures.

*They have wonders here.*

She hadn't been lying.

In our city, we'd had codexes, carvings. Nothing that couldn't be carried up. Here, they could store things indefinitely.

"Are you sure this is the way out?" I asked. We seemed very high up. "Where are our satchels?" A curving ramp delivered us out of the healer's cells down below. Each level higher, the bone walls grew thinner and more lightly decorated. We could see, as if through silk, others moving in spaces beyond the ramp.

But not many others. This city was not as populous as ours had been. If we brought our citizens here, Varat would grow crowded.

Dix nodded. "I explored while they slept."

I bet she had. The citizens of this city had never met Dix's equal when it came to survival and treachery. She could damage this city. She could get us all killed.

*How are you not dead?* I was still in shock. Even though I wouldn't wish her death now, I certainly wondered how she'd escaped it. That she had *barely* escaped was little comfort.

*That she escaped it and greeted us here is exactly why you'd need to kill someone, Kirit.* If Aliati were here, she'd be shaking her head.

Dix chuckled and held out her hands. "You know they hunt cities? I've watched them do it."

The pieces of a puzzle started to click together. The dried husks of city eggs. The exultation over Wik when he'd shown how Nimru died, taking out our own city in the process.

"We didn't see anyone walking the desert to other cities." The groundmouths were too dangerous.

Dix smiled. She leaned close and whispered, "Maybe they fly too." She said it as if she already knew the answer. As if she wanted me to ask. I heard Maalik chirp desperately from within her robes.

I fought my own curiosity. Dix wouldn't lead me into owing her anything. Still, I followed her. "Where are the satchels?"

What Dix revealed worried me. We needed a new home, but she'd poisoned them against us. They'd celebrated Wik, had let him explore. They'd made me well again. I flexed my leg. It still ached; it would likely always ache. But the infection seemed gone.

Yet the people of Varat hunted other cities. And they had a wealth of artifacts that seemed to be collected from many places.

We'd be hard-pressed to fit in, even if we could learn their language. Even if we could get everyone downtower. And there were too many of us.

But the truth still shook me. *We were never alone.*

And neither were they.

Where we hid was a gallery of sorts. They'd shaped walls from the bone ridge, much like in our own cloudbound towers. Metal poles marked boundaries between alcoves, as with the paths below. The honeycombed cells of the upper alcoves were brighter than any below. They'd polished walls until tiny portions were fingernail thin and delicate. Natural light streamed through bone in complicated patterns, many cryptic, but a few familiar: a spiral within spirals. Bird chevrons. What looked like a cascade of littlemouths down a wall.

"Look at the dark panels," Dix said. Each wall in the gallery was divided into two strips of pitch-filled carvings and then subdivided by seasons and moons. "They don't get Allsuns or Allmoons here, only two dark seasons, because of the clouds."

She'd been here long enough to know.

I stared. They marked their days with sculptures of bone and light.

And there was light to spare. Above us, bone tiers began to split and rise freely, without further carving or sculpting. The result was a slimming of the towers and a separation that added to the airflow.

The contrast between Varat's light-art and the bone carvings of the Spire also struck me. So much beauty here. The walls were calendars, like the floors were maps.

"They're artists and teachers," I whispered as we walked. "They heal, they make things, they keep records."

"They punish. And they don't make everything." Dix raised her injured hand, then let it drop. "They take things too."

I didn't want to believe her. "They're curious. Explorers."

I tried to imagine what would happen if our city descended on this place, this library, and winced.

"On expeditions, they take what's not theirs," Dix said. "Your satchels, for instance."

We needed those back.

More citizens passed, in groups of twos and threes. They did not shout, or whistle. They whispered and murmured, soft like a breeze. Their voices sounded like wings cutting through wind, echoing through the passages. Beauty, yes. Still, the quiet unsettled me.

Dix pulled me closer to the wall, out of sight of a tall figure who'd entered a larger room across from us. "Watch. Then I'll help get your things, and mine."

The citizen dressed much like the healers below, with a woven facemask and shorn hair. They pressed an undecorated wall with their fingertips. The bone panel swung outward, revealing storage: shelves of small objects made of metal and glass. When the individual held one object up, a cone, it made a whirring sound, and I could feel the breeze it generated from across the honeycomb. Like Djonn's whirlwind, but much smaller.

The breeze pulled a strange scent from another section of the tier to our nostrils. Something I hadn't smelled in days. "What's that?" I wrinkled my nose at the bitter odor.

Dix answered. "There's a large rookery just beyond these rooms. Bone eaters. Tame ones."

*Maybe they fly too.* She'd known they did.

"I'm taking you there," Dix said. "But we need to wait for the curators to leave."

I was tiring, but if I followed her, I'd get my satchel back. The plates.

So much metal and artifexing in the gallery already, and yet they wanted to keep ours too. As I turned to Wik to wonder at the differences between our cities, I realized, finally, what Dix was up to. I grabbed her hand. "She's going to steal something here. Something important to them. And then she's going to escape, and we'll take the blame."

"If she hasn't yet," Wik said, "she won't be able to now. We won't let her."

Maalik screeched.

My fist clenched tighter on Dix's hand. I wanted to shout at her, but I had no words. She'd been here while the rest of us had been trying to keep the city alive. But she'd poisoned this world against us.

Now everything was closed to us, to our city. And she had Nat's whipperling.

The curator spoke then, and a voice answered from the rookery. Their incomprehensible language fell around me like the dappled light, unfamiliar and complex. Sound patterns were starting to repeat, but not enough, not yet.

Wik shook his head. "I can't make sense of it." He kept staring at the objects the curator sorted. His fingers twitched.

I expected as much from Dix, but Wik? "You're thinking about taking some things for yourself too?"

He shook his head. "If I knew they would help the city, our city, I might. I am curious too. And I want to survive, just as she does." He tilted his head at Dix.

"You'd risk the same punishment as her?" Captured. Lost fingers. Losing the ability to climb. The ability to fly. "They caged her. And could cage us." Unless we got out of here.

A clamor of squawks broke out in the rookery. I peered through one of the thinner panels in the wall. Wik hadn't been mistaken. Enormous bone eaters stretched their wings and hissed at their keeper on the bone ledge just outside.

"Those don't look trained at all." They looked like they might bite the handler's fingers off.

Wik shook his head. "I'm not certain. They might ride them? They could use them to feed the city."

Dix *knew* they rode them. Now I had no doubt she planned on riding one herself.

Dix looked guardedly at the curator. Then back at me. Defiant. A third curator entered, carrying Dix's wings. Or what was left of them. And the broken set we'd had in our packs.

We had to hold her back. "Those are mine," she whispered.

The pulleys and battens had been partly disassembled, the straps peeled back from the wingframe.

"They're curious," I said. That kind of curiosity wasn't good for us. We wouldn't fly home from here now.

The first curator put the wingframes on a shelf. Stored our satchels on the same level. Now I was the one thinking about stealing.

But the second curator pulled four brass objects from another shelf. Sheer and solid, with a bit that turned, holding fast to a point no matter how I looked at it. "What are those?"

Dix stared like a bird admiring something shiny. But no one replied. We were stumped.

We hung back in the shadows, watching. Outside, dark shadows swooped. The rookery trainer and the curator opened a bone box and pulled out a handful of something. Reached through a grating and scattered it. The grain smelled thick and rich. Dark shadows outside went crazy, cawing and scraping, then settled down.

I heard a soft chirp. Too low to be Maalik.

Through the grating, a pile of bedraggled feathers stared back at us. "Baby bone eaters?" I whispered to Wik.

The baby stuck its beak through the grating and chirped again. One curator looked left and right to make certain they were unobserved, then slipped the bird a strip of something the color of bone. With a cheep and a loud crack, the beak withdrew.

The corners of the curator's eyes crinkled from smiling.

Meanwhile, the second curator, the one who'd taken apart Dix's wings, knelt on the floor and spread something I did recognize—another map—across the bone tier. The map was made of woven layers of the same material as their masks. Odd markings and complex hatch-work crossed its surface. Our fallen city was rendered expansively. Their city, which we'd called Varat, had the same detail, its migration circuits marked clearly.

Was I looking at a game, like Dix's Gravity had been? I saw no way to win this.

On the map, a long stone ridge bordered the part of the plain that had no cities on it. The wingbreaker-curator waved their arms and said something incomprehensible.

The other curator, who had a spiral symbol beside their left ear, withdrew a white stick from their sleeve. I recognized it. We'd made eggshell chalk in the towers as children too.

Pressing the chalk to the brownish fiber, the curator carefully marked a circle around our city and another on the map. They looked about to mark something else, but from far below, a bone horn sounded. All three curators sped from the room and down a ramp opposite the one we'd climbed. The rookery trainer followed.

They'd left the map on the floor near the alcove where we hid.

I couldn't resist. Despite Dix's hissing and Wik's muttered "Kirit!" I snuck out and knelt by the map. A ring of glass and metal lay nearby, and I placed it over the illustration of the desert around Varat, thinking it a magnifier.

As the glass covered the thick fiber sheet, an astounding

thing happened: detail sprang up in the lens, far more than I'd ever seen a magnifying lens do. Layers became visible deep below the surface. I saw the ground, and what was beneath the ground, seemingly as great as the distance we'd fallen from the sky.

Wik crept from the alcove and leaned closer. Then he shifted the lens out of the way. The depths disappeared, and we had only a simple map to look at again.

"What artifexing is this?"

Wik said "artifex" like some in our city would say "luck," with the same adoration. He placed the lens back over the sheet, removed it, then picked up the sheet and looked behind it. We could see small lines and flecks of metal in the many layers that made up the map's pulp, but nothing that would indicate some elaborate engineering. And the map was so very small. So many Allmoons of carving would be required to render this much detail in bone, so many tiers in the Spire. I moved the lens back to one of the new chalk circles. "Look. There's our city." Ours was the only one without a migration route.

Several other cities had marks by them, in pale, almost luminescent ink. *How many generations does this map span?* Many hands had worked on it.

Wik looked at the map as if he wanted to peel it apart. I stayed his hand. "It's not ours. None of this is ours. It cannot help our city."

Dix's groan from the alcove made my head pound. "It could. It *might.*"

The map captivated me. I wanted to know all of it, wanted for it to be mine more than I'd ever desired wings, wingmarkers, anything. Anything except a new home.

I stared so long I didn't see Dix emerge from the alcove until I heard metal clink in her robe. Maalik gave a warning cheep. "Dix!"

The pocket of her robe weighed heavily, and she held the pieces of her silk wings in her uninjured hand. Her ruined face looked triumphant.

Another horn blew, and we heard voices approaching. Quick footsteps, echoed on the ramp.

"In here." Dix pulled me into a dark cell covered with hangings, then led me farther along the carved passages that grew narrower closer to the exterior of the bone ridge. There were no thinned or sculpted panels in this part of the city. Wik caught up with us, carrying both of our satchels.

"Good grab," I whispered.

Following Dix, I began to hum, nervously. A breeze slapped the hangings closed over this alcove. In the darkness, I caught another slight glow behind his ear. "Wik!"

"What?"

The glow was like the marks on the citizens who'd questioned us. The same color as a littlemouth in the clouds. The speckles of glow pulsed when I hummed or spoke. "You still have groundmouth in your hair."

"I thought I got it all out," he said. He brushed absently at his ear again. The glow disappeared. "Just a trick of the light?"

I wasn't so sure, but I let it drop for now. The smell of bone eaters grew stronger. Wik and I caught up to Dix when she stopped just before the ledge.

"There!" She pointed. Several greasy harnesses made of bird-gut and fiber hung from the wall on bone hooks. "They do ride them! I knew it."

She looked at me expectantly.

"No," Wik said. "We have no idea how to ride one of those."

"We need to leave this place. The only way down is that ramp or these birds. And if we go down again," Dix said, "we'll have to find a way off the city. We'll need to run."

At the moment, I was terrible at running.

Behind us, the tunnel darkened to black; ahead, the sun shone through a bonework gate. Outside, the bone eaters cackled.

"I'll give you the bird back, after," Dix promised.

I didn't believe her, but I saw no way to get Maalik back without a huge risk now. She knew the city, and I didn't. She had nothing to lose; I had everything. Below? I might find an advantage. "All right," I said, and pulled a harness down from the wall. Over Wik's protests, Dix played with the combination for a long moment, then pushed open the gate. I stepped through.

And found myself face-to-face with a juvenile bone eater easily twice my height. It clacked at me. Lowered its beak so the sharp point was an armspan from my nose.

Dix shut the gate behind me, with her and Wik on the other side. "Throw the harness over its head and put that bit of metal in its mouth," she called. "That calms them."

We weren't high enough that the wind could hold me, but the breeze did a good job of carrying my curses away from the tower I stood on. "I hope you fall forever, Dix. I hope you land in a pile of guano so big that you can never clear it." I could hear Wik cursing too.

Dix, from behind the gate, said, "Hurry, people are coming."

The bone eater's breath was hot on my cheeks. I hefted the harness and, with shaking hands, held up the metal piece. The bone eater looked at it, then at me, then opened its mouth.

When I slipped that bit of the harness into the bird's mouth, it dropped neatly into a small divot on the sides of the beak, something too regular to have been nature's doing. The thought gave me a shudder, but I threw the harness over the bird's obligingly lowered head and moved to its side. I nearly tripped on a claw.

The bird had extended a leg for me to climb.

"Okay!" I said. I climbed on its back.

As soon as it felt weight, the bird began to move forward. Dix slid around the gate and scrambled up just as the bone eater took off, leaving Wik stranded on the rookery.

❧ ❧ ❧

Steering a bird in the sky—especially one the size of a bone eater—was as strange to me as wings were to the people of this city. I tugged at the harness and hoped the bird knew what that meant.

Dix, her arms wrapped around my waist, whooped once and then fell silent as we wobbled and glided along the bird's chosen trajectory.

For a moment, I reveled in the feeling of being in the air again. Then fear took over. I had very little control over this creature.

"Make it go faster!" Dix jerked on my robe.

I couldn't make the bone eater go anywhere, much less faster. With Dix tugging on me, I nearly lost my seat. "We have to go back!" Wik stood on the deck of the rookery.

As I watched, he tried to duck back into the passage, but then backed out again. He hid behind a large basket.

He would be captured. Would I fight for him? Clouds, yes. I yanked the reins and the bit dragged on the tender part of the bone eater's beak.

"What are you doing?"

I didn't answer Dix. I focused on forcing the bone eater's head in the direction of the rookery. The bird's body followed.

"You can't go back!" Dix's voice rang loud in my ear. "We'll be captured again."

The bird's slow turn was all I could manage. Glancing out over the landscape as we closed the distance, I wished once again that the map were mine. Below, cities walked the large expanse of desert. Groundmouth divots patterned the ground.

The outlines of old structures and dead cities etched the shadows with angles and straight lines from this height. Beyond a long ridge, sunlight glinted on more water than I'd seen in one place before. The cloud above us seemed to end over that stretch of water.

The bone eater screeched as we closed on the rookery. Other bone eaters croaked and cackled in discordant response.

Ours pulled and fought the bit once it realized I didn't know how to command it, trying to throw us off. I fought to stay on, and Dix clung to me. Sweat drenched my robe by the time we returned to the balcony. My arms shook from holding tight to the reins. Where Wik had hidden, a basket was toppled on the balcony. The curators and the rookery trainer yanked me from the bird's back before we landed. Dix toppled off behind me. Their sibilant language held a familiar note of anger.

What I had been furious with Dix for doing, I was now guilty of as well. A thief. A citykiller and a thief.

They bound my hands. Hauled us away, Wik tied beside me. He looked straight ahead, his jaw set. A bruise bloomed on his cheek.

"Can't kill anything, can't fly," Dix said. Our guard cuffed her, and she quieted.

Wik shook his head, angry. We were hauled down the ramps as two more rookery workers passed us, carrying large sacks of offal. We glanced back to see a curator outside tying these to bone eater harnesses, save for the one I'd stolen.

"What are they doing?" I asked, wanting to hear Wik's voice again and know that he was all right.

"They're going to move the city." Dix's voice was extremely level. I braced for trickery and danger.

Wik's jaw tightened. "How do *you* know?"

"Look at it. They're preparing the bone eaters right now."

If we were still on the city's back when it began to move faster, we'd have a hard time disembarking.

Our guards dragged us farther down the ramp until we lost sight of the rookery.

They pulled us, three criminals, through the light-dappled corridors of the strange city.

# 18

## NAT, MIDCLOUD

*⌒ While Brokenwings and Magister flew from low to high ⌒*

"If we want to move everyone off the towers quickly—" My words filled the cave. "We can't take too much time debating risks, looking at other solutions." I'd made my decision. I would tell them everything. I would. As soon as Ceetcee, Beliak, Elna, and the baby were safe below. As soon as the first kite descended.

Ciel would keep her promise, I knew.

But my companions in the midcloud cave waited for me to say something more, even Urie, the former blackwing. My certainty rose. This was dangerous information to share. If anyone talked—especially Urie—about what awaited us, and what didn't, we'd never get my family down the towers. There would be panic.

The cookfire popped and smoked. The remnants of the meal turned to green paste in the bone bowls.

"I'll tell you more about the city." I meant it. I'd tell some of the truth now, some later, once my family was safe.

The baby cooed.

Macal leaned closer. "I had hoped you would."

"Tower residents may despise life below," I began. "It won't be easy. I hated it. It's hot and damp, and it smells terrible. We've never seen the like above the clouds. The only advantage is that you cannot fall any farther."

Ciel heaved herself up from the floor. "Clouds." She stomped towards the littlemouth cave. Moc followed her. She could have said something. But she hadn't. She understood.

"Why can't we stay above, then?" Urie said. "Float the cities like Macal had planned? How will we live?" He began to pace behind the cookfire.

Macal put a hand on his arm. "We have to go down. Everyone has to. It's safest. We can't panic others," he said. He looked at Urie until the young man nodded. "We'll find a way." Macal looked at Djonn, then me. "A hostile environment like you describe is a lot to absorb."

"Urie's reaction is exactly why I'm worried about the towers." Worse, what would happen when they learned the rest? What would Macal do? "Any group that decides to go its own way is fewer hands to help, more possibility that people will die. We have to hold together." I stared at Djonn until he dipped his head in agreement.

Ceetcee stepped from the cave mouth and came to stand by me. "You did the right thing. Now we know. I'll make some adjustments to the kites to try to keep out the rain."

So much was outside of my control. "The ground needs to be a sign of hope—a way forward. It can't be seen as a bad place, or people won't move fast enough." If they learned the whole truth, especially. Now it wouldn't be.

Ceetcee patted my shoulder and walked back through the tunnels. "Come see what I'm working on. We'll see if Elna's awake on the way."

Beliak joined us, the baby in his arms.

Elna slept in the littlemouth cave, the soft light illuminating her face. Occasionally, she coughed. The littlemouths pulsed a flutter of alarm each time.

Ciel and Moc sat on either side of her, holding her hands. "She's all right, just tired," Moc said. "We'll get her down to the ground, and she'll be better." Ciel didn't look at me.

I knelt by Elna's side and took her hand. It felt cool, not cold. She murmured in her sleep. I wanted so badly to wake her. To talk through my decisions with her. But I couldn't bring myself to do that.

"She's worked so hard here. Tired herself out," Moc said. Worry had completely replaced his usual bravado. "She's been like a mother to me. To all of us."

"Keep her warm," Ceetcee said. "And make sure she drinks something when she wakes, has a little broth." She handed a water sack and the last bone bowl to Moc. The boy took it and settled back against the wall, watching Elna.

Ceetcee gestured for me to follow her out of the cave, to the meadow. "I think I can make an adjustment to the basket designs that will help occupants shelter from the rain if they need to. I need extra hands, though."

"Djonn can do this," I said. "You need to start preparing to go to the ground."

"We've been preparing to go up above the clouds," Ceetcee said. "The opposite direction isn't that much different."

*Oh yes, it is.* I made another decision. "I have to tell you and Beliak something more. Djonn knows as well."

Ceetcee climbed the scaffolding around the kite and gestured for Beliak to hand up her tools. Beliak switched the baby from his right arm to his left, reached into his robe, and pulled out the silk roll, tied with skymouth tendon, which had been Ceetcee's tool bag since she became a bridge artifex. She took it with a sure hand, while holding on to the scaffolding with the other. "What is it, Nat?"

"Once you are through the cloud, the wind—" I looked behind me to make sure no one was listening. Only Djonn was near enough to hear, and he already knew. "The wind disappears almost completely. At ground level, there's not enough to get up in the air on wings. That's why Ciel and I didn't come back sooner. We couldn't."

Ceetcee stayed silent for a long time. Feet crunched on lichen as Djonn approached. "That changes everything," she said.

"No it doesn't," Djonn replied. "We're still going down. We're taking precautions."

The knot of secrets was growing. Now I'd involved my family. Had I made the right decision?

Sitting down on the scaffolding, Ceetcee played with a piece of silk on the box kite. Beliak rocked the baby back and forth, keeping her quiet. His jaw tight, he stared at me. "I thought we said no more secrets. How could you keep this one from us— from them?"

"Only enough to get you and Ceetcee and Elna to the ground safe. And I'm telling you."

A brief nod from Beliak. "You're telling us. Not the city." He stood beside me below the kites, and we watched the work going forward on our escape plans. "There's still time to figure something else out. We could float plinths, we could escape that way."

"There isn't any more time." Why couldn't he see this? "If we split our efforts, we'll run out of time."

Ceetcee held her hand out to me, and then to Beliak. Wove her fingers through mine. "You helped get this started. You and Ciel. You came back up." Beliak ran his hands through his hair in frustration.

"Not fast enough. I wasn't here when you needed me."

"We managed," Beliak said. "We had Elna too. You were here, through her." He clasped Ceetcee's hand, then mine. "And I know you're doing what you can to get us down safe. I don't agree, but I will try to understand."

Our linked hands made a web. A net. We leaned on one another. All I'd wanted to do was protect them. Now I knew it wasn't enough.

My hope faltered. What if the lies had become too great, the net too weak?

Ceetcee felt me shiver. "It will be all right," she said.

"How do you know? I can't hope right now that anything will go right. So much has gone wrong."

Ceetcee looked out at the meadow and then down at the infant sleeping in her arms. "Because we can make it be all right. We've come through hard times. I helped build the kites. I know they'll work. Djonn's designs are sound. That's not hope, that's effort." She turned to me, her eyes framed by long lashes. "I'm putting everything I know into getting us—all of us—down to the ground safely. Once we're there, I'll do it again. That's how I know it will be okay."

The wind changed, and mist dampened her face. Beliak adjusted the baby's covering—an old robe. "There's no other way through," he said. "We know that now. The midcloud has been hard on everyone. No one wanted to be here. We worried for you. But being here kept us from danger up above."

I hadn't realized until that moment that if we hadn't been chased into the clouds, Beliak and Ceetcee would have been on Densira when it fell. Same as Elna. I shivered more. There was loss at every turn.

"How bad is it below?" Ceetcee asked.

I didn't want to tell her much more. "I only know what the city is like. That was hard." I shifted the subject, gently. "How did you get by?"

Ceetcee smiled at Beliak. "Everyone here helped. There wasn't one moment I felt alone. But Elna was the pin that held everyone together. She just did things, and everyone followed her lead. She knew it was all going to be all right."

The baby turned her head to look at her mother. Her tiny pink tongue darted out, then back into her mouth. It sounded as if she was kissing the wind.

There was quiet in the meadow as my family considered both my secrets and my keeping of them. The air was cool here, especially in comparison to the heat below. As they thought over what I'd said, I tried to memorize every line of their faces.

I'd lost them once. I wouldn't risk losing them again. "You'll go down with the first kite, then? If I promise to tell the others everything once I know you're safe?"

Beliak and Ceetcee looked at each other. Beliak lifted the baby and placed her in my arms. She felt warm and, again, heavier than I expected. I held her close.

I'd worked so hard to hold on to hope and strength on the way up the towers. Now I held hope in my arms. There wasn't room for any other feelings. Nothing that would hold us back.

Here, with them, it was suddenly all right to feel again. Feelings curdled in my throat. Not hope. Fear. Not waves of it, not an impending city of it, but a low, far-off beat of it, from the future. Would we survive? Would my family survive their journey tomorrow?

I knew the kite descent would be easier than my fall had been. Still.

"There's so much danger," I whispered, my hand reaching out to brush soft baby fuzz, like down, the head that fit in my palm. "How can you be here in a world with so much danger? How can I protect you from it?"

"We're born into danger. We keep each other safe." Ceetcee put her hand over mine. "We build our communities to withstand it. That's why we love. Why we fight." She tightened her hand. "If we didn't fight so hard, the danger would get in. And we can't let it."

"I want to be so much stronger." *For you, for her.*

"You are stronger than you know," she said. "We all are. Climbing all that way. Ciel too. All we have to do is ride down."

The baby squirmed in my arms and let out a yell that pierced the meadow's gloom.

Beliak looked me in the eyes. "I think you might be doing the right thing, keeping the wind secret."

Ceetcee tilted her head. "As for me, I can see both sides. But I want you to tell everyone soon. Promise?"

I nodded. I wanted to tell them also, but I was afraid. "Once you're safe."

She laughed quietly. "I'm building our rescue kite, Nat, assisted by the best of artifexes. We will get down safe. You'll see."

Her confidence warmed me. Made me feel safer too. I shifted attention to the baby in my arms. "What will you name her when you reach the ground?" I wouldn't be there then, but I wanted to know.

Ceetcee and Beliak both smiled. "We'll wait," Beliak said, "until we're all together. When you come down too. She knows she's part of a family that protects her. That's what matters now."

Ceetcee leaned over and whispered in my ear, a soft breeze. "But if you have any favorite names, tell me."

I whispered several names to her. Her eyes danced at the prospects. They were old names. Tower names. Good ones.

Names meant so many things. They told a history. What tower you lived on. I was Brokenwings and Densira, and Nat—Naton's son. What would this baby be? "What do we wish for her?" I whispered back.

Beliak laughed. "A fair wind, strong wings were the old blessings. What about a new horizon?"

It wasn't a traditional tower wish, but it was a wish we made together.

Sitting with them and talking, planning for a naming, gave me new strength for what I needed to do. There was so much beyond the clouds, so much danger. But those dangers were less than what the towers faced now.

We would see our way through it, together, and stronger for the risk.

As long as we all made it safely to the ground.

# 19

## KIRIT, BELOW

*⁓ The Skyshouter fled from a city of light ⁓*

Down the ramps, speeding over patterns of light and dark, the curators dragged us. We passed the alcove where I'd recovered. From within, the healer shouted, then emerged.

The healer gestured, "No," emphatically. Pulled at our escort's sleeves. The guards resisted, roughly.

I stumbled as the three of us were shoved and prodded down the ramps to another alcove in the bone ridge. Varat's guards stuffed us into the woven bone cage that had once contained only Dix.

With some effort, they reinforced the lock with wire.

The place reeked of old robes and sweat. A bucket, pushed into a corner and covered tight, also smelled. Pressed next to Dix, I realized she stank to the highest of clouds too. Worse than the bone eater.

Wik, on her other side, seethed. Dix grew somber as our captors departed.

"Kirit." Dix's broken front teeth turned the two syllables of my name to one. She added a pleading note at the end that held me still and wary. Worse, she stood too close, her chest brushing my shoulder, my arm pinned against her belly. Crammed into a cage together, because of Dix's escape from the same cage in the first place.

Guilt by association. Bird stealing. Lies.

Wik slipped his right hand to his left sleeve. His fingers brushed the short knife he'd hidden there before we left our dying city. "What now, Dix?" He tilted his head as if considering whether she could make the situation any worse. He'd had to duck to fit in the cage, so this made him look like a giant, looming over her shoulder.

I put my fingertips on his and shook my head. *No harm comes to her, not here. We'll never be let out if they see us as liars* and *killers.* "Maalik."

Wik's grimace deepened. "That bird isn't worth your sacrifice."

"I disagree. We need to keep him safe." Maalik was our only connection to our former home.

Dix ignored Wik, despite the close quarters. Focused on me. "Kirit," she said again. Hearing my name emerge from her lips gave me chills.

In the shadows of our bone cage, her presence was still enough to make me squirm. There were too many betrayals between us. Now she raised her hand—to beg for more favors or to touch me, I didn't know which—and I flinched. "What now?"

"We have to try again," she answered. "You have to get me off this city."

I flinched away from her. "Why should we help you ever again?"

Wik frowned at her. "We can't leave easily when the city's moving fast. As it will be soon. Meanwhile we're stuck in this cage with you." Wik's voice was cold as Allmoons winds.

All the murders and horrors Dix had committed in order to hold power in the city above. Her crimes in this new city. The fact she still held Maalik hostage in her robe, one hand clamped over his body as a warning. The things she'd done. I grabbed her, my fingers at her neck.

"Kirit, I'll help you," Dix whispered. "Let me go."

Maalik cheeped, then squawked. Dix's good hand squeezed his brown feathers tight, even as she pleaded for her life.

I couldn't let go. I couldn't kill her. Wouldn't, Wik would say. I stopped squeezing, but held on. "Give me the bird."

Dix's face transformed at the refusal, painfully highlighting the crease and dent in her skull where her eye socket had healed badly. That eye drifted. "Please." She crumpled the sleeve of my robe with her mangled hand. "Please. Help me. I'll help you."

The city rolled slightly from side to side. The motion was disconcerting. "They're moving." We'd lost our chance to leave easily.

Beyond the cage, we heard people passing between the thin bone walls, talking in their unfamiliar tongue. We saw their shadows. "Dix, quiet." We were in enough trouble. The bone cage held us apart from this city, its technology, its history. The bars and lock said this city's peace should never be ours. Because of Dix.

And because of our actions too. We'd become like her.

I let her go.

Dix pulled her way past me and leaned against the far corner of the cage. She kicked at a bar and wiggled it: loose. She pushed a piece of bone until it turned sideways. The bar had been cut carefully with a wire like the one Dix wore around her neck. She'd stolen it from the cloudbound cave, I realized, and kept it with her since. No wonder she'd escaped more than once.

"You too!" She gestured with her ruined hand.

The gap was wide enough for Dix to squeeze through. She tried to pull me after her, but my right shoulder jammed against the cage wall. The rough bone joins snagged at me. I gasped, but I was too big. The cage held fast.

Dix stood on the other side of the cage, wavering. She wanted to flee, but couldn't escape without us.

Footsteps. Just outside our alcove.

Dix froze. Wik's face turned stormy. "We're cloudfood."

But the healer stepped into the alcove. Silently, they began to unwind the wire that held our cage closed. They looked up once, their brown eyes catching mine. So like my aunt's eyes in color, like Elna's in kindness. But the healer's brow furrowed. They covered their mask with a hand and stared at us intently, willing us to understand. Pointed at us. Then repeated the gesture. *Quiet.*

Then they reached through the opening and tugged at my robe.

Wik grabbed me from behind and held on while the healer tried to pull me from the cage. A piece of rough bone tore my robe as the healer tugged. Their grip was hard; they pulled urgently.

"Let go," I whispered. I didn't want to go wherever they were taking me.

Dix shrank against the wall, trying to hide. Her eyes were wild. Maalik wriggled in her robe.

When the healer finally yanked me from the cage, I wobbled, thrown off balance by the city moving beneath me. Wik followed, and the healer let him. Both held firm to my robe.

Dix stared at the healer, shocked. Then turned to me. "Now you're a thief and an escapee just like me," she whispered. I felt nauseous, whether from the rolling motion of the city or Dix's words, I couldn't tell.

But the healer hustled us away from the paths with spiral designs on the floor. They put their hand to their lips again, pointed at all three of us, and gestured "no."

"You're helping us." I stared at them.

The healer glanced back at me, the corners of their eyes crinkling, and made a gesture that seemed very obvious: "Get moving."

We turned left and right as the healer drew us farther down the city's tunnels. Dix followed, trying to keep up. The healer picked up speed.

"Where are we going?" Dix whispered.

The healer turned, a fierce look in their eyes. They covered their mask with a hand one more time, then kept moving. Even Dix hushed.

Pulled along the corridors by the healer, we tried to stay as unremarkable as possible. Those few who walked the passages down here saw the healer's white shift and mask, their shaved head, and did not question. Once, the healer pulled us into an alcove and gestured again for silence until another Varat citizen, one with a blue mark behind their ear, had passed.

As we descended, the bone walls began to turn green and lush with moss, marked with thin patterns in purposeful places that let light in.

After working our way through the bone ridge of Varat, when we emerged onto the city's back, the sunlight nearly blinded me. The healer kept pushing us forward, towards the edge of the city's body and the moving landscape far below.

Varat's thick hide was even and almost smooth, unlike our old city. And the rolling motion of its walk was much more pronounced the closer we were to its legs.

I nearly lost my balance as Varat stepped lower, into a ditch, and then lurched forward. The healer caught my arm and steadied me. The bone eaters flew farther out in front of the hungry city, and the beast straightened its path.

We stumbled through the daylight, four now, not three. The healer was still with us. For the first time, I noticed their robe was torn at the shoulder.

They smiled, eyes crinkling above their mask. Gestured at me to move, fast.

"That healer's a gentle heart. Was for me too, once." Dix

laughed until coughs racked her chest and she had to slow down and breathe for a moment. The healer turned and gave Dix the same gesture, but didn't smile.

Dix ignored them. "Kirit, what will you do now that you have another pet to protect?"

"If they're coming with us, they're not a pet." I recalled the loud conversations outside the alcove where I lay ill. The look of disdain the five officials gave the healer as they passed. There'd been disagreement about our care.

Dix coughed again, earning her another *hush* gesture from the healer.

Above the clouds, wounds like Dix's—or any of ours—could have been a death sentence. I thought about the blackwings, and about our injuries. Was the sky more dangerous than the ground? I thought about the healer, who, for reasons of their own, was helping us escape.

Anything could kill us down here, just as in the sky, even things we could not see. But the cities themselves were more dangerous here. I shivered. No wonder our ancestors had climbed on the cities' backs. It was safer up higher.

Soon we might have to make that choice again.

Dix caught her breath. "I'm ready. Whatever comes next." Maalik stuck his beak out of her pocket and cheeped at me, but she pushed him back into the folds of fabric.

The healer pointed to ropes that hung down the side of the city. Began to descend, while the monster's motions were still slow.

"The healer's helping us," Wik reminded Dix, "as, so far, we are helping you."

"*I* have something you want," she snapped. But she looked worried. She glanced at her ruined hand, and at the ropes. The healer's shorn head could barely be seen, they were descending so fast. We had to move fast too.

Dix couldn't go anywhere fast.

It was tempting to let Varat take care of her, or the drop to the ground. But Dix was our problem.

"If we bring you with us, how do we keep you from turning wing on us and coming back around to attack?" I asked.

Wik growled, answered for Dix. "Nothing at all. Except tying her up."

"She's all bones. Not hard to carry if we share."

"So we take her," Wik said. "She causes any problems, it's on your wings."

I looked at her and almost felt sorry for her. "We get you off this city, Dix, you'll give me Maalik. That's all. We're done after that." I couldn't see the healer any longer.

Wik looked at his former captor, but spoke to me. "I'd like to drop her from something high."

"You might get your chance if she doesn't behave," I said. Dix flinched beside me.

We walked across Varat's back to where the healer had begun the descent.

"Stop here," Dix murmured. We'd been following the beginning of Varat's bone ridge. Dix pointed at an outgrowth that spread low against the city's walls. I set her down and she knelt beside it, sawed for a moment with the wire, then pulled. A piece of bone lifted away like the cover of a heartbone gap in the Spire, with a peeling, sucking sound.

The bone on Varat was healthy and alive. It grew fast. My nose filled with the smell of heartbone. Such a familiar scent, I was thrown back to the first moment I'd been shown the city's core. As a newly marked Singer, in the Spire. Here, now, things were much different.

From within the hollow, Dix pulled three wrapped objects. They glittered as she slipped them into her robe. I heard Maalik squawk.

"What did you do?" I whispered. Three objects. Had she lost her fingers as punishment? "You stole those from Varat too." I reached out to grab her arm again, and she shifted so I nearly tumbled from the city's side.

"Their artifexes are better than ours. Or the people they took these from were," she said. "We need new knowledge to survive."

*Birdcrap*. I knew she was right.

But the last thing in the world that I wanted was to be like Dix.

# 20

## MACAL, MIDCLOUD

*⌁ And the Magister hoped for a new kind of bridge ⌁*

In the towers above, Sidra and the council tried to hold the city together. Below, I worked on breaking it apart.

More than once, I caught myself staring into the mist, wishing I could talk with my partner, wishing I had her skill with people, her ability to shift a situation from disastrous to possible.

Even as Nat and I helped Djonn equip grips and weapons for our return above the clouds, we sized each other up. Would Nat be a help or a weight? My concerns had eased after his confession, but they were still there. Just as I had held concerns about Urie, above. Was he telling the whole truth?

"We'll tell them that the city is dying first," I proposed. What would Nat say in reply? Did he still believe that we shouldn't tell the others?

He dipped his head. "A good idea. We need citizens to listen, to follow directions."

"We've been trained to do that all our lives. With songs, with Laws. The blackwings are going to help us. Well, the faction of blackwings that Rya is leading will, hopefully."

Rya's stand against the Conclave on Grigrit was a good sign. She'd be the better leader to work with.

"They'll still need to be convinced. When will you tell them about the city?"

A long silence. Nat didn't comment. He was still holding something back, I was sure of it.

"Nat. A new community built on lies may be weakened from the start." The Singers had traded truth and lies. Our community would need to be more open to survive. I didn't want Nat to turn away from that.

The cave brightened with mist-light and the baby wailed, hungry. Djonn grumbled, rolled from his blankets, and slowly levered himself upright by first rolling to his knees. He sat back on his heels and, gritting his teeth, pulled himself up the wall. He wouldn't take any help. He stalked away from the noise.

Nat drew a deep breath. "Let's get ready, then. I'll say what I must to convince the blackwings we're telling the truth."

❦ ❦ ❦

On one side of the meadow, bone scaffolding propped up an irregular bone and silk mechanism. Ladders and platforms distributed the structure's weight across the plinth and secured it to the nearest tower. Ceetcee stood atop the scaffolding, working on the mechanism inside. A few of the former blackwings who'd chosen to stay in the meadow after Dix lost worked beside her.

I left the cave and caught up with Nat. Behind us, Djonn slowly descended the ladder and began to cross the meadow. He waved us on.

Ceetcee had bound her baby to her back by a swath of gray silk. A metal awl gripped between her teeth, another in hand, she pushed the butt end of a bone shaft into place on an overgrown wing cam. The holes for pulley lines and the tension clamps were missing, but I could feel how that one piece might move in my fingertips. Just like tightening a wing. Nat and I slowed to look at broken pieces of another creation trapped beneath a fallen bone shard. Djonn caught up with us.

"We'd been building two of the climbers. Only one survived the quake." His voice resounded with loss.

The surviving mechanism was part wing and part tentacle. Its articulated legs were joined and levered to be controlled from an interior platform. "It moves a bit like a silkspider," Djonn said, pointing out the new tension springs he'd added to the legs.

On the ground behind the climber, two strangers—their cloaks hunter blue—wove a fiber and silk basket large enough to carry four comfortably.

Djonn asked for the workers to stand back. He cranked the springs tight and pulled a lever. Three of the climber's sharp feet dug into the side of the bone tower like a blade into grease. Like the grip I'd been carving, only much bigger.

In another part of the meadow, three giant box-wing kite frames, the size of a quarter tier, rested.

Moc worked on one of the box kites. He threaded skymouth tendon through two pulleys to a platform below.

"We're running out of supplies," Djonn added. "We can't work on the crawlers much longer, or test anything. We need more of everything. When you come back down, bring silk, bone, more heartbone. All of it."

*Heartbone.* "You know how to make lighter-than-air." I stared at him, hope rising.

Djonn nodded slowly. We were far enough from the scaffolding now for privacy.

"I think we can help each other. Once the towers and the blackwing factions come together. Few towers have supplies now, and the blackwings control so much distribution above," I said. "We have to be careful."

The spider fascinated me. This could, if it succeeded, get more citizens down the tower. I noted one change from Djonn's sketches.

"The basket," I whispered.

Djonn coughed. "What?"

"You reworked it from your sketches in the cave."

Djonn put his hands on his back, stretching. "It's much more useful as a support crawler going down. Hard to ride in. We're going to have to lean on the kites a lot more than we thought. I'll need more supplies. Fast?"

He looked away from me at the last minute. As if he was keeping secrets too.

❧ ❧ ❧

Long ago, I'd separated from the Singers, from my family, in order to become Tower. I'd made that choice.

Kirit Skyshouter had tried to keep both groups. It hadn't worked out well for either of us. But both decisions had helped strengthen the community. I hoped.

Now Kirit was gone, disappeared below the clouds, and what the city had left was me and Nat. And whatever Nat was still hiding.

Secrets had been the Singers' trade goods for so long in the city. That had nearly killed us all.

I hated secrets.

When I'd first come to the towers, it was to be a Magister at Mondarath, a tower that had needed one so desperately few questions were asked. The towerman was bribed, of course, but that was normal back then. I'd been outside the Spire only a few times before my excursion, and then only after dark, to test my night flying. For while I was a new Magister to everyone else, I was in truth still a Singer, sent to watch the towers, to see which way their politics flew.

The secret nature of what I'd been expected to do, passing information through whistles and glances, keeping facts from citizens who needed them, all made me writhe in discomfort.

I'd been windstruck by the sheer openness of the towers,

their tiers and balconies, their shutters thrown open to the sky, children wobbling in the air on patchwork wings. The vast unguardedness of the city.

When I had set my sleeping mat down at Mondarath, I drew a first breath of that air unbounded by Spire walls and felt my loyalty to the Spire snap.

The small songs I'd made since I was a child, plucking cheap notes out on a borrowed dolin, began to change then. They became less about structure, rules, and the battles of the past, and more about daily things: meetings and kisses and partings of ways.

I longed to know the rest of the city's songs. The ones that would fade over time, on the lips of few, and then be lost to history. When Tobiat began teaching the old songs again, I listened, but I listened more for newer songs.

Now, across the meadow deep in the clouds, I heard someone singing. High voiced, but enthusiastic. I followed the voice like a thread and found Ciel helping Djonn add the spring she'd been shaping to part of the climber's mechanism. She looked up and smiled, but kept singing.

She sang something I'd never heard before. A song about walking and falling. And walking again. A toddler's song, perhaps.

I smiled to hear it. Vowed to learn it someday.

"So many new songs we get to make," Ciel said, looking at me for a moment, before she focused on the bone spring and tendons in her hands again. "If we survive."

My heart squeezed at her words. "We will. You'll have many new songs."

Ciel laughed. "I will, at that."

Her voice was still so young, and she was so determined. She gave me hope. She wasn't relentless like Kirit, nor impulsive like Nat. She was scratched and bruised, but still finding ways to help, still making her own music. Still trying. Sidra had sung too, early on. She'd sung Remembrances one last time over the loss of her father when the council fell, and then gone silent. I missed her singing as much as I was now missing her wisdom.

In the mist and haze, looking across the cloudbound meadow to the rotting stub of what was once the Spire, I promised myself the city would sing again. Better, it would be free of the secrets that had bound it for so long.

My fingers brushed the climber and a cog turned, lifting a pointed leg a handspan into the air. I spun it back quickly. Djonn looked at me. "I've been working out how we can send citizens down each time a kite or a pulley mechanism is finished. If you send me more artifexes, we can work faster still."

"Urie's aunts know more artifexes are being held on Grigrit. We'll find them." I sounded more confident than I felt, but this had to work. I would make it work. Once I would have been able to find anything. Once, the city had kept its secrets in a single place.

Now it was almost as if we'd dreamed that city, but woken to a different one. "We need to help the towers understand that a change had to happen. We have to do it quickly."

Ciel spoke again. This time slowly, choosing each word carefully. "We need to give them a song. Something to hold on to."

Nat cracked his knuckles. "Like The Rise?" He hummed a verse.

*Far down below the clouds, oh, the city did rise*

"Different, I think. I've been thinking about it a lot, but I don't have it all yet. Can we give them a few verses? Make the rest later? When we survive this?"

*If* we survived. "I think that's a good idea," I said. On our last night together in the undercloud, making a song felt like exactly the right thing to do.

Ciel began to repeat the song she was working on.

Ceetcee and Djonn joined in, learning as they sang. Soon the guards did as well. The simple, familiar melody, a modified Singer's Rise, made learning easier, new words and a growing set of verses. But it was something.

Voices echoed around the meadow too. The sound made a promise; the promise made a binding. I tried to join them, but got caught up learning the words and watching everyone interact over a song. Ceetcee leaned on Nat and Beliak. Ciel and Moc stood like fledges trained in the Spire, singing counterpoint. Elna dozed by the cookfire, listening now and then.

> Pulled apart, the sky's towers weakened, unless a bridge
>     was tied.
> While monsters clashed and the groundbound watched
>     as a city died.
> All that shook, all that fell was sky and bone,
> So two went far and two climbed home. . . .
> We're headed to the horizon . . .

The song went on, and our spirits lifted. I noticed sometimes the singers broke into comfortable laughter when they lost a line or a beat. The cloudbound had sung together before.

I noticed something else too. Nat and I were the only ones not singing.

ᔦ  ᔦ  ᔦ

The next morning, Nat and I flew loops around the nearby towers to find space for citizens from above. The mist turned to rain, and a storm threatened lightning in the distance, but Nat encouraged me to continue. Water beaded on my wings, waxed now like those of the rest of the midcloud. As we passed them, four tower trunks looked safe for temporary hang-sacks.

Nat circled the last tower, closest to the city's edge, a final time. It rose above the clouds, but cracks ran in lightning patterns across its thickened core.

Nat bowed his head as he flew. I heard him singing Remembrances.

I joined him. We sang to the tower's memory as we flew through the mist.

"Should we warn them about the cracks?" Nat said when we landed.

"If they balk, we absolutely tell them. Anything to get people to begin to move," I said.

Nat peered at me, curious. Asked, "Would you tell other towers the same thing, knowing they'd be hard-pressed to prove you wrong?"

I considered it. Would I lie to other towers? "No," I told him. No more secrets.

Above us the towers rose into the mist, and the evening darkened to night. Work on the kites and mechanicals continued by oil lamp and, when Ciel could coax them to it, littlemouth glow.

When Aliati returned after her latest run above the clouds, she pulled us aside. "I spoke with a blackwing near Varu. There are two major factions still. The group from Laria has been absorbed by Rya's Aivans after a bit of interference at a Conclave." She smiled at me. "But they're fighting others due to Laria's loss of their lighter-than-air." She paused for a long look at Urie.

The former blackwing had the wisdom to duck his head and return quickly to work beside his aunts on more lighter-than-air.

Aliati continued, "The other faction, from Bissel, Varu, and Lith, plus their allies, is currently preparing to attack the northwest again, starting with Mondarath."

"Mondarath can weather an attack. Our guards are well trained." I didn't feel as certain as I sounded. I wanted to go there first, more than ever. Or send Sidra a message.

Aliati hadn't been able to get close enough for the past several flights.

"Another worry," Aliati said. "We saw no skymouths anywhere around the towers. Not even in the clouds. And not one gryphon."

Ciel drew a long, tremulous breath. "We saw three when we came up a few days ago. If the skymouths are gone, then we need to speed up. Tell everyone to move faster." Her whole body shook as she said it.

Aliati put an arm around her shoulder. "Maybe. We're nearly ready. We've got the pulleys set up, and we'll lower the first group tomorrow."

The sun was out now, but barely visible as light in the mist. Another precious day had fallen. Nat balled his fists. "We should start now. Get them moving."

"We could, but we can't risk launching the first kite in the dark," Aliati said. "Everyone will be safer this way." She was a mote of calm in the midst of Nat's urgency. "Plus we still need a crew."

"Our pulley operators need to practice and to rest. We'll eventually need more hands to help work the pulleys, but for now, these are our experts," Djonn said. "We'll send the group down tomorrow, as planned."

Ciel nodded. "I want to lead that group, with Ceetcee steering the kite." She was still young, but her experience went beyond everyone's except Nat's. "I know the ground."

Djonn bowed to her. "And you should, Risen. But the risk—"

My niece practically glowed with the honor. "I know the risks. I want to take Elna and the baby down myself. And Beliak to help prepare for the rest to come. For Nat's sake. And the community's sake."

I felt a surging pride on my niece's behalf. I wished Wik could have seen her. Sidra too.

Moc ducked his head. "I could do that." But he looked proud of his sister too.

Aliati gestured Ciel towards the kites in the meadow.

"I don't think I'll be able to sleep now," Ciel whispered. Her voice carried in the dark.

"You'll need to rest if you're going to go back down with a kite full of people," Aliati answered. "Want to sing something more? 'Nest of Thieves'?"

Ciel shook her head at the song suggestion. "Maybe. It's hard singing when so much is about to happen."

Something had been bothering me, since I flew around the towers and saw the cracks. I found Djonn and Ceetcee. "This may be the time," I said, "to find a home that isn't another city. Especially if we don't hear from Kirit and Wik. We need to learn to live on the ground, no matter how dangerous. Or build our own city somehow. Something that cannot die."

"What kind of city?" Djonn asked.

"I'm not sure. What would you build?"

Djonn smiled and looked up into the mist. "Something that can fly, or at least float."

"I think that's a good place to start," I said.

Djonn's excitement took wing, though I was glad to note an undercurrent of caution in his gaze. He grabbed a bone tablet and began to draw. "Thanks, Macal. It's always important to dream."

As for me, I liked the idea of a flying city, but I was curious about the ground. The crushed lichen underfoot and the mist in the midcloud still felt strange on my skin. The smells here were too rich after a life spent in the mostly dry cold of the clouds. What would the real ground be like?

I'd accepted the city as it was all my life—there was nothing we were taught that told me otherwise. No songs, no Laws. Cities grew from below the clouds as plants grew from dirt. That's what the songs said, the ones that sang of bone forests. And we'd always looked up in the other direction, towards the sky. We'd always moved up, towards safety.

Children asked about the sky, its purpose, its form. As a community, we'd stopped questioning the city in the same way long ago. The towers were there; they grew. We lived on them. So the Singers had taught us. In doing so, they'd buried the fraught history of the midcloud.

Now we'd see more. We could become more. Starting on the ground and, if Djonn's ideas worked, perhaps from the sky.

After a few moments' silence, while Djonn made notes on a bone tablet, Ciel coughed, then began to sing again.

"*While monsters clashed and the groundbound watched as a city died . . .*" she started. A chill ran across my shoulders. *Died*. But I didn't say it.

Ciel nodded as we sang, then cleared her throat. Gestured to Nat: *You try.*

Nat cracked his knuckles again. Hesitated.

"*All that shook, all that fell was sky and bone,*" he finally sang. Ciel nodded.

"*So two went far and two climbed home.*"

That first line was the quake. One city knocking another to pieces. Ciel and Nat were singing now. Both of them working together to learn a song. I had tears in my eyes. This time I tried to learn the words, so I could sing it tomorrow and the next day, so the song could be shared and learned and acted upon.

I still worried that Nat would stick to his decision to tell the truth about how unpleasant the ground was. But I was relieved he'd changed his mind.

The singing went on late. A last moment together.

We offered new rhymes and ideas. Ciel discarded some, took others. I didn't mind. I loved watching her build a song. She would have made an excellent Singer, once. But no longer, for there were no more Singers.

We listened as, in Ciel's new song, the city changed from one that rose to one that moved. Where safety replaced luck.

I imagined the entire city on the move, climbing down the bone towers. Flying into the much-feared clouds. Ciel's song would help get them there. It would help, I hoped, keep us together.

*We're climbing to the horizon.*

The evacuation was a massive undertaking, even in my imagination. So many places we could lose people, or where our community, already so frayed at the edges, could come shearing apart.

"When the city dies," Nat added, "the towers will all fall. There will be no safety then."

Ciel added Nat's words to the tablet. "I'll figure out how to write that later. After the city dies. It would be bad luck before."

The roar and rumble of collapsing towers from the previous quake, the towers left in the north and south, all falling sideways and crashing into rubble, were too much to think about. I could remember the tumult but not see the actual fall. I could hear the noise, but not see the people. I could feel Sidra's hand on my arm, clinging tight, forming a net that kept our citizens from falling into the sky.

"We're looking out to the horizon," I repeated as Ciel wrote more down on the bone tablet.

Nat, beside me, echoed those words, the refrain for the middle of the song.

As work slowed around us, and the littlemouths faded into darkness, our voices carried over the meadow. We heard the other workers begin to pick up the tune again.

# 21

## KIRIT, BELOW

*⌇ The Skyshouter walked between a city abandoned
and a far-flung ridge ⌇*

If tending our dying city had been a waking nightmare, escaping a living city with Dix clinging to my back was my punishment for past wrongs.

"What does it mean that you're always on the run from one council or another, Skyshouter?" She clung tight, fingers digging in where my wingstraps once rested. "Once a citykiller, always a citykiller." She laughed.

Dix was a weight, a flesh-and-bone Lawsmarker.

I refused to let Wik carry her.

"I won't kill another city, Dix," I said as we descended the side of the giant beast. "No matter how much I want a home. We need to find a way to live like they do on Varat, without crushing or breaking one."

She laughed again. "Why not just take Varat?"

I didn't answer. Focused on putting my feet and hands in the right spots. Going down was even harder than going up. The speed with which the city was moving, led by its trained bone eaters, didn't make for easy climbing at all. My leg burned. So did my ears.

Worse, I kept looking, but couldn't see the healer below.

They'd moved quickly on the same ropes we were carefully navigating. Where had they gone?

"You are changed, Kirit," Dix said. "You've taken an awful lot of blame on yourself, haven't you?"

"You might try it," I whispered.

She hung close and murmured my fears back to me instead.

I focused again on placing my grips. The city's hide had good places to set them, long dry cracks and wide spans of wrinkles. When I misplaced a foothold or handhold, faltering only encouraged Dix to berate me more. She hissed at me.

Finally, I snapped. "I broke the Spire. I shouted it down. When we found the city, it had infections running from that spot. What blame do you take? What responsibility?"

"The city would have died soon," Dix said. "It was too big. The towers were too high. Even the Singers knew the towers' growth was slowing."

True, the most powerful Singers had known something was wrong. I remembered conversations in the Spire. Her words enraged me anyway. They hadn't done anything to help except try to maintain control. *Focus, Kirit.*

She continued, "The city's end terrified the Singers. It scared the blackwings more."

My hands burned, my leg throbbed, but afraid or not, I was not going to stop. We'd get off this city, then find another city to explore, quickly. And if we could leave Dix in the desert while we were at it, I wouldn't have any regrets. She'd used the blackwings' terror to gain power.

"Why would you want to make our ascendants repeat that?" Wik asked. He gestured to me, offering once again to carry the blackwing. The ground moved below, still slow enough to see details: silver-green spiked plants, a groundmouth hill.

I shook my head. Dix was my responsibility. My weight to carry.

Dix laughed until she hiccuped. "I'm asking the questions, Singer. You're not a good defender of the city any longer either. What happened to you?"

"*You* happened to us." Wik, descending next to me, did not mince words. "You destroyed the council, broke the city's trust. You enslaved the fledges. Your hands are covered in the city's blood. You stole from the new city. We don't want you to happen to anyone else."

She frowned. "Surely people can change?" Her voice sounded different in the warm, open air than it had above. The rhythmic pulse of the city's feet hit the ground far below, matching my heartbeat. Sweat ran into my eyes.

"What happened to 'once a citykiller, always a citykiller'?" Wik said.

I coughed. "Some do change." I hoped it was true.

The sky rolled past above us, a roiled gray cloud tinged with second sunset. Puffs of dust rose far below as each foot struck ground.

Even as we descended, the dizzy feeling of being in motion wouldn't go away. Wik looked green as well. Only Dix seemed unfazed. She hung on my back, arguing with us.

"We should leave her," Wik said again. "You could drop her."

"And drop the bird too," Dix said. "Her precious bird. Can't even fly, can it?" Her voice seemed to get louder the hotter it got.

"I've seen Maalik fly," I said. It was the truth. The whipperling had flown up several times, only to come right back to my hand. I looked at Wik. "Besides, we can't leave her here. She's our problem."

One hand below the other, gripping the fibrous ropes. The pull of Dix's weight against my grip.

Since she'd gathered her cache of stolen things off of Varat, Wik had been talking about dropping Dix. He'd proposed making her wear them as Lawsmarkers. Instead, he had to carry them, while I carried her.

I tired quickly, but I could feel Maalik moving in Dix's robe. The fast beat of his heart twitched against my right shoulder blade. Wik looked like he was chewing over ways to leave Dix sooner that involved her not being alive.

"Wik. We can't kill her either." No more killing, not if we could avoid it. Dix was half dead on her own already. And she was right: any fall would crush Maalik.

In the long pause between us, Dix simpered and looked pleadingly at me over my shoulder. I glared at her as well as I could.

"I might not have been thinking that," Wik grumbled, coming to a halt on the city's side. He made a show of checking our supplies and the things Dix had stolen. Finally he straightened. "She'll stay with us, As long as we can tie her to something so she won't get in the way or steal anything else."

Dix didn't look like she was going anywhere. The flight from Varat's cells had exhausted her. "When we get to the ground, you want to bind her hands, go ahead."

Wrapping her wounded arm tighter around my clavicle, Dix drew Maalik from her robes with her good hand. She began squeezing the bird. "No ropes."

Maalik sounded a soft trill. A warning of pain to come.

"No ropes," I said quickly.

She put the bird back in her robe and sighed. "Kirit, when will you learn? Caring about living things is inconvenient. It hurts too much when you lose them."

I couldn't not care. We needed Maalik. We'd get him back. Dix had to sleep sometime.

Maalik was Nat's favorite whipperling. His only surviving whipperling. He'd entrusted the bird to me, with the purpose of finding a home for all of us. If Maalik died, Nat's forgiveness when I walked away from the city could die with him. Maalik had to stay alive.

Our descent continued. Even Wik's hands and feet trembled with the effort. We were almost to the city's knee. Navigating over the joint would be tricky while it was in motion. The healer was nowhere in sight. And Dix wouldn't be quiet.

"You've lost your edge, Kirit. That sharpness that made you not care for consequences." Dix shook her head. The city's skin was baggier around the knee, harder to get a grip on. Dix was growing heavier. I needed a break, but I wanted to start looking for a new city quickly. And the map had indicated there was one close by.

She was wrong. I'd always cared. I just hadn't seen how widely consequences rippled. I gave in to her needling. "What do you want now, Dix?" Power? Control?

"I want a safe place for me and my people to live," Dix said.

"You have no people," Wik said. He reached the knee and tied a spidersilk line to a grip. Then threw the line down. It reached almost to the foot of the city's hind leg. "Go on. I'll take Dix for a while." We traded burdens.

So first Dix and Wik, and then I descended on the spidersilk. Wik navigated very well at first, but Dix's weight, and her arguments, wore on him, and he tired and slipped.

"Careful!" Dix cried.

"I should let you drop," Wik muttered. But for my sake, he wouldn't risk hurting Maalik any more than I would, and Dix knew it. Wik stopped and rested for a moment. Then began descending again.

She didn't listen. "You could help me capture Varat. You could live there, in that beauty."

"We would never do that." I spat the words.

The city slowed then, and the ground stopped moving so fast

beneath us. We inched down farther. The grueling descent made harder by Dix's nonstop taunting.

"We can't take her back home," Wik said. He was right, but his phrasing shook me.

Our dying city was still home to him. It hadn't been my home for so long. I wanted the fresh start.

"Who would you be in a new city, Kirit?" Dix wondered from Wik's back. "Afraid to kill anything, unwilling to fight? Certainly the city will need you to fight." As we neared the city's foot, puffs of red dust grew into small clouds that got in our eyes and mouths.

"Who will you be, Dix?" I replied. Annoyance crept into my voice. "The same as you've always been? Hungry for power? Or would you change, if you could? If we're allowing for people who have done so much harm to change."

She'd done it again, found the heart of my fears, and brought voice to them. If we found a new home, I wouldn't bring my past with me. I'd set it aside and become something new. I wanted to be one thing: one Kirit. Not Kirit Densira, Notower, Spire, Spirebreaker, Skyshouter, not Kirit Citykiller. I wanted to be me, to be home.

I wanted that home to be something safe, as Dix said she did. Something I could not kill.

"Come on." Wik tugged at my sleeve. "We're very close now." The ground's imperfections, the wide track that was the city's normal path, spread before us. The city itself began moving again, slowly at first. We were going to have to jump.

The motion of the city's foot swept dirt into the air. "Hurry," Wik said. "I can't see the ground. I don't know what a good landing spot is."

A white cloth fluttered on a small hill. The healer. Still helping us? "There." I pointed. Then I jumped, rolling away from my injured leg.

The impact hurt anyway. But when I stood, my leg seemed sturdy enough.

Dix and Wik landed not far from me, rolling in the dust from the city's motion.

The healer was nowhere to be seen. A piece of their shift was stuck to one of the silver plants. An accident? Maybe. I took it and tucked it into my satchel.

Wherever the healer was, I hoped to return the silk to them. To thank them, somehow.

When we regrouped by the hill, Dix surprised me by gently handing over Maalik without protest. "A promise is a promise."

I gave the bird a piece of the graincake I'd pocketed at the healer's on Varat. Smoothed his feathers. He lifted and flew a circle around my head, once, twice, and then settled on my shoulder and let loose a high-pitched screech at Dix.

Dix laughed. "You too, whipperling."

Wik turned to get his bearings so Dix couldn't see his amusement. It was hot on the ground, though not as hot as it had been when we first fell. "There," he pointed. "That's the city from the map."

We headed in that direction, hoping that this one would be uninhabited. Working our way around the groundmouths hiding in the dirt.

᠃ ᠃ ᠃

We'd made it a fair way over the horizon, back towards home, when Varat's bone eaters came for us.

Three dark birds cruised overhead. Their shadows patterned danger on the ground. I knew that danger. Braced for it.

"Wik!" I pulled on his sleeve. There was nowhere to hide in the open desert. The birds circled once, twice. One passed low enough that I could see its harness. Webbing covered its beak, reins reached to its crown, where a white-clothed city guard steered.

As the rider spotted us, the beast's claws reached out for me, extending, ready to grab. A cracked talon marred its left foot.

Wik let out a yell and threw his knife hard. The blade struck just above the talon, in a tender spot. The bird shrieked— a noise that sounded like the sky was tearing—and wheeled away so suddenly, the rider nearly dislodged and fell to the ground. The bone eater screeched again and spun away. Its mate followed.

Dix ran, but I stood my ground with Wik, daring them to come back.

Varat's citizens weren't used to fighting. Meantime, fighting was nearly all we knew. When they were out of sight, we turned towards the city again.

Dix's laughter trailed ahead of us like a lure. Then she yelled, "Watch out!"

I looked around wildly. "What?"

"Groundmouth," Wik said. He pointed to our left, where an invisible turmoil stirred up the dirt, just out of range. That had been close. Dix watched from a hill nearby.

Groundmouths made my skin crackle with fear, but no more than the bone eaters. I breathed deep. "If you can't point out danger clearly, and you can't go away, stay quiet," I muttered at Dix.

"I was nearly grabbed by one. You have no idea how frightening . . ." Dix trailed off. "Clouds. You made it across the desert. You have every idea." She sounded truly remorseful. That was something.

We kept moving, this time with Dix trailing behind. Bone eaters no longer pursued us. It didn't take us long to realize why. We'd crossed into the territory of a new city. This one was larger, judging by the deep tracks it had worn with its passage.

The tracks provided shade and shelter along the dusty route.

The ground was packed so hard within the ruts, groundmouths couldn't break through.

When we reached the end of the tracks, we discovered why this city had dragged such a deep passage. It was gravid. It had dug a hole in the ground, deeper than deep, to deposit its enormous eggs.

The three of us skidded to a halt before we fell into the hole, our dread and curiosity tugging at us.

"We could find another city. We don't have time to linger here." I tried to remember the locations of other cities from the map.

"No one in their right minds should disturb a city in that state," Wik agreed. "But it's too far to go around its head before nightfall." A half day passed as the city rumbled and groaned while we tried to stay out of its way. When it carefully pushed dirt up over three glistening eggs and settled itself on top of them, we walked around the city's side. There, worn ropes and pulleys hung from its flanks.

The city had settled and began to rumble, loudly. Its giant eyes slipped closed. Its towers, fairly thick and arranged in a long line down its back, outliers to either side stopped well short of the clouds.

"It would be tired after that." Dix cackled.

"Hush," Wik commanded. "We would rather it stayed that way."

The ropes and ladders that descended from the city's shoulders were old, ragged, and gray. The cams and pulleys were as complex as any wing.

What did these resemble? One of the brass plates featured pulleys. I pulled the plates from my satchel and located the right one. "Wik, look." The etching of pulleys also showed other machines, with wheels and wings set sideways. I wondered if we'd find those on this city too.

"The pulleys look ancient," Wik said.

"If this city's abandoned, perhaps we can live on it?" I suggested, though I wasn't sure how long a city might live atop a clutch of unhatched cities. "How long does a new city take to hatch?"

"Better question," Wik said. "What will new cities do to their surroundings when they hatch?"

He made a good point. "What do you think we should do now?"

Wik stopped and looked up at the city. "That's the first time you've ever asked me that question." His shoulders shook with laughter until tears welled in his eyes.

"Well?" Frustrated, heat rising on my cheeks, I pressed him. "The ground is as baffling now as the sky is to a fledge on their first flight. More so."

"Let's look?" Wik wiped his eyes. "Just us." He turned and eyed Dix, who had seated herself on the ground in the shade. "If she leaves now, she can't bother the people on Varat. I'm fine with not helping her climb up, are you?"

I nodded. It would be a welcome relief not having Dix with us.

"Come back soon?" Dix called from below, almost plaintively. She began to hum an old song, "The Bone Forest."

Dix's tune pulled me like an errant wind into the past. I heard the desire to survive at any cost in each note. And I heard something else also. Hope. Making a song for the future to learn and sing was a hopeful act, no matter what.

Our songs would have to change, but that secret hope was part of who we were, all of us.

I began to hum, too.

# 22

## NAT, MIDCLOUD

*⌒ The first kites descended, the blackwings found
fear ⌒*

As morning rain pattered the cave mouth and blew spray into
the cave, we prepared to let the first kite go.

I sat with Elna and held her hand. Her skin felt warm and
soft as ash. She was well enough to be moved, but still fever-
ish. "I'll see you soon," I whispered.

She smiled up at me. "You will. After you keep the people of
this city safe."

"And you'll watch out for my family," I told her.

My breath hitched seeing her tucked into the litter we'd
made. I'd come so close to losing her, losing them all. "And you."
I pulled close Ceetcee and Beliak, encircling the baby sleeping
slung at his chest. "Keep my mother safe. And yourselves."

Then I kissed each of them, Elna twice on the forehead. I
touched the baby's scalp once more.

My knuckles white on the litter, I helped lift it to where the
guards stood ready to fly.

The first group wouldn't descend until after the rain ceased,
but then their descent would be unstoppable. The pulleys had
been set, the kite fully rigged.

"I'll come back up, if I can," Ciel said, leaning on her brother's
shoulder. She squeezed my fingers too.

Moc looked at her, dry-eyed. "You are the one that's always leaving now," he said. "I wish I was."

Ciel's mouth opened and shut like a baby bird. "You're needed here more. You're strong enough to work the pulleys."

"I'm proud to do that for you." Moc kicked the dirt of the cave with a silk-wrapped foot. "But next time, I'll do the leaving."

She smoothed his hair. "I know."

I bowed to Ciel. "Risen. You have charge of my family now." *And my heart. And all my secrets.* I tilted my chin in the direction of the towers where the pulleys had been set. "Stay as far from the city as you can. Be ready to run."

"Put it in the song," Ciel said. "Everyone deserves to know. Promise me that?"

I wrote down the lines on the bone tablet. "I promise. They'll know as soon as you signal you're safe on the ground."

At the last minute, Ciel pressed a furled fern into Macal's hand. It resembled the spiral symbol for "home," or an old Spire mark. "When I stayed at Mondarath, after the Spire fell, I learned that Sidra loved green. Tell her we'll see her soon."

Macal nodded. "I'll deliver it."

Outside, the rain began again. Macal and I would lose our chance, especially if the weather worsened and we waited much longer. A brighter line of yellow among rolls of gray signaled a break in the rain line. If we left now, we might be able to fly with it for some time.

"Nat," Macal said, using his voice like a winghook to lift me away from my family.

"I'm ready," I said. But I was not. I'd never be ready.

I stepped back and watched my family and the guards bearing Elna disappear in the mist.

Macal and I checked each others' wingstraps, tightening them for the long climb up the vents. I reviewed the map Aliati had shared with us, marking blackwing towers and free towers. She'd given Macal his knife back, too.

When we were ready, we leapt from the cave mouth: me leading, Macal following.

We found a fast gust quickly. Aimed for the light-streaked break in the clouds.

The wind buffeted us as we tried to stay between rain lines. My hair and face grew damp with mist.

Above us were so many things I had missed. Blue sky and flying, bone-white towers and wind. The carvings and games and our history. The way we had raised ourselves up. The stars.

I whistled The Rise's melody, and Macal whistled it back across the wind.

We would give all of this up again for the horizon.

"Ready?" Macal whistled now.

"In a generation, The Rise won't have meaning." With the weather all around us, I wasn't sure Macal could hear me.

"Soon there will be new meaning to our songs. We'll sing about descending, together, and living. We'll sing Ciel's songs instead." Macal sounded so confident.

Finally, I turned for the ghost tower and Macal followed. When we landed, I pointed out the place where I'd watched a skymouth battle a bone eater, so long ago. "There was a cave, just there. You'd almost always see one."

We rested for a long time, watching, but we saw no sky-mouths. Aliati was right; they'd gone. We couldn't slow down. I'd been right to keep the wind a secret a little longer.

"We won't be welcomed, you know," I told Macal. "You're flying with a Lawsbreaker." It had been so long since I'd faced the city's justice. So long since I'd given everything up to protect my family.

Macal nodded. "A Lawsbreaker and a councilor, working together. Whatever reception we get, we'll make do. Let's go."

It was getting darker, but Macal could echo. That got us closer to the cloudtop.

After so long in the gray undercloud, would the sun dazzle my eyes in the open sky? Would the stars?

Would my family miss the light and the stars as much as I had?

As we slowly circled up, Macal caught me looking down. "They'll be fine," he called.

"I hope so." They had to be.

Spotting a stronger draft, I angled my wings to ride it. Macal followed. We caught a strong vent circling up. That much wind, and me buoyed by it, was exhilarating.

But the wind bore a scent of rot with it, from below. And smoke, though I could not tell from where. We climbed slowly until the air cleared, the sky seemed brighter, and the shadows almost disappeared.

Above us, the shifting light of sunrise crested above the cloud.

I stared at it. "It's so beautiful."

"I've seen those who'd fled their towers stare at a wingset or food like you're staring at the sun, Nat. Is it that bad down below?" Macal asked, concern in his voice.

"It doesn't matter," I replied. "There's no other way. And there's no time to debate."

Macal circled me. "True. And I worry spreading the news one tower at a time will be too slow. Especially after one blackwings faction has worked so hard to divide the towers, to remove the markets, to keep them from sharing news."

"We need to gather people instead," I suggested. I angled my left wing and circled too, until we were a slow whirlwind. The cloud below us began to sift and follow in our wake.

We tossed ideas through the air.

"We could call a Conclave, close to the Spire. Or set up a

plinth. Or we could use the song, and spread it, use the blackwings too."

I didn't like the idea of a Conclave. It was dangerously
close to what Aliati said Rya was already fighting. And a plinth
was too risky. Too easy to attack.

Macal quieted for a moment. The edges of our wings fluttered
noisily in the wind as we turned. "We could have a market. An
illegal one."

I chuckled. "We'd get blackwings and nonblackwings attend-
ing. Maybe Rya would like to host a market?"

"From my only meeting with Rya, I think it's possible." Macal broke off circling and caught another vent up towards the
towers. "If we can find her, or other likeminded blackwings."

I curved my right wing and followed Macal.

When the net fell over me, sticky and smelling of old muzz,
I was just coming out of my turn.

"Finding blackwings will be easy, Lawsbreakers," a singsong
voice said. A child's voice. Macal was caught in the same net.
He struggled and cursed by my side.

And then we were dragged kicking and shouting in the
nets up through the last shreds of cloud, into the blinding light
of day.

ᘯ  ᘯ  ᘯ

They dumped us on a towertop. Dropped the net around Macal and then me.

I tensed, ready for a fight. "You're not taking our wings. You
won't throw us from the tower."

The blackwings made no move to do so. They didn't reach
for us, didn't demand our grips, our weapons.

The net spread on the bone towertop, a knotwork of fiber
open like an unset trap.

But up close, our captors' clothing revealed colorful mending and patches. Their wings were colored with burnt bone and blacking. They weren't blackwings at all. These weren't the guardians of the southwest; these were scavengers, masquerading.

As it dawned on me that we weren't about to be thrown down in order to appease the city, our companions pulled their hoods back. One coughed into a hand to cover a grin.

Scavengers for sure.

"Aliati asked us to look out for you. To help you," one said.

I'd never been so glad for Aliati's help. "She didn't mention you to us."

The lead scavenger chuckled. "We hadn't decided yet. But Aliati spoke for you. And this one"—the scavenger gestured to Macal—"helped rescue one of our fledges." The scavenger gestured at a young woman who held a small girl tightly. "Now we've decided."

Macal looked at me and then at their still-hooded leader like they were crazy. "What was your purpose in netting us? We were coming to find *you*."

"It was faster," said the leader. "Plus it's easier to get through the blackwings' lines if we look like them." Brushing back the hood, she revealed herself.

"Raq," Macal said, surprised.

Now the other "blackwings" began folding up the net. Some near Raq chuckled knowingly. "Helps for all sorts of things." Their bags were heavy and full.

The towertop where we stood was half cracked. I imagined I felt a slight shift when someone stepped wrong. "Is this tower unstable lower down?"

I wasn't surprised to see her shake her head and smile.

"The tower's blackwings asked for someone to come and check the tower for stability," one of the scavengers said. "We—

well, our artifex"—and there she pointed at another scavenger, who waved—"helped check it and found it *very* unstable."

I had to laugh. "I bet you did." The tower was safe after all. For now.

The scavengers secured a ladder to the uncracked side of the towertop and began to descend to a safer tier. Relief washed over me. I hadn't known I was holding myself so tensely.

Raq put her hand on my arm, and I jumped a little. "Why isn't Aliati with you?" She squinted into the clouds. "Did she take a different route?"

Macal answered first. "She stayed in the midcloud to prepare for the refugees."

"She's helping with the evacuation, building kites," I hastened to add.

Raq narrowed her eyes, trying to understand. "Like bridges," Macal said. "But bigger, and they float."

Raq's eyes lost their sharp focus for a moment. "All right." She was small and dark haired, with skin like burnt bone. Her long lashes and quick smile made her seem young, but she had wind-burn lines around her eyes that came with age. That or many more days and nights spent out in the wind than most tower citizens.

More scavengers appeared, climbing down from above, swooping in and landing with great daring and little care for safety. They were young, mostly, but all were scarred and weather-worn, their clothes and markers a jumble of all towers and no tower at all.

The lower tiers were filled with bags of abandoned items, tools, and silks. Things no one wanted to carry, the scavengers gathered up.

Raq caught Macal and me staring at the goods. "Whatever you need, we're selling. Not much food, though," she said quietly. "Or at least, not enough."

That was likely true all over. "We'll figure it out once we're below."

Raq looked at us, eyes narrowed. "We're coming with you?"

"You are," Macal said. "We need your supplies. People will be glad to see you." Raq didn't seem surprised that we had plans for these goods.

Her expression didn't change. She didn't like what we had to say, but if they wanted food, there wasn't any doubt they'd need to trade just the same. Raq looked from the supplies to the sky beyond the tier. Finally she gave a sigh and a short nod. "Fair."

"You can sell supplies, not give them away. I'll help set a price," Macal pressed.

Raq grinned and her scavengers let out a hoot. "Even more fair."

I let my breath out, relieved again. Macal was good at this. As more scavengers came in over the balcony, he won them over too.

So many of them gathered together on a single tower, instead of blending in to the community or hiding below, made a raucous bunch. Their glee at occupying a whole tower—or stealing one—was tempered, it seemed, by a bit of discomfort at close quarters with so many other scavengers. Often they took off just to be alone in the sky.

The very things we loved in our towers—community and support—were not what the scavengers valued. But they seemed to love this tower.

Of course, the tower had been abandoned because it might fall, and of course it was in the southwest, smack in the middle of enemy territory.

"What can we get for you now?" Raq laughed. Her cohort slowed to listen.

"We need the blackwings," I said. We'd been ready to confront them right at their heart, on Grigrit, before we were taken.

Raq looked at us as if we were ancient and cloudtouched. "You want the Aivans. Rya has disavowed Conclaves and is pressing for bigger changes. The blackwings aren't as organized."

"What's changed?"

"The two factions? They needed strong leaders. Rya's one, but the others are still looking for someone they believe in. It's risky to trust anyone right now, but I can take you to Rya."

What game was Raq playing? "What's the trade?"

"You get us down safely. We'll help you." Raq didn't blink. "We want to go with the first groups, not the last."

The first group had already departed, but they could go with the next group. I made a quick count. Ten scavengers, plus families. That might be possible. "Definitely," I said. "As long as two of your group work the pulleys with our people. They can go down on the next kite." We'd work out the rest of the details later.

Macal looked at them and at me. "You sure?" His eyes said way more: *Don't make promises you can't keep.*

But I'd already lied to get us moving faster. No turning back. "I'm sure." I met his eyes, then Raq's.

Raq's dark robe fluttered in the breeze, billowing around her wingstraps. "Rya's got their attention. She's dynamic, radical, and strong willed, like her father. She's got a tough group of former blackwings to keep in check, but she's a good leader. You want her."

In what way was Rya radical? I remembered her from a long-ago wingfight, before Kirit was taken to the Spire. Macal said she'd argued against the Conclave. Raq said she'd called her guard Aivans. Names revealed a lot about a person, or a group: Nightwing, blackwing, *Skyshouter, Spirebreaker, Brokenwings, Magister, Singer.*

"She believes that the community's changing into something more independent, like birds," Raq said. "She's one for drama, for sure. Wears a kavik skull and feathers."

Macal nodded. "Birds won't like the idea of going below the clouds."

*Birds would hate not being able to fly even more.* "They might not like it, but they need to do it anyway. How do we convince them to help, knowing this?" I asked.

"We don't. We say, 'We have to leave.' Everyone who doesn't, dies. End of discussion," Raq said. "Especially if they think they don't need us. There are too many good people headed below to sacrifice for people who don't want to leave the sky."

If it weren't for my family, I would understand the temptation to stay. All around the tier we stood on, the blue, birdless sky and straight sweep of clouds below it was home. I'd missed it. But now I knew I'd be home when I was with my family.

Macal reached out to Raq. "Before the other blackwing factions attack the northwest, can one of your scavengers get a message to them?"

She laughed and nodded. "We'll send some back here for your market too, if they'll come."

"What are you doing?" I asked Macal.

"Making sure we talk to everyone." He looked at me. "You were right, you know. Sometimes you do need to bend the truth."

I frowned, my brows knitting together. "You want me tell everyone the truth about the ground, while you're bending facts?" My eyes narrowed farther. He was Spire-born, raised a Singer, trained in manipulating everything. "How can I trust you now?"

I heard Ciel's song in my head.

*All that shook, all that fell was sky and bone* . . .

The words echoed as the tower seemed to sway.

"You either trust me or don't. I will do the same," Macal said. Scavengers were looking at us.

He had a point, but I had more concerns. "If the blackwings and Aivans won't come, won't listen? What then?"

"They'll follow us below once they know what's at stake." Macal seemed so sure. "The market should be all we need, plus we'll start salting the wind with rumors of what you have to trade. With trade goods from all over, some lighter-than-air."

Raq's second in command actually glared at him. "Magister, you're putting people in danger. Citizens. There hasn't been a market in the southwest since the blackwings began deciding who got what, and at what cost, and keeping the best for themselves. They'll fight to maintain that." She spat onto the bone towertop.

"I'll bet you benefited from that economy!" Macal said.

I wanted to swat him. But the scavenger laughed. "Immensely."

"They might come for a fight," I said, "but they'll leave with an evacuation plan."

"And you will too," Macal said.

Raq crossed her arms over her wingstraps. "We'll see." She began organizing the scavengers. "There's one cache of honey and stone fruits left. Get it from the silkspider towers."

"Those towers need messages taken to them anyway; and a new song." I gave Raq the chips with verses from Ciel's song. The one that said *escape now, go down,* and *we are ready for you* on the back.

"Absolutely." Raq checked her wings and tightened her straps.

Macal and I watched her go. It would have to be enough. We might not be able to convince everyone, but the city's population would not be trapped here unaware. A market would let us spread the word. We'd taken a risk, bargaining with scavengers, but risk was all we had left.

I pushed the scavengers' net aside and began to prepare.

# 23

## MACAL, ABOVE

*⮕ A market, a coup, a quake; the clouds grew far too
near ⮕*

That afternoon, tower citizens came in formations of three and
more, flying in chevrons and darts. Their patterns were poorly
organized. They flew our way on thin scraps of rumor, hoping
to be first at the market.

We scanned the sky for blackwings—and Aivans—and saw
none yet.

Nat raised an eyebrow and looked at Raq.

"Families need supplies for themselves before the blackwings
take the rest," she said, staring at the cloudtop. "We might have
misled the blackwing factions as to which tower. They'll find
it. Rumor has it the market's selling hidden goods as well.
Lighter-than-air. Stolen alembics. And that there was a Lawsbreaker here." Nat. That wasn't a rumor.

The risks we were taking flew in the face of caution. We
couldn't take a safe breeze now, though.

The first formations landed on the balcony. Citizens furled
their wings and began looking through the assembled gear
and scavenged items. "Do you have apples?" one young man
asked. His eyes were deep set in the shadow of his brow.

"Not yet," said a nearby scavenger.

As citizens milled, I heard Raq begin to sing. Typical market fare, "Corwin and the Nest of Thieves," "The Bone Forest." But then she shifted it ever so subtly, to another song, a new one. A piece of Ciel's new song. I looked for Nat. "She learns fast."

As I took a small sack of stone fruit from one of the scavengers, he smiled. "She does."

How fast could a song spread? If people were hungry for it, maybe fast enough.

"What's that?" one visitor whispered to me as she held a scrap of silk. "I've never heard it before."

"Song called 'Horizon,'" I heard her neighbor say. "It's new."

The visitor clenched the silk tighter. "We need food, not songs."

"Stone fruit?" I asked like a vendor from Mondarath. Soon I was bartering as well as Sidra, and coincidentally talking about the towers, the city, the need to head lower for safety. A crowd grew around me, and I lost sight of Nat. I was good at this. I learned fast too.

People began elbowing, protesting the tight spaces of the tier in the confines of market. I recognized tower marks woven into braids, strung across necks: Laria, Varu, Bissel, Grigrit, Haim, Naza. Much of the surviving southwest. A few northeastern towers too.

"Good outreach," I whispered to Raq. "Enough to get word of the evacuation spread."

"Not yet," she whispered back, her hand on my elbow. She was right. We had to wait for the last groups, the ones marking the horizon now with dark wings. Blackwings.

"Here they come," Raq said.

The blackwings flew in tight fighting formations: hawk and bee. Some landed, but others circled, wings locked, bows drawn. Ready to take what they wanted and go.

The Aivans emerged from the crowd—which explained the suddenly congested spaces—pulling back their green and blue cloaks to reveal black feathers in their hair and on their shoulders. They formed a knot in the market.

As the first faction of blackwings landed, Rya stepped from the knot. "This market is ours. These cloudbound too."

The sunlight struck her silk wings and seemed to dance there. She'd oiled the feathers attached to her clothing, and the result cast a kind of glow around her shoulders.

The blackwings milled, waiting. Tense.

"Who speaks for you?" Rya asked.

"You'd like to know, wouldn't you?" a Laria blackwing snapped back. "Maybe no one does. Maybe we speak for ourselves."

Rya didn't bristle. Her expression remained controlled. "I think you can't agree on a leader, so you all came."

She turned her back on them, while her captains flanked the group. In the air beyond the tower, more of Rya's Aivans circled the blackwings. The market hushed, watching the coup.

Rya seemed to ignore it, turning to Raq, her gaze passing over Nat appraisingly, like a cool wind. Over me as well. "The lighter-than-air?" she demanded.

"It's safe," Raq said. "We want to barter with you, not have it stolen from us."

"As *you* stole it from us?" the Laria blackwing said. "And then lost our quadrant leader on your northern tower raid?"

Rya did not look at me. "He was taken in battle, honorably."

The Laria blackwings began opening bags and lifting baskets.

"Enough." Not waiting for them to listen, I gently pulled a basket from black-robed arms. Rya held out a hand to stay a blackwing's knife. Under her watch, I continued my business, returning things to the market. Inside the basket, metal knives and rare glass teeth glinted; nearby, wingsets from the north leaned against baskets filled—at least at the very top—with Naza silk. I could sense the knife that was hidden in each palm. I could feel the pull of want here. The menace of it.

"The people will need these things, and very soon," Nat pitched his voice so that the entire market tier could hear him. "The city is in grave danger. We must prepare. Tower by tower."

A ripple of surprise spread through the crowd.

We certainly had everyone's attention now. For better and worse.

"Why should we listen to a cloudbound Lawsbreaker?" A blackwing circled Nat. The point of her nose brushed Nat's ear; her breath lifted his hair. Nat didn't blink. "I know who you are, Nat Brokenwings. Cloudbound. Why should we care what you say?"

His fingers curled tighter, as if around a knife. Beside me, Rya's arm muscles flexed as she tightened her grip on something in her sleeve. No one else on the towertop moved, besides Nat and the blackwing.

"Cloudbound, but not dead, and more than just returned," Nat said, pushing the blackwing gently back. Raq and I stepped back as well, and Nat moved into the wider space that was left in the center of the market. "I've been to the ground."

"Like in the song," someone nearby whispered.

Rya tilted her head, curious but wary. "There is no ground."

The Laria blackwing raised her knife to Nat's throat. "So you are a liar and a murderer."

I pressed my own blade to the blackwing's side. "Not today."

Quick as that, we stood at the edge of a fight. Just as we'd planned.

I turned to Rya. "Time for truths. Dix killed your father, and now she's dead herself. Nat fell through the clouds with Kirit and Wik and Ciel. The fall broke them, but they didn't die. They walked on the ground. They saw what the city is. And what it's become. They came back to save us."

The market tier quieted, tense and waiting.

Nat sketched the city in the air with his hands. He described the bone eaters and how they fed the city. The market-goers paid rapt attention, including the blackwings and Rya's Aivans.

Sweat began to gather between my shoulder blades, beneath my wingstraps. It itched. Instead of scratching, I pressed my hands together, saying, "Our towers crushed the city. And then another city attacked, killing it. Truth: our city will collapse. We have to leave it, now."

"This is a tale for scaring fledges." Rya snorted. Both factions of blackwings did the same. Rya tilted her head and beckoned an associate forward. "Don't you think?"

An Aivan laughed, and was quickly hushed.

I had to win them back. "What did you feel when the towers collapsed?" I paused as faces turned ashen and fighters looked at one another, remembering. "In the clouds, they felt only a little shaking. It is safer down there. Lower is safer right now. The rest we can prove to you in time."

Nat turned to Rya, hands out, palms up. "For the sake of your father and what he sacrificed, come with us. Convince your people to help evacuate the towers. We can't do this without working together. We need you. You need us."

"We could fly down and see if you're telling the truth. Seems the clouds don't hold enough danger to kill you once and for all." Rya's voice was sharp.

"You might die trying," Nat said. "There's no time. The city could fall any day now."

The marketplace rumbled with dissent. "I'm not leaving."

"You couldn't get me to go into the clouds for anything."

"We will confer," Rya said, waving a hand to include the blackwings as well as her own group. "We'll send our decision with a bird."

We were losing them.

Nat sped ahead. Put a hand on Rya's shoulder. She stiffened, and her guards tried to pull him away. He didn't pause. "You don't want to leave the city, I understand. I didn't either. I dreamed of clear blue skies while I was in the clouds. Dreamed harder once I was on the ground. All I wanted to do was see the stars again."

At Rya's signal, the guards released him, but they whispered, even more unconvinced. *Damage done, Nat. Don't make it worse.*

But they hadn't walked away. Neither they nor the others from their towers had moved. They were listening again.

"No stars?" an older woman asked, holding a very thin child.

"Do you know what's worse than no stars?" Nat began. They leaned in, listening again. "Dying is worse. I want to live. I want the people I love to live. To see my family again," he said. "You do too. The city will roll, the towers, collapse. Soon. We have get everyone to go down before that happens."

Nat spoke to the crowd, but I kept my eyes on Rya. She continued to circle us both until she met my eyes again. Behind her, a young man, tall and angular like her, brown eyes, darker skin. Unsmiling. He'd tied a black feather to his wing.

Rya whistled to him, and he whistled back, an inquisitive note on the end. I'd heard their whistle code at Mondarath, but I still did not understand it.

Not knowing what they said either, Nat shifted from one foot to the other. The scavengers behind me began to whisper. Blackwings from both factions looked uncomfortable, but waited. Somehow, Rya had captured their attention. Would she lead them? Would she come with us?

We needed to tip the balance. But how?

"I need a guarantee," Rya said. "Something that will be a powerful symbol to the city that you respect me." She did not meet my eyes.

*I let you go free,* I nearly said, but Nat spoke first.

"You want a Lawsbreaker as a guarantee? I will do what you require," he said. "Do what we ask, and you can put Lawsmarkers on my wings." There was an audible gasp from the blackwings. I bit my lip, hoping that Rya still rejected Conclaves, as I'd once told Nat, below.

He was risking everything, on my word.

Once Elna had stood up against a city and spoken her mind. Now Nat had done the same.

"What is it that you ask?" Rya's captain said.

Nat spoke again. "Help us move as many people into the cloud and down as we can, taking as many supplies as possible. Bring your people. Come downtower, into the clouds with us. And then lower. And take me as your guarantee that you will be respected."

Rya turned from us then, and I could see the dark feathers that now edged her silk wings and the collar of her robe. She'd woven them into her hair too: gryphon feathers. She beckoned the other factions to her side, and amazingly, they came. Rya held their gazes. Spoke to them, and then turned to us.

"We do not believe you."

The wind whistled across the towertop, flapping robes, lifting the feathers on Rya's wingframe. A piece of scavenged metal blew sideways with a rippling sound. It crashed as it struck one of the baskets. The smell of stone fruit, mashed to a pulp, mixed with the wind.

Rya's people began to gather up supplies. The other faction started to do the same. We were losing them again. Nat looked at me, pleading. Unwilling to give up.

I spoke fast. "We need you, Rya. To help lead the city. You are a brave fighter, and a lucky one." I put emphasis on the word *lucky*. She blinked slowly. She knew what I'd meant.

Nat had offered himself up as a Lawsbreaker. Now I offered Rya a role as a city leader and a chance to clear her unspoken debt to me. "We need you to help organize the city's escape. You will work directly with me."

I'd saved her, and I'd let her go on the gusts beyond the city. Would she honor this?

After a long pause, Rya said, "We would fight well together." A small quirk to her frown.

We had already done so, it was true.

As I pleaded with Rya to listen and not turn away, two black-wings landed with Sidra flying between them. Suddenly, I felt as if the air had been kicked from my stomach. Sidra, arms bound, wings furled tight and carried by a blackwing. A bruise was beginning to color her eye.

The blackwings had taken the northwest. She'd fought hard.

Rya saw it too, before the blackwings did. Her eyes widened for a brief moment. Then she turned to us, her jaw clenched. The power balance was shifting.

She needed to act, or lose her chance, whether she believed us or not.

The blackwings had brought Sidra because we'd asked the scavengers to pass her a message. They'd thought she was important, but did not know fully how. I could not go to her. Not until we had a deal. She raised her eyes and saw me. Smiled for a moment. Not free, but safe. That was enough, for now.

I turned, as if to speak to the other faction, but then dove back into the argument, cutting between both groups. "Rya, you control the towers in the southwest. You're responsible for those people. You *must* help them move."

Rya shook her head slowly back and forth, assessing the citizens who looked at her closely now, the blackwings, her Aivans. "We will take responsibility for those towers, then."

"And the others too," I said. "All or nothing." *Remember how we once helped you, Rya.*

"And then what? We could take the lighter-than-air and fly our people higher instead."

A blackwing muttered, "Leading all the towers? Her?"

Rya looked across the tier at Nat and then at me. She inclined her head in agreement.

I answered the blackwing, "Yes, all the towers. Rya is taking charge."

A thing said by a city councilor could still ripple out and create change. The crowded tier looked at Rya with expectation. And this time, she did not falter.

"I take this responsibility in the name of the Aivans. This is a time of emergency. I'll guide you, and keep you safe."

Standing as close to her as I did, I saw her fingers shake. Heard her draw a nervous breath. Everyone else saw a leader.

We would need to work together.

"You cannot take them higher," I said. "You don't have enough lighter-than-air, or food for everyone. You would have to choose. Down is better, for everyone."

Rya nodded, accepting the argument. But another blackwing, again very young, shouted, "We can hunt the skies!"

"How many of you can live on a plinth, do you think?" I asked. "And for how long? You'll be safer, for longer, on the ground."

Nat reached into a pocket of his robe and held out the fistful of red soil, mashing it in his fingers, letting it sift out and color the tower floor. "This is what's below the clouds. There are other cities below, many of them. Most aren't as big as ours, but they aren't dying. There are places to hunt." He didn't mention for what. "And there's more space. Space enough for everyone."

That last item got their attention. Space to spread out.

One of the blackwings from the northwest shouted, "What about—"

Rya spoke quickly, before they could finish the thought. "I will take the lead on the move. We will guide our people down, in case you are right. What do you need from the towers?"

Rya became, in that moment, the face of the evacuation. She

and I would share the responsibility. She solidified her control of the blackwings. And she allowed Nat and me to tell her and the city our plan.

"Descent in stages," I said. "Occupying towers near a smuggler's cave, with hang-sacks for sleeping. We'll harvest lighter-than-air above the clouds, with several crews up here to do the work. Nat will lead you down."

At a look from Rya, I changed my words. "Escort. Nat will escort you down."

She acquiesced. "Is there no lighter-than-air harvesting in the cloud?" Rya looked confused.

"Our artifexes believe heartbone from newer growth is stronger and easier to tap," I said.

Rya looked satisfied with that. She took several volunteers who wanted to stay and assigned them to my crews. Then she sent the rest of her Aivans and blackwings back to their towers. They were all her blackwings now, and at least for the near future. She'd won, and she knew it. And we'd helped her.

She smiled at me. "We will work together, you and I." I breathed a sigh of relief.

"And you, Lawsbreaker." Rya smiled at Nat. "I will find you when I need you. You won't be far." She affixed a large Lawsmark and a black feather to Nat's shoulder. The quill poked up through his robe. "You are mine now, an example to all the Lawsbreakers below." Her voice carried across the tier. The citizens who had stayed would remember this, and the power she wielded.

Had I miscalculated? If Rya tried, she could take over everything by the time she reached the ground. Ceetcee, Beliak, and Ciel might be only subjects in her eyes, especially if Nat was forfeit.

She winked at me. "You see, Macal? We can work together."

I tried to set my worry aside.

Raq signaled two scavengers, who listened carefully to her whispered directions, then took off, three more scavengers following. We'd need everything that the scavengers could pull from the towers on our descent, and more.

When we finished, I sat quietly on the edge of the tower, wings half furled, next to Sidra. I closed my eyes, put my arm around her shoulder. "You are safe. You are free."

Sidra whispered in my ear, "I am yours." Brushed my cheek with her thumb.

I leaned into her touch. Carved the feel of it on my memory. *This. This is what I fly for.*

Behind us, Nat coughed. I opened my eyes while Sidra kept hers closed. "Yes, Nat?"

He sat down on my other side, our pinions nearly touching. "Was that a good idea? Being so honest with them?"

I sighed. "*You* didn't tell them everything."

"I will. Soon."

I was right. He had been holding back.

I looked at him. "You did the right thing. You made them want to go. They'll bring supplies until we can find food and water. We can last for days. If you need help with them, ask Urie."

Frowning, he bit into a stone fruit he'd saved from the market. Chewed.

Finally I said, "When will you tell them?" *When will you tell me?*

He drew a long breath. "There's no wind strong enough to lift a wingset, at least not at ground level. Once we go down, we'll be stuck below."

Sidra sucked in her breath through her nose and then let it out slowly through her mouth.

I tightened my grip on Sidra's shoulder and stared out at the lightning sparking the clouds below. At the spare dark purpling the cloudtop.

How could he keep that a secret from the city? From me?

But I'd done the same. Telling the blackwings just enough to get them moving.

That was our priority now.

"How much longer do we have?" Sidra asked. We were past Allsuns. Nat had said only days.

I shook my head. "We can't delay." Two moons would be up soon. The city below would run out of food, especially if the birds were gone. More, it could topple any day. "I'll bring the last group down when we're finished here. Then try to encourage the holdouts. Take Sidra downtower for me." I said it quickly, hoping Nat would understand.

He did, and stood, holding out his hand to help Sidra up. I clasped his shoulder, grateful.

Sidra looked at him in horror. Then at me. "I will not go down. Not without you."

"You must." I said it calmly, as if I hadn't been arguing with myself about it.

She stared at me. The stubborn tilt of her head told me she was ready for a fight herself. "No."

I took her hands. "My heart." I pressed Ciel's gift: a fiddlehead into her palm. "You have to. Someone needs to lead them, and someone needs to stay here for now. They won't follow Raq, and if you don't go, they may follow Rya right off a balcony."

"We could both lead them. You and I. At least you know how. Don't be a hero, Macal. Be a leader." She spoke slowly, angrily.

"You know how. Raq knows where to go in the clouds. Nat knows the ground. Go with them." My voice broke. "I will follow." I was not being a hero.

I was leading.

In the end, Sidra gave in. I held her hand until she leapt from the balcony one last time, and glided in circles towards the cloudtop.

Artifexes dragging weighted nets full of lighter-than-air followed her. As I watched Sidra's bright wings disappear, I hoped we could do this right.

Nat reached out and clasped my arm. "We'll save the city as best we can. Whether it wants us to or not." Then he leapt from the tower and followed Sidra down.

All around me, each tower learned its fate from scavengers and the Aivan-blackwings. Ciel's song began to spread.

Bone horns sounded long and low across the sky as the city began to decide what to keep, and what to leave.

# 24

## KIRIT, BELOW

*⁀ A city forgotten, the Nightwing walked away. ⁀*

Pulleys adorned the sleeping creature's back like ancient beads draping a tower resident's wings. We used them to drag ourselves over one massive shoulder.

When we reached the top, Wik brushed the dirt and rope fragments off his hands, then mine. His fingers felt rough on my skin.

Below us, the beast began to snore in earnest. Its rumbles nearly shook us off our feet. I crouched near an assembly of cleats and pulleys and held on.

"Even as old as they are, these might help us," I said, looking carefully at the bone rollers and feeds that held the lines steady and kept them moving slow and easy. They didn't look as if they would come free of the weatherworn assembly of knots and splices easily. Who had built them? Where had they gone? We heard no noises as we had on Varat, saw no evidence of recent inhabitants.

How could I carry that equipment? I'd need bone hooks, a net. Another flier on my wingtip. *No.* I closed my eyes and swallowed hard against the ache of what was gone.

That was a question for a former me.

But I still wanted the tools, though the rope was too thick to cut.

The city slept on, not noticing us.

It felt good to be up high again. Safer. Despite the rumbling.

"We could stay here," Wik said. "At least until the eggs hatch." He looked ready for a rest also.

"And then where would we go?" I didn't want to be around when a new city hatched. I gave the towers that stretched almost to the clouds a long appraising look. "Up? Like our ancestors?"

A flash of white near the bone ridge caught my eye. Then disappeared.

"You're right," Wik said, staring at a small shape on the horizon. According to the map at Varat, that was the direction our city lay.

Far in the other direction was a dark ridge that seemed to ring the entire horizon. "These tools could help our people. But we have no way of getting tools to the city." His jaw clenched and unclenched. "We just need to find a good place to make a home." Another flutter of white.

This time I was sure I saw it. "Did you see?" I pointed, just as a figure in a white shift appeared, ducking between spurs of bone. "There's someone here."

Wik, cautious as ever, said, "If there's one, there may be more."

There was a silence as we looked across the ridge, then headed for the figure. My leg cramped, and I stopped to knead the calf.

"I can't go much faster," I finally admitted.

"It's all right," Wik said. "Just give it time."

We were running out of time. How could I give any? "The city needs us to find a home. A new one, because the one we found, the one with artifexes and healers, had already found Dix."

Wik looked down over the city's side, as if a bone eater might have carried Dix away. I looked too. "She was right, you know."

Leaning unsettled my pack, and the strap slid across my shoulder. I heard a quiet squawk. Maalik poked his head from my cloak when we began walking again.

I held out a finger. He jumped on it and chirped at me. Then flew to my shoulder. "You could fly farther," I lectured him. "Practice." He nibbled my ear with his beak.

Dix had almost ended Maalik too.

As we drew closer to the bone ridge, I didn't see anyone, but I heard a very regular sound, like an insect: *kit-kit-kit*. It was close by. I stepped towards the sound. "Right about what?"

He followed me, head turned to the left, as if he was listening too. "That we need to take some technology for our city. Especially if no one is here to use it."

The ticking sound was louder now. Looking closely, I noticed the ridge was carved with intricate marks, rubbed black by time.

A white-garbed figure stood on the opposite side of a bone spur. Their face, covered with the mask, was familiar. Their gestures of "no" and "go!" were even more so.

We approached, and Wik caught the healer's arm. "Stop."

The healer held something. It pulsed against their robe: sharp beats, not the *ka-thunk* of a heart but that *kit-kit-kit-kit* sound, like a baby bird. Regular and hungry.

"What is this?" I reached for the object, and the healer pulled it away, then stepped backwards and almost fell on the uneven ridge. Wik caught their elbow. "Steady."

The healer put the mechanism in the crook of their arm and touched a lever. The sound quieted. They fended off Wik with the other hand. Eyes fierce, twisting this way and that, they seemed determined to keep him off balance. At their feet, a piece of bone had been removed from the ridge. Another hole.

Moving down the ridge from Wik and the healer, I tapped

on bone with my hook. One spot sounded different when I thunked it.

I pressed until the bone plate shifted and wobbled at the touch of my hook. When I bent my hands to it, it felt cool. Kneeling painfully, I twisted the bone plate away from the ridge and reached inside, to where my fingertips touched cold metal.

"Wik!" The thing pulsed against my fingers, just like the one in the healer's hands. When I pulled, hinged leaves of brass and a silver metal all bound in birdgut emerged from the cache. The *kit-kit-kit* sounded louder than ever. To quiet the thing, I covered it with a cloth. But I could still feel it beating in my hands. "What is it?"

The healer made a sound and tried to maneuver around Wik to get to me.

The object looked like the map Dix had found on Varat.

Etchings marked its sides, much like the plates in our satchels and up in the midcloud cave. A long fiber cord tethered the thing to the hole where we'd found it, but that barely registered to me. The brass surround of the box had the same look as the plates tucked into the Singer's bone codex from our own city, embedded in the walls of the towers.

Had we found the place where they'd been made?

The healer was speaking now, long low stretches of consonants. Gesturing for me to give them the mechanism.

I was too fascinated to comply. Somewhere, a long time ago, our brass plates had the same origin as these objects.

"There's something else in here," Wik said. He'd mimicked my actions and was lying awkwardly on his side, trying to reach for a bundle I could barely see. He tugged at it and pulled, grunting. "Yes. Here." He held out the second wrapped item. It was an enormous basket, woven shut. It stank of guano and something sharper.

The healer began to tug at our robes, our sleeves. They'd put the mechanism down, eyes wide with alarm.

Wik set the basket on the ridge carefully. Looked from it to the mechanism in my hands, which was still making that *kit-kit-kit* sound, fast and regular. Then he opened the basket, and we saw bones. A body's worth. We looked down the ridgeline and saw similar markings everywhere.

"Wik." I felt the same chill I'd felt in the midcloud towers, when we discovered a cairn.

He drew a breath. "Put that down and run, Kirit. This city is a grave."

The healer pointed over the city's side and away.

I would not put down this treasure. If this city was abandoned, this mechanism was ours. It was our heritage. I yanked the tether free, saying, "If you don't want to carry the basket, fine. I'm keeping this."

The healer's face went gray just as Wik yelled, "Kirit!"

Both of them grabbed the mechanism. Wik tore it from the healer's hands and threw it as far as he could.

"Why did you do that?"

The healer's words were short and sharp now. Furious sounds.

Wik, breathing hard, said, "It smelled like rot gas. But much stronger. Unstable. What if it exploded?"

"Why would someone put something like that on a city?" I grumbled at the loss, and at Wik's reaction. I'd been hoping to show the mechanism to Djonn, if he made it down the towers in one piece.

Seeing Wik's movements, the healer joined him in pulling me over the side of the city. The litany of syllables continued, the urgency unmistakable.

Wik gestured at me to keep descending. "The baskets of bones and the mechanisms. If there's one, there are likely more. I don't want to find out why. The healer doesn't either. Do you?"

↖ ↖ ↖

Climbing down a city's side was easier without Dix on my back.

When we reached the ground, Dix caught up with us. Eyed the healer. "You found your pet again."

"Hush." Wik lifted Dix to his back. We walked fast for as long as we could in the heat, taking turns carrying the blackwing. The healer helped too, though their eyes narrowed to slits when they carried Dix.

"What's your name?" Wik said to the healer. He touched his chest, then my shoulder. "Wik. Kirit."

The healer paused for a moment, thinking, then said, "Liope." They touched their own shoulder.

I tried the name on my tongue. Smiled, and the healer smiled back.

But Dix kept arguing. With all of us now. "We shouldn't have left the artifact, Wik. Whatever we found, it might not have been dangerous."

The soles of our feet burned. We slowed to drink what water we had. Dix looked back at the abandoned city, shaking her head.

"And that wasn't a bad city," she said.

"There was nothing alive on it that we could see," Wik said. "That's bad luck. Who knows what we'd find in the towers above."

My hands smelled faintly of rot gas. Wik smelled like bones.

"Dead isn't dangerous," Dix said from the healer's back. "Just unlucky."

Wik began echoing, and I joined him, trying to sound out groundmouths.

Our collaborative clicking drew Liope's attention. They dropped Dix and caught up to me. Stared, then tried clicking too.

"Wait," Dix cried. "I can't keep up."

"You'll have to," Wik answered. He gestured to Liope. "They were helping. Varat was helping you."

"Not all of them," Dix grumbled. "Not the best things. The best things they kept for themselves."

"Shhh, you two," I said. "I can't echo with the noise." Dix had even made a loud clatter when she'd landed on the ground.

"The mechanicals were theirs to keep or give as they chose!" Wik shouted. He'd grown angrier since the city had moved away on the plain, but now he faced Dix and loomed over her, furious. She stooped, like the thick air below didn't suit her. Like the ground pained her feet more than anyone else's. "You're out of chances," Wik finally said. "The next time you're at risk and I have the choice, I will drop you."

Dix nodded and managed to look remorseful. "You don't want what else I found, then?" She opened her hand to show me the map and the lens that the curators had kept on a shelf. The artifacts glittered in the sun.

The healer cried out and grabbed at both. Dix pulled her hand back.

"No," signed Liope over and over again. They pointed back the way we'd come, back towards the city we'd escaped.

"Dix, may you fall forever and a day." Now I knew why the fliers from Varat chased us. This map was a treasure of theirs.

From the healer's reaction, I worried they'd chase us again.

"They have plenty of these. They give these to children," Dix said, shrugging. "No one told me not to take it."

I scowled, but Liope pulled down their mask and yelled, one hand waving in the air, fingers splayed. I reached out to calm them, as they'd once done for me. They shook me off and glared at Dix.

"'No one told you not to' is a fledge excuse," Wik said. "No more." He bound her wrists and tied the other end of the tether to his waist. She trailed behind him, a foil in his wake, fighting the tether. Trying to reason with Wik.

"If we'd stayed, or kept their things, we'd be stronger now." She spat dryly into the dirt. It barely lifted a tiny cloud, didn't discolor anything. We were thirsty and hot, and now we were thieves many times over.

"We can't return it. Unless Liope wants to go back?" Wik tried a gesture towards Varat, then pointed at the healer.

Very emphatically, the healer shook their head. Pointed at the three of us, then at Varat, and signed "no."

Dix chuckled. "By helping us, this one's exiled themselves."

"That's not funny, Dix." We could barely understand the healer, but we were in their debt.

When Dix finally quieted, the *kit-kit-kit-kit* sound came again, barely audible.

"Wik, I thought you said those were dangerous." I didn't have a mechanism anymore, so I assumed he did.

"I don't have any. They seemed dangerous," Wik said.

"The healer." I pointed to their pack. One of the mechanisms was tucked inside.

A small boom, like thunder in the distance, had me looking for rain. Instead an orange glow expanded into smoke, near where Wik had tossed the artifact.

Then, one by one, we heard more explosions go off, across the city's back.

The giant groaned and roared. Tried to rise, and failed. Its towers, which were shorter than the previous city's, and far smaller than ours, shook in the air. It struggled to rise again, pushing dirt with its feet, stepping on its own eggs. Earth pulled up with its belly, exposing the remaining clutch to the heat. The soft surfaces grew cloudy and collapsed.

"That city was dangerous enough that someone wanted to

destroy it," Wik finally said, staring at Liope, and the mechanism they held.

Wik and I both grabbed for it. Liope pulled the mechanism away, making a "no" sign again and finally showing us a cord, still in place, and a switch that kept the mechanism from charging.

Dix cackled quietly. "Now what are you going to do with your pet, Kirit? Your perilous pet."

I didn't know. The healer seemed too dangerous to leave behind.

Just like Dix.

And yet, Liope had saved our lives. And we'd ruined theirs, cut them off from their people.

Wik stared west, where another city had begun moving closer. We felt it through our feet first, a city Varat's size, headed for the immobilized city, bone eaters flying out ahead, leading it.

The healer motioned with a free hand, making a similar pattern to the one Wik had made before the Varat officials.

The injured city tried to rise to defend itself. The shadow of its towers passed overhead and we hurried to get out of the way.

One less place for our people to shelter. The ground was hostile, and we had nowhere to go. The desert once again stretched before us. After working our way over a small hill, we found a small pond and quenched our thirst.

"We can't leave them both out here," Wik said. "Though I worry less about Liope than I do about Dix."

I wasn't so sure. "We must leave the device here."

Wik rose and approached the healer. They tucked the device in their pack. Growled when Wik reached for it. Gestured at us, then back at the city. Then stood and began to walk away.

"Wait." I ran after them. If my leg grew worse, I would need the healer's help. "You can stay." I made a gesture I hoped was conciliatory. Reached for the mechanism again. They shook their head.

"Get it back while they're sleeping," Dix said. "It could be useful. I can help."

"You'll stay far from that bag, Dix," Wik said. He began walking, and Liope and Dix followed. After a moment, I joined them.

ﾉ    ﾉ    ﾉ

We rested in the shade of a tall silver-leaf plant, Wik and I keeping watch in shifts. On his watch, Wik captured two ground rats. Lacking fuel, we ate them raw.

The healer never left their pack unattended. They slept with their head nested on it.

Now and then, we continued to learn each other's words by pointing at objects and repeating sounds. Sounds were beginning to feel familiar, and though our languages had been split for too long, we were beginning to reach some understandings.

At night, the groundmouth particles glowed in Wik's hair and behind his ears whenever he or I echoed. Liope pointed and murmured about them, making a spiral sign by their ear. Reaching out to touch our tattoos, and the scars on my face from the skymouth skin.

Dix walked alone, lost in her thoughts, still tethered. We let her take lead while Wik tried to brush off the glow, mostly successfully.

Later, when I looked behind his ears, and in his hair in the daytime, I couldn't see anything. "A trick of the light. Or you needed to bathe." Thinking back to the first time he'd killed the groundmouth, and the reaction of the Varat officials, I wondered. The blue marks on their skin had been the same color as the groundmouth's spray.

Our silver tattoos were from skymouth ink. Were groundmouths similar? Possibly related? I reached for any commonalities between my former world and this one.

We kept walking, our feet aching. When I stopped to rest my injured leg, Liope murmured over it, but waved me on.

After what seemed like days and nights of little progress under the cloud, the outline of our own city grew clear on the horizon. We had failed in our search.

"What will we tell them?" Wik asked. I hadn't heard him sound so lost, ever.

"Tell them about Varat," Dix said, from my back. She dug her fingers into my shoulders. "Tell them there is a city of wonders that does not know how to fight."

I put Dix down, hard, on the ground. "No." Thinking of the trained bone eaters: "They do know how to fight. It's just that they fight cities, not people."

She looked up at me, angry. "You will kill everyone then, by doing nothing." Dix waved her uninjured hand. "No city is innocent. And we need to survive. Just ask your healer."

I wouldn't give up. But I couldn't go back empty-handed. I looked long and hard at our city, its tilted spires combing the cloud.

Someone had to keep Dix, and Liope with that ticking artifact, as far as possible from the dying city.

That person should be me.

A thin breeze teased at me as night fell, this time coming from the direction of the ridgeline, still so far away. I thought I saw smoke columns outlined by the first stars.

Over the past half day, I'd started limping again. The drop from Varat had been a long one, even with the help of the ladders. The scramble off the city of graves had jarred my leg badly. The healer had been walking closer to me, helping. I let them. But I didn't tell Wik that, and I hoped he hadn't seen.

Still, someone needed to return.

I stopped in my tracks on a moonlit hilltop, and the others

stopped with me. I put my hand on Wik's chest and looked at him. "You said you wouldn't leave."

He nodded. "I won't."

"And I promise," I said, memorizing his eyes, his face, "I'll find you."

He breathed hard through his nose. "You're leaving. Me. Now." His hand covered mine, then tightened. I slipped from his grasp.

"One of us has to tell the city to set up shelter, that there's no other home yet. One of us has to warn them about the groundmouths and the cities. One of us has to keep looking and to keep these two away from our people. I'll go with them to the ridge we saw on the map."

Wik had been so strong and righteous when we'd met. A Singer, gray robed, determined. And I'd been positive I'd known what I wanted too. That surely hadn't included a Singer.

Now we stood together, looking out over the desert and the cities.

Dix and Liope ignored us, or pretended to.

Wik waited until I reached out again and pulled him close. "I don't have to go back," he said. "You don't have to keep going."

"You can get back to the city faster without all of us." I rested my head on his chest. His heart beat strong and steady. I leaned back, taking in the way his cheeks had weathered in the sun and heat, the deep shadows beneath his green eyes, and I stood high on my toes and kissed him in front of the others. It wasn't our first kiss. Not by far. But it was a long good-bye kiss, meant to last a whole walk.

He bent closer and kissed me back. Arms wrapped tight around me. We stood that way until the sun came up.

When he began walking towards our city, he didn't look back.

Before I could reconsider, I tied Dix's tether to my pack, and she, Liope, and I began to walk away too.

# 25

## NAT, MIDCLOUD

*⌁ Blackwings found the midcloud at start of day ⌁*

In the early morning light, with a dozen blackwings and Aivans following, I left the towers behind. After taking one last long look at the sole star that still hung in the dimming sky, I turned away. Dove towards the clouds with Sidra beside me.

The gray mist pulled me in, blotted the sky, then closed as if we'd never passed through.

On our way down, I taught my companions how to glide to the midcloud. How to fly a circular route with stops to rest and acclimate.

When the rain came hard through the clouds, we sheltered in the cave where I'd hidden with Djonn. The cloud rolled slowly, and thoroughly soaked us. The Aivans and blackwings stared, shocked, at the downpour. They weren't prepared to fly in it.

The wait seemed to take days, and we had no time to spare. As we sat, we ate dried goose the scavengers had pressed into our satchels, sipped cold tea from our water sacks. We napped in shifts beneath a tarp, though I could never relax enough for sleep.

The Aivans couldn't either. They muttered and whistled to each other. I wished them quiet, so I could remember the faces of my family in solitude. Sidra was quiet too.

I had to face facts: I didn't want the blackwings back in the meadow. The last time they'd landed there, Elna had nearly died, and Doran, Rya's father, had died. There were too many memories there. Too much loss.

When the rain ended, we took off again. I led them all the way into the lowcloud.

I hadn't thought about how we'd land in the meadow without disturbing the ongoing work there. Worry nagged at me as I flew. I whistled, trying to lead my charges in the darkening mist. I threw us into desperate turns away from looming towers and strange wind shadows created by the newly broken towers above.

"Brokenwings!" a blackwing shouted. "How much farther?" Rya's second, an Aivan, hushed him with a whistle.

"Not long," I whistled back.

I sighed and curled the first three fingers of my right hand in the carefully artifexed wing grips. My new wings, a gift from Raq's scavengers, shaped a beautiful wing curve. It drew me into a slow turn, and the blackwings followed.

We passed the bridge that overlooked the meadow. An iridescent shimmer made everything look mist-covered, until the three towers poked above the canopy. The skymouth hide that Elna had suggested cloaked Djonn's work from sight.

"What about now, Brokenwings?" another blackwing called. There were chuckles in the diamond formation behind me. They'd grow louder if I didn't answer.

Rya caught up to me. Flew at my pinion. "I'll take care of it," she said.

I dipped my right wing in agreement. "They don't like Lawsbreakers," I said.

"They don't like non-Aivans." Rya wheeled away, back to the noisier part of the formation.

The light changed as we dove lower. Shifted from sunlight and sepia to green and gray.

Rya's feather hung next to my Lawsmark on my new wings. She'd stopped calling me Brokenwings at the first cave. I'd offered myself in trade, and once she'd claimed me, she began treating me as an Aivan. No wonder the blackwings hated me and the Aivans distrusted me.

I was glad Ceetcee and Beliak wouldn't be in the midcloud. Aliati would see it, though. And Moc. And Djonn. I circled the meadow again. Flew a wider circle from there. Kept flying, gliding lower, putting off the inevitable.

Dark shadows prickled with beams of light when the clouds breached from below. I balked and wheeled fast. I'd flown too far down. I fought to find an updraft, a strong gust near one of the towers, and barely made it.

The Aivans who saw me turn, the ones in the middle and back of the formation, made adjustments successfully. But three fliers out front, Rya among them, flew even lower. They shouted as the wind failed to fill their wings.

I made a curving dive and grabbed Rya with my winghook. Dragged her up, then released the hook as soon as she had enough lift. Another blackwing did the same, hauling upwards on her companion so hard, I could see muscles standing out on her arms.

But one blackwing dropped away from us. He spun faster and more erratically as the wind failed to support his weight. He spiraled down and I dove for him. He disappeared out of the cloud, out of the wind, beyond where I could follow and still return.

"I am so sorry. I didn't think we would fly so low today," I whispered to the fallen blackwing as the clouds closed over him.

When I caught up with her, Rya frowned, her sharp eyes and dark tattoos forming a piercing accusation in the dim light. "What happened?" she said.

On the wing, after that, I could not lie. "The wind goes away below the cloud."

She shook her head. "Wind doesn't go away."

"I'll explain on the ground." I tipped my wings. Aimed for the cave and the towers. We landed safely in the meadow.

I'd told Rya some of the truth.

I hadn't told her nearly enough.

❧ ❧ ❧

Several Aivans circled the air above the meadow. More rested below the overhang near where Moc stood guard. When they were settled, I escorted Rya and her second to where Djonn worked. She exclaimed quietly over the artifexes' work on the climbers and kites.

While they were occupied, Aliati pulled me aside. Her grip was tight on my forearm. "Several small problems while you were gone."

I froze, bracing for the worst. Were Ceetcee and Beliak all right? Ciel? The baby?

She saw through to my worry. "No word yet. It's that we're running out of lighter-than-air. And the blackwings are pushing Djonn hard."

I flipped over the piece of bone, thinking. "Where's Urie?"

"Over by the climber with Djonn and his aunt, learning to be an artifex," Aliati said. She whistled for him. Urie waved and began to walk across the meadow. "Before he gets here, let me say this: if you and Macal are so willing to accept what the blackwings say at face value, you can clean up their mess," Aliati said.

Urie joined us. The boy's burns had faded, his eyes shone bright. "What mess?"

"We need your help, Urie. Can you take some time away from artifexing? For Macal?" Aliati asked.

Urie looked back over the meadow, his smile fading. "The

mechanisms are so intricate. I'm learning so much from Djonn. I'd like—" Then he saw our faces. "For Macal? Yes, I can." His easy smile disappeared. He glanced back over to the kite scaffolding, then returned his attention to Aliati. "Whatever you need."

In the mist above the meadow, blackwings hung and circled on the wind, looking like kaviks at this distance.

Urie watched them too, his frown deepening.

"We need you to work with the blackwings, become one of them again." As I said it, I watched the boy deflate.

"Why?" Urie asked, disappointed. I watched him slowly figure it out. "Because you need to know what they're doing down here."

But Aliati smiled. "Maybe not so naive." The boy's face slowly transformed under Aliati's regard.

"Do you think I could pull off watching them without them knowing it?"

"You might need some lessons from the scavengers," Aliati said. "I think we can help with that, especially when Raq gets here." She looked at me with eyebrows raised. "She was supposed to come down first."

Aliati gazed up at the cloud.

"I know. Macal decided to bring the blackwings down first. But she understood."

That was a half-truth. Raq had been more than upset. She'd threatened to hold supplies back. But she capitulated once Macal decided to stay above.

Now I elaborated. "He's trying to keep the city together, to keep it from panicking. From being overwhelmed by blackwings and Aivans fighting, and by fear." Aliati's eyebrows stayed raised. "Raq said to tell you she'd be down soon."

With relief, Aliati nodded. "If she'd had a very bad feeling about this, Raq would have ignored you and done what she wanted." She slung her bow, and I waved the blackwings into the meadow.

Rya took Djonn with her to greet the blackwings. As a group, most bowed deeply to her, with a few blackwings remaining standing. Few bowed to Djonn. Rya frowned. "You will treat him as you treat me." She waited until every blackwing and Aivan had bowed.

Urie joined the group greeting Rya. His black wings gained him easy entry. His Mondarath marks and the glass beads he'd found somewhere to decorate his wings caused his neighbors in the group to nudge each other. Ignoring this, Urie bowed as well.

Rya gestured towards the meadow and the gliders, to the climbers as well. Most of the blackwings paid attention. Then Rya gestured to me. Two of her guards broke away from the group. Djonn startled and began speaking loudly, but they ignored him. They walked towards me, faces expressionless. Hands at their sides. I'd seen that before, when blackwings guarded the meadow for Dix.

As they advanced, my shoulders tensed. This wasn't part of the plan.

I wanted to run, to fly, as I had when Nimru turned and saw our city lying on the desert. But there was nowhere to run in the meadow.

And I'd promised myself to Rya.

"The blackwings wish to make an offering to the city in honor of this effort," the younger of the guards said. "Rya has chosen to take you as Lawsbreaker now."

A *Conclave*. Here? Rya? She'd stood against Conclaves. Had interfered in them, had helped save Aliati. I could not speak for the shock of it. I hadn't meant for them to use me in this way.

I'd offered myself only as a guarantee. A reassurance.

Surely Rya needed me alive, to help with the evacuation?

The Aivans pinned my arms to my sides so I couldn't move.

I realized. The blackwings had lost one of their own. They weren't listening to Djonn, or me. *Brokenwings. Lawsbreaker.* Rya needed to mark her power, to seal her control.

She raised a hand. "My father died in this meadow, I am told. This is where Dix fell. We lost one of our guards to the wind today. What better place to seal our common purpose than in this meadow? With what better gift than a willing cloudbound Lawsbreaker?"

*Wait.* But they were getting their winghooks out. *Wait.* Preparing to lift me.

Now? When we had so much left to do? When citizens hung from the pulleys at the city's edge? When my family waited for me below?

Aliati, fingers tight on her bow, an arrow already nocked, moved to stand by my side. "This will not happen."

Rya crossed the meadow. Djonn harangued her from behind. "You throw your best assets away?"

She spoke loud enough for all to hear, "He offered himself freely to us. It is a skyblessing."

"It was cloudtouched, not a skyblessing," Aliati replied. "You have two people who know what it's like below, and one has taken the first party down. The other is here, and you'd throw his knowledge away?" Aliati and Rya met in the middle of the meadow and stood eye to eye.

*Wait.*

I'd offered myself. I'd known what I was offering. In hopes of saving something bigger than myself, in hopes of getting the blackwings to listen, I'd do it again.

I thought I was helping my family escape the city. I thought— somehow—I'd have more time. At least until we all got down to the ground. And that then I could talk my way out of my punishment.

"I saved you," I whispered when Rya had come close enough.

Rya's eyes glittered, dark and angry. "And if you'd spoken of the wind before we flew, or had not led us so low, that blackwing would not have fallen. I would not have needed saving."

"Nat's life for your blackwing, then?" Aliati gripped one of the Aivans by the arm and spun them away from me, hard. "They chose how they flew. But everything else falls to the clouds?" When Aliati stopped moving, the Aivan lay on his stomach on the ground, Aliati behind him, foot in his back. "What about now?"

The meadow stilled and went watchful. Every Aivan focused on Rya. All the workers in the meadow looked from me, to Djonn, to Aliati.

The Aivans held me so tight that my feet lifted from the meadow surface and only my toes touched.

Rya's slow smile shifted her tattoos so they looked even more birdlike in the cloudbound light, below the meadow canopy. "Nat's life is mine. He gave it to me above. I have witnesses."

Murmurs of agreement among the blackwings.

"And I can make this offering to the city when I like," she continued.

Both the Aivans at my side nodded. "Truth."

Rya walked slowly among the blackwings newly landed in the meadow. "You understand that here, I speak for you. You move, work, and pay due respect or you will test my goodwill. There is no person here I will not sacrifice for the good of the city."

Rya's Aivans nodded. "Truth." The blackwings followed suit.

She turned to Djonn and Aliati. "But I would not be a good leader if I was reckless with resources. You've made your challenge well. A good leader rewards sacrifice in the name of the city. I offer Nat a stay."

She waved a hand, and her Aivans lowered me but did not let me go.

My toes touched the meadow once again, hard. I bounced, and my knees nearly buckled beneath me. I could not breathe.

"He will remain my trade from the towers, their guarantee that they will work with us. And our guarantee—which I can undo at any point—that we will work with them too. We are all witnesses to this."

This time, all of the blackwings and Aivans bowed to Rya.

The Aivans let me go. Struggling to my feet, I refused to lose my composure in the meadow. In front of the watching black-wings and the Aivans.

A stay was temporary.

But with one move, Rya had stated she was in control of the meadow. She'd chosen to honor Aliati's case. She'd shown me mercy.

Had we won? I did not think so.

Aliati and Djonn hustled me inside. Djonn whispered to me, "What did you do?"

Meantime, Aliati rounded on Rya. "Your show of power will weaken us all."

"It was necessary," Rya said. "For now. Nothing will change."

Djonn muttered as we walked, "If anything like that happens again, you'll be finding your own way down."

A smile replaced the frown Rya had worn in the meadow. "It won't."

\ \ \

In order for me to avoid the blackwings in the meadow for the remainder of the day, Aliati and Rya agreed I would inspect the tower pulleys at the western edge of the city.

Ceetcee had set the first descent lines there. From these towers, she and Beliak gone below the clouds with our baby, Elna, and Ciel.

Ceetcee's knots and lines secured the blocks and lines

high above the cloud base. I looked at the ropes she'd touched, the braces she and her assistants had driven into the towers. As I flew, I glimpsed color below the cloud. Mist ebbed and flowed.

The muted reds and dark grays woven in the cloud were as beautiful as the stars from the night before.

A new kite hung from the pulleys, awaiting its next crew. Four pulley operators sat on a nearby ledge, eating graincakes. Among them, Dojha, a long-ago flightmate, waved as I glided past.

When I came back around, she'd made room for me on the ledge.

"A whipperling came back this morning." She beamed. "The first kite made it down all right."

The weight I'd been carrying since they left lifted. "All of them? Elna? The baby?"

Dojha smiled, a dimple creasing her cheek. "'All okay' on the message chip with Ceetcee's mark."

It was enough. It would have to be.

❧ ❧ ❧

When the midcloud light faded again, I returned. I felt my way along the darkened tunnels leading back to the main cave. Rya and two of her captains sat with my companions around the fire. Urie brewed tea over the flames. In the distance through the mist, I could see hang-sacks and plinths being strung between tiers on other towers.

Urie handed me a warm cup of tea, then gave one to Rya. He looked at Rya with curiosity. "Risen."

Rya bent her head at the neck. "You are welcome, Urie."

Aliati bristled, but she recovered quickly. "Urie? If you find Moc in the meadow, he might have time to teach you some night flying."

Urie looked from one woman to the other. Finally, Rya nodded.

"He's just outside, with the scavengers," Aliati said. Urie didn't wait for more. He stepped back towards the cave mouth and unfurled his wings. When he leapt from the cave ledge, I heard Moc echo and saw a glint in the silver cloudlight, a wing curve arcing gracefully on strong wind and patched silk. Urie disappeared as he took a turn around the tower, obviously enjoying the flight.

My heart caught in my mouth once more. To give this all up. To spend the rest of our lives on the ground.

To be safe. Eight days. Tomorrow, more kites would descend. Work in the meadow had sped up.

Aliati took Djonn's hand and squeezed. "It's going to be all right," she whispered. I hadn't noticed him shaking before, but now he was.

"Exhaustion," Aliati whispered to me. "The blackwings are pushing him very hard. It is too much for him."

It was a lot for anyone.

Rya looked like a nest of bees hid behind her eyes. She, too, was troubled. Out of her altitude. She looked at me. "We're not the enemy."

Aliati snorted. "You could have fooled me."

"We need to keep the evacuation moving. More towers are on their way down, we've got maybe a few more days by Macal's estimate, and not near enough kites. And the new blackwings aren't yet completely loyal. We don't have time for dissent."

We had a common goal, but little more in common. We needed to find some way to bridge our experiences, before it was too late.

I stood. "Come with me, all of you."

Rya looked shocked, but Aliati and Djonn stood, followed by one of our meadow blackwings.

"Let's go." I offered Rya my hand.

"Where are we going?" Rya stood, ignoring my gesture. She followed us through the narrow tunnels.

When we reached the littlemouth cave, Aliati hummed until the creatures glowed.

Rya gasped, peering closer at the walls, until Aliati pulled her away. "There's more to see."

When we exited into the night-darkened meadow, Aliati kept humming. Slowly, the littlemouths in the meadow lit up as well.

I turned to her. "I thought you might like to see where your father fell. Where Dix's man killed him. Where dissent and betrayal ended his life."

Rya stared at the place on the ground where I pointed. "I knew he died here. I didn't know why. Or exactly where."

"We need to work together. No more surprises," I said. Rya nodded.

Aliati was quiet, so I spoke. "Djonn has the last word on everything. Aliati and I are his seconds; orders come from us." I had little to lose.

Djonn looked up, gaze shifting between the three of us. "That would be good, until we are on the ground."

"Are we agreed?" Aliati said, looking at me and then at Rya.

"Yes," Rya said, still staring at the ground. Her Aivans mirrored her motion.

I spoke once more. "We thought you might like to sing Remembrances. We'll join you if you like."

There was a long pause accompanied by the sound of our feet on the cave floor, heading back inside. Then, finally Rya's voice, softer than I'd ever heard it. "I'd like that."

And for a moment, we were a community, saying good-bye, together.

# 26

## MACAL, ABOVE

*⌁ Above the cloud, time grew short for those who stayed ⌁*

The danger of more tower collapses sped up time, even as it seemed to slow our movements and our thoughts.

The blackwings and tower leaders worked together now, coordinating the creation of large kite spans from all the remaining silk in the towers, caging of silk spiders and bees, and sending those downtower. They flew escort on tiers of citizens going lower to ease the apprehension of so many evacuees. Across the more stable towers, scavengers helped gather supplies for Djonn's designs. The climbers he'd already built in the midcloud crawled their way up the towers daily, transporting lighter-than-air below as quickly as those who had stayed could make it.

And each day, as I watched more citizens disappear below the mist of the upper cloud, my throat squeezed shut.

There still were too many of us still above. We couldn't possibly all get away.

But I wanted to believe we could. Each last one of us, blackwing or citizen, Singer or Tower, elder or fledge.

The tower abandonment song came to mind again, and I brushed it away.

Up was no longer safe. We'd chosen a safer course, to the horizon.

For many Allsuns, since the Spire rose above the clouds, the towers had been organized to obey Laws. Fortify and Gather were useful now; one word, and most citizens except the very young knew what to do and how. But the days were growing few and there were still too many holdouts.

"Macal!" Urie hailed me that morning as he circled up to the heartbone tapping platform where I was working. "We've got all the silkspiders below. They're thriving in the damp. Who would have guessed?"

I smiled. "And Sidra? How is she holding up?"

Urie chuckled. "She's got most of the camps organized, everyone on hang-sack rotation so that they are well rested, citizens cataloguing supplies, blackwings jumping at her orders. She couldn't be better. Except . . ."

I waited for it. I knew what was coming. "Except she wants me to come down before the work is finished."

Urie wouldn't meet my eyes. "She sent you this." He held out another fiddlehead. "Said you would understand."

I did. The fiddlehead meant life, and living it. "Tell her I hear and understand." I pressed the fern between my fingers. "But Djonn sent a message that we're so close to having enough lighter-than-air to float all the kites, I can't go yet."

"The next kites are ready to leave now, and Djonn's got some extra foils hooked up that will scoop the wind above the clouds and help float the kites." Urie sounded unsure. "It looks very smart."

Everything Djonn designed was smart. I was almost ready to believe he could fly without wings at this point. "How is he?"

Urie shrugged. "No one sees him except Nat and Aliati anymore, he's working so hard. They bring him food, make sure he rests. I suppose he's fine."

"And the blackwings?" I knew Nat had asked Urie to work with them.

Urie grinned. "They're all right. They tried to organize a kite for themselves, but Sidra wouldn't have it. They've been descending in groups of three or four, sometimes after a long shift on pulleys."

I frowned. "How many are safely on the ground now?"

"About a third of the city, we think. We've lost the last of our whipperlings. Most haven't returned even once."

So they'd been sending kites down blind. I turned my head towards the work platform. "Check for any remaining silk and supplies anyone was hoarding in the towers. We'll need it, I think. Make sure everything's moved that can be moved? And then get down as low as possible. If you have a chance to get on a kite, take it. Tell Sidra to do the same, even if I am not there yet."

Urie nodded. "I'll see you soon, then."

The traps were slowly filling with heartbone, but it was a strange color. We wouldn't be able to distill gas that lasted from this, I could already tell. Clouds, we were cutting it close. "Yes, you'll see me soon."

Urie took off, and I flew to the next tower being tapped, where three of Rya's blackwings worked. They, too, had been getting off-color heartbone. "Head for the center of the city, see if there are good sources there."

They flew fast against the setting sun.

We were running out of time, and we knew it.

↘ ↘ ↘

Later that day, I went to see the last five artifexes still tending the stills and keeping the fires banked. Slowly, a large skymouth husk was filling with gas, but the heartbone smelled smoky in the alembic. The alembics themselves looked like they'd seen better days too.

"I think that's one of the last batches."

One artifex—a young woman—turned to me. "At least the still is working again." Her voice wavered with exhaustion and relief. "We might be able to do one more batch."

For a moment, I was lost in the memory of Doran and Dix mining this stuff from the Spire, of what it had been used for last: to destroy the city council and begin a war. Below, Djonn worked with some of the very blackwings who had helped Dix do this, who'd helped imprison him. But now it was to save the city, not destroy it. If we could continue to come together like that, we might survive.

What we once feared would now help save the city. Or at least the part of the city that was most valuable, the community here, the people.

At least, I hoped it would.

The lighter-than-air we'd just mined was the last batch we needed to match Djonn's request. "Good work," I said.

*We could get this gas down and begin to pack up our equipment. We could leave.*

The young woman turned back to her task. But one of the blackwings working with her followed me outside. "Are you sure we're safe up here still?" he demanded. "There are fewer people each sunrise. More are sneaking downtower into the clouds, to safer places."

I silently wished those flying in the dark down the towers good luck and good health. "I can't blame them, can you? They are afraid."

"They should be given Lawsmarkers, held up as examples." The blackwing was outraged.

"Would you go down, if your duties were discharged?" I asked slowly, thinking things over. A few moons ago, this balcony would have had excellent views of Viit and Densira.

Now it was sky and cloud, with a few dark birds dotting the space between.

"Wouldn't you?" The blackwing stepped closer.

"I'm in charge up here. I'll go down last." I didn't want anyone else to suffer for the decisions I made.

Long ago, the Singers would have made the same sacrifice, before they became too busy saving their own skin. Long ago, they would have put the people of the city before themselves. Perhaps I was that kind of Singer. But I also wanted to hold Sidra again, wanted to seek out our future together, wanted to help lead the new community. And I most certainly didn't want to die.

"You should go. We'll find someone to do your work."

And I turned my back to him so that he wouldn't see the hope in my eyes that he would stay.

A rustle of silk, wings unfurling. Then I was alone on the towertop.

❧ ❧ ❧

That evening, sitting in the workers' tier at the base of Varat, I found myself surrounded by comforts the city could not take with it. With only a few of us left—seven at my last count—there was plentiful food, and enough water, finally. We slept on soft cushions from Amrath. The young artifex played her dolin. And when I woke, she had departed for the clouds, and there were even fewer of us than yesterday.

The heartbone had changed color on every tower we searched. We were done with that. The only thing left was to distill it into gas, and that could be done below, closer to the kites.

Across the gaping places where towers had been, a flock of dark birds flew in a thick formation. They lifted above the city and flew out over the clouds.

The bats were long gone. We hadn't seen a gryphon or a skymouth since the city shook. And now what seemed to be the last of the birds were fleeing.

I looked at my five companions. "It's time," I said. "Find a kite and head for the ground."

There was no hesitation, no protest. They hastened to gather the alembics, the heartbone. Their panniers and nets were packed as quickly as I'd ever seen. Then those flying the alembics down took off in pairs, the equipment held between them in a net. The others, carrying supplies, waited until they could spread their wings and join them below. One by one, they leapt from the tower balcony.

For a moment, I watched them go.

Then I took off as well, for a final circuit of the city, tower by tower.

One last journey seeking out stragglers and anyone who might have been left behind.

I passed Mondarath and Varu, flew close by the space where the Spire had disappeared below the clouds, and gave my attention especially to the silkspider towers, which had been stripped of their riches. At each tower, I called out a warning to any residents remaining. I heard no answers.

At the one surviving bee tower, I found two young whipperlings, both hatched that morning and abandoned. I tucked them in pockets in my robe. "You'll be safer here."

At Grigrit, I flew close to the tiers, listening again. All I heard was the whisper of wind through bone. At Haim I hailed the air, and none answered.

I was the last person in the city, the last to fly the sky and the tiers here. And for one moment, with the sky wide open and blue, towers still standing bone white and beautifully stark against the sky, I did want to stay. Or, rather, I couldn't bear to leave.

Then I curled my fingers in my wing grips and began the slow circle to the undercloud below. Down, first to join my companions in the cave, and then to the kites.

As I passed below the clouds for the last time, the cold, damp wind felt like tears on my cheeks.

# 27

NAT, MIDCLOUD

*In the cloud, some stole away, taking kites for their own*

Crews worked day and night at the edges of the city now.

Moc and I took a turn running the pulley cables alongside several blackwings and Aivans. Our arms strained as we and three blackwings slowly lowered more citizens, easing the thick fiber and tendon lines through the bone supports and blocks.

Throughout the midcloud, the remaining blackwings had shifted from nervous and troublesome to officious and demanding, even of Rya. Would she need to make another grand gesture? So far, the answer had been no, but I tried to stay on her good side. Her Aivans had increased in number as more blackwings wore her black feathers. They were much kinder.

The next descending kite crew included Sidra, as well as a number of Aivans and blackwings. We worked the pulleys in near silence, ignoring the blackwing who called me Brokenwings.

Now the Aivans did nothing.

"Nat, where's Djonn?" Sidra whispered. "He should know there's trouble again with the blackwings."

"Helping Aliati and Raq, I think," I whispered back.

When I'd last tried to speak to Djonn, Raq stopped me at

the littlemouth cave where he'd been resting. "Let him be," Aliati had said.

"What's wrong?" I wasn't going to be blocked that easily. Not after everything.

Aliati looked at me, and Raq put one arm around her shoulder. "Djonn's sick, Nat. Yesterday was hard on him. Everything here is killing him slowly. The damp, the stress. His spine's been twisting more each moon, since before we came below the clouds. It's crushing him. He's working through the illness, but this project may be his last." She took a deep breath.

Raq had squeezed her arm, comforting her.

Then she'd said, "If we need to, we will take him away to let him rest. You'll understand?"

I hadn't, but I'd agreed anyway. An artifex had disappeared in the middle of the night, as had an entire kite.

Now, watching Sidra prepare to descend with her own kite full of former enemies, I worried more.

"Hush, you two," an Aivan silenced the blackwings. "We're all city now. Respect for those who help you." Sidra nodded thanks as the blackwings quieted.

Moc grumbled, "Respect for blackwings." I stared him to silence. The fledge still had no sense of caution, and needed one.

"Will you be all right with them?"

Would any of us? The rest of the crew included several from Mondarath: Urie and Dojha. Sidra smiled. "We'll be fine. We're taking a bit of Macal's hope with us." She showed me the fiddlehead fern, which she'd pressed between thin bone plates.

The winches and pulleys groaned as we lowered the kite. Soon, we lost sight of them in the cloud. With their descent, I knew far fewer people here than I did on the ground.

Among the tower survivors, fights and squabbles broke out. The tower leader from Amrath demanded the right to challenge Aliati for the truth about the ground.

Aliati met her in the air, and Amrath was quickly knocked into the meadow. The scavenger went back to work muttering, "Challenges. Here, in the clouds."

All I could do was bite my tongue and hold my temper, and hope Rya would continue to bring the blackwings under control. Preferably without using me to do it. Or Moc. The young man had been teased particularly hard lately.

"Lawsbreaker, get me battens!"

"Singer fledge!"

"There's no talking to them! They could kill us all," Moc complained to the pulley crew as we helped lower another kite. A climber descended next to this group, making ready for us to load a third kite on the pulleys if we needed to.

Moc had worn his hands raw working the pulleys. He'd worked hard while ignoring all the yelling. I'd seen him helping repair the kite mechanisms with the artifexes who had come down from above as well. He was as exacting as his twin, and as diligent.

But the blackwings couldn't resist needling him.

Moc was seething after the latest round of muzz-fueled name calling. "They're chafing. There's not enough of anything here for them to do except sewing and making bone battens. There's plenty of that. That doesn't excuse it."

Moc looked at his hands, roughened by a recent shift harvesting more battens, and nodded. "Truth."

He looked at the tower and up into the clouds. "Let's finish this."

He sounded so much like his twin. Determined. Strong.

That afternoon, we rigged a third pulley system at the base of the cloudline. Several of the last kites were ready to put into position. It was grueling work.

The pulleys—a hundred of them—had held all the weight we gave them. And the latest kite-tiers had wind scoops, giving them more lift. They could be steered much more easily than the first box kites. They were bigger too, each holding several tiers of people. The lighter-than-air that supported them was among the last in the city.

*Macal's inspiration,* Djonn wrote on a message chip. This was widely shared among the towers, and a cheer went up around the meadow.

"And cloudbound ingenuity and discipline," Rya added. She hung with me by the pulleys, checking them carefully. "We work well as a community."

I had to agree, for the most part.

Still, the proximity of the pulleys to the base of the clouds worried Rya. "This is a dangerous place. I don't want anyone to risk a fall. Weren't there safer places we could have secured those?" she'd asked.

She wouldn't let me forget the loss of her blackwing when the wind gave out. But I knew the answer to this question.

"On the contrary." Using Aliati's sketch, I showed her what would happen if the city fell away from the pulleys. "The mechanisms won't work. Lower gives us a better chance. We're running out of time. We need all the chances we can give ourselves."

I had my own concerns I wanted to bring up with Rya too. "We're running out of resources as well. I've noticed supplies missing, a whole stretch of prepared kite boxes gone."

Rya, still looking at the kite being strung on the pulleys, its leading curve trying to lift in the wind, narrowed her eyes. "Nat, who would do that? Scavengers? Moc?"

"Not Moc. Perhaps blackwings?" She was not going to pin this on scavengers either.

"The blackwings are well in hand. But I haven't seen Aliati all day," she said. "Nor Raq."

I bristled at the accusation that those two might be causing anything to go missing. *Caution, Nat.* I'd needed to ask, despite the risks. "Moc and the scavengers have worked as hard as any-one here, getting supplies down, building kites. They wouldn't steal."

Rya blinked, her tattoos patterning her dark skin like shadows. She tilted her head, birdlike, inquisitive. "Tell me more."

"There's at least two kites' worth of supplies missing. And we still have people above the clouds who we'll need to get down. We can't lose any more supplies."

Macal had sent word he'd be heading down today, but we hadn't seen him yet.

The wind picked up and rain began to spit in our faces. The pulley operators lowering a nearby kite worked carefully. I could see it descending, the lighter-than-air buoying it as it bounced down the tower.

When the big kite, packed with remaining citizens, had moved beyond the clouds, Rya returned to the cave and I followed.

Only a few remained in the midcloud. The cave echoed, empty. A blackwing stood in the meadow, coiling lines.

"Where are you taking those?" I asked, thinking of the missing supplies.

He drew a knife, preparing to defend his find.

Rya emerged from the cave but was not close enough. I was. "Nat, stop him."

*Resources. Lifelines.* The community needed those. I grabbed the ropes back from him, and as we struggled, the city rumbled.

The blackwing let go and ran to the ridgeline. He began to climb it as he unfurled his wings. Below us, the meadow jolted. The holes in the platform began to tear, spilling lichen and ferns. The blackwing fell to his knees.

*What I'd give to know I'd see my family again.* I'd promised I would.

"Get to the kites!" Rya yelled.

I vowed I'd make it back to the ground.

I grabbed the lines the blackwing had dropped and ran through the cave. At one of the few towers that still had hang-sacks strung from it, I shouted to see if anyone needed aid. A young man with a small child came out, and I grabbed them and flew them to the nearest kite.

When I went back to the meadow again, it was empty. The jolting ceased. For a moment, the city was still. Then for several moments more.

Rya stood in the cave mouth, looking over the meadow. "What just happened? The city lurched. We should fly." She seemed calm, but she was right. We had to go. The last kites were on their pulleys and already several were being lowered much faster than we'd ever tried before.

Macal was still missing.

Rya ordered the remaining artifexes to bring out all their lighter-than-air: a jumbled collection of enormous husks and smaller balloons. We took those to the city's edges. But instead of the organized process we'd executed so far, the balloons were tied everywhere too fast. There were too many on one kite, not enough on another, or one level of a kite had too many. They began to descend anyway, filled with panicked citizens and blackwings.

The city shook again. Nothing as vigorous as a rumble. Just a shudder. "Hurry!" I shouted. I grabbed a pulley rope and began to help lower another kite through the cloud.

When a rope began to fray, I doubled it with one of my reserve lines. I saw others, including Rya and Moc, doing the same.

When the last kite on our stretch of pulleys had been lowered past the cloud, I prepared to follow them. The crew made room for me and held out a net in case I fell.

As I prepared to fly, one last flier approached. Macal?

But the farthest kite was having trouble with its pulleys. Their lines were fouled, twisted, and they lurched sideways, spilling contents, panicking. I lost sight of the flier.

I climbed back up the pulley line, hoping to reach them, but my crew began to panic too.

Returning to my kite, I hung on as the wind faded, then surged again. We slowly inched towards the base of the cloud. Were the lines long enough? They had been, but with the new jolt, had the city shifted for the worse? Was the lighter-than-air enough?

Around the city's edge, our last kites descended out of the clouds.

Before we ran out of line, when the wind was still ours, we unfurled the windscoops. They expanded with a snap and ballooned out, catching as much wind as they could.

We did not fall.

Instead we floated, slowly moving away from the city on our borrowed wind from above.

The ground became clearer, the city below, enormous. The horizon a thin line against the red.

Among my crew, a young blackwing passed out from fear. "Easy," I said. "We will be all right."

A child nearby stopped crying and huddled near the bottom of the basket instead.

When the kite jerked and swayed as it lost wind, the lighter-than-air supported it. We drifted down slowly. We were so close.

But with a final rush of air and movement, the city rolled. Where it had been braced on Nimru's towers, it now hung in the air. Then with us still attached, it rolled farther. The towers began to crack loudly.

Only two kites on nearby pulleys were close enough to hear shouting. "Let your chute go!"

The nearest kite tilted. Its crew slid, one person dangled,

their wings open, useless. Then the crew deployed their wind-scoop and drifted free of the pulleys. I cried out with relief.

From our vantage below it, the kite seemed to drift away from the city.

In fact, the city was tilting away from the kite.

Our own ropes began to pull taut.

"Cut the lines!" I shouted. I reached out with my knife to the one closest to me and began sawing at it. Crew on the kite's other side did the same.

We floated away, descending a little too quickly, as the city continued to tilt from us.

More people ran across the ground far below, fleeing the shadow overhead. "Hurry!" I yelled as though they could hear me.

When our city finally fell, we watched from the air as it crashed in on itself, spraying bone shards and undergrowth everywhere.

Birds scattered and—high above—the air roiled as a sky-mouth tried to fly free of the wreckage. Its long, invisible arms inscribed the clouds to tatters, as if it were trying to hold everything together and failing.

# 28

## KIRIT, BELOW

*⌁ On dangerous ground, the Skyshouter searched for home. ⌁*

"Why are we going to the ridge and not home?" Dix asked, half asleep.

*Because there is no home yet. Because there are no cities on the ridge.*

"Because smoke sometimes means people," I said. How far could it be? It had been seven, maybe eight days since we left our city.

"It looked, from the Varat map, like at least two days' walk, maybe another half day after that. If you didn't stop for the hot parts of the day," Dix cautioned. "The ridge might be worth looking into, but what if our people can't make it that far on foot?"

*What if we don't make it that far?* Especially with Dix going so slow.

I lifted Maalik from his resting place in my robe. Fed him a small bit of the food I had left. The whipperling had begun losing feathers after the devices went off. He shook when I held him.

He looked like he'd been through quite a fight. We both did. My resolve grew.

*If Dix stole Maalik again?* I would get him back. *If he couldn't fly when I needed him to?* He would have to.

Before I'd made Wik begin the long walk back towards our city, I hadn't worried as much. Now, almost alone with Dix and Liope, I worried all the time.

The healer cast anxious glances at the ridge, but stayed with us.

I spent my time echoing, keeping Dix from the grasp of groundmouths. Nodding encouragingly as Liope tried to echo too. When it grew too hot, we set up Dix's wings as sunbreaks. We tried to sleep in their minimal shade. When it cooled, we began walking again.

"I have a worry too," Dix said close by my ear one morning. "What if your healer is with us for a purpose?"

"They can come or go whenever they like." I didn't like her tone.

"They could also be trying to infiltrate our city. It's what I might have done."

I shivered. "It *was* what you did. But why would *they* do it?"

"To seek out our artifexes. To gain our wingmakers. To kill our city."

"Our city is already dead, Dix." *You helped kill it. So did I.*

"True. But the people are not. We still have some knowledge Liope's city wants."

Until I knew what game Dix was playing, I couldn't trust her words. Nor could I trust Liope. "Then we are well matched," I finally said. "Three citykillers, together. Far from any city."

One foot before the other. Each step, progress.

The earth beneath my feet, so different from the bone tiers. The healer caught up with us as we stopped to rest.

While Dix dozed, Liope gestured to my satchel. Hoping to distract them from the map, I drew out one of the brass plates from the midcloud.

They stared, tracing a finger along the etchings of the cities, the markings that looked like stars upside down. "Serrahun," they said, pointing at a creature on the plate, then back the way we'd come, towards Varat. They sketched Varat in the sand with a finger. Then drew several figures dressed like themselves beside it.

"Serra," they said, putting their hand on the city. Then they put their other hand on the figures at the same time as the city. "Serrahun." I perched on the edge of understanding.

Then Liope touched my shoulder, pointed at Dix, and tapped their own chest. "Hun."

I pointed at another city on the brass plate. "Serrahun." The healer shook their head. *No.*

I took in the rolling hills and watched the distant sky, hoping to find safety as we walked towards the ridge. The healer's word whispered in my ears. *Serrahun* could be a word for community. For home. For safety.

For too long now, our city hadn't served as a safe place, and we needed one badly.

We began walking again, Liope whispering strange words to us as we drew closer to the ridge. Me trying to learn, hoping to keep my people safe, determined to find a home.

ใ  ใ  ใ

Through one long night, then another. When I could, I carried Dix. When I couldn't, she fell far behind and we had to wait for her to catch up.

I tired of her whispering, "Kirit," in my ear.

Liope walked beside us, silent. Once, they offered to carry Dix, shifting their pack to the front. They dropped the black-wing on the ground, muttering angrily when she whispered too much.

We'd made no further headway on trying to understand each

other, and the healer was growing more restless as we came closer to the coast.

As the first sunrise lifted above the horizon, the light shifted.

The morning was clear and, for the first time, slightly cooler even in the sun. A breeze—an actual breeze—came from somewhere ahead. The ragged silk of my robe fluttered in it. A flock of unfamiliar birds spilled from the ridgeline and fanned into the sky.

"Might be wind up ahead," Dix said.

We were halfway to the ridge when an enormous crack sounded across the plain, followed by a roar that did not cease. A cloud of dust billowed.

From the direction Wik had gone. The direction of our city, our towers.

*No.* Not yet. The city couldn't collapse yet.

But we turned and saw the dust billow as the distant city rolled to its side.

Our time had run out.

I dropped Dix. She fell hard to the ground and cried out in pain, but said nothing.

The dust rose higher still until it blocked out the sun. It rose to the cloud. Joined the cloud and the ground in a wall of gray.

The healer stood and watched. "Serra-nar," they murmured quietly. They sliced the air with their fingers. Then they silently reached out to Dix and lifted her to her feet.

Even I could figure out what that gesture and the word "nar" meant.

I scrambled up the ridge until I could see bone tiers splayed broken across the ground. Large kites bigger than any plinth or wing, drifting away on the spare breeze, buoyed by lighter-than-air.

More tiers and bridges fell through the cloud above. The

rumbling did not stop, and the ground beneath us started to shake.

The kites descended around the city, into the dust. They were too far away. I could not reach them.

But two kites careened towards the ridge, one drifting low, the other high and erratic. Those I thought I could reach, maybe help.

Leaving Dix and Liope behind, I stumbled, then ran.

# 29

## MACAL, BELOW

A sudden, unexpected flock of whipperlings and kaviks sped through the midcloud as I circled down. Flying too fast to avoid me, they swirled around me screeching. A cloud of black and gray feathers caught me up. The beat of wing against air filled my ears.

Then the flock passed, diving straight through the clouds and disappearing. Mist pulled along in their wake and stretched into thin, grasping curls, as if it, too, wanted to cling to me, then flee.

Concerned, I began a fast dive towards the meadow. When the city jerked and shook, there were no birds left to screech an alarm. The only sounds were the crack of bone and heavy objects falling.

Several pairs of silk wings, tiny at this distance, flew out from the meadow and the cave beyond.

I followed them, whistling my windsigns: *Magister*. I got no answer, nor had I expected any. I pursued the fliers anyway.

The city jerked again before I reached the closest set of pulleys. I wasn't surprised to see the kite descending, its pulley crews already sliding down the tethers behind them.

I flew to the next tower and found a last kite. Empty, save for two blackwings—one older, one much younger—frantically trying to untangle a twisted pulley line.

"I can help," I shouted.

They made room, and I landed on the kite's box frame. When

the city shook this time, I held on to the lines, as the black-wings did.

"We should cut the lines," the older blackwing said, fear pitching his voice higher.

"Don't! It's not safe." I saw only five goosebladders of lighter-than-air tied to the kite. Not enough by far, especially if the kite dropped precipitously. "We can lower ourselves. Let me show you."

I reached for one of the sacks of lighter-than-air and the younger blackwing drew his knife. "What are you doing? We need those."

"I'm going up to untangle the lines. I'm taking this as a safety precaution." I tied a tether line to the kite as well. Then reached for the goosebladder. They let me take it. "It will only be a mo-ment." I spoke calmly to try to soothe them, but they were so afraid. Anything could spook them.

I climbed up the left pulley line, the thick fiber rough on my palms. My legs shook from exhaustion with every rope span I raised myself, but I kept going. Let my momentum be driven by the remaining lighter-than-air. When I reached the spot where the right pulley had snarled, I used my bone hook to tug loose the fiber that had hooked around its sister line, yanking it into a half-slipknot. A few shakes, and the line came loose. I looked down at my companions in triumph, just as the pulley blocks above my head and the lines they were attached to swung violently away from the tower trunk.

The air dragged at my robes. The tower loomed over me.

"Cut the lines!" the older blackwing yelled again. The rope I clung to began to vibrate as they sawed at it.

My safety tether stretched and tightened at my waist when the kite dropped away.

From below, gravity and the tether dragged at me, but my hands were locked around the line above.

Then a crack ran through the tower, a sharp edge where smooth bone had been a moment before, a jagged line that oozed where the blocks had been secured.

The pulley block broke loose with a shriek, hitting me hard on the chin. It smashed into the goosebladder. I fell backward towards the kite.

I smelled gas. And smoke.

My wings wouldn't open.

*Oh, Sidra.*

*My city, I couldn't hold you.*

I fell into the shattered air.

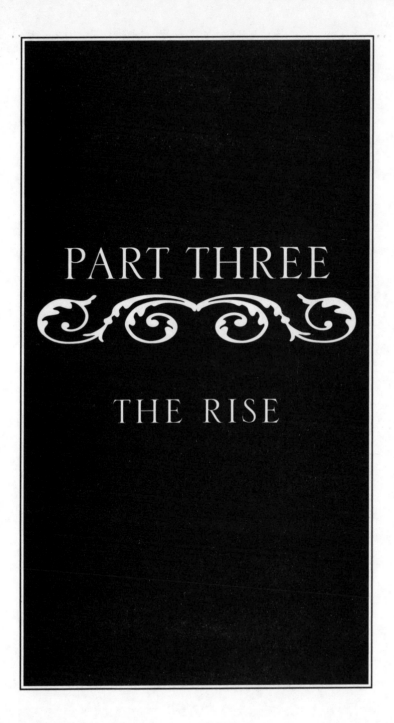

# PART THREE

## THE RISE

# 30

## NAT, BELOW

*⌐ The kites float and crash, all down so fast ⌐*

In the billowing dust and wind, three kites already on the ground broke from their tethers. They began to drift.

Our own kite swung lower in the sky as the crews on the ground fought for control.

Another kite crew dropped fiber ladders, like trailing seams in the air. Several citizens shimmied down. When they reached ground, they tethered the ladders to anything heavy they could find: enormous bones and crushed ore that projected from the ground. Anything immobile.

Two more kites bucked their anchors and rose through the dust. One was sucked into the whirlwind and smashed to the earth.

I leaned out of my kite and scanned the ground, looking for three figures: Ceetcee, Beliak, Ciel. I couldn't find them.

"Nat, can you see what's happening?" My crew stayed calm, but only barely.

"Some, but not enough," I answered.

More kite crews slid down the lines of their surviving craft, two to a line. Using their heft to anchor the silk and bone rafts, these crews leaned groundward, desperate to make contact in the blowing dust. They disappeared and reappeared in the debris. Desperate shouts and more came running to help. Two kites were finally caught and re-anchored.

When the large wave of dust washed over the third, tilting, kite, it disappeared.

The cloud of bone and earth rose around us. It rolled over people on the ground and hid them. In the air, we covered our faces with silk and closed our eyes against it for as long as we could. We shielded our mouths and tried not to breathe too deeply. Still, the dust abraded our eyes. Caught in our teeth.

With a roar that made the air tremble, the impact rolled over us.

We fought for control of the kite. Steering, altitude, direction.

I pointed and yelled commands to the kite crew, adjusting tension in the foils, trying to keep us from tipping over in the blast. My ears reverberated with wind, and also with fear for those I loved. Fear for me.

We rolled in the maelstrom. In the sand light I couldn't know who else was trapped with us.

The kite rattled. Dipped. I pulled two more crew onto the cams that controlled the wind scoops, and we adjusted tension and ballast until our pitching craft calmed.

"Stay as centered as possible," a crewperson from Bissel tried to direct the twenty citizens in our kite. A young man began to weep silently, mouth open, tears streaming, while he worked the pulleys.

The gray, biting cloud surrounded us, nearly as hard and impassable as the ground. I squinted through my thin silk robe. Tried to see what lay ahead. We battled to keep the kite upright on the buffeting air.

The seams of the silk boxes frayed in the dust, thinned at the corners, and readied to tear.

"There's clear air!" Lari, a guard originally from Mondarath,

shouted, and our windbeaters, on my command, used the scoop
to row us towards the clearer sky.

But the windscoop wasn't enough.

"Do what I do," I said, and tied a tether around my waist.
Lari didn't question, just looped a harness of her own. She began tying knots.

On the next kite over, I heard Rya shouting for her blackwings to row the air faster, to crank the propeller Djonn had
installed on their kite.

If I leapt into the wind, holding a tether, I wouldn't do anything more than drag the kite down faster. That was not a
solution. But there were other ways.

"Here," I said, pulling a small sack of lighter-than-air from
the kite beams and handing it to Lari. "Take this." I took one
too.

We could float and pull the kite.

Lari stared at me as if I were insane.

"Do you want to live?" I shouted.

She nodded. Then she attached the lighter-than-air to her
wings, and we prepared to leap from the leading edge of the
kite.

"Go!" I shouted. The wind that would normally buoy me up
wasn't there, and my stomach dropped in anticipation of the fall
and at the thought of dragging the kite down.

Instead, the drop was only a dip. My momentum drove us
forward on the thinner air. Behind us, the kite jerked and began to budge.

Others, also winged, took our example, and as we reeled
back in, they launched in twos and threes, until we had a rotation of flying wings that yanked the enormous kite across
the sky.

Sweat mingled with the dust in my hair and on my face,

turning to paste into my eyes and mouth. I couldn't stop. The kite had to get out of the cloud. Lari retched, but she too kept flying.

Somewhere out there, Moc and Macal, Aliati, and Raq all steered their kites, hopefully in safety. We hadn't prepared for the cloud, or the impact. No one from the towers would have experienced this kind of impact and lived. Not before Kirit, Wik, Ciel, and I had.

For a moment, the sole kite I could see was Rya's. A cloud of dust passed between us and then I saw only shadows and heard echoes of her commands.

Then we were clear of the dust and into the open air. As we drifted free, we emerged far over the desert. Much closer to Corat's remains and the other cities than I would have liked.

Behind us, our city's collapse had settled to a rumble. I couldn't see anyone on the ground until my eyes stopped watering from the dust. Where was my family? Had they gone far enough away?

Now I could only hope.

Our crews reeled us back to the kites, and we began to let down our ladders.

Below, a large group huddled on a hill beyond the dust, their robes caked with grit. That they'd gotten well out of the way was a relief. That they'd been on the right side of the city, away from the towerfall, even more so. But the dust had lapped at their heels. I heard coughing and retching.

Another kite emerged from the cloud, its box-wings gray with dust. Two fliers, buoyed as we'd been with lighter-than-air, tried to drag the kite, while others rowed from behind. The huge wing lumbered forward.

"I hope no one was still above," said a young blackwing from Grigrit beside me.

All I could do was stare. "We got as many away as we could." We hadn't done near enough.

Twenty kites in the air right now, more on the ground. Still more had come down over the past days. There were a few kites still above, I knew. Had they begun their descent? How many people had been left behind?

With the dust, we couldn't see the city. Not yet.

The young blackwing readied his wings in order to fly from the kite down to the people below.

"Don't!" I said, my hand on his shoulder, tight.

Confused, he asked, "Why not?"

"Djonn told everyone to stay in the kites before we left," I said. The young man blinked, not understanding. I fought the controls for a moment, and tried to explain. "Stay in the kites until you can go down the ropes or are on the ground."

The blackwing glared. "You can't tell me what to do, Broken-wings."

I shrugged. "True. But now that I have, I might not feel as bad when you get hurt."

That was a lie. But my words worked. The blackwing stood down.

On the ground, a small group moved away from the unfurl-ing dust, towards the group on the hill. I watched as they raced before, then beside the dust cloud. Then it engulfed them. My stomach dropped with fear. It was all I could do not to jump the impossible distance to help them myself. If I'd had wings and wind, I would have.

Instead, we worked the kites hard to stay on the edge of the driving dust, falling ever lower, until we were racing along the ground, our tethers dragging. We braced for impact.

I hated falling.

"Hold on!" I shouted. Everyone grabbed for the handgrips we'd sewn into the kite.

In the next closest kite, Rya's assistants shouted, "Brace!" When their kite hit, pieces of the bone frame snapped and a wing crumpled.

Then the ground came up fast for us too. Battens broke and silk tore, but the kite's main frame held. Skidding to a stop, we stayed safe in the inner nest that Djonn had designed. Then the kite flipped and we tumbled out. I landed hard on my side, knocking the wind from me. I heard a cry of pain next to me: the young blackwing.

Unlike the last time the ground and I met, I stayed conscious. I did not break.

Behind us, two more kites came crashing and thudding down. I rolled to my knees, surveying the damage. Torn silk hung from kite frames. Crews splayed on the ground, some already rolling to their knees. Struggling to my feet, I ran to help those who'd been injured in the fall, Lari on my heels.

We used broken battens and torn silk as bandages and splints for as many as we could, but what we needed most were blankets to keep the injured from shivering from shock in the hot sun, and time to get everyone to shelter. We had neither, not at first.

Where was my family? They'd made it to the ground, but now? I tried to focus on what was before me, what I could help fix. Hoped they were helping others, or someone was helping them. Which kites had brought blankets? Which had water or food? I could not tell anymore. Kite crews were picking through supplies spilled at the crash sites, shouting when they found what they needed.

On the ground, we were all scavengers.

And although my kite had crashed, many stayed aloft, as Djonn had meant them to. Dozens of kites hung in the weak air, buoyed by their clusters of lighter-than-air sacks. A few had whirlwind propellers that Djonn built before the end. One of the windscoop kites was still in the air also.

"Should we stay up there or come down?" one crewman asked from a kite still in the air.

I stumbled. I'd focused on getting everyone to the ground safely.

But then Rya was by my side, giving orders. "Come down however you can."

I interrupted, shouting before anyone could be injured. "Bring everyone down the ladders. Don't try to fly."

A ripple of quiet came after that last phrase. A child asked, "Why not?" Their voice pierced the quiet.

I took a deep breath. "Because the wind is not as strong down here. There's no updraft."

Rya looked at me hard, realizing now what I had known all along. She opened her mouth to accuse me, but before she could, I continued, telling everyone within earshot the truth, "There's not enough wind down here to fly. But you will not fall."

The quiet grew. I was encircled by it. A ripple of muttering and whispers emerged from the quiet. People began to step closer.

Then Rya groaned. "Lawsbreaker. You lied to us all!"

Her guards closed once again around me.

❧ ❧ ❧

When the dust began to subside, those who had boarded kites in the final panic began searching for their loved ones.

A jumbled refuge rose on the safe side of the fallen city. I peered into makeshift silk and bone tents as Rya pulled me through our city's temporary shelters. As we walked past kite groups, I looked for Ceetcee and Beliak. I tried to spot Ciel. Or Elna. Rya spoke to survivors and climbed to the kites still aloft to talk to the crews there.

She would not let me out of her sight. Even as she sent her Aivans with messages to those still in distant kites: "Use ropes to descend. Don't fly."

"I can help with this," I said.

"You've done enough, liar," a blackwing said.

Instead of quieting him, Rya smiled, her eyes angry and hard. "That's as good a name as any."

Word spread, too late for some.

A young man tried to fly from his kite, against orders. He crashed to the ground near us. When I tried to help, his family shouted until Rya pulled me away.

"They do not want you anymore, Liar. They don't trust you."

From their perspective, I'd caused this. I wouldn't trust me either.

Without much breeze, the dust settled very slowly. Tempers rose. And worry with it. No one was able to get too close to the city because of it, but people began to come out of the cloud. Everyone sought someone they'd lost.

When I found Ceetcee and Beliak, they'd draped damp silk rags over their faces, and over the baby's. She rode in a sling tucked tight against Beliak's chest.

"You're safe." I stumbled, knees weak, eyes blurring.

Beliak caught my arm. "We're fine." He paused and coughed. "There's news."

I braced myself, my eyes scanning for the others who'd descended with him. I already knew the name he would say.

"Elna's alive, but ill, Nat. She's worse from the landing and the dust. You should come." He pointed back into the dust.

"You left her alone?" I broke into a run, with Ceetcee at my side. Rya allowed it, waving off her guards.

The dust hit hard the first time I took a breath. Bone and dirt filled my mouth, abraded my throat. I choked, then coughed until I was nearly sick. Fighting through it, I spotted a tent in the dim light, made from several pairs of useless wings and a tarp. "How could you leave her here?"

Inside, Ciel knelt on the ground beside Elna's litter. "We couldn't move her."

Elna's skin had the texture of beeswax, her thin, pale hair lay plastered to her forehead, and her breath was so shallow it was almost not there. I knelt next to Ciel and took my mother's hand. Squeezed it. I never wanted to let go.

A slight pressure in return meant everything, even as she struggled to breathe.

"I'm here. I'm back." I hoped she'd hear my voice and wake. For now, her hand on mine was enough. Her breath in the tent, the soft whistles and wheezes. I held on to her for a long time as the dust settled around the tent. And she continued to hold on to me.

\ \ \

When the Aivans caught up with me, they brought medicine and Rya's demands.

They would move Elna to a tent near Rya where a healer had set up a small station. They would move me too, into what Rya called "a protective wing."

When my mother's breathing had steadied, I did not fight the move.

The four of us—Ceetcee, Beliak, Ciel, and I—carried Elna into the dust, her litter tented with silk.

After she was settled on a clean mat, the Aivan healer made a poultice from their precious stores. I relaxed a little. Ceetcee and Beliak stayed close.

I'd imagined our greeting on the ground for so long, all through the time we'd worked to evacuate the city. I'd imagined, also, telling them what I'd done. How I'd become Lawsbreaker again. Now, Ceetcee hugged me, hard, eyes brimming with frustrated tears. "The Aivans say you must stay here with them."

With mixed relief and dismay, I realized the look in her eyes wasn't anger; it was fear. "Rya says it's for your safety, and also because you made an offering?"

"It was the price of hope," I said. "Elna's safer, and my family too." I was less so, and that was all right. Rya's guards took my elbows to reinforce the message.

"You didn't ask us what we wanted," Beliak said. Ceetcee held on to my hand.

I struggled against the parting. Each time was harder, not easier.

"We remind you of the promises you made. And your family. We know you sometimes leave out facts," one blackwing said. Ceetcee winced, her arm still around my waist, the baby now slung on her back.

"Your family will be well cared for. Rya's promise," the guard repeated.

"He'll go with you. Just give us a moment." Ceetcee coughed to cover the crack in her voice. She leaned on my shoulder, and we let the baby kick at us. Nothing felt safe, but for a moment, I felt slightly better. She said, "We'll stay with Elna, in shifts."

That helped.

The baby kicked again, and I cupped my hand around a tiny, soft foot. A foot that hadn't yet touched the ground.

I had no more tears left, only dust.

ϟ ϟ ϟ

The blackwings led me to Rya, pulling me forward, since I couldn't turn my eyes away from Elna, from Ceetcee, from the tent silk swinging closed behind us.

Ceetcee and Ciel followed for a short way, along the path from their shelter. They lifted healer supplies and tucked them into their robes. They began moving through the tents and shelters, looking for injured to help.

Sidra wove in and out of the crash sites, handing out strips of silk for bandages. Asking questions. Her voice was hoarse. All our voices were.

I could barely breathe. It wasn't the dust or the smell. The Aivans' hands at my elbows kept me moving forward while I looked back.

As the blackwings led me away, I heard Sidra ask, "Has anyone seen Macal?"

# 31

KIRIT, BELOW

*⌒ While the Skyshouter found the ground hard and vast. ⌒*

"Kirit, wait!" Dix stumbled after me.

I would not wait. Could not.

I ran towards the ridgeline to catch the escaping kites. If I couldn't help my city, I could at least help those right in front of me.

My steps took me away from our collapsed city and the dust cloud that surrounded it, but I couldn't turn back. The runaway kites drifted closer to the ridge.

Dix dropped farther behind with each step. "Kirit! I can't run."

"You have to!" Leaving her wasn't an option. She'd head right back to our city. I couldn't let her do that. Liope, who'd been keeping pace with me, slowed for Dix. She gestured to me to go on.

I'd climbed an incline that would take Dix some time to navigate, even with Liope's assistance. My leg ached, but I didn't care. From my vantage point, I could see the collapsed city better. I could see many more kites floating nearby, survivors descending from them to the ground. Worse, I saw crumpled piles of silk and bone on the ground.

Sounds of crying came from one of the two kites floating

towards the ridge. People were still on these kites, that was for sure. "I'm coming!" I yelled. My voice cracked. I don't know if they heard me.

The distance over the tumultuous earth was much farther and more complicated than if I could fly it. *No.* I wasn't going to waste time wishing for wings and wind. I'd get there as best I could, and I'd help them.

One kite moved erratically to the north, and one floated straight enough that I imagined it was being steered.

"Lighter-than-air," Dix panted as she and Liope reached my side. "We did it."

*We.* She'd been part of the original draining of the Spire's heartbone to make lighter-than-air. She'd used fledges to do the work. She'd been ruthless. And now? Now she was here with me.

I shook my head. "There's no 'we.'"

Scrambling up over the ridge, Liope and Dix still in tow, I let my anger build. Dix had helped kill the city too, by draining the heartbone. She'd sped up the process as much as I had.

Lighter-than-air was helping to save tower residents now. At least, it was keeping them in the air, away from the sharp rocks on the ground. The kites bucked and wobbled as they neared the ridgeline.

If Wik had been with us, we might have moved faster. Gotten there sooner.

I'd sent him away.

The strain on my leg was searing. The terrain abraded my blistered feet, and I had to slow. The healer caught up with me and offered their shoulder. I leaned on it and we moved faster together.

"Liope, thank you," I whispered. "For helping."

They smiled at me over their mask. Tilted their head in what seemed like a "what are you waiting for?" gesture.

Dix, unwilling to be left behind, stood in our way. "Don't you want my help?"

The healer and I moved around her and began to walk the ridgeline, moving higher. "You didn't offer."

"I've *been* offering," Dix said.

"Stealing. Nagging. I should have left you in the desert." She'd end up tormenting another city.

She sighed, a long, tortured sound that matched the breeze on the ridgeline. "I can help too."

*Fine.* "You follow, and help if you can. My sort of help, not yours. I think we can catch the northern kite if we go farther up the ridgeline."

"How are we going to do that?" Dix looked more than doubtful. "You can't fly."

I could barely run, though with Liope's help, I was faster.

"Wish you had a bone eater now?" Dix asked. Was she heckling again? Or sincerely wishing for one? Either way, her words were no help. We didn't have wings or a bird.

*Sometimes you need to find the right question.*

My mother's words. I wasn't hearing them in a fever, or in a panic. They were just there, calm and clear. Out here on the ridgeline, her words meant something different than they had in the bone towers. They inspired me.

"No bone eaters around. What *do* we have?" I asked.

"Sore feet. The people in the kites don't have anything but bad luck," Dix muttered.

That wasn't true.

"They have me. They have us."

Painfully, I began moving over the ridge again. The breeze tossed my hair in its braid and kicked my robes before I realized that it wasn't just a breeze. It was real wind. Stronger than any I'd felt on the ground so far.

Maybe I *could* fly there.

Instead of going towards the kite, I coaxed Liope to climb higher on the ridge. I hoped there would be more wind. My wings were broken, but I wasn't the only one with wings here.

"Where are your wings?" I held my hands out to Dix.

Dix turned from me. "No."

I waited. "You can start walking away, then. I won't slow down for you again."

"You're just like your mother," Dix muttered. But finally she pulled the parts of her wings from her pack and gave them to me.

They'd been pieced apart in two places by an expert, silk panels and battens separated for inspection. Otherwise, they were in good condition. To put them back together, I would have to sew.

I hated sewing. And I had no kit.

But Dix had the wire around her neck. And I could unravel thread from any silk. "Give me your necklace," I said.

She shook her head and backed away, nearly stumbling down the ridge. "You take everything."

I had no problem doing so. I didn't need to say it. My outstretched hand and my stubborn stance did the work for me.

Dix gave in and unwound the wire from her neck. "I want it back."

The wind had shifted, and the kite slowed, still high, still out of reach, but if I was quick, maybe I'd have time to catch it.

I snapped a small section from the wire and handed the rest back to Dix. Looped it in half and wound one end of the wire around the other, until it formed a sufficiently straight needle that could carry a thread through cloth. Then I got to work patching Dix's wings.

I stabbed myself in the finger and cursed. A spot of blood welled. The healer reached out and took the needle and the wings from me. Their stitches were quick and sure. They handed Dix's wings to me, and I could barely see the patch.

Still it had taken too long.

The kites had drifted, one back inland towards the desert, the other, farther over the ridge. I could barely see the top of it. Dix had curled up on the ridge, pillowing her head on her pack.

"Get up. We're going." I prodded her with a blistered foot.

She slowly rose, groaning. "Why do you need me?"

I flexed the wings, their dark silk stained and faded in places. Put my hands in the grips, which I'd restrung. The wings felt sturdy and responsive, but I'd never flown this way before. If Wik had been there, he would have been the one I asked to watch out for me. Instead, I had Dix.

"I need you and Liope to come get me if I crash."

Dix snorted, a bit like her old self. "All right."

The wind on the ridge was stronger than I'd felt anywhere since we crashed. Was it strong enough? The kite drifted farther from me with each passing moment.

One way to find out.

I leapt from the ridge, and the wind filled my silk wings. For a moment, I hung in the air. Moved forward. Flew.

But when the wind gave out, I tumbled down the side of the ridge.

Though I wasn't that high, I hit the rocks hard enough to jar me. I scraped knees and elbows. In the distance, Dix cackled like a bird. Liope stared at me with eyes round as eggs.

Dusty and bloodied, I was still able to stand on my own. Dix's wings were unscathed. Tough, like their owner.

"Birdcrap!" I yelled at the ground.

Dix stopped laughing. "Kirit!"

The healer was climbing towards me and pointing at the kite. The wide silk spans slowly moved away as a strong gust pushed it up the ridge. Towards the water. "Serrahun?" they said.

The kite was not a monster, but it was like home. Could I take the risk of misunderstanding?

"Yes," I said. "Serrahun."

The shouts from above grew louder. *There's another way. There's got to be.* I started walking in the direction the kite was headed. Too far. I wouldn't make it.

*Why was no one else from the towers chasing them down? Didn't they know that they've lost this one?* I wasn't certain they did.

It didn't matter. We'd lost too much, and too many people. I could make this right.

Liope had turned and was berating Dix in their unfathomable language. They pointed at Dix's robe. At her hands.

Dix shouted, "Might be it's time to just cut losses. Isn't that what *you* did when you walked away from the city in the first place?"

I shivered even though it wasn't cold. "We didn't walk away. We were looking for a new city." The words sounded hollow. I could have gone up. I could have helped Nat get the community down to the ground. "We are not walking away now."

Nat had every right to be angry with us as he climbed up the towers. I could hear his voice now. He'd be even angrier when he learned we'd failed. And now I'd gone off again, chasing a kite.

"I won't accept any more losses," I shouted, pointing to the erratically drifting kite. I wasn't getting any closer. In fact, I was farther from both kites *and* the city now.

I considered Dix, still very far away. Liope had a tight grip on the blackwing's robe now. They pointed at Dix and then at the sky.

Dix finally held up her hands. Shouted, "You want to get up in the air?" She pulled a wrapped packet from her pack and waved it. The healer stepped back, relenting.

I walked back down to meet them. In the packet were the metal windups Dix had stolen from the archive. The ones that reminded me of Djonn's propellers.

For once, she looked unsure. "I think these will work."

"This isn't a good time for guesswork," I said. "We need to catch that kite."

The kite was slowly getting lower, and precariously closer to the ridge. My chances were better on the ridge, but only if we hurried.

Dix wound the stolen brass cone and pulled a bone pin from the top of the mechanism. The propeller inside began to spin and didn't stop. I felt wind stir around me. She handed the propeller to me. "Hold on tight." The cone generated enough push that I stepped back hard. When it wound down, I was breathless.

"Turn them around, attached to your wingframe, and you go up. If they don't pull your wings off first."

"That's some artifexing." We'd never seen this kind of mechanism in the city.

"Wind them again," Dix said. She showed me how to twist the parts against each other just so. We sat and wound two cones until my arms ached. We began to attach them to my wings, but Liope waved their hands and moved the propellers to my shoulders. We secured them near the strongest wing hinges with silk and wire and bone. Then I locked my wings.

"This is more skytouched than jumping off the cliff," I said.

"Careful when you pull the pins on them—they could take your fingers right off," Dix added just as I was about to set out. "And you'd better hope you can land when they stop spinning."

"They'll get me there?"

She nodded. "They should. As far as I understand them."

This was not reassuring. Still, I climbed up higher on the

ridge in an attempt to catch the kite. The healer stayed with Dix. Both watched me carefully.

"Such space," I breathed.

I would fly it, with help.

Beyond, the ridge wall that I'd seen on the Varat—or Serra, as the healer called it—map was a sharp dip and more ridge. Columns of smoke rose in the distance. And water. So much water. It spread to the horizon, glittering in the afternoon light.

# 32

## NAT, BELOW

*⌒ A city's secret discovered one night at last ⌒*

We passed by more shelters, all upwind of the city, most made of discarded wings. Citizens' faces showed as much bewilderment as I'd felt the first time. A small girl with Mondarath markers around her neck asked me, then others, "Are we dead?"

"We're not dead," Rya's guard said.

"But we're below the clouds? We fell through?"

"We did. And we lived," I said.

Others looked at the ground beneath their feet, tested it by stepping hard until it crumbled. They rubbed it between their fingers.

The air began to clear. The giant city on its side, the smaller city crushed beneath it, and the horizon beyond all became more visible.

I hadn't thought much about what would happen once we were on the ground. I hadn't thought at all about what would happen when people saw the city, the horizon beyond.

As the dust settled, some stood and stared. The gray expanse of the dead city registered in their eyes.

"I heard stories it was alive, that it ate people," a woman whispered. She pulled her children back inside their shelter.

Others climbed higher, to see the horizon. A knot of panic

and excitement built among five blackwings who'd pulled themselves up on the city's leg. "There are more!"

A man wearing hunter blue robes, still dusty and shocked,
looked to the blackwings. "What will we do?"

Rya struggled to gain their attention. Climbed up on the city's
leg too. She put up both hands for calm. "We are safe here, for
now. Don't worry."

It didn't work. More people climbed the ropes to the city's
leg. Milled around Rya, tightening their panic to a sharp point.
I pulled against the guards. "Let me help."

But they wouldn't.

When Ciel wove through the crowd, tugging Sidra with her,
few noticed. Until they began singing.

The song was familiar now. It had been a call to action. Now
it was a mote of calm in the panic.

> *All that shook, all that fell was sky and bone,*
> *So two went far and two climbed home*
> *On birdback, through cloudburst, so close to home*
> *Across desert, through illness in search of home*

The community drew close around them, listening. Sidra began to speak. "Macal, when he gets here, will tell you that this
is the beginning of something new," she said. "Until he arrives,
I ask you for patience, for calm. We are building our community again. You must give us time to do that."

She stepped back, and Rya stepped forward, taking Ciel's
hand. "We will make a new place here, safe for us."

It was a start. Some left humming Ciel's song. Others moved
to help the wounded.

"Thank you," Rya said to Ciel and Sidra. "We'll find Macal."

Sidra nodded. Still hopeful. "With a little structure, everyone's calmer."

Ciel looked at me for the first time in a long time without glaring. She passed me a bone chip, an old challenge marker from the Spire. "Sometimes secrets are kept with the best of intentions."

I was, for the first time in a long time, left speechless. I squeezed her hand.

"We'll take that into consideration, fledge," Rya said. "Someday, you'll make an excellent Aivan."

Ciel smiled and turned away to follow Sidra back towards the fallen towers, to search for Macal. I recognized that look on her face from our climb, ten days ago. That look said, *I'll do what I want.* It buoyed my heart to see that in all the destruction.

Rya led me away from the crowd. Her eyes on the horizon, she asked, "Where do we go, Nat? Which city is ours?"

I shook my head. "Kirit and Wik are searching."

Rya's eyebrows shot up. "The Spirebreaker and a Singer? That's who you left in charge of preserving our community?"

I didn't answer. I'd wanted us all to go up. To return together. I'd left hoping to see them again, and fearing I wouldn't.

Kirit and Wik must have seen the city collapse. If they didn't return soon, they were lost. My hard-won conviction dwindled. "They deserve our trust."

Rya looked at me for a long moment. "I don't owe them anything."

"It's the truth, all of it." Standing before the fallen city again, with my family on the ground now, I understood their impulse. Now I wanted to go out and search for a new home too.

"I don't believe you." She tapped my Lawsmarker. "You are a liar."

"I saved the city with my omission. We got almost everyone down." I kept my words simple, but I was fuming inside. "You cannot think I meant to harm anyone."

"True. But the city may never forgive you. And if I suggest

it, I will be seen as weak." She inclined her head, but minimally. "We'll keep you with the Aivans for your safety. We'll care for your mother as a hero."

It was too much. "I'd rather be with my family."

"You would endanger them too, then. What happens when there is no new home?"

Rya's second in command shifted uncomfortably. "There will be a new home. Won't there?"

She turned his way, smiling. "Of course. But it may be different from what we know now."

We kept walking, past shelters made of wingsets.

A ridge of bone stretched for several days' walk beside our dead home, the tiers and towers piled one atop another. Moss and pieces of calcified bridges stuck up through the tier in the vast expanse of dust and ruins.

"Rya?" Two blackwings carried the young councilor from Amrath on a stretcher of silk and bone battens. She pointed with a finger at the city. "What is that?"

"That's the city, councilor," Rya answered.

The dark body of the city had already begun to collapse in on itself. The smell was only going to get worse. No one cared, not yet. They were just staring, with the same shock I'd felt when I first saw the city, a lifetime ago.

The councilor from Amrath looked from me to the city. "It *was* alive. You told the truth."

❧ ❧ ❧

"Nat."

I woke in the dark. Aivans snored around me, wrapped in feather-decked cloaks.

At first, I thought the voice was a shred of a nightmare. One had wrapped me tight with visions of falling, a baby's cry. My first inclination was to reach for my family. Then for Maalik.

But my family sheltered elsewhere. Kirit had my favorite whipperling.

I was alone, among strangers.

Rya's captive.

Then the voice came again.

"Nat!" Close by my ear. A young voice, trying to whisper, but her range was too high, her intent too urgent. Ciel.

I hadn't seen her since that morning, when she gave me the challenge marker. I rose quietly and stepped from the tent as if I needed to relieve myself. No one moved.

"You have to come," she said. "Moc and Beliak found something."

Found what? I retied my footwraps and straightened my robe. "Is Elna all right? The baby? Ceetcee? Beliak?"

"They're fine. Elna's improving. The baby is eating."

Relief. *Did they name her yet?* In the confusion of yesterday, I hadn't asked. I couldn't ask Ciel as she led me away from the shelters, to the city's moldering side. I still yearned to know.

In the cool night, the smell wasn't any worse than it had been during the worst of our first days here. Ciel still wrinkled her nose, but she didn't say anything more, except, "There."

The moon was just about to set, and it cast a silver-gray light across the city's corpse, and that of the smaller city crushed beneath. Beliak crouched so close to the edge of the hole where the city's belly had rested that I worried he would slip.

Moc stood below the shadow of the city, knee deep in mud. His hand rested on a smooth curve, mostly buried in the muck. In the low-slung moonlight, the shape looked almost blue, with an oil sheen. "What is it?" I was still rubbing the dreams from my eyes.

"It's warm. Still alive." Moc's voice was filled with wonder. "I think it's a city. A new one."

In the muddy expanse, I saw what had been exposed when

the city toppled and the mud settled. The egg ran the length of the cavity and was sunk deep in the mud. "Moc, get out of there!"

The boy grinned at me in the dark, his teeth flashing. "I can't."

He must have been in there since evening at least.

"They were scavenging," Beliak explained, pointing to Moc and Ciel. "I tripped and nearly fell in. Then Moc *did* fall in. When he spotted the egg, Ciel came and got me. Look at the size of that thing!" He bent his head, then looked at Moc from under heavy brows. "Besides, we need your help to get Moc out of there."

The pit's sides were slick with footprints and slide marks. It was obvious he'd tried to get out by himself. "I'll get a rope."

"I'll stand guard," Ciel said.

Beliak held out a hand, and I gripped it tight. "You're all right?"

He nodded. "Everyone's fine. Ceetcee will worry I've been gone so long, but I'll tell her I was with you. She'll be relieved."

In the darkness, I stole a rope from the growing cache of supplies behind Rya's tent when the guard went to relieve himself. Once on the ground, with several artifexes still missing, including Djonn and Aliati, Rya had centralized the rest, and stored all their tools in one place. This made pilfering a long tether rope from one of the fallen kites a fairly quick proposition.

We lowered the rope, and Moc tied it around his waist, using a Singer knot that wouldn't slip. Beliak and I pulled him from the pit. His feet squelched loud enough in the muck that I worried we'd wake the nearest shelters.

When we freed him, Moc was covered in mud. Even behind his ears. Still, he was unfazed.

"We have to tell Rya," Beliak said.

I agreed. "Tomorrow." The egg wouldn't hatch tonight.

"How many towers do you think this city will have?" Moc asked.

As he spoke, a tall figure approached the city. Someone who could get past Ciel without her sending up an alarm. I let out a low whistle.

"No towers," Wik said. "Not at first."

Moc nearly fell back into the pit in surprise. Then he threw himself at his uncle. "You're back. You found a new city, then!"

Wik slowly shook his head. "We found several, but none we can go to. Many are dead."

"Where's Kirit?" I asked. "What happened to her?"

Wik looked along the fallen tiers to the horizon. "She's still searching for a home for us. She won't stop looking."

Ciel came running. "Nat has to return. Rya's guards are waking."

My questions hung in the air, unasked, unanswered.

❧ ❧ ❧

The next morning, Sidra came to the tent.

To the guards, she said, "I'm on official business of the council. Rya knows."

They acquiesced, bowing. As she and I walked to the shelters, she whispered, "Rya knows I'm council, at least."

"Rya needs to know what Moc and Beliak found. Everyone does. No more secrets." I ducked under the silk-draped opening of Ceetcee's tent. Beliak and Wik were already there. I hadn't greeted Wik last night, so I bowed to him now. Because I didn't know how to honor him, I sputtered for a moment. Eventually I settled on a name. "Returned, you are welcome."

He looked pleased, but hesitated. "The blackwings may not feel the same way."

"When we find Macal, he and Rya can straighten the blackwings out," I said. Sidra nodded agreement, but her expression glazed with worry.

Wik said firmly, "They'll find him. He's always been lucky."

"How can you be optimistic while under Rya's thumb?" Beliak asked. "And you, while hiding here. I'm losing hope. The egg? The other cities being dead? What next?" He didn't look angry, only sad and worried. He clasped my hand again.

"We need to tell—" I started to list names in my head. "Everyone."

Sidra's forehead wrinkled. "Are you sure? Won't this frighten people, that they're living next to a city that might hatch anytime?"

It frightened me. But I nodded. I was sure. They needed to know.

Ceetcee looked at me, clear-eyed. "That's what we need now. Everyone. Together."

Wik rose. "I'll go too." He ducked out of the tent with me, Sidra behind us.

Four guards passed us. They carried a body on a span of bloodstained kite. A torn Magister's cloak dragged behind them on the ground. They weren't headed to the place where we'd begun burying our dead. They were aiming for where the city sheltered now, in low tents.

I recognized the shock of hair, the cloak, but not much more. But Wik knew. He reached out. Asked quietly, "Alive?"

Sidra stepped towards the bearers like the air was too thick, like a sleepwalker, about to slip from a balcony and fall.

One of the bearers was from Mondarath. Minlin, tears streaking her cheeks, slowed the rest to let Sidra to take Macal's hand gently in her own. "Breathing, but barely. We found him in the lower tiers, near the city. The kite frame saved him," Minlin said.

Macal's cheekbones were crushed from the fall, his chin swollen, eyes blackened and pressed shut. Although a leg was temporarily splinted, he moaned when the blackwings shifted the silk too quickly.

Sidra sucked her teeth and put a hand on Minlin's arm. "I'll stay with him. Take us somewhere safe." She reached as if to brush mud from Macal's hair, then stopped, her hand hovering in the air above him. Then she drew a deep breath and dropped her hand to her side. "Take us to Rya's tent."

Minlin and the other Aivans began moving slowly forward. I stayed still. "That's safe?"

When I protested, Sidra raised a hand, but kept walking with the litter. "We don't have much medicine, and the Aivans do. We need a place for him to rest, out of the community's eye. He helped them evacuate. It's as safe as anywhere, hopefully. Until we find a better home."

I swallowed hard. No one had told her yet that we might have to stay here for good. I couldn't bear to do so now.

Macal took a shuddering breath, and Sidra looked at me. "I'll go with them. Try to keep him alive. But Nat? Wik?"

"Yes?" We both answered.

"Be quick. And keep people away from that egg."

╲ ╲ ╲

We heard the fledges before I saw them. Five of them, the tallest near wingtest age, the youngest just ready for flight.

But not anymore.

They crouched by the city's leg, impervious to the smell. Peered into the pit. "It's enormous," said one.

"I still think it's a bone or a bird's egg," whispered another, streaks of mud light on their dark skin.

Another fledge, carrying a younger child, laughed. "Maili, you're wrong. There's no bird that big."

"What happens if it hatches?" said a third, wearing a torn robe and their first patchwork wings, still.

"The slowest ones get eaten!" the oldest shrieked and chased the rest of the fledges back to the shelters. Five fledges, all running back to their families, to share the news of their find.

"Wait," Wik shouted. Two of the fledges halted in their tracks. "Go get Rya and Beliak. Tell Beliak to bring whoever's with him."

It was time to tell everyone.

The fledges were quick. Rumor was quicker. Wik held the curious off with a Singer's resolve.

"Dirt and bones," Rya whispered when she'd had a good look. "Liar, did you forget to tell us this too? Do these monsters come out of the ground?"

I ignored her name for me. "Wik says they do. I've never seen anything like it before." *Would it hatch something small enough to climb, or kill?*

"Look at it! Fascinating. Like a birds' egg," Rya said.

Beliak, arriving with Ciel, disagreed. "It's dangerous. The size of it. Think of what happens when it hatches."

Wik agreed. "When it hatches, it'll be hungry. We need to be far away. Worse, there are other cities out there, some trying to kill the others. They'll kill us alongside if we stay."

He described the cities he and Kirit had seen, and who they'd found there.

Rya's face went completely calm. "Dix."

Wik turned to her, touching her feathered shoulder. "You have control of the blackwings—the Aivans now—she's not a problem any longer."

"I disagree," Rya said. "As long as she's alive, she's a risk. Perhaps even when she's dead."

"She's with Kirit," Wik said.

"Then she won't be alive long," I said with confidence. I couldn't imagine Kirit letting Dix live.

Wik looked at me for a long time before he said, "Don't be so sure."

Rya paced in front of the hole, the drooping, graying skin of the toppled cities, the egg. "We'll post a guard here, to keep the curious away. And we'll sort out some way to drag the egg to a new location, a safe distance. Or . . ." She paused, tapping a finger against her lips, "We can raise this city. Properly. We might train it."

"That's skytouched," Wik said.

Rya gave him a long, appraising look. "You are a citykiller. I choose a different path. The carrion birds have already begun stripping the dead city. When they're done, we can live in its bones. That can be our home until the new one is grown large enough," Rya continued. "*You* haven't found us another one, so we'll make our home here. When the new city hatches, we'll take care of it."

"You can't mean it," I said. "This is no place to live, among the dead."

Rya looked at me. "Being here feels a bit like being dead, doesn't it? Below the clouds, no sky, no wind, everything heavy. We are not made for this, but we will get used to it. And somehow, we'll fly again. We'll rise with the new city's towers."

Wik sighed. He reached into his pocket and withdrew an intricate map. "This came from a city about two days' walk from here. We called it Varat. But it will be more than two days' journey away now. The city moves."

Ignoring our questions, he spread the map against one of the city's claws, and took out a lens. "Varat was here. There are cities walking these routes, here and here. This, I think, is the dead one we found. And this is our own city. That small city is the one that attacked."

"We named it Nimru," I whispered.

"This other city has artifexes?" Rya asked. She put her hand on the map. "We'll need this."

Wik nodded. He let Rya take the map. "But they can't understand us, nor we them. And Dix has already broken their trust, stealing from them. They'd attack us if they saw us coming."

"Then maybe they won't see us coming," Ceetcee said. "New tools would be helpful while rebuilding."

Quiet overtook the group. Wik shook his head. "I can't advocate for that."

"Wik, why didn't Kirit return?" I wasn't sure I wanted to know the answer.

"She's determined to find a proper city, with no one on it. Somewhere safe."

As he said that, Ciel's face closed up like a trap. "We can't climb towers again. Not here, not anywhere. We'll kill another city if we do." She looked at Wik, at Rya.

The sun had risen above the clouds, blocking the light. The day grew darker. A few citizens passed us by, but the Aivans kept most away.

Rya looked at all of us. "But if we don't," she said, "we'll never fly again. We'll be always at the mercy of the ground. I need your help." She looked at me. "Yours especially."

We waited, and listened, while she laid out her sense of the community's needs.

Rya gestured across the destruction of the city, the fallen towers, moss, bone shards, and crushed birds. "We need to make our home a fortress. To keep our community safe. And to keep the blackwings from learning about Dix until we have the community's support. Until it doesn't matter anymore. We need to find a way forward, to fly again." She looked at Wik and Ciel. "We need to gather all the supplies. We need more artifexes."

Ciel stared at Rya. Her fists clenched and unclenched. She looked at me, then back to the Aivans. Rya didn't notice. She was so busy trying to picture the future of the city, she ignored the youngest among us.

Then Urie came running, the sound of his feet on the ground breaking the tension.

"Sidra sent me," he said.

Rya looked at him, alarmed. "Blackwing, is Macal worse?"

Urie bowed. He glanced at me, but he turned to Rya. Her feathers were dusty and her voice raw, but he stuttered in her presence. Finally, he spoke low, and with awe. "Risen, she sent me as Macal's second. He still lives, but I am yours. Not the blackwings' any longer. I wish to be of use. To help artifex for you."

"Not Risen. Aivan," Rya corrected gently.

"Aivan," Urie said. "I am honored. I will follow you and Nat anywhere."

"There is nowhere to go," Rya said. "Nat has lied. Kirit has failed. We need to find food, clean water, to begin again. And we will start here."

She pulled a feather from her pocket and gave it to Urie.

He tied it to his shoulder, delighted.

"Rya—" I started. This was time to discuss, to plan. Not to fortify.

She held up a hand. "We clear the area, we defend the bones of the city from any challenge. We can live beside it, use the skin for shelters, footwraps. Begin to see what grows here. We need to begin again. Just like Ciel's new song says. Everyone must help."

Urie focused on her words, but he looked concerned. "Djonn's climbers and kites 'become real in the sky,' yes. But no one's seen the artifex since before the collapse," he whispered. "What can I help build in his absence?"

"I need you all," Rya said. "Urie, I need you to help run messages. Ciel, you can make new, hopeful songs."

But Ciel's gaze turned bone-stubborn. She turned to me and whispered, "I will never live inside the city's skeleton. We need to fly. And we need to find a home for us, and for the silkspiders and the—" She bit her lip before speaking louder. "We have to find a place that's better."

Rya focused on Ciel. "We need to, yes. Still, your songs helped give us a way to live now. If it will help your city, will you write us more?" Rya said. Her tone was kind, inviting.

Ciel, storm-faced, walked away without answering. Past the small group of fledges camped by the tethered kites.

Rya blinked and took a deep breath.

"I need you too, Nat," she said after a pause. "You can redeem yourself. You can help the community recover."

"How?" I watched Urie look from Rya to me. Rya hadn't asked him to do anything besides run messages. He followed the conversation, waiting.

"You can help me find a way to fly again. If that means attacking Varat for their tools, so be it. Otherwise, you find another way."

I thought about my options. Looked at the intricate map. If this was an example of Varat's power, we would lose. And helping Rya fly again? Impossible. I needed to stall her.

"You'll need all of us for those things," I said. "Ciel included. She's not a fledge by any means. Let me go get her. But I need to do it without guards."

She held up a hand, considering my request. Turned to Urie. "I need you to find those who can help me build, who can lift us into the air again."

"I can help," Urie said. "I helped Djonn and my aunts with the kites."

"Then you'll know what to look for," Rya said. "Very helpful."

Urie, looking slightly disappointed, said, "On your wings, Aivan."

When he'd departed, Rya looked at me for a long moment, then nodded. "Go."

❧ ❧ ❧

Ciel had traveled a long way down the bone collapse in a short time. When I found her, she was repacking two small bags for better balance on the uneven bone shards.

"Where will you go?" I asked quietly.

"I am NOT a fledge. No more than you are a liar. I'll go find another city, maybe. Or I'll find Kirit." She slipped her basket over one shoulder. It glowed slightly when she spoke. She crossed the other sack over the other shoulder. That one clanked.

Alone? I doubted it. "What's in the bags?" A sneaking suspicion began to rise. "Ciel?"

She whistled, and Moc came over the rise, carrying two panniers. Both also carried wing frames, furled.

"We're going to look for Kirit. To warn her about Rya. Kirit can't come back with Rya seizing power."

"Rya wouldn't harm Kirit." I couldn't imagine it.

Moc looked shocked. "Of course not! But Rya would never let Kirit leave. She'd keep you both as Lawsbreakers. Like Dix wanted to. Especially with Kirit befriending Dix."

"I doubt that's what's happened." Wik hadn't explained. "And Rya's not like Dix."

Moc reached out and touched the feather at my shoulder. "You sure? What happened to wanting to save the city? Are you giving up?"

My family needed me here. My city needed me. The feather on my shoulder swung back and forth, a pendulum of accusations. I hadn't given up. I'd given myself to Rya in trade, as a Lawsbreaker, in order to speed the evacuation. To earn hope.

And I'd lied. Maybe I deserved what I got. "I can be more help here."

"You were trying to help already," Moc said. "You're not a Lawsbreaker. Don't let her repeat names at you until you believe them."

Ciel added, "You might check the city's supplies. Rya has collected the kites and ropes, yes, but also the lighter-than-air! She pulled a lot of it off the kites. And the kites themselves? She's talking about dismantling those."

Ciel turned and looked out across the landscape, towards the desert. At what was left of the towers: a treacherous scrabble of wobbling debris. Bonefall piles. It opened to ankle-twisting gaps, large chunks of bone, rotting plants.

Ciel and Moc made ready to climb into it. To disappear.

"Walk away with us, Nat. Keep looking for a better place," Ciel said. "We can't live on this city's back, or its bones, or by Rya's rules, but we can live somewhere. We'll find it, and Kirit, and everyone else can come live with us."

"What about Macal?" I scolded. Had they forgotten their uncle?

Ciel looked sad.

"He's very ill. The healers have him." How could she not know? I watched Moc wobble on the bones.

Ciel shook her head and scratched her scalp. "You've seen Sidra today? You should talk to her."

Only early this morning. "She was at Macal's side. She sent Urie to Rya." Hours ago now.

Moc said, "Rya moved Macal into her quarters at midmorning. She's trying to help. But if Macal dies, half the city may follow Sidra and the tower leaders. Rya knows it. She wants Sidra's support. Didn't you see that when she was talking to you? She has to consolidate power. Worse, if the blackwings hear Dix is alive, they might split away to follow her, not Rya."

I touched the feather at my shoulder. Without wind to make flight easy, Rya had to find a new way to inspire her followers. She might grow desperate.

Ciel walked a few steps forward, clanking. She looked like she was trying to hide something. I recognized the sound from the time I'd carried something similar.

The brass plates.

"If you're so sure the community's splintering, why not support the tower leaders? And why are you taking the brass plates?" I lifted one from the satchel, and she grabbed it back. "And the littlemouths?" That glow from the other satchel was unmistakable. "Ciel—"

"Because the groups are too small, the frustrations so large. Don't you remember The Rise? We could start attacking each other." She sighed with frustration. "I want to preserve something of what we were."

The brass plates were our city's artifex heritage. They contained knowledge well beyond what any of us understood. The littlemouths had always been Ciel's charge. "Maybe Rya should have those, or the artifexes. Didn't you hear her? They're needed."

"We're taking them somewhere safe," she said. "Everyone should be able to have these. Not just one group." She looked at me accusingly.

Ciel's braids were once again encrusted with red dirt. Moc's hair as well. She'd tied her new footwraps with bird gut and sewn on hard dried-skin soles. I recognized these. Moc had cut these from the city's skin and begun trading for gossip almost as soon as we landed. Now she looked ready to walk away on them.

"We'll find Kirit. Wik said she wasn't giving up, so we aren't either. We'll get help," Ciel said. "The way things are going here, you're going to need it."

"What help could Kirit possibly be?" I said. "She walked away. She's with Dix." The thought was ludicrous. "Go, then," I said, a sour taste in my mouth.

The twins scrambled across the bonefall and out into the desert.

❦ ❦ ❦

When I returned to her camp, Rya was waiting for me. Wik sat on the ground, the map spread before him.

Rya's guards checked through my satchel. Searched my robes.

"What are you looking for? I have nothing that you don't know about."

"Liar," she said, not unkindly, as if she did it for the guards. Then her voice changed, became softer still. "A kite crew saw two fledges walking the bonefall this morning, but only reported it when they didn't return. No one can find Ciel, nor her brother, Moc. You said you were going to talk to her. Instead, they've fled the city and supplies are missing. Did you see them go?" Her men were searching through the bags and baskets, even the ones from the scavenger market. They'd lost something.

"What are you seeking?" If what Ciel had said was true, and Rya had been gathering all our resources into a central location, they sought something important.

"Do you remember the littlemouths from the midcloud?" she asked.

I nodded. "Of course." Ciel had taken care of those.

"And the silkspiders?"

"We packed several hatches in the kites." I didn't know which kites, or how many survived.

"They're gone, as are the artifexes plates. I think your fledges took them." Her voice rose an octave. "All of her verses about working together. About new horizons, and now she's made off with the city's treasures, into the desert."

"Maybe she had a good reason? Maybe she thought our plans were dangerous." I didn't mention that I'd heard what they were looking for. Perhaps I could get Rya to understand what Ciel and Moc feared first.

"What do we need littlemouths for?" Wik said. "Down here, they're not likely to matter much."

Rya was quiet. She tilted her head at me, then at him. "Don't you see them as lucky?"

"Not really," Wik grumbled. "People make their own luck."

"I disagree. The littlemouths are important. They inspired me in the clouds. Kept me going." I'd never told anyone that. Now I felt protective. "They were our connection to our community for a short while, too. Our bridge."

Now the twins' hiking out beyond the outer tower collapse began to make more sense. They'd taken more than the brass plates. And the guards had lost sight of them. I would not lie about where they were to Rya, but I wasn't going to offer any details either. Soon, the twins would be out of sight.

Rya smiled slowly, looked at the guards. I realized now one was a blackwing, the other wore an Aivan feather. Rya's voice was still worried. "Your family wishes to see you. They'd like you back in camp with them. I have reason to want that."

I wanted that more than anything. "What's the cost?"

"The littlemouths, Liar. I want them. And your help developing a plan to keep the community together, to fly, and to train the new city." She glanced at Wik, at the blackwings. "You endangered us by keeping truths from us. You cannot lead. So I must. And you must help me." Then she whispered, for my ears only, "Before Dix returns."

*Is that all?* "That's a great deal to ask."

"You'll have help." She beckoned a guard. "Bring Urie. He can assist Nat."

Moments passed. The guard returned, with Urie, breathless, and two blackwings in tow.

"Did you find the artifexes?" Rya asked.

Urie shook his head. "I saw something on the horizon instead."

The twins? I hoped not.

Rya raised her eyebrows, interested, but her jaw clenched.

Urie continued, unaware, "Another city. Moving away from us, I think." He looked at Rya with a bit of fear in his eyes, but only a bit. "It's enormous."

"Could we reach it?" Rya's guard asked. "Climb it?"

"We could get there, but it might take days. Aivan"—he addressed Rya with that same tone of awe—"what would you do?"

An enormous city on the horizon might not be moving away from us. Especially if it hadn't been there that morning. "How fast is it moving?"

Urie shook his head. "Not fast. There was a big flock of birds around it."

Rya waved a hand. "Leave it for now. If it's moving slowly especially, we can consider it once we decide what to do with the egg. Once we fly."

Urie, disappointed again, ducked his head and chewed his lip. He was thinking something over.

"Rya," I cautioned. I saw Wik's lips move. He put his finger on the map, in the shadows. "Varat. We have to prepare. Be ready for another city to attack."

The name of the city they'd discovered. The one Rya had wanted me to attack. The one that had moved away. And was coming back.

"Nonsense. Why would a city come here?" Rya said. "We will stick to the plan. How do we go on if we cannot fly? Flying is what we know best. How can we possibly train a new city? Or defend it? We'll fight better from the sky. How else do I keep the city's loyalty?"

*Who are we as a community if we're grounded?* That was her true question. One I couldn't answer. I opened and shut my mouth like a fledge.

Her guard poured Rya a bone cup of stale water. She grimaced as she sipped. "We must return to the sky," she said. "We must be ready to fly as the city grows. Safety is in the air, not on the ground. Your lie cost us so much, Nat." She frowned. "It may have saved us, but how do we live?"

I didn't know the answer to that either. I thought of Maalik. Imagined his return. "Maybe it's only temporary," I said. "Maybe we will fly again." Inwardly, I cursed myself for ever grasping at hope, making promises I couldn't keep.

Another of Rya's guards approached the tent entrance. Rya quickly shook herself ready. By the time the young blackwing had reached her, Rya looked once again confident and sure. Two blackwings waited at the tent entrance.

I was rattled at the change in her. But I looked at Urie, and he was transformed too. Not afraid any longer.

Urie stared at Rya, boldly. "The blackwings wish to work on this together, with you."

Rya's captain looked at us and raised an eyebrow. "You can help the Aivans distribute food. Or find for the lead artifex. What Rya's asked of you. We searched most of the bonefall closest to the city. Tomorrow we'll search the remains of the hightowers. The blackwings know all this. You can help."

"I don't want to just help," Urie said. "I want to work by your side. As I did with Macal. I meant the flight problem. The blackwings wish to take that project out of your hands. They're suggesting I be in charge because I worked with Djonn."

She put the water down. "Not an option, Urie. You don't have the experience." The boy's face grew cloudy. Rya saw it and said,

"I need you as a tether, a liaison. I want to call all the blackwing factions together. Urie, go tell them, and invite guards and hunters from the towers too. And any tower leaders who survived. We'll have a ceremony—Remembrances, and also something new. We'll declare the kind of community we want to be now."

"I'll tell them." Urie turned and left, but his face was a storm cloud.

"Rya," I cautioned. "Declare? What about defending? Rebuilding? What about asking everyone to decide? What about not looking away from a moving city? One that is coming closer?"

Rya raised her voice, so that the guards outside could hear. "As you once said, Nat, asking everyone to decide takes too long. We have an egg that might hatch into a city. Another one on the move. We have people to feed and clothe and keep out of trouble. They all deserve to know now what we're up against, but not until we have a concrete plan. They'll figure it out soon enough. They can relay it back to their towers."

"They'll tear you apart if you fail," I said.

"No," she said, looking at me sideways and pinching the bridge of her nose. "They'll tear *you* apart. You are the Liar. If they do, then we will be free to go on. If they don't, we'll continue in this way. Unless you can give us a sign of luck to come."

The littlemouths again. She wanted their light, their luminosity—a sign that we could carry the past forward.

The one thing I could not give her, because Ciel had taken them, for the one thing I wanted most: my family. "Do Ceetcee and Beliak already know what you plan?"

"They do. And they'll agree to helping the cause you've given us." Rya stretched "cause" out long enough to be two words, considering it. "Flight."

She continued, "Ceetcee's already working on a launcher. This is a good way to unite everyone and keep us together. If we need it, defense is also easier from the air."

Rya pointed through the sheltering silks, and I looked out at the place where the Aivans had stretched a kite and were slicing it apart with their knives. They were cutting shapes from the stretched cloth, but strange triangles, too small for wings, or at least smaller than what I was used to.

Djonn's windscoops. The last things he'd made for us, to free us from a dying city. They were what Macal sacrificed himself for. A new kind of city. A new way of living.

I looked openmouthed at Rya.

She beamed, pride showing through her worry. "Flying again, of course. We are working on the right technology to get us back up in the air, and Ceetcee and Beliak are being amazingly resourceful, especially when it comes to modifying some of the existing kites and crawlers."

"What do Macal and Sidra have to say about this?"

Rya bowed her head, confirming what I'd feared. "Macal once saved my life. I owed him a great debt. I tried to save him, but he says nothing any longer, Nat. I am sorry."

The news kicked the wind out of me. Just this morning, Macal had been alive. There had been a glimmer of hope. Now it slipped through our fingers. I heard Wik gasp.

We'd argued, and disagreed, but Macal had been a good man, a good leader. His loss ground me away. But Macal was Wik's brother.

"Wik, I—" There weren't enough words. I stood when he stood, rocked by his—and the city's—loss.

Wik strode from the tent, fast. A guard blocked me from following. While Rya struggled to hold the reins of the city, I still couldn't leave until she let me go.

I turned back to her. "What will you do now? Who will speak to the towers for you?"

She'd squared her shoulders. Closed her eyes so her tattoos

looked like a mask. "I will speak to the towers. We'll fly together. We'll use what we have and unify the city, in Macal's name."

I didn't like the sound of that. "In Macal's name? With the kites? We need those!"

"I disagree. They can be used to make many things. We will use them to fly. Macal's dream was to save us. And I will save us. You will find the fledges and bring back what they stole."

"That's not—" I began. But Rya stood. A guard walked me from the tent. I was dismissed.

# 33

## KIRIT, BELOW

*⁓ Stolen objects lift wings up high ⁓*

Atop the ridge, the giant kite rippled in the breeze, closer now.

I adjusted the straps on Dix's wings, feeling the once-familiar weight on my shoulders, heavier now with the mechanisms. Pushed my fingers into the grips. The strange landscape made each motion new again.

I tightened the harness one last time. Double-checked the battens and grips. My heart thudded, nervous.

*Now or never, Kirit.*

Maalik grew restless and climbed on my shoulder, then flew to a safe perch on the ridgeline.

Instead of a disaster, the first failed flight had helped me figure out and recalculate how much lift I needed. It gave me a good guess as to what might happen with the propellers' lift. How much curve I'd give my wings. "No time to hesitate." My mother's favorite phrase.

Reaching over my shoulder, I pulled the propellers' pins with my fingertips. With a whir, they began to spin. I lifted up, into the breeze.

The wind caught me, and I straightened out. I flew.

Then I wobbled. Even with the wind bellying the silk and the propellers pushing me forward, I still felt extremely unsteady. But the forward motion drew me closer to the kites.

I didn't care how I looked while getting there. *Don't crash,* I whispered.

Controlling the powered wings in a real wind gust was a different risk. As the breeze picked up, I tried curling my wings and immediately rose higher—a different angle than I was used to.

*Stay calm, Kirit.* If I threw myself out of the weak wind by panicking, I wouldn't reach the kite.

I could see part of it now, knocking against the rocks above. The large frame had caught on something, and the wind battered at it but couldn't blow it away.

Still wobbling, I dipped, then recovered. But my toes scraped hard against a jutting part of the ridge. I hissed at the pain and kept my body as straight as I could. It was much more work to glide here, though I felt the wind increasing as I flew higher.

The propellers made everything more difficult. They thrust me forward instead of buoying me up. Unaccustomed to their motion, I pitched wildly again, and then fought my way level. I yearned for the wind I could feel just a bit above, the strength that I could see pulling at the kite.

But if I looked down, which was dizzying, I could barely see Dix's black cloak against the ridge. The healer's shift stood out, stark and white.

The wind increased, and I fought to keep level.

Then the little propellers sputtered, first one, then the other. Then they stopped spinning. I had barely enough momentum to glide and turn. The wind pushed me sideways, to the water, then dropped me towards the ridge just below the kite. Close enough.

I stumbled again when I landed, jarring my ankles and knees with impact, but managed to stay on my feet on the uneven ground. I bit the inside of my lip to distract me from the ache in my leg, then put the windup propellers in my satchel and furled Dix's wings.

By the time I got to the kite, my arms and legs shook with exhaustion. Huge expanses of patchwork silk billowed in the sky above the ridge, ripped free of the bone frames.

Listening for sounds of survivors, I scrambled up. When I got to eye level, I saw the left box frame of the kite was bent at a sharp angle. The sun gave the resulting crumpled shape a jagged shadow, which made it hard to see if anyone was still inside.

To my right, against the ridge wall, the kite's tether was twisted around a rocky outcropping. The full outline of the box kite appeared as I cleared the last part of the ridge. A broken frame on one end revealed where the edge had snagged and torn. The frame dragged against the ridge and turned the kite one way and the other, but the rest still floated on the breeze, hanging out over the cliff edge and the rocks below.

"Hello? Anyone?" My voice bounced off the rocks. No answer.

Pale yellow silk from the kite made the gray cloud above look even darker. I scrambled for the fabric and tried to reel it in, but it was too strongly hooked. So I climbed the tether and peered inside.

Empty.

Where had they gone? There was no sign of the citizens who'd ridden in this escape craft.

A snapping sound from the tether drew my attention. The line looped and twisted over the kite, and the kite itself was upside down. The frame was still trying to fly on the wind with no one to steer it. My breath caught.

Across the landscape, bone eaters wheeled and banked, marking territory in the sky and on the ridge.

Not again. My heart sank.

I could hear the bone eaters' cries in my memory as they stalked the midcloud meadow, where the council—and my mother—had fallen. I wanted to chase every bone eater from the air. This ridge was not for them.

Then I heard shouts from a section of the ridgeline just out of sight. Several people clambered over the ridge near me, battered, as I was, but upright. I didn't recognize any of them.

"On your wings," one called. "Mercy on your wings!" said another.

The familiar greeting, after all this time made laughter bubble from my lips. Still shaking, I made my way down the ridge to see how I could help and lifted a young boy who'd cut his foot. I carried him as best I could, back to the peak where they'd crashed the kite.

"Did Nat and Ciel survive the climb?" One must have, for these refugees to be here.

A woman nodded. "Both. Brokenwings and the Singer fledge. They sounded the alarm. Ciel was a wonder with the kites. She came down first."

"And Nat?"

"He kept everything moving, Skyshouter." The woman laughed. She knew a name for me, but it was a northern name. Even as Brokenwings was a southern one.

I didn't care what they called us at that moment. Knowing Nat and Ciel had made it to the clouds was enough.

And at least one of them made it back down, only to find no whipperling waiting for them, and no new city to live in. I calmed, sobered. Soon Wik would be there to explain, but would it be too late?

Would Nat forgive me again?

I put my hand over the pocket in my robe where Maalik had nested. Empty. The whipperling had flown below. Dix stood near him on the ridge.

I whistled, but he didn't fly up to meet me.

Above, the huge box kite hung in the sky. As it gently rocked on the breeze, its crew below picked across the ridgeline for the supplies they'd jettisoned.

It was hungry work. Other survivors from the kites had figured out how to lower buckets and toss nets to the water like we'd once done in the air. They came back with a strange, slick creature that flopped in our hands, unable to breathe the air. They'd built a fire on the rocks. The smell of cooking wafted up.

As they worked, I heard a laugh. Dix had finally made her way across the ridge. She rested there, but not for long.

I couldn't see Maalik.

A shout went up among some of the crew. Two southwestern hunters. "Dix Grigrit? Is it you?"

She frowned, her broken teeth hidden, her wrecked face pale. "Who's asking?"

There were only two blackwings among the whole group, but the idea that she'd reconnected with any of them, that scared me more than the heights, or the propellers.

"We flew with Dix once, at Laria. Are you she?"

Dix's good eye stared at them. They didn't recognize her. She swallowed. "I flew with her too. She was smart as they come."

The blackwings shrugged, even as the other crew muttered about Dix. "Figured you were too old to be Dix," one said.

"Not really," she answered. She was about to say more, but the kite's tether loosened and began to slap the air near us. She ducked low.

I scrambled after the tether lines, skidding on the rocks and tearing my footwraps. One of the blackwings joined me in the chase. The box kite hung in the air above us, its lighter-than-air balloons drifting behind. Its silk spans billowing in the breeze. Its crew looked up at it, then at the ridge, then at us.

The healer from Varat, who'd finished bandaging the young boy's foot, joined me in chasing down the kite tethers. Dix did the same.

Once we'd caught all the tethers and managed to wedge several of them under rocks, I built up a cairn with loose stones from the ridge.

Dix brought me a piece of graincake and then handed Maalik to me. The bird nestled happily in my robe while I stared at Dix's retreating form. Whispered, "Thank you."

She paused, then kept walking down the ridgeline.

Meantime, the blackwings pitched in, unaware of the exchange. Soon we had a fairly tall pile of anchors built up beneath the kite. And as the evening wore on, the kite rose in the air, lifted high on a proper breeze.

Oh clouds, a strong breeze—moving soft across my cheeks.

A whisper of wind in my ears.

I lifted my arms to catch it, and the wind slipped through my fingers like spidersilk. There wasn't enough strong air this low to lift me.

No wind, no ride.

I let the breeze trail across my fingertips and flap the edge of silk on my wings. Overhead, out of reach, the breeze filled the silk of the kite.

And beyond it, I saw the second kite's wide spans, coming closer.

# 34

## NAT, BELOW

*⌁ And friends gather to bid a love good-bye ⌁*

At the edge of the bonefall, near where Ciel and Moc had disappeared, I heard a noise. Sidra knelt there, beside a figure wrapped in silk.

She dug at the packed dirt with her fingers—raw and bloody—and a bone hook.

I didn't know what to say to her. We'd never really been able to talk. She'd teased me once, long ago, but I hadn't known how to respond. Later, I'd felt awkward about what Macal might say to her about me: that I always flew too high, too fast.

In the midcloud, she and I had worked side by side to rig the kites and the climbers, but there'd been no time for true conversation. How could I dare speak to her loss? Interrupt her mourning?

More footsteps on the bonefall. Wik, walking quickly.

Rya's guard stood a little ways away, out of earshot. When the former Singer approached, the guard let him pass.

Sidra didn't look up. Wik knelt. Reached out to touch her shoulder. Hesitated.

In her grief, she reached up and clasped his hand. They grieved in silence.

My choices were all bad. I coughed, hoping it would be enough. It wasn't. "Sidra," I finally said, as softly as I could. "I'm so sorry."

She looked up at me, her robes torn and hair snarled. Her eyes were unfocused at first, but then they drew down on me, two arrows that pierced straight through me. "You brought this to us. He wasn't supposed to be a hero of the city. He wasn't supposed to die."

She put a hand on the dead Magister's chest. "And I won't let them have him. They aren't going to train a new city by using Macal as bait."

"Who would suggest such a thing?" I was astounded. For Sidra to carry Macal's body out here by herself meant rumors were flying.

"There's been talk," Wik said. "I've heard it." His voice cracked. He did not let go of Sidra's hand.

I'd heard murmurs too: that the egg had moved, that it was about to crack. But nothing like what this implied. I looked back at the impassive guard. They hadn't heard us.

Sidra didn't answer my question either. She released Wik's hand and dug at the ground with the bone hook. "Macal and I fought before he went into the clouds. Before he left to see what was wrong with the city. I wanted him to lead, but I didn't want him to be a hero. I wanted him to be *honorable*. I wanted so many things for him. I didn't see what he was. Who he was. I got so caught up in supporting the *idea* of him that I didn't see him. Or me."

She began digging again, her face wet with tears.

Wik touched his brother's forehead.

I heard the resonance in her words. "Sidra. Wik. I promise you. I'll live up to Macal's trust. I'll be better than I've ever been, for the sake of the city. For Macal. For all of us."

I would not let the people of the city tear themselves apart. Not while I lived and could make a difference.

Far from the rest of the city, Wik and I helped Sidra bury Macal.

# 35

## KIRIT, BELOW

*⸺ Stowaways steer by a different star ⸺*

I chased the wobbling second kite. I didn't hesitate.

Whatever I found inside when I caught the glider, I would deal with it. I would not turn away.

The second kite drifted erratically, then regained control once more.

That made the kite easier to catch, but it was troubling. Was anyone steering?

I drew close enough to spot the kite's tether, tangled and dangling out of reach. I jumped for it, landing painfully, but holding the spidersilk line. "Got you," I whispered.

Liope helped me drag the line to the ground and pile stones over the tether as an anchor. I climbed up the stones, wincing. My leg felt as if it were made of fire.

I'd look after it later.

When I pulled myself over the side of the kite, I found three figures huddled together against the cold, faces buried in each other's shoulders. Asleep or unconscious? It was difficult to tell in the dark. Two shivered; the third, sleeping between them, felt too warm to the touch, even in threadbare robes.

Up this high, the gentle sway of the basket occasionally gave way to the pitch of the kite bucking against the wind as it fought the tether. I hoped Liope was paying attention, watching for me.

"Hello," I called, shaking them. Strewn clothes and belongings traced the kite's path across the ground. They'd been jettisoning things? Trying to go back up?

The nearest sleeper raised her head. Looked at me groggily. I gasped. "Aliati!" Hope buoyed me.

"Kirit?" She blinked and wariness took over her gaze. "Where are we? I thought we'd floated out over the water. I thought we were dead."

"You're over a ridge overlooking more water than I've ever seen, but you're safe. You're at the edge of a desert, where the giant cities graze on—" I searched for a word to explain what we'd seen in the desert. "They're like skymouths, but in the ground. And the cities fight each other." It sounded like a child's story. A scary one. Aliati blinked again, confused. I tried again, simplifying what they needed to know: "You're in a kite. It's still aloft, and I've got it tethered. Safe. For now."

Aliati rose and walked unsteadily on the kite's surface. She brushed the other sleeper's shoulder. "Raq, wake up."

The woman lifted her head. Her shirt was streaked with vomit. She looked miserable. With all the movement, the third passenger moaned too. Djonn.

Still alive. But barely. Burning with fever.

What were they doing here? "You made it off the city! How did you drift so far?"

Aliati smiled. "We stole Djonn, before the city and the blackwings worked him to death, before he worked himself to death."

"What do you mean, steal?" I didn't think I'd heard her correctly.

Raq laughed. "We scavenged him. We cut the tether lines, and the kite floated away, as it was supposed to."

Aliati frowned. "But we'd miscalculated. The kite went too high too fast, then down too fast. We couldn't control it. Had a hard time steering at the lower altitude. The changes made us ill. And then Djonn didn't get better."

Raq looked at Aliati, then Djonn. "He's not been able to eat, and even a few sips of water make him cough like he's drowning in it."

"Will he die?" If they'd stayed with the city, this might not have happened.

"He might," Aliati said. "He's been ready for a while now. He wanted to see the ground first."

Now I knew why no one had chased this kite. No one knew it was gone. "The city needed Djonn; Nat and Ciel needed his knowledge. And you stole him?" Something must have spooked them badly. Clouds. "What made you take an entire kite barely filled?" I couldn't stifle my anger. From what I'd seen, so many could have come down in this kite.

"The kite *was* full. With scavengers, because the city had already gone back on a promise. Scavengers decide when to get off on their own, and that's just what happened. They've scattered. They'll be all right. Or they won't. It's their choice. And Djonn already had trained six more artifexes in how the kites worked. He needed to rest," Raq said.

I sputtered. Scavengers didn't know a thing about surviving on the ground. "There are predators out there. Things they can't see! Other cities!" *What if the scavengers found Varat? The treasures there?*

"It's true. We left without permission, from you or anybody." Aliati's chin tilted, and she smiled defiance at me. Raq came up beside her, and her smile mirrored Aliati's. "It's what we do."

"The scavengers have to come back." The groundmouths alone would get them. "I can tell them how to survive in the desert."

"If they want your help, I'm sure they'll ask," Aliati said. She held out her hand to me. "But this kite is ours. It's not a bad view. You know you have a home here if you'd like it."

No time to think of a home for me yet. Not when many still needed a safe place to live. But I was curious. "How do you plan to live here?"

Raq raised her hands to the silk. "We don't know yet. We could hunt from here. We saw many birds. If Djonn could recover enough to help us figure out the controls, or we could find some more lighter-than-air . . ."

A kite might be a strange home. Aloft, it would raise us above the hostile ground. I pushed the memory of bone towers and blue skies away. A kite was a start.

Aliati got serious. "But first we need to find medicine for Djonn."

I knew one place there were healer supplies, but likely Varat had moved. They had medicine. And healers. And were now lost to us.

But we did have one of Varat's healers. They'd helped us. Dix still suspected them.

Would they help us again? Had they been exiled for helping us escape? Or would they betray us once they knew more about our city?

I brought out the last of my water and shared it with the others, thinking hard.

Then I descended the rope, hoping I could communicate what we needed from the healer, hoping they could help.

Halfway down the kite's rope, my leg aching with exertion, realization hit me. *Dix had stolen Maalik from me in the healer's cell. She'd stolen artifacts. What else did she have in her robe pockets?*

Getting Dix to answer a question like that without her seeking to benefit selfishly was a lot to hope for. But I was willing to try, once more.

We needed Djonn. The city needed him to recover. I imagined the kite city that Aliati dreamed of. I wished Djonn were awake, or Ciel and Ceetcee were here. Remembering how they'd built wonders in the caves out of silk and bone, I wanted more of their help now.

I landed on the rocky outcrop and tested the tether. "You're anchored!" I shouted. "You won't blow away." Aliati threw me another tether line just to be sure, and I locked that one under a cairn of rocks too.

When I reached the middle of the ridge, I didn't see Dix at first. Then a flap of black robe from a nearby cave caught my eye. I climbed up to her. "What have you found?"

"Shelter," she said. "And strangers." She pointed back towards the desert.

At first, I couldn't see what she saw from here. Then I did. Two figures on the horizon, still far from us, walking our way.

"Aliati!" I shouted, hoping she could hear. "What can you see?"

Aliati waved. I saw the flash of a scope. She was looking. While we waited, I turned to Dix.

"We need your help. I can never forgive you for what you did, but I can hope that what you will do will be better."

Dix chuckled. "Where did you learn this? I know it wasn't Ezarit. I flew with Ezarit. She was all ambition. No forgiveness."

"She forgave. She didn't do it often, though."

I didn't tell Dix that I'd also had Elna's example. Elna was the one who forgave. Always Elna, soothing, supporting, showing us the way. I learned ambition from Ezarit, but Elna, when I needed it, was the one who saw me through. Who forgave my crimes large and small. I hadn't realized I'd needed her so much.

Dix was quiet for a moment. "Maybe edges aren't always—" She didn't continue. She stared out over the ridge instead.

"Once, I had a flock of blackwings at my call. Once I had influence. The ear of important people. I can't lie. I want that again."

I didn't hesitate. "You can't have it. I won't let you. Ever."

She didn't look at me.

"But you can help people. If you want." I explained what we needed. I was ready for Dix to bargain, but she handed over the medicines in silence, then gave her satchel to Liope. I pointed to the boy they'd bandaged, and to my own leg. Then I gestured to the kite in the distance. The healer looked through the contents of Dix's satchel, exclaiming and glaring at Dix.

I put my hand on their arm. Pointed at the kite. "Our friends." No reaction. I tried another word, knowing I risked getting it wrong. "Serrahun." They slowed and nodded.

When I pointed to the kite again, Liope stood and began climbing towards it. *Serrahun* wasn't a word for a city with people on it. Not anymore at least. It was a word for home, for community.

$$\text{\v{k} \quad \v{k} \quad \v{k}}$$

Dix watched the healer go. "I don't want to help people. Not like that one seems to. I want them to help me." She turned to stare over the ridge again. Then she pointed at the smoke rising from vents near the water. "Notice that smell?"

I had. It smelled like rotten eggs. But after the stink of a dying city, the scent was a minor irritant. "It's gas?"

Dix nodded. "The people on Varat steer their city away from it. They're much like us, Kirit. They're as superstitious as we are, but about different things. They couldn't understand our wings, but they have propellers. I don't think they actually made them. I think they collected them from elsewhere, or inherited them. From what I saw, I think they are archivists, *not* artifexes. I think they're trying to learn how to artifex, but what if they do that by taking from others? How do we defend against that?"

Her dark eyes moved from the smoke vents back to where I sat, and from there to the two tiny figures moving on the horizon. Then to the collapsed city in the distance. "Those two know where they're going." She smiled a gap-toothed grin. "Maybe we know them." I saw fear in her eyes.

"Do you want to be known?" She hadn't wanted the kite survivors to know she lived, and so far, she'd stayed far from their camp.

But if the approaching figures were people she'd hurt, they deserved to know.

"I don't know anymore," Dix said. "It's pretty awful, not knowing what I want."

I felt no pity for her. I still didn't trust her. But hearing her words, I realized the ground had changed Dix, as much as it had changed the rest of us.

She stood and moved into the cavern. "If I can, I'll help figure out the source of the smell. See if we can use it. I won't interfere."

I left her to it.

Aliati called down, "I can't tell who they are, but I think they're ours. They are carrying wingsets."

I scratched a message on a piece of bone from the broken kite and attached it to Maalik's leg. "Please fly," I whispered, hoping the whipperling would recognize the shape of wingsets and head for them.

Maalik stretched his wings and lifted on the ridge breeze. Instead of circling back to me, he flapped hard and turned towards the figures on the horizon. As the sun set below the cloud, the brave bird returned, exhausted and wobbling in the air, to collapse on my shoulder, trembling. The message chip tied to his claw rested on my collarbone. I stroked Maalik's feathers flat. Then I read the brief message. There were two symbols carved into the bone: Ciel's and Moc's marks.

When their figures sharpened on the horizon, I wound the propellers, reattached them to my wings and flew to greet the twins.

╲  ╲  ╲

"I remember a Rya," I said. "She was always very serious. She's leading the blackwings?" Doran's daughter, a blackwing leader. That hurt a little.

"She's good at it," Moc said.

Ciel rolled her eyes. "She's learning. She's charismatic, but she's still learning."

We'd climbed into the kite, taking turns helping Aliati and Raq tend Djonn. Below us, the other kite survivors and some scavengers had regrouped around the kites. They'd set up camp on the ridge and in some of the caverns high enough on the ridge to be well out of reach of the two vents that spilled noxious smoke over the water.

Ciel had opened her satchel and moved some of her things into the kite. She looked prepared to stay. When she began to hum, then continued to sing softly, the darkness lit with a soft blue glow.

"Littlemouths!" I couldn't contain my joy at seeing them, despite my confusion over everything else.

Their effect on Liope was more gradual. At first, they avoided the glow. Then we had to take turns nursing Djonn because the healer refused to leave the space where the littlemouths rested.

Then we heard Liope humming, trying to follow Ciel's tune.

"Are all the other city's residents like this?" Ciel asked.

I shook my head. "They're all different, I think. Just like us." Though this one was particularly unfathomable, even after our time together. "We would need to work hard to understand each other. I hope we can someday."

When Liope returned to their attention to Djonn, they had

a faraway look in their eyes. Their gaze kept drifting back to the littlemouths. Once, they spoke a word and touched my tattoos, then gestured at the glow.

I'd forgotten, in the long time away, that my scarred skin would sometimes pulse with the littlemouths. I could see the glow on Liope's fingertips. The intent look in their eyes.

Once again, I wished we could understand more than a few gestures. Liope touched the back of their neck, where their blue tattoo was.

We weren't alone. We were similar. But not similar enough.

Shaking her head at the healer, Dix had disappeared into the depths of the caves, muttering, "Spy."

"There's a thing you should know," I said to my five friends in the kite. I told them about Dix, our journey across the desert, and her words the night before.

Moc growled, "I will never forgive her."

"It sounds like she doesn't want you to," Ciel said. "And she's Kirit's find. Kirit scavenged her. She gets to decide what happens to Dix."

Raq's mouth quirked into a smile. "You'll make a good scavenger," she said, clapping Ciel on the shoulder. Aliati leaned in, chin over Raq's shoulder, admiring the littlemouths. "She already is, it looks like."

"What we have to decide," I said, "is what we do now. There aren't enough of us here with the two kites to defend against an attack, but Dix doesn't think the other cities will come to the ridge."

"I don't care what Dix thinks," Moc muttered.

"The right information can sometimes come from the wrong source," Aliati said. She frowned. "Just depends what we do with it from there."

"Rya's going to force the city to stay where it is. She's going to try to defend the new city, make a go of things there," Moc continued. "She thinks we're just fledges, so she talked over us. Over Urie. Over Ciel. We heard everything."

That had been a failing with Doran too. "Nobody is 'just' anything," I said. I remembered something Ezarit had said to me long ago. "Don't let anyone tell you who you are."

The littlemouths' glow dimmed as Ciel stopped singing. "Can we begin again? Here?" The breeze came in over the kite and teased her brass curls. Liope stared at where the glow had been.

A city might not attack the ridge. One might attack our once-home, though. From what Ciel had said, below those bones, a new city was readying to hatch. And Nat and Rya seemed in no hurry to move away.

Should I send Maalik now? Would they pay attention?

It was tempting to stay here. To leave the other city behind. To start fresh and let the disaster on the horizon be someone else's problem. I knew people who would be happy to do that. Who'd fought hard enough that they deserved to do that.

But that wasn't who I was.

With Djonn still ill, though improving, the solutions I needed would be harder to find. I hoped Ciel had been paying attention to the artifexes.

"I need to go back," I said. "And I need your help to do it."

In the dim light, I began to explain my plan.

# 36

## NAT, BELOW

*⌒ Before Brokenwings takes a leap too far ⌒*

Singing Remembrances was a sad but welcome break from living in the shadow of the fallen city and fear of what was to come. People streamed from their shelters, and we walked with them to where we'd say our good-byes.

Rya led us to a site near the anchored kites. She'd chosen a ceremony location as far upwind as possible.

We were still too close to the stench, if anyone asked me. But Rya hadn't asked.

She allowed me to walk through the shelters without guards trailing. "You don't cause as much trouble on the ground," she'd said.

I'd done my best to reassure her this was true. I'd promised to sing Remembrances. And if someone called me Liar today, even Rya, I would try not to challenge them.

Better, I would help Rya test the launcher Ceetcee had built. A first step towards flight, we hoped. To do so, I carried a medium-sized ballast sack, filled with scraps. It weighed a bit more than a fledge.

So much could weaken the community as it began to heal from the fall and prepare for the future. We needed strong leaders to help. Macal was gone. Sidra still mourning. And I'd promised myself to Rya.

The day before, a blackwing had been dragged right into the ground. Rya had sent four guards out to investigate, and two had come back. "There are creatures like skymouths in the ground," Wik had explained to Rya, to the council. Councilors from Amrath and Bissel had scrambled to reassure people that these groundmouths were not a sign of worse to come, but without Macal to guide them, panic had bloomed.

"I hope the ceremony and the launcher test will help give them hope," Rya murmured.

As we walked, they called out to her. "What next? How much more bad luck?"

I cast an uneasy glance at the horizon. The approaching city had moved closer overnight. Its bone eaters were a black cloud above it, but it still had a large distance to cross. Rya's guards had begun gathering weapons, but she had not yet told the citizens.

Still, Rya kept walking as she answered their questions. "We will face whatever is next together." Only I was close enough to see the pulse of tension at her throat.

At least for now, citizens fell into step behind her. They trailed their worries behind them, their losses.

At the site Rya had picked for Remembrances and the launcher demonstration, a crowd of blackwings and a few Aivans waited for us, Urie among them.

"When will we fly, Rya?" he asked.

While Rya had transformed herself for the day by adding a mix of feathers to her robes, from bone eater top feathers, to smaller gryphon pinion feathers, Urie had stripped his few feathers away.

"We must fly again," Urie said to those who would listen. "For the good of the city. We can't fight or flee danger when we aren't on the wing. We can't defend ourselves." Citizens pressed close, listening.

Minlin, one of Macal's guards from Mondarath who had been seen recently with the blackwings, pointed to the horizon. "Another city is coming. We have to fly now."

The crowd began to murmur, Remembrances almost forgotten.

Urie had wanted so much to be important. Had loved working with the artifexes in the meadow. Rya had given him small tasks. Minlin too.

"We will fly!" Rya said. "And soon."

She was still learning to be a leader on the ground. Meantime the blackwings were growing stronger again. At exactly the wrong time.

Minlin continued to speak. "You've built a mechanism to launch fliers. You've been working on it for days. Let's use it, before the other city gets too close. Put us back in the air."

Rya nodded and gestured to the sack I carried, and the launcher at the other side of the site. "The launcher has not been a secret. We'll test it after Remembrances. When we know it works, we'll move forward. You must be patient."

"It is time to try it now. To reclaim the sky," Urie said.

Now Rya stepped up, balancing on a large piece of bone. She raised her hands, and her feathered robe swung, as if in a breeze. She spoke to everyone, not just Urie and Minlin. "This is a beginning. Not an end. A time to remember and move forward. Then we *will* regain the skies."

The blackwings, led this time by Minlin, began to chant, "Fly. Fly. Fly."

Rya's face fell.

Minlin shouted, "We need to do something, Rya. Another city is coming. We have no defense." The crowd joined her.

Beliak, on the edge of the crowd, shouted louder, "We have defenses. All of us, together. Look what we've survived. Let's remember our dead now, and heal the living. Then we'll test this launcher in a way that doesn't reduce our numbers further. *Then* we can deal with the approaching city. We have the time. Let's use it."

Beliak always spoke his mind. Amidst my fears, I felt so much pride that he was not afraid to disagree. With anyone.

The crowd quieted, and Rya nodded her thanks to him. She was younger than Kirit; still, her stubborn expression reminded me of my lost wingmate. She could lead, if she could keep control of the blackwings. But this small rebellion would hurt her as much as the groundmouths had.

"We will fly again," she said. "But first we must learn how to live *here* and fight here. Together. To defend what's been entrusted to us by our city." She looked behind her. "To earn the future."

"What holds us back," the Varu councilor countered from below, "is lack of action. We cannot fly if we don't take risks. Don't you trust the work Ceetcee and Beliak have been doing?"

Rya stared at him. "You would also press us forward too fast, risking our own people? Is this what Macal would have done?"

"Urie, Minlin. Councilor Varu. Macal trusted you," Sidra added. "I trusted you. Why do you do this now?"

Urie turned on Rya. "You said we could be like birds, escape the towers. We fell. You said we could become strong, but we live in the mud. We can fly away, or to the attack. Do you not want to try, now?"

They were afraid. They wanted strength. Fearlessness.

Rya weighed her options. "I want us to fly on our own again. Perhaps very soon. But only after carefully testing the mechanism."

The crowd made restless noises. Minlin stepped forward. "There isn't enough time to be careful."

Rya stepped from the bone platform and stood nose to nose with Minlin. "Are you offering to fly?"

The crowd quieted, waiting with a bone eater's focus to see what would be left for its meal. Sidra retreated through the crowd. I moved to follow her, but Rya's guard put a hand to my chest.

An Aivan brought Minlin a pair of wings. She turned to the climber, braced atop a broken bone tower, rising two tiers above the mud. Her face looked more uncertain now.

She'd meant to pressure Rya, not risk herself. Urie, too, looked away.

Rya's challenge had quelled them. But the crowd grew noisier. Someone shouted, "Not Minlin!" Another, "Take the Liar instead!"

Rya glanced at me. The crowd was turning on her, on us.

*They will tear you apart.*

The sun sank below the cloudline. The ground steamed, and heat rippled the horizon.

Rya tried to calm them. "We'll need more bravery if we're going to keep other cities at bay," she said. "I see now that we must move forward faster. But I do not think this is the right time, unless you would sing Remembrances for one more."

The crowd disagreed. "Fly," Urie shouted. "Fly!" the crowd responded with one voice. Minlin grasped the wings the Aivans held out.

If Minlin failed, after Rya's challenge, the crowd would blame Rya. We could lose more leaders in the process. But Rya didn't see the risk. And neither did Minlin or the blackwings.

While everyone focused on Minlin, I dropped the sack I carried and stepped behind the climber's base. Djonn had been working on spring tension for the legs, back in the meadow. I found the catch that held it. With a quick motion, I released the spring tension on the throwing arm. When Minlin gave the signal to launch, the mechanism didn't move.

A blackwing saw me and guessed what I'd done. "Liar! What gives you the right to interfere?"

A soft rain began to patter on the ground, making dark spots in the red dust, drawing wet lines on my skin and caking mud in the creases between my fingers and in my hair. The air smelled cleaner, even as everything below the air got messier.

There was no good way forward. The people would not follow me. And if Minlin failed, they wouldn't follow Rya either. And Minlin was not ready to lead.

"I have the right," I said. "As much as anyone."

The restless crowd slipped and skidded on the softened ground, their footwraps growing heavy and slick with water.

*Liar.*

I heard it before the first handful of mud hit me. A blackwing and her mate, both smiling and laughing. The mud slid down my arm as they turned back to Urie and Minlin. A child caught the game. I heard a badly thrown handful land behind me, striking the launcher, and Minlin.

"Liar!"

"And your family too!"

❧ ❧ ❧

They might just tear me apart, as Rya had warned. But the community had to stay together.

On the horizon, I thought I saw a flicker of bright wings. Not the dark feathers of bone eaters who flew circuits around the cities, but brighter things by far. And then they were gone, a mirage.

Once, I'd thought nothing could be worse than falling through the clouds. Once, I'd preferred the ground to falling.

Now, before the gathered crowd, in front of shelters made of discarded wings, a dead city at my back, I knew there was something worse than falling.

Failing.

The blackwings gathered with Urie and Minlin at their center. Rya's Aivans were arrayed around her. A struggle seemed imminent. All that Macal and I had tried to do by bringing the community safely to the ground threatened to unravel.

"I'll test the mechanism instead, Rya," I said. "There is nothing wrong with it, nor with the artifex who worked on it."

Before I could rethink, I climbed to where Minlin had stood moments before.

The crowd whispered. But Ceetcee shouted, "You cannot do this! You are needed here!" She turned from me to Rya. "Do not let him do this!"

Pitching my voice louder, I added, "I was less than truthful about what we would face on the ground. Some of it"—I gestured towards where the city's egg lay—"I didn't know. But I did know there wasn't enough wind to fly on the ground. I should have told you." I turned to Rya. "I made a promise."

Rya, a ruff of feathers at the neck of her cloak, her eyes outlined with crushed blacking, nodded acknowledgment of Ceetcee's words. She turned to me. "Do you do this as my Lawsbreaker? You could die."

The crowd quieted. Rya held their attention again.

I had no wish to die. But this was my chance to redeem myself. To keep Ceetcee safe, and Beliak too. To turn the blackwings' defiance into a way forward, for all of us. I nodded. "I do this."

Minlin tried to give me her wings. "I'll use my own," I said. I whispered to Wik, who left the group at a run.

"Haven't enough people died already?" Beliak said. He held the baby so I could see her.

"When will you name her?" I asked, trying to distract them. To remind the community what we fought for.

It was the one question to which I desperately wanted to know the answer.

"You won't be around to see it!" Ceetcee said, angry. "Why ask?"

"The flight might go well," I countered. *I wanted to be around.* I needed to do something for the city.

"Staying on the ground will go better," Beliak said.

Falling was my greatest fear. I'd fallen on my wingtest, in the Spire, through the clouds. Macal had seen me fall, had caught me. His dream for community had to be earned. Beliak had been right. Now I could pay Macal back.

"You will have no time to recover from a dive," Rya said. "One mistake, and you'll be dashed to the ground."

"I understand." I thought of Maalik, trying to fly, then tumbling to the ground. My mouth went dry. I thought of my father, risking his life to save the city.

"Adjust the throwing arm to Nat's weight," Rya said.

Ceetcee stood firm. "I refuse."

"Someone else will, then," Rya said.

Ceetcee capitulated. Changed the counterweights on the articulated bone leg, even as she tried to coax me to change my mind. "You don't have to do this," she said. "You take too much responsibility. We need you. Not a hero of the city."

I checked my wings, tears prickling my eyes. This was a way to end the debate. To get us moving forward. Beliak stood still as bone, watching. Letting the baby suck on his finger.

"Maybe we need heroes too," I said. "We can best defend the city with flight. Rya is correct. I took flying from you. I want to give it back. Varat, according to Wik, is tall and mobile. It's coming here, there is no doubt. But if we can fly, we have an advantage, we can turn their attack. We can keep the egg safe. Keep us safe."

Beliak broke his silence as Ceetcee threw up her hands, furious. "Someone else can do this. Why does it have to be you?"

I pointed at the horizon, far from where I thought I'd seen wings earlier. More bone eaters, circling, in formation near the city on the horizon. Clearly visible now. Moving faster. "Because we are out of time."

The previous battle with Nimru was still so fresh that I imagined I could smell Varat approaching, feel its footsteps reverberating beneath my feet. Soon, we would.

I was a hunter, a defender of my city, my family. Still the memory made me want to run. Instead, I stood fast in front of the launcher, while Rya helped Minlin down.

Wik returned, my wings in his hands. He'd attached small sacks of lighter-than-air as well as ballast—in the form of bone chips—to the wings. "Coming down may be harder. You're sure?"

"I'm sure." I'd seen Djonn testing something like this at the midcloud, but he'd opted for the bigger kites. With the launcher, it could work. I climbed in. That's when Ceetcee began yelling at me in earnest. Wik pulled her and Beliak back from the launcher.

Up in the launcher, I could almost feel the wind.

I looked down at Rya. She had the crowd's attention now. The blackwings had dissipated and were watching intently from the outskirts. Urie himself had stepped back to make room if the mechanism failed.

I'd been frightened many times in my life, but never with such an audience. I tightened the wingstraps and put myself in the hands of those who were winding the tension spring again.

Before me stood citizens I'd been fledges with, some I'd represented on council, some who'd supported me when I'd challenged the city, and many with whom I'd fought. They stared up at me, whispering. Beyond them, a broad span of desert, and then the approaching city. Birds circling on the horizon. Somewhere in between, I thought I saw a glitter of pale wings again. I blinked and it was gone.

*Brokenwings. Liar.* I was none of these. Not any longer.

"To the flier!" Minlin said. The crowd echoed her.

I focused on the baby's head, her eyes, closed tight, her fingers curled to fists. On her future, not mine.

"Ready," I said.

I heard them crank the climber's legs down. Felt tension build at my back and feet.

Then I heard Rya say, "On your wings, Nat. Mercy on your wings."

And the climber flung me into the air. The rush of wind felt so familiar. The wild forward pitch did not. But, for a moment, I flew.

When I dropped my ballast, I rose higher, gliding on the light air, thanks to the gas in the pieces of skymouth hide that hung from my wings. I was flying.

I made it farther than I thought I would too.

I made it halfway to the oncoming city, getting a close look at their bone eaters, when my altitude began to drop.

One of the gasbags was leaking. I could hear it hiss. My left wing dipped hard, and I spiraled, watching the ground get closer. I tried to curve my wings to capture more air. Failed. A shadow passed overhead.

I couldn't scream. I couldn't brace. I closed my eyes.

With a jerk, I was yanked out of my fall and lifted.

"Caught you," said a voice I hadn't heard in several moons. Kirit.

# 37

## KIRIT, BELOW

*⁓ Against all odds wings finally soar ⁓*

We'd worked for days on my plan, building the new wings.

Using the supplies Moc and Ciel had brought and making the modifications that Djonn dreamed up when he wasn't sleeping, a new kind of glider emerged from the wreckage of the first box kite.

The objects Dix had stolen from the other city became our salvation. We reworked the kite so that it could steer with them. We kept them wound. Ciel prized apart one and figured out, with the help of the brass plates, how she could make it stronger and run longer. She and Aliati made several more out of bone.

As I sat on the ridgeline the second day at sunset, sewing extra panels on a new set of wings, Dix approached.

"Do you know if they have an alembic with them?"

"Aliati and Raq? Yes, they brought one. Why?" I couldn't imagine she'd find heartbone down here.

"Because the gas that's coming from vents near the water might be distillable, like heartbone, but much faster. Like rot gas. We could turn it into something that works like lighter-than-air."

We couldn't spare the hands, but we needed the gas, if it was possible. "We don't have time for distractions."

"I am trying to help," she said.

She was being true. "This doesn't mean you are forgiven," I cautioned.

"I understand. I don't deserve to be," she said, quieter than she used to be.

Aliati gave her one of the alembics. When Dix succeeded at harvesting the gas—a dangerous task—she distilled it.

She brought the first sack, floating on a string, to Djonn. Transferred the gas to emptied ballast balloons and went to make more. The balloons filled fast. I followed her down to the cave.

In the quiet, while she began distilling the gas again, I had to ask a question I'd wondered about for a long time. "Why did you hate me?"

She shrugged. "You were the Spirebreaker. And Ezarit's daughter."

"Why did you hate her?"

"Ezarit?" Dix laughed softly. "She made it easy."

That wasn't an answer. "She had what you wanted. You were jealous? So you—" The wingtest. The attack on the council.

"At first, yes. I was turned down for Singer. They offered it to her instead, and she refused. Then Civik chose to betray the Spire."

*Civik. My father.*

Dix continued. "All that hurt. I vowed to be better. Then Rumul offered to help."

"You were a Magister. That is a great honor."

"But I wanted so much more. Rumul expected much more of me." Dix looked younger as she spoke, despite her injuries.

"And then he gave you that more."

Dix nodded.

"And you took it farther."

Her hand stopped. Hung in the air over the alembic. "It's true. I did that." She didn't elaborate or try to excuse herself. "I might do the same again."

I hated her then. I could not forgive her. But she kept working. She was helping. We needed all the hands we could get. And I respected the fact that she wasn't trying to win us over with lies. But she'd be a problem when we regrouped with the rest of the community. "You cannot stay here," I said.

She saw me looking at her work. Her neat, exact movements with the alembic. "I know. I don't belong in the world that's coming next, Kirit."

Her words, out of nowhere, shocked me. No scheming. No attempts to win something. I couldn't answer. She kept speaking.

"I'll take my leave once we get the gliders rigged. We'll launch you right, and then I'll go. The scavengers might have me. If I prove myself."

They might. Or might not. "I hope you're not waiting for me to beg you to stay."

She shook her head. "I'm not." And she kept working.

❧ ❧ ❧

When we were ready, we took the transformed second kite. The foils were smaller and sleeker now. The craft steered easier too.

Ciel, Moc, Raq, and I crewed the kite. I tucked my wings inside its main basket. Below us, Aliati and two of the survivors from the other kite ran with the tethers along the ridgeline, getting us enough momentum to rise higher in the air than the lighter-than-air could push.

And we flew. The propellers buzzed, and the cams we'd installed in the wings helped us turn. With Moc and Ciel functioning as the hands, and Raq working the windscoop as a tail while minding the propellers, we began to turn a slow, climbing circle on the updrafts to build up height, and then headed for the interior, moving faster than I expected.

The healer had demanded to come with us in the kite, to stay close to the littlemouths. Now they crouched in the bottom of the basket, terrified and airsick.

But Ciel whooped. Moc let loose a long shout of happiness. And I felt the wind on my face. We were flying again. It was a different kind of flight, but it didn't matter.

"Don't crash!" Moc shouted as we passed a peak on the ridge.

I wasn't about to. We kept building up speed so we could make it across the desert.

Once we arrived, we wouldn't be able to land. I would have to anchor near the city. I hoped we'd be able to talk Rya into moving away. I hoped we could carry some citizens with us, while others followed on their own kites, to the ridge, where we'd be safer.

But once we'd anchored, getting going again would be slow, dependent on the lighter-than-air—if we could get any, if they had some left—and the propellers. We'd come in like a gryphon or a kestrel and leave like a float. That was fine, as long as we could leave with the citizens aboard, or give them means to escape.

We gained altitude and finally got a good look at the city. Liope joined us, looking at the shelters that had sprung up around the fallen beast. Eyes glazed with tears, they looked back at me, then back to the city.

The collapse had driven a deep valley into the ground, covered with bone tiers that stretched far from the decaying frame of the giant. Below it, I saw the curve of an enormous egg, and I sucked my teeth.

"Can you see it?" I asked Ciel.

"It looks lighter than before," Moc said.

"Serrahun," Liope whispered.

Then, briefly, motion out of the corner of my eye. Near what must have been a set of tents and shelters, someone had rigged up a mechanism. As we watched, it flung a person high into the air. Their wings filled and they kept going, gliding a wobbly path.

"Oh," said Ciel and Liope both at the same time. The little-mouth on Ciel's shoulder glowed at the sound of their astonishment.

Below us, people ran, trying to follow the flier along on the ground, unable to catch up. They saw us too.

The pair of wings began to falter. "Go closer," I said.

"We can't!" Ciel called back. "We'll lose too much altitude."

I began to slide my rebuilt wings over my shoulders. "A little lower. Now."

When I jumped off, they'd rise back up. But there wasn't any time to plan. Ciel did what I asked, and I climbed over the basket and stood on the silk and bone wing.

"Kirit!"

"Wait!" I'd know that wingset anywhere, and I wasn't going to let him fall this time.

I flicked the propellers on, dove from the kite, and spread my wings.

❧ ❧ ❧

When I caught him, Nat struggled for just a moment. I circled lower, flying back over the dead city and brought him down in the center of the shelters. He stood then, wobbling, and turned while I let the last of the lighter-than-air out of my own wings in order to land. The ground caught me hard, and I stumbled. Nat reached out a hand to steady me.

"You came back," he said, dusting himself off to avoid meeting my eyes.

"I couldn't miss an opportunity like that, could I?" My voice cracked when I said it.

Finally, we looked at each other while we furled our wings. People came near, clapped us on the shoulders, and tried to pull me away. Wik stood a few winglengths off, near a woman draped in black feathers who looked unmistakably like Doran. But I couldn't look away from Nat.

He was bruised and battered; I was scarred too.

I grabbed his shoulder and pulled him close enough to crush him, wings and all.

He squirmed, then wrapped his arms around me too. For a moment, we were back on his mother's balcony, talking all night, looking at the stars. We were six Allsuns old and just learning to fly. We were walking through the undercloud, falling out of the wind. He was hauling me out of the meadow, away from the fallen council; I was leaving him to climb alone back to the clouds.

We were all these things in one.

I pressed my forehead to Nat's, and he met my eyes.

"You are such a bonehead," I whispered. "I'd catch you again if I had to."

"I'd catch you too," he said, low enough that only I could hear.

My almost-brother, my wingmate. Forgiven and more.

Maalik circled and dove, finally landing on Nat's shoulder. The whipperling chattered at me.

We didn't let go of each other until Ceetcee and Beliak came running, yelling at Nat for every stupid thing he'd ever done. And then, over Beliak's shoulder, a baby cried and they all started laughing.

The tiny creature kicked at me, and I tickled its feet, amazed at how small it was.

The others crowded closer.

Only then did I reach out and lace my fingers through Wik's. Pulled him close, into the knot of friends and companions. "I promised I'd return."

# 38

## NAT, BELOW

*⤳ A city approaches, the Aivans want war ⤳*

At the center of our ruined city, our tight knot of companions had only a moment together before Ciel shouted from the kite above, "Look to the horizon!"

The approaching city was indeed moving faster, headed towards us. Its bone eaters, loaded with sacks of carrion, flew out front, goaded by riders on their backs. The ground began to resonate beneath Varat's feet.

Overhead, Raq, Moc, and Ciel circled in their strange kite, recalibrating their wing angles as they tried to stay above us.

"Their lighter-than-air might run out soon; their propellers will need to be rewound," Kirit said. I heard Ciel calling orders. A figure in a pale shift slid down a rope from the kite, and landed gracefully on the ground.

"Who is that?" I asked as the figure waved at Kirit.

"Someone who helped me," Kirit said as the stranger began to walk towards us. "Liope. A healer at the other city, the one we call Varat and they call Serra. They risked their life, though it's not fully clear why."

I stared at Kirit. Siding with another city. Not destroying Dix immediately. Did I know her any longer? "What did you do?"

She frowned. "We've learned much. We can help."

"Take the stranger," Rya ordered her guards. "And Kirit too."

"Hold on," Kirit protested. "You need me. I think we can avoid a fight. We're going to try anyway."

*Avoid a fight? Kirit?*

Two Aivans tried to catch the stranger, who dodged the guards by racing them over the uneven terrain to come to Wik's side, where Rya looked at them warily, her knife drawn.

The attacking city drew closer.

Wik didn't raise his weapon. "I want to hear what Liope has to say."

The stranger pointed to Wik. Reached into their bag and pulled out an intricate mechanism, which was softly making a *kit-kit-kit* sound. He hissed in alarm. They pointed to Wik again.

"What is this?" Rya said. "Take this person and their artifact away."

"Wait." Wik looked hard at the stranger. "We took something that didn't belong to us. From Varat. Didn't we?" He pulled the map and lens from his satchel. The healer nodded.

The stranger held up the mechanism, made a gesture as if offering it to Wik. They pointed at our group gathered on the plain. "Hun."

Kirit pointed at the dead city, and at all the people there. And at the kite. And the horizon. "Serrahun." Serra. Home.

Liope looked at us, then at the fallen city. They took a deep breath and held out their hand for the map. When they had a firm grasp on it, they handed Wik the mechanism.

A trade.

"What is that?" Rya asked.

"Like rot gas," Wik explained.

Kirit added, "But in this case, I think it is a peace offering."

"We have to prepare to fight, Kirit. Not exchange presents." Varat's bone eaters were audible. "Why now?"

"Now, Nat," Ciel shouted to us from above, "because we have

more in common than we thought." She hummed and Kirit hummed until the littlemouth on Ciel's shoulder glowed. A corresponding glow appeared on Liope's shoulder.

Liope saw the glow and smiled. "Littlemouth," they whispered.

Kirit's shocked expression told me this was a new development. "Hope," she whispered.

Then the stranger stepped away from our group and began the long trek towards the oncoming city. Varat seemed to slow as Kirit's healer stepped into its sights. But no arrows flew. No bone eaters attacked them. Not yet.

"Ready weapons." Rya signaled her guards. "Kirit, if you plan to fly for us—"

"We need to wait," Wik interrupted. "Let Liope try. Our ways aren't like theirs. We're not the only city anymore. We have to hope they'll see it too."

"I disagree," I said. "If Varat is attacking, we must be ready to fight." Ceetcee cradled the baby, her eyes were wide as she watched the city. She headed to the kites for safety.

"I won't abandon the old city or fail to defend the new one," Rya said. "No matter what." Her Aivans shared out weapons. Wik took a bow, a sheath of arrows, and a knife. I found a passable bow as well. "If Varat reaches the towerfall, we'll fight."

"From above and below," Kirit said, nodding. "But if Liope can turn them, or we stop them, that would be better."

Beliak checked my wings for me. "That flight was the stupidest and bravest thing you've ever done. Don't do it again."

I chuckled. "I'll try." Then I tightened his wingstraps. We made ready for a fight, or maybe for a tentative peace, if Kirit was right.

Raq and Ciel began tossing down tethers. "We can take five

at a time!" The other kites, farther away, set up high-flung archer stations.

As each fighter grabbed a wingset from the shelters, the area around the city became less of a settlement and more a wide swath of footprints.

Liope reached Varat. Their figure was nearly lost in the oncoming city's shadow.

Above, the kite was still circling and had dropped two ballast sacks: one split on impact and spilled dark ridge rock. Rya picked up a piece of the rock and looked at curiously. "What is that?"

"It is a chance to start again," Kirit said.

We climbed the ropes to the kite and gathered the lighter-than-air. When we were ready, we launched from the kite wing, aiming for the oncoming city and its enormous black carrion birds.

\ \ \

The last time a city loomed on the horizon, there'd been four of us to stand in its path. Now there were many more, both in the air and on the ground. Not all could fly. Those who couldn't armed themselves still and headed onto the plain to stand between the oncoming city and ours.

From the air, they looked like bugs scrambling towards a giant. But just four of us had toppled a city once. Perhaps, now grown in numbers, we could successfully turn this one away.

Beside me Beliak, Kirit, Wik, and Urie attempted a bee formation. We all moved slower than we were used to with the lighter-than-air, rather than wind. Kirit and Wik dropped wing-hooks and towed us, propelled by their stolen spinners. Others circled slowly in the air over the settlement, ready to advance if the other city crossed Rya's line.

We'd locked our wings and had nocked arrows. When we got

close to Varat, I saw that five figures stood on the city's head. They'd dropped a net over the side, where Liope approached.

"The council leaders," Wik called.

The five watched the scene impassively.

The air suddenly filled with feathers as one of the bone eaters dove at me, and tried to knock me from the air with claw and wing. I fired one arrow and nocked another.

Wik, leading Beliak and Urie, dove after the bird.

When the healer climbed into their city's net, Kirit cheered. A dirty, grayed shift flapped in the wind, a mote rising quickly on the city's dark expanse.

With a screech, a bone eater tumbled from the sky, an arrow through its enormous eye. The net stopped. A horn blew, a high bright note.

Two more bone eaters beat a path back to Varat.

Meantime, the city still moved forward, bearing down on the bonefall. We were running out of time.

Riders on the other two birds tried firing at us. The carrion sacks they bore threw off their aim. Even so, an arrow caught Urie's wing, and he spun, tumbling.

One of the five council leaders began to haul the netting up again. In short measure, the healer reached the top of the city. Now we would see if it mattered.

Meantime, the last two bone eaters still came at us.

"Cut the lines to their sacks," Kirit yelled, "instead of the birds or the riders! The city will stop following!"

*Clouds, if Kirit's gamble doesn't work, we'll have to fight for our city against these same birds and riders. Is it worth the risk?*

Kirit dove for one of the sacks, a long knife drawn. She sliced her glass-tooth blade through the rope, nearly severing it. The carrion sack hung by a thread. Beliak followed, cutting the final cords, and the sack dropped to the ground.

On the back of Varat, Liope joined the five councilors.

The city slowed, but with one sack left ahead of it, it did not stop.

The other bone eater rider goaded his bird into flying faster. The city looked from the food at its feet to the food getting away and slowed even further. It snapped up the sack and swallowed it, then looked for more.

A horn sounded. High and bright. Varat came to a halt with an enormous groan.

In the air, our lighter-than-air was starting to give out. "Land or turn back?" I shouted.

"Land!" Wik yelled. Rya seconded. We curved our wings to spill wind and foil the propellers. Then hit ground in the vanguard of our community.

"Watch the feet!" Rya called, as several guards got too close. Varat's enormous footstep knocked two hunters and a blackwing over, and they were barely pulled to safety in time.

The city had stopped before Rya's attack line, circled by its remaining birds.

"They could still attack us; we need to drive them off forever," Rya said.

But I understood now, why Kirit hadn't wanted to fight. Why Liope had risked everything to return to their city. We couldn't just fight. "We have to change strategies."

We weren't alone any longer.

And neither were Liope's people.

The battle that had almost happened could have ended both our communities. Now that we knew of each other, we needed to learn different ways.

When Varat turned, it did so slowly, moving away from us with pacing steps. One of the bone eaters swooped out in front of it, leading it back to its normal track. I breathed deeply, relieved.

"You gave them back the map," Rya said, when Wik met us on the ground. She was angry.

He nodded, unfazed. "It's theirs."

"The map could have been useful," I said.

Kirit joined us. "Perhaps someday, they'll let us borrow it."

By the time the sun passed below the clouds, we watched the giant move into the distance. Ciel and Moc began to turn the kite towards the ridge, pointing the way for those who wanted to go now. They signaled that they were running out of lighter-than-air.

I still stood cautious guard. Without air cover, we were vulnerable. But the battle avoided gave me great hope.

"We need to leave soon," Kirit said. "We have people who need us at the ridge. If we use the kites that are tethered here, we can move everyone. There is water and hunting. Come with us?"

I wanted to go, but for different reasons.

Though Varat was headed away from us, we had no way of communicating with its inhabitants. Kirit seemed to think the ridge would be safer if there was a new attack, with our people together.

Ceetcee and Beliak hadn't packed to leave yet. Moving Elna would take careful planning. "We'll go or stay, where you're needed," Ceetcee said.

They waited while I went to petition Rya.

"Why do you need my leave?" Rya said.

"Because I made a promise, up above the clouds. I'd go with you as Lawsbreaker, if you helped evacuate the towers. I do what I say I'll do. And you have not yet released me."

"You no longer need to ask." She laughed. She pulled the marker from my shoulder, but left the feather. "I remove your Lawsmarker. Offer you Aivan status. You're free to do what you want." The air cooled more, and a teasing breeze lifted the feather on my shoulder. "Your sense of honor is to your credit. I release you."

While Varat moved farther away and my family watched me, I made my decision. "I'll go to the ridge."

Rya smiled. "You've earned it."

I looked at Kirit and Wik, at my family, and made ready to head for the horizon. A fledge—Maili, I remembered—came running across the dirt, nearly tripping in the last few steps.

She grabbed Rya's robe. "The egg cracked. The city is hatching."

We wouldn't be going anywhere yet.

# 39

## KIRIT, BELOW

*⁓ Another city awakes, friends seek farther shores ⁓*

I was eager to leave. To go to the ridge, to fly. Even more eager when I saw the cracks in the city's egg.

But Rya asked for help, and I could not turn away.

"The fledges and the wounded must go to the kites," she said. This time, blackwings and Aivans alike followed her, coughing in the dust kicked up as we retraced our path. "Urie, you're in charge of that."

Urie spun fast, bowing just a little to both Rya and Nat, "Yes, Aivan. Risen." His dirt-streaked robe billowed as he headed for the tents first, then the kites. There was little sign of the dissent Nat had whispered to me about on the way here.

Rya waved Minlin to her side. "Bring all the nets to where the new city lies." To the rest of the Aivans and blackwings: "Clear the area around the pit." Her voice was firm, her commands clear.

"What do you need from me?" She seemed to have everything under control.

The ground rumbled.

"Another crack!" a fledge yelled, as if no one could feel it.

We ran towards where the old city's moldering body loomed over the pit. In all the mud and gore, the egg looked very pale, almost glowing.

When Rya turned to me, I saw the young woman I'd met many Allsuns ago with her father, independent and strong-willed.

"Can you take care of them, Kirit, if—" She didn't finish. A loud, sharp noise echoed across the ground.

I drew my bow, answering her unfinished question, "Of course I can. But . . ."

She slowed. Watched me nock an arrow. Held up a hand. "Don't kill it. Whatever you do."

Laughing under my breath, I said, "I won't kill anything. But if it's down to you or the city, I'll wound it like crazy."

She laughed, nervously. "Thank you. You'd make a good Aivan."

I had to smile. "I like you too, but I'm not a good follower."

She laughed.

Nat met us at the lip of the pit. We moved the fledges back from the mud-slick edge as they excitedly pointed out the widening fractures on the side of the egg.

Finally, Urie came and led the fledges away. Desert dust billowed as they fled to a safe distance.

If this was anything like a whipperling hatching, it would take a whole day for the city to emerge. Still, my heart was already pounding.

This was a city. It wouldn't be anything like a bird hatching. *What would it look like? What would it do?*

"What will it *eat*?" Nat said, as if reading my thoughts. "We need to have something to feed it." He was right.

A lone bone eater coasted high above us, and I eyed it appraisingly. Nat put his hand on my arm. "Don't feed it a bone eater."

"Why not? Our city ate them all the time."

He pinched the bridge of his nose. "Not first. First tastes are important. The city needs to not think of bone eaters as food. Not at first."

I narrowed my eyes. "You are an expert now at cities?"

There was a loud crack from the egg, as the fractures split wider. Rya chuckled. "No one's had time to become an expert, but it is a good point from a trained hunter." She signaled to Wik. "Can you take some Aivans out and find a few of those . . . What did you call them?"

Wik blinked. "Groundmouths?" He gave a long sigh. "I could find some for you. I'll need guards who can echolocate. A very large net. And all the muzz we have left."

Rya grinned. Another loud crack met the sound of wet surfaces pulling apart. "You should hurry."

Wik and several Aivans left at a run, headed for the closest stretch of ground with visible divots in the earth.

Through the crack in the egg, a small—relatively speaking—horn emerged. It kicked at the shell until cracks ran everywhere.

Nat gave a low whistle. "That is going to be a big city."

Bits of shell fell to the ground, landing hard enough to shake the area where we stood. A rush of fluid muddied the earth below the egg.

We could see the grayish inner membrane, and something curled tight inside. A nostril flared. A blue eye the size of a small child slowly blinked.

After another long moment, the city uncoiled and stuck its head out, then lay its chin on the mud. Its eye slowly closed.

"Is it dead?" Rya's second in command asked.

Nat shook his head. "Sleeping. This is tiring work."

Before he'd finished speaking, the city opened its eye again and pulled a clawed foot from the shell. More eggshell broke off and clattered to the ground.

We spread out on the bonefall, waiting to see the city in full, but also ready to run.

"Rya, don't get too close," her second in command called.

Nat looked at me across the crowd. He remembered watching the old city eat. We both backed up several more paces and encouraged the others to come with us.

The new city made a rumbling sound high in its throat. Its gray tongue poked out, tasting the air, and then it yawned. A few tooth points were barely visible on its jaw. Its gums were the color of stone fruit.

I kept a firm grip on my bow while Rya knelt, at a safe distance, looking in the city's eyes. "Rya . . ."

With a slick rolling motion, the city darted at her, rumbling. Rya held her ground. "Nets!"

The city's hind legs got tangled up in the shell, and it tripped, then righted itself and tried to scramble up the bank of the pit.

Nat and two blackwings threw the joined netting over the city's head and the front part of its body. "That's as far as it'll stretch."

"Control the head, control the city," Rya murmured. She took two of the net tethers, and we each took two more. As the city shook its backside free of the eggshell, we looked at the pen Rya's men had built in haste.

"That's not going to hold it," she said.

The city tried to spring forward again, but the thick nets held.

"Could keep it in the pit for a while," Nat said. "Build a cage over it."

"Like the skymouths?" I whispered, remembering all too clearly the push of their bodies against the nets in the Spire.

Nat shivered. "Nothing like the skymouths. This would only be until Rya tames it or retreats."

Wik returned with his haul of groundmouths. Most of the

hunters were covered with the same goo that had struck him when we killed the first groundmouth. The iridescent tinge to it was visible in the dim midday light.

He measured a piece of groundmouth carefully with his hands, slicing off a city-sized bite. He gave this to Rya. "Don't move too quickly. You're not its parent. It could snap your hands off, even without teeth."

Rya frowned, concentrating. She knelt on the edge of the pit, her feathered robe growing muddy. The bird skull slipped around her neck. She brushed hair out of her eyes with one shaking hand, leaving a trail of groundmouth slime.

She held out the food to the newborn city.

The beast stretched its head to her hands, nostrils blowing like a small storm. Its gray tongue emerged again, curling around her hands.

"Rya," I said. "That's too close."

"Wait." She waved me off. She didn't take her eyes off the city.

"It's not going to be your pet," Nat said. "It will be too big, very soon. Be careful."

"Shhhhh," she whispered.

The tongue drew back quickly, yanking Rya into the pit and the mud. She scrambled to get out of the way of the city's feet.

"Ropes!" Wik called. "Quickly." He nocked an arrow as well. "Say the word."

"Not yet!" Rya scrambled up on the city's back. The dorsal ridge was barely apparent, white points on the gray, mottled skin. The city didn't seem to mind her weight. It smacked its jaws together and swallowed the morsel of groundmouth, then opened up for more.

Wik cut another slice and Rya's second in command reached for it, but Wik shook his head. "For now, just Rya. Soon, perhaps everyone else."

The city ate until the sun passed below the cloud again, then collapsed in the mud and snored.

We helped Rya from the pit and stretched the strong nets over the expanse.

"That won't hold it for long," Nat observed. "You'll need something stronger."

"Maybe," Rya said. "Maybe not." She'd lost her bird skull in the mud, and needed a sand bath more than anyone.

She posted three guards at the pit and ordered the remaining citizens to move their tents at least thirty city-strides away.

"What will you do while the new city is growing?" Many of the Aivans and blackwings had decided to remain with her. Many from the old city's towers had planned to make the journey to the ridge. Now that they understood how big the infant city was, I saw several more groups packing to leave.

She looked at the bone shelters slowly growing from the old city. "We'll have much to do."

"The ridge kites will always be open to you," I said. Sidra came to join me. "They were Macal's idea, originally. I want to honor his memory. He was and will always be a bridge between us."

Sidra took Rya's hands, ignoring the grime on them. "You'll need food and clean water, especially at first. Kirit says the ridge has that. We'll help."

"And we'll keep an eye out for approaching cities," I said. Varat, which we would call Serra now, had retreated far away.

"I appreciate it," Rya agreed. "We will send traders to you. The new city will always be here for you and your ascendants too, should the kites have trouble."

We sealed our agreement by carving two spirals in a bone shard, symbols of the old city and the newborn one. Then we clasped hands. "I wish you only good luck, Aivan," I said.

Rya bowed to me, "On your wings, Risen." Her smile was genuine. I beckoned Ciel forward. The young woman bowed to both of us, her cupped hands extended. They looked empty. Then she began to hum.

Two littlemouths glowed. "For you," Ciel said. "But don't let the city eat them."

Rya laughed. "I won't, I promise."

Our ancestors made a decision like this, once. To climb higher. To stay on the ground.

Some of us would stay with the new city and wait for it to rise. They would keep it safe.

Some of us would go across the desert and try a new way of living.

We made the decision knowing for the first time in generations that we weren't alone on the ground. Knowing that each choice would take work and sacrifice. Knowing we would need to rely on each other.

No city could stand alone now.

ᐟ  ᐟ  ᐟ

When the sun rose, there were far fewer tents in the shadow of the old city.

Those who could began the walk through the desert, towing the kites above.

Ceetcee and Beliak waited with Nat, their belongings bundled into satchels and packs.

Urie returned from his duties with the kites. "Everything is ready," he said to Rya.

Rya regarded him. "You're certain you wish to stay? You will be under my leadership."

He nodded. "There is much to build here."

"We'll take all but two kites," I said, looking at the long stretch between here and the ridge. "Are you sure?"

Rya shook her head. Her horizon held only the hatchling for now. "I knew long ago we were changing as a people. Becoming something different. I thought that meant we would fly. I know better now. It is the Aivans' duty to tend the new city. We are sure."

Ceetcee's baby kicked in Beliak's arms and began to scream, but the city didn't wake. As Beliak rocked her back to sleep, I looked up at the cloud above us, and the kites floating in the dim predawn light. We had a long journey before us.

Wik, his hand on my shoulder, touched the baby's cheek. "What's her name?"

"We'll know when we get there," Ceetcee said. "When we get home."

# EPILOGUE

## KIRIT, HOME

On a morning like this, joy is a sky filled with birds. It is the sound of laughter, of wind ruffling a patchwork wing.

My son, Mac, wobbles on his first flight, quietly intense. Aliati and Raq fly a spidersilk net beneath him. There's no room for error as he sweeps a small circuit through the sky and returns to our platform.

His face is a geometry of excitement when his feet touch the silk. The moment his wings are furled, he runs to me, then past me, past Wik, all around the room. All unconstrained energy, until he flies once more, into my arms. "Did you see?"

"I did, and you flew beautifully." I wink at Raq as Mac's aunts glide home, their windups churning beneath their wings.

Mac's best friend, Eza, swings on a tether around the tier divider from the next platform. She is a year older, and has opinions. "You did nicely, Mac. I watched."

Eza, being Nat's daughter, can do nothing so easily or so well as annoy Mac. This has been true every day of Mac's life.

"You did not watch," Mac says. "You had your own lessons."

She smiles, chewing a piece of dried fish with loud smacks. "I watched." Eza sticks her tongue out.

Mac looks up at me, his gray eyes showing all the suffering that his face will not reveal.

"Eza can watch you fly. But she can't interfere," Wik says. "Don't let your friends get in your way, Mac."

"She's not a friend," Mac mutters, but he gets the point. Turns back to me. "Do you fly today?"

I smile. "I must. We need bone and brass. Rya says they need dried fish and more silkspiders. Their last batch of spiders died. Liope wants more lighter-than-air for Serra."

"You always have to fly," Mac says.

"It's a long way. Easier than walking. Wik will stay with you, and if either of you need anything, ask Ceetcee, or Elna." I pause, looking down at my son's tousled hair, his hawk nose. "Do you mind that I go?"

"No," he says, and hugs me tight. "Because you always come back."

Across the platform, where the new kites are being added, I see Nat, Moc, and Beliak putting in battens according to Ciel's latest plan.

"I'll return," I promise. I watch the kite rise in the air and tether itself loosely to the rest of our platforms, supported half on lighter-than-air and half on the near-constant offshore wind.

Tiers and tiers of kites, lifting into the sky, filled with friends and family. And below, more living in the cliffs on the ground.

White and yellow banners curl in the morning air, marking our city's boundaries. We tried many names for the kites and the platforms: after the old towers, after our families, after battles fought. In the end we decided that we are one city for now—a city of wind and wings—not disparate tiers. Not yet. We call the city Horizon.

As I prepare to fly, Ciel's and Elna's voices drift from a neighboring kite, raised in song.

Verses familiar and new follow the breeze, describing our fall, and our rise. We sing to remember and to teach. We weave new words with old.

We lift on the wind. We soar.

# ⁓ HORIZON ⁓
## by Ciel

As bridges burned, Mondarath fought above the cloud
While far beneath, four struggled to rise again, proud.
When monsters clashed, the groundbound watched a
    city die.
Pulled apart, towers weakened, unless a bridge was tied.
All that shook, all that fell was sky and bone,
The Magister sought the cause alone
Then two went far and two climbed home
On birdback, through cloudburst, so close to home
Across desert, through illness in search of home
Above the clouds, destruction vast, the Magister flew
    alone
Skyshouter and Nightwing climbed new cities formed
    of bone
And Brokenwings returned to find his mates.
A midcloud discovery, as the world quaked
Within the cloud, the rescue started
While Skyshouter found a city's heart
The artifex's craft became real in the sky
An old foe appeared, strange rules they defied
While Brokenwings and Magister flew from low to high
And Skyshouter fled from a city of light
The Magister hoped for a new kind of bridge
The Skyshouter abandoned city for far-flung ridge

The first kites descended, the blackwings found fear
A market, a coup, a quake; the clouds grew far too near.
A city forgotten, the Nightwing walked away.
Blackwings found the midcloud at start of day
Above the cloud, time grew short for those who stayed
In the cloud, some stole away, taking kites for their own
On dangerous ground, the Skyshouter searched for home.
The kites floated and crashed, all down so fast
While the Skyshouter found the ground hard and vast.
A city's secret discovered one night at last
Stolen objects lift wings up high
While friends gather to bid a love good-bye
Stowaways steer by a different star
Before Brokenwings takes a leap too far
Against all odds wings finally soar
A city approaches, the Aivans want war
Another city awakes, friends seek farther shores

Chorus
We're looking out to the horizon,
We're headed for the horizon.